T5-AFQ-058

WET

RUTH CLAMPETT

To Karen,
wishing you a sturdy bridge
and a joyful journey ♡

Wet
Copyright © 2015 by Ruth Clampett
All Rights Reserved.
ISBN: 978–0-9966857–1-9

This book is a work of fiction. Names, characters, places and incidents are either products of the author's imagination or used fictitiously. Any resemblance to actual events, locales, or persons, living or dead, is entirely coincidental. No part of this publication can be reproduced or transmitted in any form or by any means, electronic or mechanical, without permission in writing from the author or publisher.

The author acknowledges the trademarked status and trademark owners of various products referenced in this work of fiction, which have been used without permission. The publication/use of these trademarks is not authorized, associated with, or sponsored by the trademark owners.

Cover Design:
Jada d'Lee
www.jadadleedesigns.com
Cover Photograph: iStockphoto

Editors:
Angela Borda, and Melissa of There For You Editing
www.thereforyoumelissa.wix.com/there-for-you

Interior formatting:
Christine Borgford of Perfectly Publishable
www.perfectlypublishable.com

To the colorful characters
that have passed through my life,
the mime, the sprinkler man, the dreamers
Your little gifts
a dramatic phrase, a sad laugh,
a wink, soft kiss, or whispered secret
I've carried with me
so they could one day be
part of my stories.

CHAPTER ONE

THE FACE OFF

I love the earthy smell when the afternoon sun hits the grass still damp from an earlier rain. I want to toss my tools aside, take off my shoes and let my feet sink into the ground, leaving my footprints in the grass.

I remember when I was a young boy, eager to help my dad with his work, he would give me a shovel and teach me how to dig, turning the soil so we could discover what was wrong down below. Now years later, even though I'm a landscape architect and work at a drafting table instead of a field, I feel like I haven't stopped digging.

Part of me misses this kind of labor. I'm never more at peace than when I'm outside working with the sun on my back. I take a deep breath with my face tilted to the sky, and then kneel down to finish my task.

I've just started screwing the sprinkler head into the new connection when the bush next to me starts ringing.

What the hell?

I lean in closer to the shrub to make sure I'm not imagining something. Sure enough, the damn thing rings again. I lift myself off my knees, and stand with my hands on my hips, peering down into the clusters of leaves.

"Did you hear ringing?" a voice calls out behind me.

I turn to see who I assume to be Mrs. Jacoby walking bare-foot across her lawn. I blink rapidly and tighten my jaw to keep my mouth from falling open. My teenage memory of meeting her doesn't do justice to the woman before me.

I can't remember when I've had such a visceral reaction to a woman. My blood heats up the longer I gaze at her.

She's a knock-out—wavy, auburn hair, skin the color of cream with a shot of coffee, and electric blue eyes. Throw in lush lips that look made for kissing, a perfectly curvy figure, and she's skating on the edge of being too good to be true.

I silently nod and point to the bush just as it rings again. By the time she's up next to me, I can't decide if I should look away or just continue to enjoy the view.

She's in those tight, stretchy pants and a tank top, and with the way her breasts dance as she approaches, I'm pretty sure she's not wearing a bra.

I take note of her fiery expression.

The ring comes again and I glance over at the landline re-ceiver in her hand with an arched brow. "Did you dial this bush? 'Cause it doesn't look like it's going to take your call."

She chews on her bottom lip and narrows her eyes at me. "Who are you?"

"Paul, from Sprinkler Brothers. You may not remember, but we met way back when I was helping my dad during summer breaks."

Her eyes grow wide and she can't hide her surprise. "You're Paul Junior?"

"The one and only."

"How old are you now?"

"Almost thirty. Like I said, it's been a while since we met—I was eighteen that summer." I lean back, stretching to my full height and slip my hand in my back pocket.

She studies me as if she's seeing me in a new light. I know from my parents talking about clients that we're not that differ-ent in age.

"Wow, you look so different. You're all grown up."

My eyes skim across her barely covered breasts, and down to the swell of her hips in those skin-tight pants.

Damn.

I give her a lazy smile. "I could say the same about you."

She follows my gaze and looks down at the way she's dressed. I wonder if she realizes that she might as well be naked. She quickly folds her arms over her chest.

The ringing shrub is starting to annoy me. "Doesn't this damn bush have voicemail?"

"I hate voicemail," she grumbles.

"Ah, I see. So this is your phone."

Grinning, she nods.

"What's it doing in the bushes?"

"I threw it out the window."

She threw it out the window? "And now you want it back?"

She lets out a long sigh. "I suppose I do."

I sink to my knees so I can run my hand under the bush and over the wet soil. When I retrieve the phone, I rub its surface along my thigh to brush the loose dirt off.

She ends the call from the landline phone she's holding and reaches for her cell phone.

I'm still on my knees when I hand it to her. It feels a little weird, but I like this view of her. Actually, I think I'd enjoy any view of her.

She turns to check her messages and the phone practically explodes with prompts. She sighs again. "It still works."

I nod toward the cell phone as I stand back up. "Someone's anxious to reach you."

She rolls her eyes. "Maybe I should just leave it in the bushes."

"Be my guest."

She squints as she sizes me up. "So where's your dad?"

"I've been helping him out on the weekends since his knee surgery. He only trusts me with his best clients."

"Your dad is such a sweetie. He takes care of my friend's place, too."

"And your husband's family."

She scoffs. "I have no husband."

I offer up some insincere sympathy. "Oh, I'm sorry. I didn't know."

"Don't be sorry. He's long gone and good riddance."

"Okay, then." I shrug. If she's good with it, I sure as hell am, too.

I can feel all my red flags popping up as I tread into my danger zone. My attraction to her builds with every minute I'm in her presence.

Sliding my finger under my collar I pull it looser. I try to think about anything but her being single. "So do you have kids?"

"No." Her expression softens, and she falls silent.

"Well, I guess that's good then. Divorce is tough with kids."

"Besides, I'm not sure it could've happened. All work and no play made the Mister a very dull boy."

"Really?"

"And it's not like I'm overly needy or anything. I just have needs that most men would like attending to."

I swallow hard. "So those kind of needs."

She lets her gaze trail from my chest down to my boots. The look in her eyes is hungry, like she's going to eat me for dessert. "I'm sure a man like you would understand."

I take a sharp breath. "I understand one thing for sure."

She looks up at me expectantly.

"Your ex is an idiot."

A wide grin spreads across her face. "Oh, I like you. Come on, it's hot out here. Let's go inside to cool off. I've got some fresh lemonade."

She doesn't wait for my response but turns on her heel and heads toward the house.

Her ass looks amazing as she walks. I chuckle too loud as I follow her without any hesitation.

She turns, her long hair swinging over her shoulder. "What's so funny?"

"My dad only sends me to work on clients' homes where the women are married or old."

She laughs out loud. "I bet! Look at you."

"He sure got this job wrong. Hey . . . what about me?"

She steps right up to me and looks at me with those big gorgeous eyes. "You're hot . . . and I bet you're a handful of trouble."

"Maybe. But I'm pretty sure you are, too."

She winks and keeps walking.

Holy hell. I feel the adrenalin of my pick-up days shoot up my spine. *What I could do with this woman if I was still a player.*

Once we're in her kitchen she pulls out a chair for me as she heads to the fridge. "So lemonade or something stronger."

"Got any beer?"

Grinning, she takes out two bottles. I notice there are already two empty ones on the counter with their labels peeled off in shreds. No wonder her phone got thrown across the yard. She notices me staring at the mess.

"Yeah, I was having one of those days."

When she slides into the chair across from me, she glances down at her outfit, pulls her low neckline up a little higher and pushes her hair off her face. "I forgot you guys were coming today, and I really wasn't expecting company. I should change into something more presentable."

Despite all my efforts to play it cool, I doubt I can hide the weight of my lust for her in my expression.

"Not on my account. I like that outfit."

"Hmmm." She takes a swig of beer as she studies me, the corners of her mouth turning up.

I nod at the buzzing cell phone she set down on the table. "Is that your ex trying to reach you?"

"No, not my ex."

"Oh, so there are others."

Of course there are others . . . I mean, look at her.

She rolls her eyes. "It's that damn profile on my Tinder page. I made a mistake saying that I have *a very open mind.*"

"Why is that a mistake?"

"Oh, you wouldn't believe the weirdos that contact me."

I take a long sip of my beer as I watch her. This woman is making my head spin. "Do you mind me asking something?"

"Not at all."

"Why are you using Tinder? I have to think that men are falling all over each other to be with you."

"That's the thing. I don't want to *be* with anyone. I've done that and I like being on my own."

Puzzled, I point to the phone. "So?"

"You really want to know? You won't judge me?" She pauses and appraises me like she's trying to determine if I can be trusted.

I nod—my curiosity piqued.

She squares her shoulders and boldly stares me in the eye. "I want sex, lots of sex. Nothing more. I'm only looking for hookups."

I cough, almost spitting up my beer. *Is she serious?*

"Initially it was my girlfriend's idea. After the crash and burn of my marriage she knew that my self-esteem was low, and thought if I had some fun I'd realize how *hot* I am." She laughs and rolls her eyes playfully.

"I can't believe you ever questioned that," I reply.

She shrugs. "My husband's lack of interest preyed on me after a while."

I shake my head in disbelief. Her ex must be nuts.

"I'd always been a 'good' girl, so I thought my friend was crazy to suggest doing hook-ups on Tinder . . . but I agreed to try, and for the most part, I've had fun."

"I bet you have." I grin, imagining how men must react to her. A few years ago she would've been my ideal woman.

She taps the phone with her manicured nails. "And Tinder is an efficient way to sort through the crowd."

"Then why did you throw your phone in the bushes?"

She leans back into her chair. "This last creeper pushed me over the edge. He wanted me to wear a latex body suit and sit on him."

My eyebrows knit together. "What?"

"Exactly! So you can see why I'm agitated!"

"So you're not a fan of squatting in latex body suits?" I ask, trying to keep a straight face.

"Hell no. I want hot sex. I'm not interested in being taken to dinner, or saran- wrapped for some kinky weirdo. Is there anything wrong to just want to get screwed?"

I shake my head. I can't believe this woman. She's already drained her beer and she's at the fridge getting us two more.

"Well, I don't think there's anything wrong with that at all," I say.

"You're a man. Tell me if I'm being unreasonable. If you saw me on Tinder would *you* want to straight-up screw me?"

I set my beer down. "Um, Ms. Jacoby."

"Oh, for God's sake call me Elle."

"If I was a Tinder guy I'd really want to do that, Elle. But I'm a *take you to dinner and get to know you* kind of guy."

She laughs loudly and waves her hands toward the ceiling. "Damn, can I get a break! My sprinkler man won't even screw me!"

I pick my beer back up. "I'm not a sprinkler man."

She purses her lips together and her smile fades. "I'm sorry . . . I offended you."

"I'm a landscape architect."

"That's so hot."

I shake my head in reproach. "Remember I'm just helping out my dad until he's fully mobile again after his surgery. Regardless, fixing irrigation systems is an honorable profession."

"Right, sorry." She glides her fingers along the curve of the beer bottle before looking up at me with a coy smile.

"So is sex really all that matters to you?" I ask.

"Maybe it won't be when I finally get some that's satisfying."

Oh, good Lord. How much restraint can one man be expected to have?

I let out a sigh of regret. "Well, I'd love to help you out but I don't do casual sex. Been there, done that."

I square my shoulders after making my declaration. After almost two years of following my abstinence program, I can say I'm confident I've moved on from my sex-obsessed ways, but it still makes me cringe with a sense of loss after the words leave my lips.

She pounds her fists on the table. "My timing is always shit. So if I'd met you during your *been there* period you would've screwed me?"

"Without a doubt. Screwed is too simple of a word for all the things I would have done to you."

I take a deep breath and glance over my shoulder at the kitchen layout. "I'd have you bent over your kitchen island as we fucked, or your legs would be wrapped around me as I took you against that wall."

"You're killing me here! Are you good in bed?"

"Good?" I smile, remembering those days. "That wasn't the adjective most women used. What do you think?"

"My guess is a big fat *yes*."

Leaning back, I stretch out my legs under the table. "Let's just say, back in the day . . . I'm not ashamed to say I did all right."

She huffs and folds her arms over her chest. "I bet you did. And I bet you have a big cock too."

Good Lord, no more beer for her.

My eyes roll back. "You've got a filthy mouth."

"So what. Do you?"

"Have a big cock? Is this information you really need to know?"

She looks down under the table. "Ha! You've got big feet!"

Jesus, this woman.

"And you're so tall." She grabs my hand. "And you've got thick fingers. You know what they say . . ."

I watch her trail her fingers over mine as she gives me a sultry wink.

I lean over, and whisper into her ear, "I've got a huge cock."

She looks drunk with lust as she bites her lip. "Hung like a horse?" she whispers.

"Yep."

"Oh for God's sake." She scoots her chair closer. "Show me."

Her eyes are twinkling, yet it's hard to tell if she's teasing or not.

"Yeah, sure." I take a long draw from my second beer.

"Come on," she presses, seeming hopeful.

"I can't."

"Why not?"

"Well, besides the fact that that would be a complete violation of my new lifestyle, I'm hard right now. I don't want to scare you, Elle."

"Ooo," she moans.

"Not to mention, you have quite a beer buzz going on and I don't play that way."

Her cheeks grow pink as she picks at the label on her beer bottle.

"That's gallant of you but I don't think you'd be taking advantage of me, if that's your concern. Besides, I'm four years older than you. Some people might think I'm taking advantage of a younger man."

I arch my brow and shake my head.

She tries to peek under the table. "So are you really hard, or are you messing with me?"

"Maybe. Maybe not." I set down my beer. "But I've got to go. I've got another client's system to check out, since I'm the sprinkler man and all."

"You aren't going to let go of that are you? Is this some kind of cruel punishment?"

"No." I can't resist giving her a hard time. "Are you always this direct?"

She blushes an even darker pink. I could totally get addicted to this woman.

"No, since I've been single I'm usually just flirty, but as you said, I've had a few beers and you're incredibly handsome . . . I really didn't expect to look out my window and see a man like you on his knees."

"So I should be flattered?"

"Absolutely. You caught my eye, and then got me all hot and bothered. How tall are you anyway?"

"Six foot two."

"And you work out. It's not just your fine body, it's your face . . . something about that sharp jawline and your green eyes." She fans herself. "Oh my."

"You're pretty amazing yourself, even if you have a filthy mouth."

She gets a devilish look in her eyes. "So can you show me your jumbo cock then? I promise not to touch it, so you won't be breaking your rules."

What's in this beer? I'm seriously considering her offer.

"This is the weirdest customer conversation I've ever had."

"*Please.*" She tugs on my index finger and something about that makes my cock harder and weakens my will.

"You're one pushy woman."

"If you show me yours . . . I'll show you mine." She skims her fingers down between her breasts. "I've seen you admiring them."

That captures my attention but I'm not sure I trust her. "You're crazy."

"I may be crazy, but I've got great breasts."

"So tit for tat, or shall I say tit for cock?"

She laughs with delight. "Yes!"

She's so damn cute when she laughs. I'm going to have to tell Dad about her so he never sends me here again. I'm liking her way too much. I mean, I'm seriously considering showing her my cock and that's testing my *Abstinence Until Love* program. Who am I kidding? It's a complete violation.

Still the longer I look at this sexy woman, the weaker I get. My resistance is crumbling like a soft-baked cookie.

She sets down her beer and runs her hands over her breasts slowly. *Damn.* I'm doomed.

Standing, I polish off my beer before I set the empty bottle down on the table. I nod at her. "Well, it's really hot when you touch your tits but are you going to show me?"

"Are you?" Her eyes grow wide like she can't believe I'm going to do this.

I narrow my eyes and slowly start to undo my belt. I'm feeling that mind-bending surge of lust from the old days right before I'd score a particularly hot woman. My heart is pounding, and I can't believe I'm caving.

She runs her fingers along the hem of her tank top and then slowly inches it up. I start to drag my zipper down so I can pull out my cock but it's not going smoothly. I'm so fucking hard it hurts and it's making everything tighter. It's going to take some maneuvering to get it out. The whole time I'm screwing around with the zipper I'm cursing myself inwardly for being so weak willed.

"Do you need help?" She's grinning like it's Christmas morning.

If she could only know the kind of help I'm picturing.

I huff. "I can do this. It's just what we were talking about is making this difficult. If I'd known I'd be playing show 'n tell I would've worn looser jeans."

She waves her hand at me. "Move your fingers," she says.

I rest my hands on my hips as she fixes her stare on my crotch.

"What?"

"Oh my God! It's huge! Is that anaconda in your pants really you?"

"Of course it's me! What do you think it is?"

"I knew a guy once who stuffed socks down there."

What do you bet it was her ex?

"Are you serious? What the hell good is that? As soon as your pants are down the jokes on you."

She shrugs. "Why do women wear padded bras? False advertising I guess. So seriously, is that padding or the real deal?"

"Let me put it this way . . . why would I stuff socks down my shorts to go on a work call? I had no idea you were going to be intrigued by what kind of heat I was packing."

"Good point."

I look at her tits that are still covered as I fumble with my zipper again. Her excited nipples are so defined through the fabric that they give the term 'perky' new meaning. I have this kid-like compulsion to not show her mine until she shows me hers. It's ridiculous because at this point I may never get my jeans open. "Well?"

She pulls the fabric up excruciatingly slow as her gaze fixates on my fingers trying to work the zipper further down. When the bottom of her breasts are exposed I start rethinking my *done that* stance. I can already tell that her tits are epic, making me reconsider shifting back into the *been there* category.

Her nipples are hard for me. My cock is hard for her. It all seems so straightforward.

Wait, what the hell am I doing?

"Hurry and get that bad boy out so I can imagine licking it," she purrs.

Licking it? I stare at her mouth and wonder how my dick would look between her pretty lips.

I can picture her on her knees gazing up at me through those thick lashes. My blood starts to boil as I slowly burn for her.

For a second I'm ready to throw all my hard work out the window, but then in my mind I see my dad's face and it's jarring—reminding me of my promise to him and to my sponsor. It pains me when I carefully zip my fly back up.

She gives a little pout and fondles her breasts to tease me. "What are you doing? Are you really going to turn me down?"

I close my eyes and chant my oath to myself.

God grant me the serenity to accept the things I cannot change, like the fact that I'll always be a horny bastard

The courage to change the things I can, like not screwing every broad that asks me to.

And the wisdom to keep my cock in my pants . . .

I open my eyes with renewed resolve.

"Sadly, yes I am."

She pulls her shirt down low and full-on pouts.

"Believe me, there will be regret. However, I made a promise to my dad and a promise to myself. I used to be completely out of control, but now I'm a reformed man."

"That sounds so dull." She sighs and leans forward on her elbows. "I mean, what fun is that?"

"When I meet *the one*, it will be worth the wait. I want what my parents have."

Her eyes go soft. She glances down at the table and rubs her fingers over the surface deep in thought. When she looks back up at me her eyes are glassy. "I wanted that once and even thought I found it, but I was wrong. I really hope you find it, Paul Junior."

Her tender reaction makes me think there's more to her than this vixen. I smile at her. "Thanks, Elle. And I hope you find the right guy to give you all that great sex you deserve."

Before she lets me out the front door she turns to me, suddenly seeming more sober. She stares in my eyes. "Should I be embarrassed? Maybe it's the beer, or maybe the heat, but there's something about you. You brought the wild side out of me."

I shake my head. "No, in another time it would've been perfect. You're seriously hard to resist, Elle."

"I'd say I'm sorry if it was too much, but honestly I'm not. Regardless, please don't tell your parents how forward I was. They're such nice people. Well, I haven't met your mom yet but she's so lovely on the phone."

I smile to reassure her. "Don't worry, it's our secret."

Once I'm in the truck I pause before driving off. Did I really just turn down sex with the hottest woman I've seen for a long time, maybe ever?

As I fire up the engine and gun the truck down the street my mood swings between feeling proud of myself for sticking to my plan, and idiotic for not encouraging her to lick my cock. I adjust myself and try to focus on the road. My raging hard-on better calm down before I get to the Anderson's house.

CHAPTER TWO

THE CROUCHING TIGER

I'm on my second tumbler of coffee thanks to my sleepless night. It was the Elle effect, visions of my hands on her tits and my cock in her dirty mouth. I haven't jerked off that many times in one night since I was a pent-up teenager.

My phone rings and the number looks vaguely familiar.

"Paul Junior?"

No one calls me that except provocative Elle. "Ms. Jacoby?"

"I thought we'd gotten past such formalities."

I smile thinking of her inching her tank top up and how enticing her breasts were.

"I suppose we have. Good morning, Elle. What can I do for you?"

She lets out a long sigh. "Well, besides the obvious, I'm having a situation in my yard."

"Okay. What's that?"

"I was cutting some rosemary sprigs for my roast chicken when the sprinklers went off. And let me tell you it was quite a show."

She's such a tease. "Can you elaborate?"

"In that spot right next to the ringing bush, the thingy shot right out of the ground with a gush of water behind it. It's like my lawn had an enormous orgasm."

I can't hold back my laugh, but a second later I'm pissed at myself for getting distracted on the job. I never finished securing the sprinkler head once she stepped into my focus with her ringing phone-in-the-bush situation.

"That's a very vivid description, Elle."

"I thought you'd like that. So what can be done since the gusher was dramatic? I've shut off the system until you can fix it."

I'm tempted to rush over but then I remind myself of the risk.

"Actually I can talk you through it. It's a simple fix."

There's a long pause. "I was hoping you could do it for me."

"My day is completely booked," I lie.

"You can't squeeze me in?" she asks in a breathy voice.

Oh God, my cock is twitching thinking of squeezing *in* her. "Really Elle, let me explain it and you'll see how easy it is."

I can picture her pouting.

"So you know the thing that shot out of the hole? That's the sprinkler head. If you know where it is, pick it up."

"Give me a minute."

My mind wanders to sexy places and I slide right into the danger zone. I wonder what she's wearing and if it's low cut. I let out a moan remembering her hard nipples.

"Do sprinkler heads turn you on?" she asks in a playful tone.

Shit I didn't realize she didn't put me on hold. "No, not sprinkler heads. Actually I was remembering our almost show-and-tell last night. So are you wearing a bra now?"

"Wouldn't you like to know? If you came over and helped me with this head situation you could find out for yourself."

I swallow thickly wondering what kind of sexy bra she must wear. I bet it's black.

"Sorry . . . back to the task at hand. All you have to do is get on your knees, take the head and push it deep in to the hole."

"Oh, baby. I love it when you talk dirty to me."

My cock is no longer twitching but throbbing at the idea of her.

"Can you do it?"

"Say it like you mean it."

So that's how she wants it. Why am I surprised? "Get on your knees right now and shove it in the hole like a good girl."

She giggles then takes a deep breath. "Can I touch myself while I do it?"

"No!" I start palming myself, but she doesn't need to know that.

"Okay. It's in really deep. Now what?"

"Screw it."

"What?" Her voice genuinely sounds aroused.

"Screw it in tight."

"Yes, sir."

A minute passes and I'm still stroking myself while thinking about her bent over.

"Sir, we have a problem. It won't screw in. I think the threads are messed up."

"All right, I'll come over after work."

"When?"

"Don't worry, you don't have to be there. I'll bring a new head."

"Oh, I'll be there. Do you want me to wear a bra?"

I let out an exasperated groan. "Yes. And if you have a pair of baggy ugly sweats could you wear those too?"

"You told me not to touch myself while you were being bossy, but I may have been touching myself anyway. Have you?"

I can tell from her tone that she's teasing but I want to believe she means it.

"I'll see you at six, Ms. Jacoby."

"Yes, sir."

It's five forty-five and I'm halfway to her house when I pull off the road and pick up my phone. I'm relieved when Jim answers immediately.

"Hey, Paul. What's up?"

"I need some counsel. I'm feeling very weak."

"Who is she?"

"One of Dad's clients. I was at her house yesterday."

"Is she attractive?"

"Unbelievably. I get worked up just thinking about her."

"What's her ass like? Shit. I'm sorry. Forget I asked that."

I can't help it. It makes me feel better that even Jim isn't perfect. "Her ass is amazing. Really round and tight."

"Damn. Look, it sounds like this woman is pushing all your buttons. Is there any way you can avoid her? Can someone else be sent out to the job?"

I think about getting Gabriel to do it but this strong feeling comes over me that I don't want him near her. He'd fuck her for sure and then be an asshole about it.

"No, I'm the only one until Dad is back on his feet from his surgery."

"Well then use the visualization techniques we've worked on. And get in and out as quickly as possible. Any lingering around leaves you vulnerable."

I consider what he's saying and repeat it in my head to make sure I've got it clear.

"Got it. In and out. No lingering."

"You're strong, Paul. Just remember your promise to yourself. Self-respect means everything."

"It does." I hated myself when I'd sneak out of a woman's bed in the middle of the night and not even remember her name. Although I'm pretty sure I'd never forget Elle.

I think I'm clever by not ringing the doorbell and instead, let myself in the side gate to go straight to the backyard.

The last laugh's on me, because when I step into the yard I see her in a chair just to the left of the repair sight. I immediately glance away and keep my eyes focused down.

"Hello, Paul Junior."

I don't look up as I lower myself to the ground. "Ms. Jacoby."

"Thank you for coming. Did you bring your head with you?"

I feel a sweat break out across my brow. "I did." I pull the sprinkler head out of my jacket pocket and wave it like a flag. I try not to look at her but the way the sun shines on her bare legs catches my eye. Her legs are crossed with one foot tapping the air. She's wearing sandals with dangerously high heels. My gaze travels up higher to see her skirt has ridden up her thighs. *Holy hell.*

"Nice sweats," I mumble.

"I don't do baggy sweats. But you'll be happy to know I'm wearing a bra."

The sweat is now trickling down my neck.

"A really sexy bra, if I do say so myself."

She leans forward as she fingers the stem of her wine glass slowly. Her blouse dips open and reveals her overflowing cleavage and a hint of black lace. The view is everything I hoped it would be.

I turn back to the hole in the lawn and shove the head inside. But despite my maneuvering the damn thing won't screw in. I pull the head back out and run my fingers inside the tread of the pipe in the ground. "Damn," I curse when I realize what the problem is.

"So it wasn't just me?" she asks.

"No, it wasn't. I'm going to have to dig this out and I don't have the tools here to do it with me. I came in my car. I'll have to come back."

"Tsk, tsk. What a shame." She uncrosses her legs and then slowly crosses them in the other direction. It's hypnotizing. If she does that a few more times I'm sure I'd be under her trance.

"Sorry about this."

"Oh, it's fine. So where are you off to now?"

Standing up, I brush off my knees. "I'm having dinner with my folks tonight. We do it every Thursday. They're old-fashioned when it comes to family."

She studies me with a faraway, kind of sad expression. I

wonder what her family is like.

"Really? That's so sweet," she says, her tone sincere.

"And my mom's a great cook."

"Lucky man."

"I am."

Her message prompt goes off on her phone and I notice it's tucked into the edge of her seat next to her naked thigh.

"More potential conquests?" I ask nodding to the phone.

She pulls the phone out. "Here let me look." She reads the screen and then rolls her eyes. "Why does everyone want to tie me up?"

My eyes bug out imagining her tethered to my bedposts naked. "Seriously?"

She nods. "I'd show you but you need to leave."

I glance down at my watch and I know I should leave but the horny man inside of me opens his mouth before I can stop him. "No, I've got some time."

She stands up and smooths her skirt down. Her legs go on for miles. I can imagine them wrapped around me and I want it bad. I try to remember Jim's advice but it's all fuzzy in my head right now as all the blood is going to my cock instead of my brain.

She turns and walks across the grass and along the brick pathway with a swagger. Despite her high-heeled sandals she strides with confidence. I walk stiffly after her thanks to my stiffy.

Once inside, she pushes me down on her couch in her den, and then steps away. She returns with a glass of wine for me, and her glass refilled. As she sinks down onto the cushions I'm acutely aware of her thigh pressed up against mine as she holds up her phone. I take a big gulp of wine and try not to look down her blouse.

She taps her screen. "See, here's a picture of Richard, who's apparently a dom."

I squint at the screen to see a beefy guy with tattoos holding handcuffs in his hand and a four-poster bed behind him with only a sheet over the mattress.

"Is this a potential hook-up?"

"Indeed it is. He wants to see me tonight in his lair. He's insisted actually."

"Really? So I'm guessing Richard won't be bringing you flowers and taking you out for dinner."

"Is that what you do with girls you date?"

"Yes," I lie. I haven't actually done that yet, but when I meet the right girl I will. It's part of my master plan.

She sighs so loud it's practically a swoon.

"Lucky girls. Are you for real? You know, you're pretty dreamy—a stand-up kind of guy, who spends time with his family. To top it off you're so easy on the eyes."

Would she still think I'm dreamy if she knew what we did together in my wild fantasies last night?

She holds up her phone. "So no, if you read the text you'll see that Richard only wants to tie me up and fuck me repeatedly."

My chest tightens and my fingers clench into fists. "How repeatedly?"

"Well, he says in every orifice."

I angrily grab the phone from her hand. "Are you serious? What the fuck?" I read his message and then turn to her. "You aren't going to meet up with him, are you?"

"No. He doesn't appeal to me at all, and I don't want to be tied up and fucked in every orifice."

"Glad to hear it. Hey, show me the latex guy you told me about."

She takes her phone and runs her fingers over the screen until she finds what she's searching for. She hands me the phone.

"This guy is perfectly ordinary looking. Good looking even. What the hell?"

"I know right? And I even think he's married on top of it. See how there's a thin stripe of skin that's lighter on his ring finger?"

"Asshole!"

"So you see what I'm up against?"

"I do."

This woman deserves better. Too bad I can't be her knight

in shining armor to save her from all these perverts but I have to hold my line with her. Besides . . . I've been accused of being a pervert because I'm obsessed with sex, so who am I to judge?

"So is there anyone at all on this Tinder thing that appeals to you?"

"Well there's one I'm considering."

"Show me."

She scans through what must be a long list of men before she clicks the screen. "His name is Scott."

I study the screen. "He looks all right. Does he want you to dress up in something weird?"

"No, he wants to meet at a wine bar."

"You sound hesitant."

"I don't know. He said that he liked that I was naughty and we haven't even met yet."

"Hmmm, well if you talk to him like you do to me I can see why he'd say that."

Her cheeks blush. "I guess you're right."

For a second I wonder if all of this sexy talk has been an act with her, but then she opens her mouth again.

"So if you'd screwed me when you had a chance, things really would've been so much simpler."

"You and your pretty mouth."

"Well I wouldn't have to go see if this guy's a creep or not."

"True . . . but there's nothing simple about me, Elle. And if I'd screwed you, you'd know that."

"You love to taunt me don't you?"

I stand up. "Just a little bit.

I want to do so much more than taunt her. It's taking everything I have not to reconsider her offer. It's not just the sex, there's something about her that makes me want to know the sides of her she hasn't shown me yet.

"This has been enlightening, but my number one woman is expecting me."

"Should I be jealous?"

"Definitely. My mom is awesome."

She pushes me in the shoulder. "Get outta here."

Two days later I'm on my knees in her yard again. The grass is still damp, but warm and it has that freshly cut smell. I appreciate her Studio City neighborhood with the understated ranch homes with good-sized yards. It's certainly different than some of the lame postage stamp-sized quasi yards on the other side of the hill due to the overbuilding epidemic. *Crazy L.A. real estate.*

Elle's stretched out on the nearby chaise lounge sunbathing just to taunt me. If she hadn't pushed her skirt up high and stretched out those long, shapely legs I'd probably be getting this job done more quickly.

She glances up from her magazine. "So you really don't have a girlfriend?"

"Nope."

"And you don't do hook-ups?

"Not anymore."

She lowers her sunglasses and gives me a skeptical look. "And you don't miss sex?"

"Of course I miss it. Some days it's all I think about, but I'm committed to this program."

She pats the chaise lounge next to her. "Time for you to take a break. I want to hear all about this *program*."

I drop the shovel, and lift up, brushing the dirt off my knees. She gazes at my body as I approach her. I can tell she's checking out my junk again. There's nothing subtle about this woman. I grab the iced tea she left out for me and down half of it before I sit on the chaise and stretch out.

"So this program? Are you going to be a priest? Is that it?"

I scoff. "Hardly."

She throws her hands up in the air. "I give up! What then?"

"I'm doing this program my dad talked me into joining. It's called AUL, short for *Abstinence Until Love.*"

"Seriously? And why did your dad think you needed to be a

part of something so insane?"

I rub my hands hard over my face. She isn't going to let this go. I'm not sure how to tell the story without sounding like a complete asshole.

"He walked in on me."

"Screwing a girl? What's the big deal about that?"

I fold my arms over my chest and keep my eyes focused forward. "He walked in on me with three women in my bed."

"That you were fucking?"

"Well, generally speaking. I was only fucking one at the time but there was other stuff going on. We'd been at it all night."

Her mouth falls open and she leans over and slaps me on the arm.

"You stud! You beast!"

"It's not as impressive as it sounds. I practically gave Dad a heart attack and I was drunk out of my mind at eight in the morning. I didn't even know the girls' names."

"Oh . . ."

"And the reason he came into my apartment is I was late meeting him on an important job."

"Ooo, you really screwed up."

"Big time. He threw out the girls and then made me take a cold shower. And the first thing he told me was that he was going to tell my mother, Millie, all about it."

"The mom you mentioned adoring . . . your number one girl?"

"The very one. He knew it was the worst thing he could say to me. I'm her favorite and the apple of her eye. I can bear almost anything but disappointing her."

I look at Elle and she actually looks distraught.

"Oh that's awful."

"So he gave me a choice. I guess he'd been hearing stories about my antics for a while. He said he knew I had a problem— that sex had become an obsession and my constant need to scratch the itch was ruining my life. Doing research he'd learned about this program through the church he wanted me to check out. If I was willing to commit to it for four months, he wouldn't tell Mom."

"Abstinence Until Love? That sounds like something a church would come up with."

"I do it in conjunction with Sexaholics Anonymous, which isn't run by the church. Although they let them use their community room for the meetings."

She gives me the side eyes. "Are you kidding me?"

"It was a joke to me at first, but once I stopped rolling my eyes at the meetings, it started making sense."

She licks her lips. "You were a sex addict?"

"I still am . . . always will be. It's all about managing the disease."

"Oh, the irony! You are a reformed sex addict and I am sex starved. What a cruel world this is."

I give her a big grin. "It *is* ironic."

She pushes her sunglasses back up and hikes her legs up so her entire thigh is exposed. "Well at least we have one thing in common."

I look over at her.

"We both think about sex all the time."

Elle's in the house when I finish the repair and run a test to make sure that it works as it should. As I finish up I think about the part of my addiction story I didn't share with Elle. I've never told anyone about the call I got from the health office two months after my wild foursome, that I needed to come in for testing. I never heard the STD's the caller mentioned, since my mind went black and my body into shock when he mentioned AIDs testing. *AIDs?* Had I become so cocky with my lifestyle that I forgot I was playing with fire?

That was a week I'll never forget, starting with punching a hole in my living room wall after the call disconnected and messing up my drafting hand. I ended up on my knees in church that night knowing full well that if I had one or all of the things the caller mentioned, my prayers won't do me a damn bit of good.

That night I made a promise to God and myself that if I came out of this clean the next woman I took to bed would be the one I'd fallen in love with. Little did I know that love was a language I had to learn to speak, and after all this time I still haven't found the girl who could inspire me to learn.

The humiliation of going for testing was profound and as I waited my turn surrounded by people I would have previously looked down upon, I realized that I was now one of them. As the minutes ticked by I promised myself I would never end up in this fucked-up situation again.

So no one knowing this would be surprised that I've stuck to my program religiously and have not missed a meeting. I knew the grace of God was with me when my results came back clean, and I sure as hell wasn't going to test Him again.

I knock on the back door to let Elle know I'm leaving. When she swings open the door she's got lipstick on and those sexy high-heeled sandals.

I swallow hard and try to look away as I point to the backyard. "You're all set. I tested it and everything's working as it should."

"So no more lawn orgasms?"

I grin. "Nope." I turn back to the yard. "Sorry, lawn."

"Well, I suppose that's good. Thanks for taking care of it."

"No worries. Hey, you look nice."

Too nice. I'm imaging her naked with just the heels on, my hands running up her inner thighs as I part them. I take a deep breath. I need to get out of here before I lose it completely.

She smiles. "I'm meeting that Tinder guy, Scott."

"At the wine bar?"

She nods and twists her bracelet around her wrist.

My brows knit together. "Are you sure?"

"You jealous?" She winks at me.

I know she's teasing but it's a hit in the gut when I realize I am. However, I'll never admit it. Jealously has never been my thing. I just move on.

"No. He just better treat you right."

"I'll make sure he does," she says with what feels like a false bravado. "Besides, it's just a meet-up tonight."

"You've got my number. Call me . . . you know, if you need anything."

She leans on the door jam and studies me in the most unnerving way. "Thanks, Paul. I will."

The next morning I pick up my phone three times and set it back down. I glance at my watch and the roll of blueprints next to me. Screw it all. I open the contact list on my phone and rub my finger over her name.

She sounds a little worse for wear when she picks up.

"So how'd it go last night?"

"Paul Junior? Is that you?"

"You can drop the junior now, you know."

"What if I don't want to? It sounds so . . . I don't know . . ."

"Are you high?"

"Nah. Maybe a little hungover. Or maybe a lot. There's a lot of wine to drink at the wine bar."

I grip my phone tighter. I don't like that she drank that much with a dude she didn't know.

"So how was the guy? Was he what you expected?"

She sighs. "Even better. The man has unbelievable swag. You should have heard him and his sexy talk. All the things he wanted to do to me."

"Really?"

"Oh my. Yes, really. And he licked my fingers. Sucked on them actually."

"He what the fucking what?"

"Oh, I know it sounds weird but it was so hot. My fingers in his mouth as he gave me that smoldering look . . . damn I was so wet. As a matter of fact I think I still am."

I take a sharp breath as I imagine Elle wet. My cock comes to life in record time. I desperately try to refocus on the conversation.

"I'm sorry but I'm trying to picture his fingers in your mouth and how that can be hot. The dude sounds freaky if you ask me."

She giggles. "He told me he wanted to taste my pussy . . . over and over."

I hold the phone away for a second to compose myself. "In the wine bar?"

"I think he meant at my place."

"Sounds like a winning evening."

"Well, I'm seeing him again tonight."

"I guess it doesn't take a lot to impress you," I say as my grip tightens on the phone.

"What?"

"I don't think you know him well enough to have him at your place."

"I may be new to this hook-up thing, but I'm not a dim-wit. You don't have to worry—I'm going to his condo. He lives in those fancy new high rises downtown. He's so sophisticated, Paul."

Really? The finger-sucker is sophisticated? He sounds like a douchebag. I remember the call I got back in the day from the health department. "Promise me you'll use condoms."

"That's the sweetest thing anyone has ever said to me," she teases.

"Promise? Take some in your purse."

"I promise."

When we hang up I have to take a long shower despite being late for my meeting. The entire time the water rains down on me I'm jerking off thinking about tasting Elle's pussy. I'm so screwed.

"Paul, I'm just checking in because this is the second meeting in a row you've missed."

"Yeah, sorry Jim . . . it's just been a really busy week at work."

Liar.

"Have you talked to that woman you told me about?" I pause fighting with myself as to how to answer. "Have you slept with her Paul?"

"No." At least I can say that.

"Do you want to?"

"Every motherfucking minute of every day."

Jim lets out a long sigh.

"This is your test . . . your big test. We all have to face them. You need to stay away from her."

"Okay."

"Don't give me lip service Paul. I mean it."

"What if I can't?"

"Remember how you told me how worthless it made you feel when you were out of control? Is it worth it to get that low again?"

I think about Elle's ass with my hands gripping it and I'm at a loss for words.

"It's not worth it Paul. You've said it before, and you made a promise to God and yourself. You want to find a good woman to marry and have kids. You don't want to be getting blow jobs in dive bar bathrooms."

My cock twitches as I picture Elle on her knees. "I don't?"

"You don't, Paul. You've told me again and again, you want what your parents have. You aren't going to find it with a girl like her."

"She's not what you think."

"Paul, you need to be at tonight's meeting or I'm going to have to reconsider being your sponsor. Do you understand how important this is?"

I close my eyes tightly and try to remember my oath. "Yes. I'll be there tonight."

The SA meeting that night gets me back on track. I even get my ass up in front of the group to confess how meeting Elle had gotten me off track.

"Off track? Is that a euphemism for admitting that you're screwing her?" asks George the perv, who gets off on women mud wrestling.

"I'm not screwing her," I reply.

"But you want to," Austin says with a nod of understanding. He's the youngest in our group. He's still in college and I'm pretty sure before he joined our group his college major was screwing anything that stood still long enough.

"So damn badly," I say.

"Are you jerking off a lot?" Austin asks.

I lower my head so I don't have eye contact with Jim when I nod. "Yeah."

Jim clears his throat. "What did we talk about, Paul."

"That jerking off all the time only fires up the obsession and that I should avoid thinking about her if at all possible."

Jim nods. "Unless this is a girl you want to date as a possible future life partner, and you certainly haven't made her sound like a viable prospect, you need to step away."

"He's right," George states. "Pardon the pun, but it only gets harder the longer it goes on. You remember how messed up I got over that mud-wrestling stripper I thought I wanted to marry."

Comparing Elle to George's stripper is just wrong, but I know these guys have my best interest at heart. Besides as beautiful and fun as Elle is, I don't see a dirty mouthed divorcee looking for hook-ups on Tinder as the mother of my future children. My mom definitely raised me with an old-fashioned attitude about marriage.

I have a moment of clarity and decide I'm going to talk to my father when I'm over for our next family dinner about not handling her yard issues anymore.

Everyone is being unusually civil at our family Thursday night dinner. It's a surprise since my siblings and I usually revert to our childhood selves and goad each other into stupid arguments.

Watching whomever gets pissed and storms away from the table has become a regular source of family entertainment.

"Paddy, pass the green beans," Ma says to my brother.

"You really should start steaming these, Ma. You could reduce the calorie total by almost 150."

"But then they'd taste like shit," I respond.

I may be twenty-nine going on thirty, but my dad still gives me a scowl for my use of foul language at the dinner table like he did when I was a kid. Despite that, he nods in agreement at my assessment.

"What kind of man counts calories?" my sister, Trisha asks while rolling her eyes.

"An accountant," Ma answers with a warm smile. She always defends my nerdy brother.

"So Paulie, do you think you could take care of another client for me this week? The Andersons contacted us about drip systems again for their vegetable garden."

"Sure, Dad. I'll give them a call. Speaking of your clients, I wanted to tell you something about Ms. Jacoby."

"How is sweet Elle?" Ma asks. "She is always so lovely on the phone and she pays her bills so promptly."

"Well, she's fine, but I guess her marriage wasn't. She's divorced now."

Both Ma and Dad's mouths drop open in unison—to them divorce is like a capital crime.

"What? Why?" Ma asks. Her Irish brogue is thick, and her accent always gets heavier when she's upset.

"Apparently they were incompatible," I reply, leaving out the fact that it was specifically in bed that they were incompatible.

"Tsk, tsk. Well, thank heavens they had no wee babes yet. I bet he was a cheater," Ma says.

"Only a man who had lost his mind would cheat on that darling lass," says Dad.

"Anywaaay . . . I know your rule about me not working with clients who aren't married, and she's Ms. Jacoby now," I say.

My sister gives me the evil eye like she can see right into my dirty mind but then follows it with a confused look as to why I'm trying to get out of working with her.

For some reason my parents skip over my plea.

"I never understand women who don't take their husband's name. I don't buy that nonsense that it was because she was established with her own business," my dad says.

"I kept my name," Trisha says.

"Well if your husband had been a real man he wouldn't have put up with that."

"Dad," I say as I watch Trisha's face get red, "let's not get into this again."

Dad looks down at his plate and stabs the potatoes with his fork.

Everything is silent for a minute while we chew our food until Ma clears her throat.

"So, what do you think, Papa?" She nods over toward Patrick who knows the calorie counts for everything, and can do a balance sheet like a champ, but can't add one plus one when it comes to women.

Dad looks doubtful as he squints considering what she's thinking. It's creepy how he always seems to know what's on her mind since they usually communicate telepathically or something, but after she winks at him he nods.

"Okay, invite her to dinner next week."

"What?" I clutch the end of the table so hard the table tips.

"Ma's matchmaking and doing a hook-up for Patrick again," Trisha explains.

I'm pretty sure my firefighter sister, the upstanding citizen that she is, doesn't actually mean 'hook-up' but just hearing the term applied to Patrick and Elle fills me with rage.

"What's this? So I can't fix her sprinklers but Patrick can date her?"

"Well you guys have opposite problems don't you?" Trisha says.

"How's that?"

"You can't keep it in your pants, and he never seems to get

his out of his pants."

"Trisha McNeill!" Ma yells.

"You know I'm right," Trisha says leaning back and folding her arms over her chest.

"Paddy's older so I think a divorcee is okay," Dad says. "And as for you, Paulie, I'll handle Elle from now on."

"Awesome," I grumble.

I get up from the table, go to the kitchen and come back with a beer. I'll need more than a beer buzz if sexy Elle gets served up to my clueless brother next week.

CHAPTER THREE

STAND AND DELIVER

"You aren't going to believe this."

My hand tightens over my phone. "Elle?"

"My lawn is orgasming again."

I feel a blow to my pride. "But everything was so tight when I left."

"No, that backyard issue is fine. My poor old gardener took out two more heads this week in the front. I swear the man is blind."

"Old or not, that's messed up. He should replace them."

"I tried to get him to do it once and it was a disaster. Ask your dad."

I'm reminded of dinner with the family last week.

"Speaking of my dad, he told me he wants to handle your account from now on." I feel bad as soon as the words come out of my mouth.

"What? Why? Did I do something wrong?" She sounds more upset than I expected.

"No, of course you didn't do anything wrong. Remember how I told you he won't let me see young unmarried clients because of my issues?"

"He thinks you'll have sex with me?" She sounds hopeful and it breaks my heart a little.

"I'm pretty sure he doesn't trust me. I mean look at you."

"You think I'm attractive?"

"How could I not? Even if I were blind, your voice is beautiful."

"Oh, that's so sweet. Well, you know how I feel about you."

I let out a long sigh. "Elle . . ."

"Don't you want to see me?" she asks with a sad lilt to her voice.

"Of course I do. And you're making it sound like you still want to have me work on your yard?"

"Yes . . . I do," she says softly.

"Okay, let me finish up here and then I'll be on my way." As I hang up guilt starts crawling up my spine but I do my best to say the hell with it.

When she pulls open the door I sense that something is wrong—something more than our discussion about my dad. *Damn, what is it with this woman?* I want her to give me her real smile, not this half-baked smile.

I nod toward the yard. "You wanna show me where the old guy messed up my work?"

She sighs. "Thanks for coming."

"I'm your man."

She looks up at me and blinks repeatedly.

"Your sprinkler man," I add, correcting myself.

She blushes and steps out the door until she's standing next to me on the porch. I notice she's barefoot and wearing no make-up. She looks prettier that way. I like it.

She walks to the middle of the lawn and points to the areas of destruction.

"Damn. Does your gardener have issues? What does he have against sprinklers?"

She smiles. "I know, right?"

"You should fire him."

"Actually he's so old he can barely push the lawnmower anymore. I could never fire him. I'd feel terrible."

I bend down and pick up one of the broken heads.

"Can you fix it?

I wink at her. "Baby, I can fix anything."

She turns away and I realize her expression has fallen.

"You okay?"

She nods. "I'm going to get some coffee. You want some?"

"I'm good."

I watch her walk away and I can't shake the feeling that something is really wrong.

When I'm done with the work I let myself in the house and pause in the entryway before walking further in. Everything is in hues of grayed blues and cream. The floors are whitewashed wood, and a quiet beach landscape painting hangs over the couch. It's sophisticated and more serene that I would expect from saucy Elle.

"Elle," I call out.

She doesn't answer and I pause wondering what to do.

Hearing a sniffle, I walk past the living room toward the light-filled den. I spot her curled up in the corner of the couch.

I notice her eyes are red as she brushes a tear away.

Damn it all. I feel so fucking awkward. I pick up the box of tissues on the coffee table and thrust it toward her.

She pulls a tissue out and looks away as she dabs her eyes.

I sit on the edge of the couch. "You want to talk about it?"

She shakes her head. "No."

We sit silently for a minute. I twist my fingers together and look over at her.

She has a glassy stare, her gaze focused out the window.

"You sure, Elle?" I ask. My voice has an edge. I can't hide my anxiety.

She nods.

I rub my hands over my knees and slowly stand. "Okay then, I think I'll take off." I've taken several steps toward the door when she clears her throat.

"I don't think I'm going to do Tinder anymore."

I stop and turn around. "What?"

She picks at something on the sofa arm and doesn't look up. "No more Tinder for me."

As thrilled as I am to hear it, I'm worried about what happened to lead her to that decision. Judging from her demeanor, it must've been bad. I sit back down on the sofa. "Seriously? You're really done with it?"

She nods. "D-o-n-e, done. Maybe I need a hobby or something instead," she says with a forlorn expression.

"Hobbies are good," I agree, my tone encouraging. "I know it's not really a hobby but I work out a lot and it's a great stress release."

"I was thinking more along the lines of something brain numbing like Sudoku or needlepoint."

"Sorry, but I can't picture either of those satisfying you. How about tennis? Do you play? I used to, and there are great courts you can pay for by the hour down on Whitsett. Why don't you come with me and we can just knock the ball around . . . how does that sound?"

She looks so deep in thought that she doesn't appear to be listening to me. "Maybe I should join your no-sex club." She nods her head. "ASU or whatever you called it. Would you take me with you?"

"ASU is a university in Arizona, it's AUL, and I'll take you if it's what you really want but you've got to tell me first what happened."

Her expression gets dark. "He called me a slut," she whispers.

My head jerks toward her. "What?"

"Scott, that guy from Tinder, called me a slut and a whore."

There's an explosion in my chest. It's fury weighted with the gut-kick that I didn't protect her from the very thing I feared.

"When did he call you that?" My fingers curl into fists.

"During the sex." She looks at me wide-eyed and in that moment she looks like a little girl. "He pulled my hair hard, and told me I was a dirty whore . . . that he couldn't believe he was fucking such a nasty slut."

I have to focus on breathing so I don't explode. "What did you do?"

"I just laid there stunned. And when it was over he couldn't stop talking about how friggin' great it was."

"Damn," I say shaking my head.

She curls up tighter. "I just wanted to feel sexy and independent. Like those girls on those racy cable shows."

I inch over closer to her and when she doesn't flinch I slide my arm over her shoulder. When she leans into me I pull her closer.

"Oh, Elle. Those girls are fictional characters and that guy is a fucker. You know he didn't mean that, right? That's what gets him off . . . it's not you."

She leans into me but remains silent.

"When did you have sex with him?"

"A couple of nights ago, and still I can't get over what he called me . . . all of those awful things. I'm just so angry with myself for not following my instincts when we first hooked up. Yes, I want hot sex but being told I'm a trashy whore feels abusive, not sexy."

"Have you talked to him since then?"

She shakes her head. "No. He's left me a few messages to hook up again but I haven't responded."

"You want me to tell him to fuck off?"

Her eyes widen. "You'd do that?"

"Sure I'll do it. He won't bug you again." I crack my knuckles as I think of pounding his face in, even though I won't have the chance to do more than threaten him on the phone.

She drops her head against my shoulder. "You're really something Paul. Thank you for offering but I'm going to have to do it. I need to stand up for myself, but it means a lot that you want to help."

"Okay. Well, you know where to find me if you change your mind."

She wipes her tears away again and sits up straight.

"You know I never thought being a modern woman who

embraces her sexuality would be so difficult. Why can't I enjoy this side of me without being made to feel bad about it?"

"You shouldn't feel bad about being true to yourself," I agree.

"Before I got married I used to underplay that side of myself because I wanted to be noted for my intelligence and abilities but look where that got me. It feels like finding a man who embraces my sexual side while still respecting me may be impossible."

I rub my palms over my knees. "When it comes to sex, men think with their cocks. And we all know cocks are defiant assholes and have minds of their own."

"Is your cock like that?"

"Well he sure as hell used to be. It's taken two years of meetings for him to understand that I'm the boss now."

"What if I never find a man that wants what I want?"

"You will, Elle. You just haven't looked in the right place yet."

She smiles at me. "Hey, I forgot to tell you. Your mom called and invited me to dinner."

I scowl inwardly. "Yeah, she mentioned she might."

"She was talking up your brother, Paddy. What's that all about?"

"She has a second career, my mom."

"Which would be . . ."

"Matchmaker."

"Ooo. She's setting me up with your brother? Is he hot like you?"

I have to choke back a laugh. "Well, we're pretty different. He's an accountant and he's four years older than me."

She scrunches up her nose. "An accountant? That's not nearly as sexy as a landscape architect."

"And sprinkler man," I tease.

She pushes me on my shoulder. "Is he addicted to sex too?"

Embarrassed I look down. "Ah no, . . . He doesn't share my affliction apparently."

"Okay . . . so he isn't as hot as you, he's an accountant, and he isn't hot for sex. So why do I want to date him?"

"To make my parents happy."

"Ha! Your parents! Do you want me to come? I'll come if *you* want me to."

"Don't do me any favors. Besides, you'll have to deal with my sister, Trisha. She's a mouthy firefighter married to a florist. It's like a bad sitcom."

"Will her husband be there?"

"He usually doesn't come. He uses the excuse that he's working but I think he's scared of my dad who's convinced he's gay."

"Just because he's a florist?"

"My dad's really old school. I'm hoping he'll ease up if they ever have kids."

She breaks her first smile since I found her on the couch. "Oh, I've got to come now. I'm so curious."

I'm picturing Elle in her high-heel sandals and bare legs for miles. When my mom gets one look at her it'll be the last invite for our family dinner. Ma is looking for breeders for her boys, not hot babes.

"Okay then. Just remember that I warned you." I give her shoulder a squeeze and then scoot to the edge of the couch. "I better go."

"If you must," she says.

I glance down at the coffee table and something catches my eye. There's a short stack of books and the top one's cover intrigues me. Its title is in bold red letters: *Broken,* and the picture is of a pissed off guy with tattoos and no shirt on.

I pick it up to examine it more closely.

"What's this?" I ask.

She tucks her face into her folded arm and groans before mumbling something.

"What was that?"

"It's a book I just read."

"What kind of book is this?" I wonder aloud as I study it.

"A romance." Her cheeks are pink and she looks away.

"What the hell kind of romance is this? This dude looks like he's going to beat the shit out of someone. Is it a gangbanger romance?"

She giggles softly. "No. It's an erotic romance."

"Well seriously? What's romantic about this? Shouldn't there be a girl in a low cut pirate dress about to kiss this guy? I remember my mom having some of those in the house."

She grins. "Pirate dress?"

"You know what I mean. The kind that's low cut with laces and her tits busting out. If she were on the cover I bet this dude would be a lot less pissed off."

I reach for the next book in the pile. This one has a guy in a suit with his head cropped off and it's called, *Deal or Die*. "Is this a romance, too?" I ask, not hiding the disbelief in my voice.

"It is indeed."

I flip through the pages. "Is there a lot of sex in these books?"

"Does the sun shine?"

"Is it hot?"

"I thought it was." She pulls *Deal or Die* out of my hands. "I burned out two sets of batteries on this book, but I doubt that will happen again."

Oh damn, picturing Elle burning out batteries with a vibrator between her legs will require a long shower for me tonight. "Why's that?"

"He talks dirty to her a lot." She glances down to where she's twisting her fingers together.

"What kind of dirty?"

"He calls her a slut and a whore."

"I see. And when you read that you thought it was hot?"

"I did . . ."

"But it's a lot different when you're the one being called a slut?"

She nods and her eyes tear up again.

I slide back against the cushion of the couch so that our shoulders are touching.

"We've talked a lot in my group about watching porn vs.

reality. It's easy to get desensitized as to what is good for you and the woman you're with and what isn't."

She sighs. "Sex can be confusing."

"Mind-blowing and amazing, but yes, confusing too." I flip through the rest of the pile. "Hey can I read one of these?"

"Why would you want to?"

"Maybe to understand what makes the female fantasy psyche work."

"Are you sure?" She sounds nervous.

They must really be dirty. "Yeah, I'm sure."

She grabs the pile and sorts through it. "Here, read this one."

"*Torched?*"

"It's so hot."

"Seriously? I mean with the flames in this picture it looks like his head's on fire so I guess that's hot."

"Well, I think the story is hot." She gives me a demure smile.

"Okay. That's good enough for me." I turn the book over in my hands a few times. "I better get going."

"Hey, Paul Junior?"

"Yes, Ms. Jacoby?"

"If you ever decide to be a man-whore again will you have sex with me?"

I kiss the top of her head. "You'll be first on my list."

This time, as I lift off the couch and say good-bye, her smile is genuine.

That night I climb into bed and crack open *Torched*. I'm not even to the end of the first chapter when the main dude, Luke, is fucking this Lucia chick in the back of his parent's tasting room at their vineyard.

I shudder at the dialogue and descriptions—throbbing clits, massive cocks and all the wetness. It all starts with the guy ripping her panties off. Have you ever tried to rip off a pair of panties? It's not like they just pull apart. Those things are sewn to stay together, and I gave a girl a skin burn once trying to yank off that lacey shit.

But the best are the orgasms on command. "Come!" he commands. And she does.

I roll my eyes. *Right. If only . . .*

I close my eyes and imagine I'm hearing the buzz of Elle's vibrator as she reads, dropping the book on her bed to circle her nipples while the vibrator gets her off. Now that's my kind of erotica. I sigh as I grip my hard cock. It's going to be a really long night.

The next evening the phone rings just as I'm finishing off my second scotch and watching the game.

I glance at the screen. *Damn.*

It's her. *Elle,* with a capital E.

The girl that kept me up late last night jerking off. I've got a little buzz going from my couple of drinks and talking to her right now is risky.

I clear my throat and try to push my dirty thoughts aside. "What's up, Elle?"

"Hi, Paul," she says in that breathy voice.

I'm already getting hard again. *Damn.*

"I just wanted to let you know that thanks to you I'm feeling so much better today."

"That's great," I say, impressed with how much better she sounds. "And what brought that on?"

"I was thinking about what we talked about . . ."

I can't resist the impulse to fill in all the blanks of what she wants to tell me . . . *and the dirty book I gave you to read . . .*

"And it occurred to me," she says earnestly.

. . . how much I want you, Paul . . .

But when she finishes her thoughts it's nothing like what I thought she would say.

"Why should I let one bad apple spoil the whole bunch?"

I sit straight up. *What the hell? Can we hit rewind?*

When I reply my voice is louder than intended. "Did you

really just say that one bad apple shit? My mother used to tell me that. Have you ever considered that the whole bunch on Tinder could be bad apples?"

"You're so funny!"

"I'm not joking," I say.

"Seriously Paul, I've decided to throw myself back into the game."

"But Tinder's not really a game, Elle . . . it's more like the mosh pit. What if you get head butted again?"

"I've realized the mistake I made. This time I'm going to spell it out to the dude before we get to the sexing."

"Spell it out, huh?"

"Yeah, no weird stuff like latex or furry suits. No demeaning talk or behavior. No bondage. No threesomes."

"Or foursomes?" I ask.

"Ewww, no!" she says.

"Are you trying to make me feel bad?"

"What? No, why?"

"I told you about my foursome."

"Oh, I'm sorry. I forgot about that. That was when you were a man-whore."

"Yes, thanks, although I prefer the term 'sex fiend'."

"Well . . . that's still what you told me."

"I did. So see, I'm the very guy you wouldn't want to sleep with."

"Ummm."

"Yet, you pretty much asked me to screw you when we met. Do you see how complicated this is?"

"Can I ask you something, Paul?"

"Sure, why not? You know so much about me already."

"Did you do men too back during your sex fiend days?"

I almost drop the phone. "Sex with dudes? No! Why would you ask that?"

"So your orgy was really just you and a bunch of women. Did you have a harem or something?"

"I could have."

She huffs into the phone. "Oh really? A harem? What if you're making all this stuff up? Why should I believe you and all your big talk?"

"If you don't believe me, I don't care. It doesn't change anything."

"What if you made up all those sexy stories . . . like that you were addicted to sex. What if you're really more like your accountant brother?"

I feel the vein pop out on my forehead. Why is she screwing with me?

"I know what this is about," I whisper in a dark voice.

"Oh yeah? What's that?"

"You're provoking me, trying to get me to come over there and fuck you and break my oath. Well, it's not going to happen."

"Good!"

"Yup, good."

"Because you know what, mister? You don't fit into my profile anyway."

"Oh that's rich. You must have one hell of a profile."

"Well look at you. You're searching for a little complacent wifey who will roast your chicken and birth you a bevy of babies."

"Roast my chicken? What's that a metaphor for?"

"It's not a metaphor, it's dinner."

I roll my eyes. "You're pretty weird, you know."

"And you don't want to fuck anymore and nothing's weirder than that . . . so who's calling the kettle black?"

"Who says I don't *want* to fuck? I never said that. I want it."

"Really?"

"Sure." *I want it bad.* So bad it hurts, but I don't tell her that.

"So it's that you just don't want to fuck me?"

"Oh, I want to fuck you. Right now I want to throw you on the bed and ride you so hard you won't be able to walk the next day."

There's a long silent pause. *Maybe that was too much.*

"Ms. Jacoby, are you still there?"

"I'm here, Paul Junior. I'm just distracted thinking about you throwing me on the bed."

"And mounting you?"

"Yes."

I hear a soft moan.

"And fucking you hard?"

"God, yes."

"So you really want that, do you?"

"You're cruel. Are you going to make me beg for it?"

"Maybe."

"Please . . . Paul, are you touching yourself? Because I am."

I pause.

"Maybe."

"Mmm."

I feel myself unraveling from this conundrum of a woman with her dirty mouth. I've never known a female I couldn't figure out at all until I met her. When I hear her moan again my mind goes to a visual of her with legs spread and her hand in her panties. I swallow hard.

"Elle, what are you thinking about when you ride your vibrator?"

"That I'd rather it was you."

Damn. "Yeah?"

"Or more specifically, your anaconda."

"I bet you'd like that." My fingers tighten over the phone, my other hand tightens over my cock.

"You can teach me to be bad. Is that big-boy hard?"

I tighten my grasp. "Does the sun shine?"

"You're killing me here, Paul. Please come fuck me."

Oh for God's sake why am I being tested like this?

My heart is pounding as I hear that little bastard speak up— the annoying voice that lives in my head.

You fuck her Paul, and then what? How will you feel in the morning?

My mouth is dry as I respond to her plea with unbearable regret.

"No. I just can't."

It's another tortured night and it's becoming apparent I'm on a slippery slope and losing more self-control by the day. No more drunken late night phone calls with Ms. Jacoby. That's for sure. I can't even believe the stuff I said to her. *Ride your vibrator?* What the hell am I doing?

I go in late to work the next morning so I can go straight to a meeting. Jim studies me as I approach him.

"Rough night?"

"Yeah, and rough morning too."

He nods with a sympathetic gaze. "Well you came to the right place."

That afternoon at work I finish going over the plans for tomorrow's meeting at the Taylor project when a thought occurs to me. I call my old hook-up buddy Gabriel. Thank God I'm so much calmer than I was earlier.

"Hey, Gabe, you free after work to catch a beer?"

"I'm free now. My day's over already. You still at work?"

I glance at my watch. It's not that early before the time I usually take off. "I could head over there now."

"Brennigans?"

"Yeah, I'll be there in about twenty."

Gabe's already parked at the bar with a beer and watching the game when I walk past the studio techs and grips that are gathered around the pool tables. The wood paneling on the walls makes everything darker through the haze of smoke wafting in from the patio. I buy a beer and then nod to him for us to move to a booth. He's changed out of his working gear. I almost didn't recognize him all cleaned up.

I still can't believe that Gabe stayed in L.A. after high school to work for my dad while I went off to college.

"What's up, Paul? We haven't done this in a while. You still watching your partying?"

"Yeah . . . among other things."

"He gives me a knowing look. Well, your dad says you're doing great, but if you don't mind my saying so it doesn't sound like you're having much fun."

I hate admitting to myself that I miss when we used to go out looking to score.

"How about you?"

"No complaints. I've got season tickets for the Clippers and I have plenty of other fun too."

"Got a girlfriend yet?"

"Hell no. Who needs the headache? I'm still playing the field . . . sampling all the flavors. Why settle for one, when there's so many to choose from?"

He holds up his beer in a toast and we clink bottles.

I lean in toward him. "While we're on the subject there's something I want to ask you about."

"Yeah?"

"Tinder."

He chuckles. "So you're telling me you're ready to have fun. Are you going to start clubbing with me again?"

"No, I'm helping a friend."

"Sure you are. That's as good a bogus reason as any, my man."

I glance around our booth and make sure no one I know is nearby. "Can you show me how it works?"

"Yeah, no problem. It's a really easy way to get laid. I use it all the time."

He pulls out his phone and opens the app, flipping through the most recent women interested in connecting with him. He swipes the screen to the right when he's interested, to the left when he isn't.

"So what happens to those girls?" I ask.

"Poof. They're gone."

"Whoa. Really?"

"Yeah, see how easy it is. And only the ones you keep can

contact you. That's how you arrange the hook up."

"Can I see who you've kept?"

He hands me his phone. "Be my guest."

I'm stunned as I scan through all of the women he's saved. All of them are do- able, some actually hot. How out of control would I have been if I'd had this when I was on the prowl? "And all of these women live in close range?"

"Close enough. I'll drive farther if they really turn me on."

With the next sweep of my finger across the screen I freeze. *Elle.* She's wearing a low cut shirt and posed provocatively. She looks like a girl who'd like a little trouble. My heart is pounding.

I hold the phone out to Gabe. "Who's this one?"

He sighs. "Hot, right?"

I nod. My mouth's suddenly dry.

He shrugs. "I can't get her to respond to me. She hasn't accepted me yet. According to her start date she's pretty new to Tinder, so who knows what's up with her. But believe me, the minute she does respond to me I'm going to nail her."

I let out the breath I've been holding. I'm surprised how relieved I am that she hasn't accepted him. That feeling is followed by feeling like I'm going to have to kick his ass if he ever nails her.

"So what can you do?" I ask.

He shrugs. "Nothing. I can't send her a message or do anything unless she accepts me. Hey why don't you get on? Maybe she'll accept you."

I glance back down at her picture and become anxious, like I don't want her on this site . . . other men looking at her, wanting her like I do right now.

He shows me how to check out her other pictures and her statement. I almost knock my beer over as I read it.

I'm a caged bird finally set free.

I want to live big and try things I've never done.

I've got an open mind, and a free spirit . . . are you ready for me?

Let's connect . . .

The flush moves up my chest so fast I get dizzy. What the

hell, Elle? Does she not understand that men are animals and she's just asked to be fucked, drawn, and quartered?

Gabe's expression becomes suspicious. "What?"

I rub my hand over my face before studying her pictures again. "Damn, Elle."

"Dude. Do you know this girl?"

I nod.

"Can you introduce me? She's off the flipping charts."

I shake my head.

"Oh I see how it is," he grumbles. "I'm your hook-up pimp. Well screw you."

I throw a tip down on the table and grin. "Screw you too, buddy. I've gotta go."

When I get to her house, her car is parked in the driveway and the porch light is on. I have to ring her doorbell twice, and when she answers she has one sandal on, and the other one in her hand. Her eyes grow wide when she sees me.

"Hey, Paul. What's up?"

She's got that lipstick on again.

I realize I didn't think this out very well. I shouldn't have just shown up impulsively.

"Do you have a minute?"

"Well, I'm on my way out . . . but I guess I've got a sec. Come on in, I've got to get my other shoe on."

I follow her into the living room where she sits on the edge of a chair and straps on a sandal that's even higher-heeled than the last pair I saw on her.

"What's up?" she asks as finishes the buckle and runs her hand up her calf. I'm disappointed when she stops at her knees.

"I want to talk to you about Tinder." I jam my hands in the pocket of my jeans. She looks up at me with narrow eyes.

"What about Tinder?"

"I saw your profile."

She arches her brow. "You have to join Tinder to see my profile."

I shake my head. "My friend was showing me how it works and you were one of the girls in his line-up."

"Oh really?" Rising, she puts her hands on her hips. "What's his name?"

"Gabriel."

She nods. "I remember him. That guy is a friend of yours?"

"Yes, we used to be really good friends. He also works for my dad."

"I wasn't interested."

"So your instincts aren't all bad. He's one to stay away from for sure."

"Hmmm. Maybe I'll check him out again. Gabriel you say?" She picks up a sparkly bracelet off the table and snaps it on.

"Where are you going?"

"Out."

"To a Tinder hook-up?"

"Nosy aren't you?"

"Show me."

"Show you what?"

"On your phone. I want to see who you're meeting."

"Why do you want to see who I'm meeting? Jealous?"

My stomach churns. *What if she's right?* "No, I'm not jealous. I'm going to screen him for you."

"Oh really?" She steps out of the living room and returns with her phone. She sits next to me on the couch, close enough that I can smell her perfume. Damn, she smells good—like a rose that's just opened in the garden.

I watch her bring up the app.

"His name is Stephan. He's an architect."

"Impressive," I say.

"He designs buildings."

"So much better than a sprinkler guy." I point to her phone. "Let me see Stephan the builder." I study the screen and chuckle. "Look at that. His hairline is receding. He'll be bald in five years."

She grabs the phone out my hand. "What are you talking

about?"

Leaning closer to her, I point to the screen. "This isn't just a high forehead."

She purses her lips. "I don't mind. Some bald guys are sexy."

"As long as you don't mind hair all over their backs."

"Excuse me?"

I shrug. "It's a phenomenon. Their hair falls off their heads right when it starts to grow on their shoulders and down their back."

"Ewww! No hair on the back!"

She pinches a part of my shirt near the back and starts to pull upward. "I want to see. Do you have hair on your back?"

I brush her hand away. "Of course not. I'm Irish. We have sleek backs and great heads of hair."

"Oh really?"

I lean my head toward her. "Care to see for yourself?"

She pushes her fingers through my hair then grabs a bunch and tugs. "Wow, you've got a lot of hair."

I groan. I love having my hair tugged at. "Do that again."

She pulls harder and I groan louder. "Keep that up and the balding guy is going to be very disappointed when you don't show up."

"Oh yeah?" she asks as she rakes her fingers into my hair and then tugs so hard it brings tears to my eyes.

"Hell, yeah." I reach up and wrap my fingers tightly around her wrist and then regretfully pull it away from me.

Before I know what's happening she eases me forward and then yanks my T- shirt upward.

"What the hell . . ."

"Shhh. I've got to know."

She bunches my T-shirt up near my shoulders, then lightly rakes her fingernails over the surface of my back. She sighs.

"What?"

"No back hair."

"I told you."

"Mmm, and you've got a really nice back, too."

"You think?"

Her fingers slowly run diagonally from my shoulder to my waist. "Who has muscles in their back like that? Do you lift weights or something?" I can hear the admiration in her voice.

"Something like that." I wish it were okay for her to keep touching me. I've missed being touched and now I'm kind of aching for it. But if she keeps it up, I'll be more than touching her.

I point to her phone. "You know Stephan has beady eyes."

She stops stroking me and pulls my shirt back down.

"No he doesn't. His eyes are seductive, not beady."

I shake my head. "What if he's another asshole?"

"He isn't. I asked him all the questions and his answers were spot on. He likes to worship a woman."

I roll my eyes. "He did not say that."

"Indeed he did." She grins.

"Let me guess . . . and his bed's an altar."

Her eyes widen. "He said that too!"

"And you believed that crap?"

She stands up and straightens her skirt. "Okay, you've made your point. Geez, you're like the big brother I never had. This has been fun, but I don't want to be late."

Turning, she walks toward the front door and I follow. "Can I just say one more thing about Tinder?"

She picks her purse off the side table. "Be my guest."

"Your profile is screaming out for the wrong kind of guy."

She stops in front of the door and turns to me. "Is that so?"

"Yeah. You might as well say 'Hey, assholes . . . I'm easy pickings'."

The edges of her mouth turn down. "Gee, thanks."

"It also makes you sound like an idiot."

She purses her lips and opens the front door. "I'm leaving and you're an asshole."

I step up to the door and press it shut. "I'm not trying to be an asshole, I just need you to understand you're at risk."

She lets out a long mournful sigh as she opens the door back up. "I can take care of myself. Go home, Paul."

I lean into her close to her ear, my lips grazing her wavy hair. "I'm a caged bird finally set free . . . are you ready for me? And that sexy photo of you that makes you look like a pin-up girl. What the hell, Elle?"

She turns and looks up at me with those big eyes. Her gaze is intense and the energy between us is charged—like power-grid-amped, nuclear power plant sizzling. I want to press her against the wall and grind against her while I kiss her senseless.

"You know something, Paul? I don't think you're ready for me . . . but you know what?"

I swallow hard. "What?"

"Stephan is."

She turns on her heel and walks to her car, rocking those high heels like a runway model, leaving me in her open door-way with my mouth agape.

CHAPTER FOUR

THE HOT SEAT

I'm uneasy as I inch my way down Franklin Boulevard driving to my parent's. The streets are clogged with hipsters at the coffee houses and juice bars powering up for the night of partying up ahead. I chuckle knowing I'm heading to a family dinner. What is my life?

You're so cool, dude.

To top it off I'm having reservations. Considering how my last encounter with Elle went, I'm not sure how it's going to be seeing her tonight. I tried to back out but my dad wouldn't hear of it.

"Your mother is expecting you, Paulie."

Yeah, they aren't super flexible about the dinner thing. I think my mom would like me to still be living at the house like Patrick. I love my parents, as a good son would, but living at home could never happen again. I moved out at eighteen and never looked back.

I find Ma in the kitchen checking on her special meatloaf. Trisha is next to her and beating the hell of something that must have once been potatoes. Dad is in the living room with Patrick, probably giving him advice about women. He needs it.

Desperately.

Suddenly the absurdity of this evening hits me and makes me grin. Patrick and Elle are as likely a pair as oil and water.

She's so forward that she'll scare the hell out of him, and he's so dull that she'd have trouble staying awake through a single date. I relax and decide to enjoy the inevitable fail of an evening.

When the doorbell rings, everyone pops to attention and Ma hurries to the kitchen sink and washes her hands. She's still drying her hands with the dishtowel when Dad answers the front door. We both lean into the hallway to see what's happening.

"Oooo. Oh my," my mom says as Elle steps inside. She has a big smile and is holding what looks like a pie.

Ma sets the dishtowel on the counter. "What a pretty lass she is."

I'm too dumbstruck to respond. Elle's hair is pulled off her face and looks smooth, not her usual wild and wavy. She's also dressed like a librarian in a longer skirt, sweater, and flat, slipper-looking shoes. If I'd passed her in the street I'm not sure I'd have recognized her.

Patrick practically trips over his own feet to get over to her while Dad handles the introductions. Ma turns and winks at me before hurrying forward.

"Welcome to our home, Elle!" Ma announces halfway down the hall.

I can't hear Elle's exact response but she extends her free hand and shakes Ma's with a sweet smile. I didn't think she had it in her to be so demure.

Ma gestures to the couch and then takes the pie out of Elle's hand so she can bring it to the kitchen. When she returns she holds it up close to my face.

"She. Baked. A. Pie," she says like Elle just won a gold medal.

"I can see that."

"She's perfect for our Patrick!" After she sets the pie down she claps her hands together with a victorious smile.

I can't help but give her a worried look. Has she lost her mind? "Because she baked a pie?"

"It's not just that!"

"Then what?"

Ma practically swoons. I've never seen my mother like this.

"She's just lovely, Paul." She points into the living room. "And look, they're hitting it off already."

I glance at where she's pointing. So now Patrick staring at Elle's breasts while she talks to Dad indicates a sure-fire love connection. I roll my eyes.

"Don't book the wedding venue yet, Ma."

"Don't be such a downer. She's lovely and so sweet—and she baked that pie from scratch!"

"But you haven't even talked to her yet. Talk about judging a book by its cover!"

"True, but I can tell she's something special. And did you see the way Paddy looked at her. He's smitten for sure."

"How could that be when he doesn't know anything about her yet? Didn't you warn us to stay away from divorcees? What happened to all your rules?"

Ma puts her hands on her hips. "Paul Fredrick McNeill! If I didn't know better, I'd say you're jealous."

I nod with a deadpan expression. "Yeah, wildly jealous. I wouldn't stand a chance with a girl like Elle."

Ma nods too eagerly. "You may be right. You are a bit of a rogue you know, and she's a nice girl."

I bite my tongue. There's no use sullying Elle's good impression with talk of Tinder hook-ups and a coffee table stacked with porn books pretending to be romance novels.

I look at the pow-wow still going on in the living room. The circle is wider now that Trisha has joined in. I turn to Ma. "So you think Patrick is going to win her heart with his thrilling stories from the world of accounting?"

"Stop!" she says as she grabs the dishcloth and snaps it at me, before joining the rest of the family.

I open a beer and linger in the kitchen a few minutes longer. I'm in no rush to join the Patrick hook-up party.

"Oh, Paulie," Ma calls out as a summons.

I sigh, set down my beer, and surrender.

"Hi, Ms. Jacoby," I say as I approach. Now that I'm seeing Elle up close it really rustles my jimmies. Is the get-up she's wearing *Irish Catholic family cosplay* or something? She looks like she's heading out to her job at the library. I'm holding back a snicker so hard that my lips are tingling.

She reaches out to shake my hand and when she does I realize I've never held her hand. Damn it's strong but so soft at the same time.

"Hi, Paul Junior."

Dad laughs. "Oh you don't have to call him Junior, lass. We call him Paulie."

She grins like she knows how much I'm not enjoying this. "Paulie. I like that. Hi, Paulie."

"And what shall I call you? Is it Eleanor?"

She arches her brow with pursed lips. "No, Elle will be fine, thank you."

Ma turns away from me. "And Patrick was just telling Elle about his promotion at work. Weren't you, Paddy?"

He nods as his cheeks color. "I'll be a senior manager now, just below being a junior director."

Oh for fuck's sake. Soon he'll be the VP of senior mid-level bottom-feeder ass- kissers.

"Impressive," Elle says in a breathy voice. "Why don't you sit over next to me and tell me more about it."

By the time we get to the meatloaf she's mastered gazing at him like he's the most interesting person in the world, while Ma and Dad keep mentioning his accomplishments to keep the conversation going.

Trisha, for once in her life, doesn't say much, but the shit-eating grin she has watching me slowly get riled up is really pissing me off.

The family and Elle are drinking some pussy chardonnay that you couldn't pay me to gargle with. When I go into the kitchen to get another beer, Trisha follows me in.

"What's up, Paul Junior?"

I narrow my eyes. "Screw you."

"What, are you pissed because there's finally a skirt more interested in Patrick than you?"

"Yeah, I'm devastated." I take a long swig of my beer and then wipe off my mouth on my sleeve. "Completely devastated."

"It's got to hurt. I mean she's really cute."

"You think?" I ask, studying Trisha. Maybe she's gay too, and she and her husband Mikey are beards for each other. Talk about a marriage of convenience.

"Super cute. Have you ever seen Ma this amped up?"

"Not since Prince William and Kate got married."

"Right!"

I decide to push the envelope. "So when they get married do you think they'll live here with Ma and Dad . . . you know since Patrick still lives at home?"

"Good question. Maybe. But doesn't she have a house or something? Weren't you there recently helping Dad with a job?"

I slap my hand over my forehead. "What's in that damn meatloaf? Are you people all high or something? I was joking Trisha! They're not getting married!"

"How do you know? Daddy asked Ma to marry him on their first date."

"That was decades ago, when they lived in a tiny village in Ireland where Dad could either marry Ma, or his second cousin. Times have changed, Trisha, or haven't you noticed?"

"Jealous," she says with a taunting expression.

"Shut up," I growl.

"Jealous! Jealous!" She spins on her heel and goes back to the dining room with me following close behind.

I sink back into my dining room chair with a huff and dig into my meatloaf.

Taking a sip of her wine, Elle watches me over the edge of her glass I stare back and raise my eyebrows with a *what-the-hell* look.

When her eyes dart over to my mom and then my dad, and sees they're both focused on their dinner, she looks back at me with a piercing intensity.

I take a long sip of beer as I glare back. She holds her gaze without blinking.

Game on, Elle. But damn, the woman has focus. My eyes start to water from the pressure and I turn to Ma as I blink.

"I like Elle's outfit, don't you, Ma? It's much fancier than what she wears at home."

"I do," Ma says with a smile.

Elle gives me a dirty look with a headshake so subtle that I doubt anyone else notices.

"What do you mean exactly, Paul?" Patrick asks, his serious accountant expression on his face.

"Oh you know at her home she had those tight stretchy pants on and a little tank top on during my first visit to her place last week," I say as I fill my spoon with a pile of buttered peas.

Patrick's eyes widen as he glances at Elle and then looks down at his plate.

Elle's cheeks color. "I was wearing my work-out outfit. And in fairness I wasn't expecting anyone at the house just then."

"Riiiight," I say before leaning back in my chair.

"I think it's lovely that you work-out and keep such a nice figure," Ma says.

"What kind of working out do you do in an outfit like that?" I ask.

"It's a Pilates spin-off. You know, working with resistance."

"Resistance? How do you do that?"

"With exercise balls, and various elastic straps."

I rest my elbow on the table and rest my chin in my hand. After she's had a bit of time to fidget, I tilt my chin up and soften my expression to give her, what has been termed, my panty-decimating smile.

I clear my throat. "Really, balls and straps?"

She shakes her head briskly. "It's a great workout. I swear," she says sounding a bit frantic.

"Well, I'd *really* like to see that sometime. You and this resistance thing."

In the downcast light of the light fixture over the table I can see her cheeks are turning hot pink.

"Me too," says Patrick the dork. He has no fucking clue what's going on.

Elle looks like she's just steps away from losing her cool entirely.

It's at this point my dad announces that he'd love some of that pie Elle brought. Ma jumps up and starts clearing dishes. After they gesture at Trisha and I, we pick up the cue to help clear too.

Dad pushes his chair back. "What would everyone like with dessert? Tea, coffee? I think I'd like a hot toddy with the pie? How about you, Millie?"

Ma nods her head.

The way the three of them scurry to the kitchen it's obvious that it's a ploy to get Patrick alone with Elle.

He keeps nervously folding and unfolding his napkin in his lap. I turn toward him. "Hey, Patrick, show Elle the animal shapes you can fold out of napkins."

She turns to him with a bewildered expression.

"When I was in school I worked summers at the country club," he explains to Elle.

My work here is done, I think as he clears a space on the table to fold his napkin.

Everyone is bustling about the kitchen as I lean against the pantry door. While I sip my beer, Ma keeps peeking through the crack in the door to spy on Patrick and Elle.

"Oh, he just folded his rabbit!" Ma says to Dad.

Even Trisha rolls her eyes.

"What do you imagine she thinks?" Dad asks.

"Well, she's smiling at him. I think it's good. It shows he's not just about numbers and tax write-offs."

Oh for fucks sake. He's folding a fucking napkin in the shape of a rabbit.

Ma peeks again and then turns back to us. "He got up and left the room. Paulie, go ask if she'd like a spot of tea or some coffee. I don't think she should have a toddy since she'll be driving."

"Sure thing, Ma."

"Hey, Elle," I say as casually as possible as I approach the table.

She sits up straight and pulls her shoulders back when she sees me.

"Hi Paulie."

"So where's Patrick? Did you scare him off with your dirty mouth?"

She gives me a stern look and shakes her head before glancing toward the kitchen door that's still closed.

"He got an emergency text from a client, so he excused himself to email them some documents."

"That's Patrick!" I say with a grin.

"He'll be back very soon."

"Sure he will."

I pull out Patrick's chair and flip it around before I straddle it and sit, resting my arms across the back of the chair.

She turns to study me, her expression full of apprehension.

I lean as close to her as I can without tipping the chair over.

"So what's with the get-up?" I ask with a low voice.

She shrugs. "Whatever do you mean?"

I wave my hand over her outfit. "The librarian get-up. It's so . . . unexpected."

She looks away but I notice the corners of her mouth turn up. "I guess I'm just full of surprises."

"And you bake pie from scratch, and can charm the pants of my parents with a single smile."

"All good things, I'd say."

"I guess so. But where's Vamp Elle? Where's she hiding?" I lift the edge of her long skirt up a bit and pretend to peek underneath. "Is she hiding under this granny skirt?"

She slaps my hand away.

"You think you know me so well."

"I mean, don't get me wrong, librarians are hot. I slept with one once who was smoking."

"Is this during the man-whore days?"

I nod. "She talked a lot while we screwed, and she had a

dirty mouth like you except she used a lot of big fancy words, too."

"Is that so? Is this supposed to be of interest to me?"

She crosses her legs and when she does her skirt slides up and I swear I see a hint of a garter holding up her stocking.

Oh damn, does she know that garters and stockings are my weakness?

My voice breaks a little when I lean toward her even closer. "Why are you messing with me, Elle?"

She folds her arms over her chest. "How am I messing with *you*?"

"My brother? Really?" My fingers tighten over the top of the chair. "Do you honestly think he's going to give you the hot sex you're searching for?"

"Looks can be deceiving, you know."

"Well tonight, that line certainly applies to you, but Patrick is pretty much a *what-you-see-is-what-you-get* kind of guy."

"I'll find that out for myself, thank you."

I lean back and grind my teeth. "Why are you trying to make me jealous? And not even over someone worth being jealous about?"

Her eyes widen. "Jealous? You don't want me. Why would you care if he does?"

I growl with frustration. "Like it's that simple."

"Isn't it?"

"Next time you come over I won't be here. It just messes with me being close to you."

"How so?"

"I'm a man, Elle. Just because I'm trying to abstain doesn't mean I don't desire you."

She bites her lip. "And being close to me stirs that up?"

"If I had my way right now, I'd push all of these dishes over, lift you up until your ass was on the table and then I'd have you for dessert."

She swallows hard. "Dessert?"

"I bet you'd be extra sweet."

Elle loops her index finger under the collar of her sweater and then pulls it away from her flushed skin.

"Please . . . stop. It's cruel to tease me like this."

"So I'm getting to you?"

I can hear her short breaths and her eyes look wild. "Paul," she whispers.

I notice footsteps behind me.

"Paul, what are you doing?"

I look up to see Patrick sliding his cell phone back into his shirt pocket.

"Keeping Elle company." I slowly lift myself off the chair and turn it back to face the table. "She was sitting out here all by her lonesome self and I felt bad about it."

"Well, I'm back now," Patrick says right as the rest of the family joins us with the pie and clean plates.

We all dig into what could be the best apple pie I've ever eaten. I'm even considering helping myself to a third piece when Elle announces she needs to get going. She explains that she has an event meeting first thing in the morning.

Although I'm not sure what kind of meeting that is, it gives Elle a new dimension to think she has important work to attend to. I must be an ass because I've never asked about her job or career. How lousy is that?

Patrick, the gentleman, stands up to pull out her chair. He insists on walking her out to her car but first she has to have the royal McNeill send off. Ma gives her one of her crushing hugs, the kind where you end up buried in her bosom and unable to catch your breath. Thank God for the growth spurt that assured I'd never be victim of the ample bosom hug again. Elle isn't so lucky and she gasps for a breath when Ma finally releases her.

She gets more of the same from Dad. "Hope to see you again soon, lass," he says with a wink and nod to Patrick.

Trisha asks for Elle to email the pie recipe, which almost makes me laugh out loud. The day Trisha bakes a pie is the day I grow a tail—a spiked one at that.

I pull Elle into my arms next and hold her too long. "Thanks for coming, Eleanor," I say softly and I run my hand along her back. Dad pries my arm away.

"She needs to get going, Paulie," he states in a low voice.

She's mine, I think silently.

Mine, I think as she steps away from me.

What am I doing? I shake my head to knock my possessive thoughts out of my head. She's not mine and likely never will be.

Patrick helps her pull on her sweater and opens the door for Elle and I wonder if I would've done the same classy moves. He's smitten for sure—it's written all over his hopeful face. Maybe my parents think he deserves her. Surely he would treat her like a queen, and as for me, I bet Dad thinks I'd consume her with my insatiable sexual appetite until there was nothing left.

Patrick's outside for a long time, so long I consider going out there to see what the hell's happening. Ma keeps distracting me though with things like helping Trisha load the dishwasher and bringing in firewood from the back porch.

When Patrick stumbles back into the house his face is flushed.

"What's up, dude?" I question.

"What do you mean?"

"You were out there forever, Paddy!" Trisha says.

"Was it that long?" he asks, pretending to be clueless, but he breaks out in a grin.

"Did you ask her out?" Dad asks looking hopeful.

Patrick's taps his chin in thought. "No. Not yet. I will though."

"Were you making out?" Trisha teases.

My stomach turns imagining his pokey tongue in her mouth.

"No! She just met me!" he says.

I fold my arms over my chest. "So what were you doing all that time?"

He pulls down his shirt cuff. "Giving her tax advice for her event management business."

He looks pleased with himself like that's sexy—like he's

scored big with her.

"That's hot," I say, nodding.

Dad shakes his head at me.

"What?" I ask with a shrug.

"I like that Patrick was showing her he cares about her business. That's very gallant of you, my boy."

"Gallant? Is that an Irish thing?" I wonder out loud.

"Shut up," says Trisha.

"She's really nice," he says with a big grin.

"Nice?" I repeat.

"Yeah, nice."

And very naughty, too.

I wait until the next night to call her.

"So you and Patrick, huh?"

"Is that you, Paul *Junior*?"

I grimace. "Yes, it is *Eleanor*."

"I don't like to be called that."

"And there is nothing junior about me—so we're even."

"I really enjoyed meeting your family."

"I bet."

"They're very colorful. And your parents are so sweet with each other. How long have they been married?"

"This year will be thirty-six years."

"Wow . . . and they still love each other."

"Isn't that the idea?"

"Sure, in a perfect world."

"Well, they put up with each other."

"You're such a romantic, Paul."

"Well I'm more romantic than Patrick, but believe me, that isn't saying much. Is it true he was giving you tax advice when he should've been kissing you against your car?"

She sighs. "Tax advice . . . yes, that was so sweet. And he offered to come clean out my rain gutters."

I huff. "His dating skills are impressive."

"Do you even begin to understand how sexy a man who is

handy is to a busy woman like me?"

"Well, I'm handy, too. I'm handy as hell."

She moans. "Well if you keep teasing me like this, I'll start breaking things around here just to get you to come by."

I laugh uncomfortably because I sense she really might do that and I know I'm playing with fire.

CHAPTER FIVE

THE SIDEWAYS SAMBA

Jim catches me in the parking lot at the church. "Hey, Paul."

I nod his way. "Jim."

"Good to see you here. So how are things with that woman? Have you been able to avoid her?"

"I haven't gone to her house in ten days."

"Okay, that's good. Have you talked to her?"

I turn my car keys over in my hands. "Yeah."

"How do you feel when you've talked to her? Is the desire less intense, or more?"

"I can't say less. I'll doubt I'll ever say less when it comes to her, but I'm keeping my promise to myself."

"Good." Jim nods and unfolds his arms from his chest.

"And she's still doing Tinder so that's a big fucking red flag."

"Yes it is, my man. Yes it is."

That evening I wonder who else Elle has hooked up with. Or maybe Stephan 'the architect' was her dream man giving her multiple mind-blowing orgasms. Will sex be her salvation, or her downfall like it was for me?

I pick up the phone and press her name on my contact list, only to put it down again, releasing a long sigh.

A second later the damn phone rings and I look down and see it's her. The timing is so weird that there's no way I'm not going to answer it.

"Elle?"

"Hi, Paulie."

"What's up?"

"I need you."

There's a long pause as my mind flings about every single scenario those three works imply. Yet in my heart I know this woman . . . she's teasing me.

I'm not going to make it easy on her.

"How badly do you need me?"

"So badly," she says with a breathy gasp. "I may come undone unless you can take care of me."

"What do you need from me exactly?"

"I'm in the dark, Paulie. I thought you could give me light."

"Do you care to elaborate? 'Cause if this is depression, I can't say I'm your man."

She scoffs. "Depression? No, I have a burned-out light bulb."

I'd be pissed if it were anyone but flirty Elle. "So you need me to change a light bulb? Are you screwing with me?"

"No, I'm not, and once you see how heavy the light fixture is you'll understand. Besides if you came over to change the damn thing, I *could* be screwing with you. This light fixture is right over the bed, and you should know that I'm someone who likes to leave the light on. I want to see everything."

"Everything?"

"Oh yeah."

Naturally that makes her Tinder escapades pop into my head. "So how did things go with Stephan? Was he a freak like the others?"

"Actually, not at all. He's a gentleman."

"Good in bed?" My hand tightens over the phone. I'm desperately hoping she says they didn't get that far.

"Really good, actually. Very attentive."

"Great," I respond with the most contrived enthusiasm in my life. "So you've found your stud."

"I wouldn't go that far. He's got issues I'm trying to figure out."

Smiling, my grip on the phone eases. "What kind of issues?"

"Well, at first I thought it was really sweet when he jumped out of bed right after sex to get warm washcloths for both of us. He even took the time to clean me up."

"You mean like a sponge bath?" I ask, trying to imagine what kind of man gives sponge baths after sex.

"Sort of like that. I didn't mind. It felt good."

"Okay, then what was weird? You said there were issues."

"Well when I wanted to get wild again he said I had to take a shower first."

"Are you serious?"

"And he showed me the detachable handle in the shower, if you get my drift."

"He likes everything squeaky clean?"

She giggles. "Apparently. I mean don't get me wrong, I'd prefer a clean person over a sloppy one, but this was a little over the top."

"Did he have those large pump containers of hand sanitizers everywhere?"

She lets out a squeal. "How did you know?"

"I just had a feeling. And I bet he makes you take your shoes off when you come inside."

"Yes! Yes!"

"Are you seeing him again?"

"Actually I invited him to come over tonight and he asked what day my housekeeper comes. When I told him tomorrow he said he had work to do tonight but he could come tomorrow night."

"Awesome. You sure know how to pick 'em, Elle."

"Well at least I'm having some fun . . . and putting myself out there."

"I'll tell you what. Tell Sterile Stephan that you're busy to-morrow since after work I'm coming over to change your light bulb, and I'm messy. Yeah, tell him I get sweaty and dirty when I work at your place and so it probably wouldn't be a good night for him to come over."

"Do you really get sweaty and dirty when you work?"

"Do you want me to get sweaty and dirty?"

"Oh, yeah. That's hot. Hey, can you wear a wifebeater shirt and not shave so you have scruff?"

"What? Why?"

"I want to see your shoulders. I bet they're built. Do you have any tattoos?"

"I'm not telling."

"Tease!"

"Anything else, Ms. Demanding? Work boots? A hardhat?"

"No, but worn tight jeans would be good. Oh, and a tool belt!"

"You're kidding, right?"

There's a long pause. *She isn't kidding?*

"Ummm. Do you want me to be kidding?"

"Hey! I know what this is about!" I slap my hand down on the counter. "What are you currently reading?"

Another pause.

"A book," she answers quietly.

"And the name is . . ."

"Duke's Revenge."

"Sounds like a Pulitzer."

"All right smarty pants. You know it's erotic romance so just deal with it."

"I'm dealing. And what does Duke do for a living?"

"He's a construction worker."

"Let me guess, and he has scruff, worn jeans and a tool belt."

"Maybe."

"Does he wear that tool belt to bed?"

"I don't know. So far all the sex hasn't been in bed."

"Whoa. He's a stud! Where's the sex happen?"

"Let me think . . . in his truck, the construction elevator, on top of her desk, in the back room of her studio . . . and I'm only three chapters in."

"Does he ever actually do construction?"

"I don't know, and frankly I don't care."

"Well I hope this woman he's screwing has a good job. Somebody needs to bring home the bacon."

"She's an architect!"

I laugh. "And she's the designer of all the stuff that he doesn't construct because he's too busy screwing her."

"Okay Mr. Judgey. Can you be there at six? I have a meeting that may run late but I'm sure I'll be home by then."

"See you at six."

When she opens her front door and sees me her expression is crestfallen. "What?" I hold my arms open.

"Where's the wifebeater?"

"I don't have one. And for the record that's the worst name ever for a shirt." I glance down at my T-shirt from the Gap. I wore the tight white one but I guess that doesn't cut it. I rub my chin. "Look though, I didn't shave."

"But your jeans aren't tight."

"Elle, I can't wear tight jeans. You know why."

She blushes. "Oh yeah. The anaconda."

"So are you going to invite me in? I'm here to help you, so it would be nice if I could actually come inside."

She pulls the door open farther and gestures me in. "Sorry about that. Come in."

I glance back at her and she's pouting.

"Oh for God's sake, what now?"

"No tool belt?"

"I don't need a tool belt to change a light bulb."

She looks serious for a second and then gives me a big smile and links her arm through mine. "Come on, let's go to my bedroom."

We stop in the back porch for a ladder and the bulbs. "Hey, what's that smell?" I ask, my mouth watering.

"Lasagna. I thought I'd make you dinner since you came to

help me. Can you stay?"

"Hell, yes! I'm starving."

She stops and turns toward me. "You want to eat first?"

"If it's ready."

Only minutes later she's served up the most amazing looking lasagna with salad. She pours us wine and then stops mid pour.

"I better not give you too much wine. You're going to be on a ladder."

"Oh, I'll be okay. I can tolerate good wine. Besides, you can catch me if I fall."

She winks at me and keeps pouring.

I'm on my second serving and she's barely taken a bite.

"Hey, why aren't you eating? This is so good. I had no idea you could cook like this."

"I have all kinds of skills you don't know about."

I study her. She's right. There's a lot I don't know about her.

"Well, tell me. What else are you good at?"

She runs her finger along the glass. "My career."

"Tell me about what you do."

"As a corporate event coordinator I oversee the planning and execution of events and conventions for my clients."

"Sounds like a big deal," I say.

"I think it is. My job is to be on top of every detail so that things run smoothly both leading up to and during the event."

"I bet you do a great job."

She smiles at me. "Well, I do take pride in being able to charm even the most difficult client."

"Well, you have charm in spades, so I bet you're good with clients. As for the running smoothly I'll take your word for it. You certainly seem on top of things here." I glance around the house and take in how well designed and maintained everything is. I like her taste; it's sophisticated yet still feels comfortable.

She smiles broadly. "Thanks. I love the home I've created here. It's really nice of you to notice."

I shrug. "It would be hard to miss."

"Oh believe me, my ex took all of that for granted."

"And what did I say about him the first time we met?" I take a long sip of my wine while I see her expression shift from one of disappointment to glee.

"That he's an idiot!"

"That's right. So here's to you, Elle. You're an impressive woman." I lift my glass and take in her smile.

Her eyes soften and as we click glasses I realize that she needs to hear this much more than I could've ever imagined. I make note. I may not be able to give her everything she wants from me, but I can give her that.

"Careful!" she calls out as I get higher on the ladder.

I regard her with an arched brow. "You drank more than I did."

"That thing is deceptively heavy," she warns, pointing at the hand-painted glass light fixture.

"Don't worry, I'm pretty strong." I hold one hand up against the glass dome as I unscrew the base with the other.

"Well if you'd dressed as I asked I would see all your muscles and how strong you are."

"I'm plenty strong. And if this thing is that heavy, I hope you are too because I'm going to be handing it to you in a minute."

"I'm super strong," she replies with a grin.

When the screw is loose enough to drop into my hand I slowly pull the dome away from its base. Damn, she's right. This sucker is heavy.

I hold it out toward her. "Ready?"

She bites her lip and reaches toward me. "Yes." I ease the dome into her arms and she pulls it protectively to her chest before resting it on the bed, then offers a replacement bulb up to me.

"Screw it in tight," she says with a grin.

"It's the only way I screw." I give her a sly smile.

While I replace the bulb I notice her step over to the side table where she's left her glass. She takes several sips of wine. She seems a little buzzed.

"So this Stephan dude. Is he really that uptight about being clean or were you playing me?"

"No, he's really that way."

"So do you see a future with him?"

She scoffs. "It's highly unlikely."

"Then why bother?" I hand her down the burned out bulb.

"Why not?" she says. "He makes me feel great."

I glance back up to focus on the work. Repositioning this dome back in place is much harder than it looks.

"Damn!"

"What?"

"I can't get this heavy bastard aligned correctly."

"I told you it was heavy."

"You weren't kidding. I've never seen a light with glass this thick. What the hell?"

"Believe me, if I could've done this myself I would."

I peer down at her. I can tell she means it. "Well, I'm glad you didn't. I'm surprised you sleep with this thing looming over you as it is. A lot of people would be in a state of terror every night. I mean what if the thing fell? It'd be certain death."

"I like the thrill of uncertainty, and besides, I love the Venetian design."

I roll my eyes. *She loves the design.* She won't love it so much when it splits her head open.

I finally get the base screwed in and carefully pull my hands away to make sure it stays firm. I let out my breath when it remains in place, and I test it with a few attempts to jiggle it. It's solid.

On the way back down the ladder I glance at Elle and realize I can see down her shirt. A real gentleman would turn away, but instead I lean forward to improve the angle of my view. Her breasts are noteworthy. I'd love to have my hands full of them.

I crane my neck out. My forward sway causes me to lose balance and a feeling of doom engulfs me. I'm going down.

A millisecond later she grabs me from behind. Her arms are

wrapped around my thighs and her face pressed against my lower back.

"Whoa!" she exclaims.

I take a sharp breath as I grab onto the ladder and steady myself. When I'm finally down on the floor I turn toward her.

"Thanks."

She looks up at me, and smiles. "Any time."

I trace my finger under her chin as she gazes at me. Have I ever fully noticed how beautiful her big blue eyes are?

This woman.

"What?" She tips her head to the side.

"What do you mean *what?*"

"You look like you want to kiss me."

"Hmmm."

"So what are you waiting for?"

She wants me to cave in and break my promise to myself, but then what? I share her with Mr. Clean and the Tinder Posse? That's not the relationship with the future mate I've been waiting for.

I pinch the ends of a lock of her hair between my fingers. "I don't want to kiss you."

"Are you sure?"

I stare at her lips. They are exquisitely, infinitely kissable. Of course I want to kiss her but I can't tell her that.

"Yup."

She inches closer to me, her breasts skimming my chest. I can feel the heat shimmer off her. "Really sure?"

I swallow hard. I stare at her as she waits for my response, and realize this is a defining moment between us. Am I going to surrender to my lust and accept from her what it is I really want? I can picture fucking her so vividly. I can even hear her moaning in my head. How bad would it really be for us to just own it and go at it until we're satisfied? But would we ever really be satisfied or would it just be the beginning of my downward spiral into my obsessive ways?

My weakness fills me with shame and I turn away.

I notice her blinking rapidly as my rejection hits her. She's out the bedroom door before I can even say anything. I find her in the kitchen.

"Elle?"

She's taking the lasagna pan out of the refrigerator. She ignores me as she pulls out one of those plastic food storage things and slides several pieces of lasagna inside. The room is silent other than the popping sound of the top closing over the bottom of the container. She pushes the full plastic box toward me.

I clear my throat loudly and when she looks up I gesture toward her bedroom. "Hey, about what just happened."

"Nothing happened." There's no tone or inflection in her voice.

"Look—"

She cuts me off. "So something's just hit me, Paul."

Stepping up to the kitchen island where she's working, I tighten my fingers over the edge of the honed marble top.

"And . . ."

"I hate being rejected. Rejection makes me sad. And I lived through an entire marriage being rejected. So I really don't need it from you."

"I understand. I'm sorry I make you sad."

"I'm sorry, too."

"I'll leave now if you want me to."

She nods. "Yeah, maybe you should."

I feel unbelievably bad. I'm such an asshole. She deserves better.

"Okay. If that's what you want." I pick up my jacket. "Thanks for dinner."

She points to the box. "That's for you."

"You didn't have to do that."

"I wanted to. You really seemed to like it."

"I did. I like your lasagna a lot."

She gives me a tiny smile.

"And I like you a lot."

She arches her brow. "You like me? So what, you want to be friends?"

I nod.

"With no benefits?"

I shrug. "Yeah."

She shakes her head and laughs. "What am I going to do with you? Well, let me think about that, okay?"

I smile. "Yeah. And I'm going to bring this plastic thing back when I've eaten all of this and make you laugh again."

"And while you're at it, bring my book back."

"Torched? Did that book really get you off? I mean, that shit was crazy. Who talks like that in bed?"

"It totally got me off, and it will again as soon as you bring it back here."

"Can you tell me what man speaks entire sentences when he's fucking a hot woman?"

"Well apparently you don't. But I'll never know that for sure." She winks at me and leads me to the hall. We're almost to the front door when her doorbell rings.

"Expecting more company?" I ask.

She looks at me with wide eyes. "No." She peeks out the door viewer and jumps back. "It's Stephan! I thought he wasn't coming tonight."

"You want me to sneak out the back door?"

"Don't be silly. I'll introduce you. You can judge him for yourself."

She opens the door. "Stephan!" she says like she's thrilled to see him. She gives him a big hug. "I thought you said you weren't coming!"

"I couldn't stay away."

She pulls the door open wider and when he comes in he looks up and our eyes meet. He's taller than me and thinner. He's blond and looks like an underfed Viking.

At least he's not wearing a wifebeater and worn jeans. That would piss me off. Instead he's wearing a black turtleneck.

Poser.

I wonder if he smokes a pipe.

I raise my hand in greeting. "Hey Stephan. I'm Paul. Elle's

told me all about you."

She smiles and nods as he studies her. "Has she now?"

"Paul's a friend of mine."

"A *good* friend of hers," I add.

"Really?" His gaze darts back and forth between us like he doesn't know what to make of us.

"Yes, matter of fact I had an electrical problem and Paul came by to fix it for me."

I nod. "Yes, her light bulb burned out."

"Light bulb?"

The pipe-smoking Viking appears ruffled.

"Gee Elle, you struck me as the type of woman who could handle anything, certainly a burned out light bulb." He gives me a wary look.

Ha! *He's suspicious of us now.* I should feel bad for being delighted, but I don't at all.

"Oh, Paul is only telling half the story. Aren't you, Paul? The heavy hanging light fixture was the issue." She punches me semi-playfully in the shoulder.

I nod. "Really heavy."

"And as a matter of fact Paul was just leaving."

I'm being asked to leave?

Well screw that.

"I *am* leaving. Great to meet you, Stephan. And thanks for the lasagna, Elle. Sorry we made such a mess in your bedroom. I think I got some dirty footprints on your bed."

The expression on the Viking's face is priceless. I think I'm seeing some shades of green breaking through the bronze toner it looks like he's sporting.

Elle starts scurrying about to push me out the door and distract him. Is the Viking's booty-call a bust?

"Bye!" I call out right as the door shuts.

I'm sitting in my car, contemplating going back inside, when my cell phone goes off.

It's a text from Elle.

   Dirty footprints?

I text back a smiley face.
Her response makes me smile.

Asshole.

Chapter Six

THE MAN TRAP

That night as I lie in bed I think about Elle and how I wish I knew what to do about her. She's the most unpredictable woman I've ever met. One minute she's getting me worked up with that dirty mouth, the next she's baking lasagna and apple pie like one of those 1950's T.V. moms.

It's confusing because I'm constantly fighting off the urge to get close to her. Maybe it's because I grew up being taught that divorce damages people and they carry that into their next relationship. I can't disagree since Elle still talks freely about her disappointments. My mom taught us to never date a divorced woman or we'd regret it . . . what would guarantee that the same thing wouldn't happen to us?

Besides, after how I've changed my life, could I really date a girl who was willing to screw everything from a germ-a-phobe to a finger sucker? Where would I stand in her illustrious Tinder line-up?

I toss and turn until I finally make up my mind. I'm going to tell Ma that she can finally hook me up with that Sunday school teacher at her church. Maybe it's time I see if what I think I've been wanting was worth the wait.

At our family dinner Ma glances up at me with a hopeful look. "Are you serious, Paulie? You're really going to let me introduce you to Lourdes?"

"Indeed I am."

She claps her hands together. "She's the sweetest lass, and has the most gorgeous shiny black hair. It's curly, with ringlets down her back. Oh, Poppa! Just think of the babes!"

Dad gives her a warm smile. Hell, they're practically goo-goo eyes. He must really want grandkids too.

Trisha sets down the chicken leg she's been gnawing on. "Is Mercury in retrograde or something? Ma's pulling off two set-ups in one month. Surely this is a new record."

I shake my head. "It's not a set-up. Lourdes hasn't agreed to go out with me yet."

Ma has a smug smile. "Oh yes she has! She hasn't left me alone since I showed her your picture!"

I narrow my eyes at her. "And what picture was that?"

"The one of you crossing the finish line," Dad says.

I feel my ears get hot as my blood pressure goes up. "You showed her that high school track picture?" This picture was infamous in my family for reasons I try not to think about.

Trisha starts howling like it's the funniest thing she's ever heard. "The one where his thing is falling out of his track shorts?"

"That's the baton," Ma insists.

"How many times do we have to go over this Ma? The relay baton is black not flesh colored."

"Enough!" I roar.

"Stop provoking your brother, Patricia," Dad demands.

"Lourdes said you look like a young Ryan Gosling," Ma says to distract me.

Trisha rolls her eyes. "Apparently a really young Ryan Gosling."

"And that you're quite the athlete," Ma continues.

"She did," Patricks agrees. "I was standing right there."

"Great! Who else witnessed this? Father Murphy?"

Ma shakes her head. "No, although I did show him the

picture and he said you're a very fine specimen of a man."

"You showed it to your priest?" My temples are throbbing. Maybe my head is going to explode.

"Of course, he always asks about you."

"But not as much as Lourdes does," Patrick says.

I pound my fist on the table. "If we don't drop this now I'm not calling her!"

The resulting silence is deafening. They must really want me to take her out on a date.

I decide that I better go to church with my clan to see what I'm getting into. For all I know she may be trying to set me up with some well-meaning girl with bad breath. To impress the ladies I put some effort into my appearance, I even wear a sport- jacket, which makes my mom swoon. She struts into church like we're two peacocks.

Honestly, I tune out the sermon, it's not really my thing, but I like the choir part. This church has an impressive group of singers. That's what you get for living in a city of wanna-be performers.

When it's time to go socialize Ma links her arm through mine. Everyone seems surprised to see me. Has it really been that long?

We're near the table with platters of sugar cookies and bunt cake when a small sparrow of a woman catches my eye. She's tiny with huge light-blue eyes, but the most startling thing is the contrast between her porcelain skin and her thick head of black ringlets that trail down her back. She looks like she's from some kind of mythical world.

She gives me a shy smile and twists a ringlet around her finger.

Ma pulls on my arm and nods her way. "Lourdes," she whispers.

Smiling, I nod. I have to admit there's something very in-triguing about her.

Right as we approach, a little kid grabs her, throws his arms around her waist, and cries out, "Miss Solaris, Cindy said I was ugly."

She gently pushes him back so he can look up at her and she runs her fingers through his hair. "Jeffrey, sometimes kids tease each other just to get a reaction. And look—it worked. The best thing you can do is to ignore such silly comments. You're very handsome." She taps him on the tip of the nose.

He instantly blushes and breaks out into a wide grin. "Thanks, Miss Solaris!" He runs off, and all is well in his little world.

Damn, if only life were that easy.

Ma seizes the moment. "Look who I have here, Lourdes. It's my Paulie!"

I smile, reach out, and shake her hand. "But you can call me Paul. It's much more dignified."

She smiles back. "I'm happy to meet you, Paul. I've heard so many nice things about you."

"All lies," I tease. I look to our right where the little boy ran off. "You were really good with him."

"Oh Jeffrey. He's such a sweetie . . . such a sensitive boy. All the girls love him but he just doesn't get it. Of course one day he will."

"I sure wish you'd been my Sunday school teacher."

"Yes? Who was yours?"

"Old Mrs. North. She used to smack our hands with rulers when we didn't memorize our Bible verses."

"She did not!" Her rosebud lips are making a little "O" shape. I bet those lips would be fun to kiss.

"She did!"

Ma scoffs. "Quit telling stories, Paulie!"

"And you're much prettier than she was. I'd have had a crush on you like Jeffrey appears to have."

Lourdes cheeks color. "That's very sweet."

I decide to just go for it. She's certainly pretty and kind, and Ma likes her. That's as good a start as any.

"So Ma here wants to set us up, don't you Ma?"

She smacks my shoulder. "Paulie!"

"Well don't you?"

"Yes, but you don't need to advertise it. I thought you were smoother than that."

I wink at Lourdes. "Sorry I'm not smoother."

The corners of her mouth turn up. "Oh, I like a man who's direct. That's very refreshing."

"Would you like to have dinner next week, say Friday? There's a new bistro on Melrose I've heard is good."

"That would be lovely, thank you."

Pulling out my phone, I put her number on my contact list and then call her so she has mine. She looks happy. This dating thing is very different than hooking up.

"So is it true you said I looked like a young Ryan Gosling?"

She throws her hands up to cover her face. "Oh my goodness, I'm so embarrassed!"

"It's okay. I considered that a compliment."

She inches her tiny pale hands down. "Oh, it is a compliment. He's a very handsome man!"

I grin at her. "Well thanks again. I'm going to get Ma home, but I'll look forward to Friday."

"Me too!" she replies.

Ma gives her a squeeze before we go to find Patrick and Dad. When Lourdes waves good-bye, her sweater slides down her arm and I notice a tattoo that looks like a cross on her wrist. It kind of weirds me out. What if she's a religious fanatic? She probably wouldn't put up with my apathy. I decide not to worry about it before we've even had a date.

As we walk away Ma turns to me. "Goodness, Paulie! Where'd you learn to be so dashing?"

If she only knew about how wild of a player I was. I'll spare her the truth. "It was all those old Cary Grant movies you used to watch, Ma."

She grins widely. "Of course! Oh, how I love that man!"

Over the next few days I wonder how Elle is doing but I don't call her. Is she still with Sterile Stephan the sponge bather? I wonder if he ever got over my comment about dirty footprints on the bedspread.

I decide to wait to talk to Elle until after my date with Lourdes since I want to give Lourdes my full attention. Little did I know that I'd have a big old surprise at our weekly family dinner.

Trisha looks like the cat that caught the canary. "Patrick has a date!"

"You do? With who?"

"Well, Elle of course!" Ma says with a grin.

"I'm taking her to the science museum Sunday. They have a kinetics exhibit I thought she'd like," he replies.

"What makes you think she'd like kinetics?"

"She said something that night at dinner about how things are always on the move for her."

"And to you that translated to a kinetics exhibit."

His expression falls and I feel like an asshole.

"You know what, Patrick? Actually, that's a really cool idea for a date. I like it. It's different."

Ma gives me a smile of approval.

"She seemed excited about it," he agrees. "And I hear you have a date, too, Paul."

"Yes, I'm seeing Lourdes tomorrow night."

"That's outstanding." He gives me a thumbs-up. It's like the two of us for one brief moment finally have something in common.

Later over banana pudding I ponder Elle agreeing to go out with Patrick. Now that we've established we're friends I can't believe she'd do it just to make me jealous. Maybe she really wants to go out with him. I guess stranger things have happened.

I had sworn to myself that I wouldn't compare Lourdes to Elle, but I found myself doing it anyway just minutes after my conversation with Lourdes starts. She's very sweet and attentive but I miss Elle's sass, and even her dirty mouth. Who am I kidding? I especially missed her dirty mouth.

I guess the upside is that with Lourdes' conservative dress and mannerisms I haven't been thinking about sex at all. It's kind of liberating and disappointing all at the same time. She talks about her work being a teacher's assistant at St. John's. She's almost done getting her teaching credentials and now she's anxious to move up to being a full-fledged teacher.

Her eyes light up when she talks about how much she loves children and that she can't wait to be a mom.

I note that's a big check on the future mate list of requirements. I really want to have my own family one day.

As the night progresses I discover that there are surprising things with Lourdes though. For one thing she ordered her steak bloody—that's just disgusting. She also makes a big point of closing her eyes and tipping her head down before she starts eating, and I've already dug in when I realize she's praying. I awkwardly drop my fork and pretend to join her. I mean I knew she was religious but she must be really religious to do that in a restaurant. We get an impatient stare from the waitress since she has to wait until we're done to grind the Parmesan cheese over my side of spaghetti.

At the end of the evening I drive Lourdes home and walk her to the door, where she thanks me and kisses me on the cheek. She doesn't even invite me in. It's not like I really wanted to go in, but I've always gotten some kind of offer from other women. I don't even know what to make of that. I feel like I've entered an altered universe where at the end of the evening you get dry, precursory kisses on the cheek instead of wild-monkey sex.

The whole drive home I try to make sense of it. She's certainly the most proper and nice girl I've ever gone out with. She's smart and pretty. But hell, I didn't think about screwing her once all night. I'm not sure how that will work.

Maybe I'm mixed up in the head. This is probably a good issue to bring up with Jim and the guys in my group meeting Tuesday.

Lourdes and my second date is just as surreal because we go to see a movie and after several failed attempts where she pulls away from me, she finally lets me hold her hand. I feel like I'm back in junior high.

When she calls me a couple of days later to invite me to dinner at her place I'm surprised. I'm not exactly excited about seeing her but decide there's no harm in one more attempt to see if there's anything between us. Dating is such a novel concept in my life. It's sure a lot of work but it seems to pay off for plenty of people. I figure I shouldn't give up so easy.

Saturday I take a shower and shave before changing into clean clothes, then stop at the florist and buy a bouquet of flowers.

Lourdes answers the door wearing a black dress that has lace running up her neck and down her arms. Through the lace covering her wrist I spot not just the cross tattoo peeking out, but an identical one on her other wrist. She looks particularly pale tonight, with porcelain skin and soft red lips. Her hair is pulled up and I realize that everything's just more ramped up than our last dates. After taking the flowers with a smile, she pulls me inside.

I squint as I enter her living room. The walls are dark red and there are candles lit everywhere. There's even some heavy-duty classical music playing. It certainly isn't what I would have expected from Lourdes. I have a fleeting thought that maybe she's a witch and she's going to cast a spell on me. I half expect bats to start flying out of the fireplace.

She goes to the kitchen to put the flowers in a vase and I realize that the brightly colored bouquet I got couldn't have been more wrong. A bunch of dead red roses would have fit in this room better. Am I in a Tim Burton movie?

I step farther inside to study the paintings all hung in fancy gilded frames.

Every single one is with a crucifix painting or Madonna and child.

What the hell? I lean into the doorway to the kitchen and wonder if I can make a break for it but she sees me.

She returns to my side with two tiny looking wine glasses.

"What's this?" I ask.

"Absinthe."

I sniff it. "Is this some weird booze or wine?"

"Sort of." She gives me a demure look and takes a tiny sip.

I take a larger sip and almost spit it out. *Damn!* My throat is on fire.

"Too strong?" she asks.

I nod my head while I try to stop coughing. Meanwhile she keeps taking small sips and the fumes don't seem to bother her at all. For a tiny thing she's pretty tough.

The weirdness continues through dinner where she serves up some strange soup she probably cooked in a cauldron with thick bread that has a tough crust. I'm pretty sure I'll have to stop for a burger on the way home.

I find myself absentmindedly taking sips of the absinthe. Maybe subconsciously I'm hoping to numb my mind and after a while it's working. We move to the living room for dessert. I'm halfway done with my dark chocolate mousse when I get the guts to confront her.

I sweep my arm across the interior view. "So what's this all about? Are you a goth or something?"

"Something like that."

"I've gotta say, I wasn't expecting this. At all."

She licks the chocolate off her spoon and sets it down.

"Really? What were you expecting?"

I shrug. "I don't know. White wicker furniture and pale yellow walls. English landscape paintings. Like you see on TV shows."

She laughs softly. "Sorry to disappoint you."

"I don't know if I'd say disappointed, just surprised." I take a sip of the weird wine and realize I've almost finished my second glass.

She refills it.

"Are you really into *Phantom of the Opera* or something?"

Her eyes grow wide. "No. Actually my home is a reflection of my spirituality. It's my refuge here, akin to a place of worship. I hope you know how rare it is for me to invite a man here, but I feel a really strong connection to you, Paul."

"You do?" I can't help but be surprised. She may have been attentive during our dinner date, but that little peck on the cheek when we parted didn't say *strong connection* to me.

"Definitely, I had to pray on it before I understood His will where you're concerned."

The hair on the back of my neck stands up.

She slides off the couch and down to the floor. I'm wondering if she dropped something, but suddenly she pops up, kneeling right in front of me. Just the sight of her kneeling is making my palms sweat. There's no way I'm letting her give me a blowjob. It's not just that I don't want dark red lipstick all over my cock, but this is all wrong and not just because I'm abstaining until I meet the right girl. As much as I love a good blowie, even I have my limits and she's freaking me out.

I grasp her shoulders. "Please, Lourdes, get up."

She gazes up at me, as she rests her hands on my knees. "Paul, I want to offer myself to you."

Suddenly a quick blowie sounds preferable to getting naked between the sheets with goth girl. I will my cock to behave despite the sex offerings, and clear my head as best I can in order to reply coherently.

"Offer yourself? But we haven't even gotten to second base yet. Hell, we haven't even kissed!"

"Yes, although I knew you were the one when I met you, I was waiting for a sign."

"A sign? What sign was that?" 'Cause right now all I'm seeing is a big fat stop sign . . . the same dark red as her walls.

"I was waiting for a spiritual sign. I want to be frank and speak from the heart. I want to offer you my virginity, and I hope you understand how sacred that is."

I don't know if it's the heat from the fireplace, or this screwy wine but for a few seconds the room goes black. When my vision clears she's patiently waiting for my response. *Damn this isn't just one of those freaky dreams you have when you mix too many different kinds of booze.*

"You're a virgin?" I whisper.

"Spiritually I am."

"What the hell does that mean?"

"When the Lord gives me the sign that I'm supposed to give myself to a man, I say a prayer to resurrect my spiritual virginity."

Oh, that's rich. And I thought Elle was way out there. "I didn't know there were virginity do-overs," I mumble.

She nods, lifts herself off the floor and reaches for my hand.

I wipe the sweat off my brow and close my eyes to keep the red room from spinning. "I'm dizzy," I moan.

She places her hands on my shoulders and I immediately sense the teacher of small children in her as she speaks to me in a soothing voice. "It's okay. It must be the absinthe. Here, lean forward and drop your head between your knees. Stay like that. I'm going to get you a glass of water and a cool cloth."

I nod as I drop down and face the fabric of the couch. "Yeah, water please," I mumble.

I hear her walk away and my mind races, trying to figure out what to do. I don't want to hurt this girl's feelings but she's a whack-job. I'm half waiting for someone to pop out and say I've been pranked. My mother would lose her shit if she knew how much she missed the mark on this girl.

When she returns I slowly ease up and take sips of water

while she studies me. I shake my head. "You know I really didn't see any of this coming from our previous two dates."

She nods with a solemn expression. "I know. I keep this side of myself very private. It's precious and should only be shared with someone who appreciates it."

"And that would be me?" I ask with my eyebrows scrunched together. I've never felt so freaked out by a woman.

"Yes, I'm certain it's you."

She leaves the room again and returns with a small fancy bottle filled with a clear liquid. Before I can ask about it she lowers herself to her knees again and offers me the bottle.

"This is holy water from Lourdes in France. Will you sprinkle it on me?"

I take the bottle and hold it up. It looks like tap water to me. "Are you sure this is holy water?" I wonder how many guys have sprinkled this stuff on her and then taken her virtual virginity or whatever the hell she called it.

"Yes." She tips her head back like wants me to pour this over her head or something.

"Umm, Lourdes?"

She lowers her chin and looks at me. Her expression is so peaceful it's creepy.

"I'm not sprinkling anything on you. I mean that's really cool of you to resurrect your virginity and all that for me, but I think I have to pass."

"What?" She frowns and looks so crestfallen that I have to imagine not a lot of dudes have turned her down. "I was so sure," she whispers.

"But I'm not so sure."

"Maybe we should just try."

I hand her the bottle of water and stand up, scanning the room for where I left my jacket.

I'm almost to the front door when I turn back. "Actually, I'm super-duper sure, like one hundred percent sure, and I just remembered that I have a really early meeting tomorrow."

"On Saturday?" she asks with a pout as she slowly stands

up.

I nod. "Yeah, but thanks a lot for dinner."

Her eyes narrow but I shoot out the door before she can do her voodoo stuff on me.

I don't think I've ever felt as relieved as when I hear that click as I pull the door firmly shut behind me.

Chapter Seven

Get a Leg Up

In the gothic aftermath I try not to call Elle to vent. God knows I try, but the compulsion is stronger than my will. I need to hear her voice. I know it will ground me.

"Hey, Paul Junior. What's shakin'?"

I let out a big sigh of relief remembering that not all women are scary.

"I've been dating."

"Dating? You mean like with a girl?"

"Not a girl, a woman," I huff.

"Oh yeah, sure . . . sorry. You know what I meant. I was just stunned. What compelled you to go on a date?"

"Maybe you've inspired me the way you just put yourself out there."

There's a long silence.

"What?" I ask.

"Well if I inspired you, why didn't you ever take me on a date? Am I merely a conduit or something? I know, me and my filthy mouth represent everything you don't want to have in a woman. Right?"

The fact that she'd be pissed off at my omission didn't occur to me. As I try to figure out a pithy answer she jumps in.

She sighs. "So how was the date sex? Was it hot?"

"I didn't sleep with her."

"Seriously?"

"I'm serious."

"Then what did you do? And don't tell me you talked."

I lean back in my chair and stretch out my legs. "Well we did. And we ate food. And we saw a movie."

She chuckles. "Sounds freaking awesome. What did you see?"

My mind races but comes up empty. "I didn't pay much attention. Some historical chick flick."

"Did she at least give you a hand-job in the theater?"

"No. See . . . there goes that filthy mouth of yours."

"What's wrong with her? Has she even touched the anaconda?"

"Nope."

"You know, I've got to say Paul . . . your street cred is going down the toilet."

"Well, this girl's . . . different. It's kind of hard to explain. Hey, what are you doing?"

"Watching the game."

"What game?"

"What else? My kick-ass Trojans and those wimpy UCLA Bruins. Some serious booty is getting kicked tonight!"

Oh, for God's sake. This woman likes football? It's almost more than I can take.

"Can I come over and watch with you? Is the Viking there?"

"The Viking?"

"Balding, beady-eyed Stephan."

"Stop it with that! No, he's not here. He's on a business trip. Besides he's only for sex. He probably doesn't even watch football. He's probably reading the Atlantic in his hotel and wondering about the future of urban planning in undeveloped countries."

"And smoking a pipe," I add.

"What? Mr. Clean would never smoke a pipe! That's a dirty business."

"Of course. I should have thought of that," I agree. "So I can come over?"

"Sure. I'm wearing grubby sweats, but we're just buds, so that's cool. Right?"

"Yeah, very cool."

I show up at her front door with a six-pack and I blink when she opens the door. Her hair is in a messy bun, she's holding a bowl of popcorn, and her tight sweatpants have a hole in the knee, yet she's the sexiest thing I've ever seen.

"Hey, you," she says, nodding her head to the right. "Come on in. It's second quarter and my boys are up by ten."

"You need to know that I'm UCLA all the way, baby."

She almost drops the bowl of popcorn. "What the hell? You better be joking!"

"I'm not." I pull open my jacket to reveal my UCLA T-shirt.

Huffing, she turns toward the den. She doesn't even look back to see if I'm following her. Finally, she turns and makes a face at me. "Hey traitor, you coming or what?"

I grin and follow her down the hall. Once we settle in, she pretty much ignores me for the second quarter. She also yells at the TV a lot. This side of her is a revelation. I wish Dad were here, he'd be in heaven. None of our women-folk can stand football—even my butch sister, the firefighter.

To consume the beer I brought, I have to go to the kitchen and find a bottle opener all on my own but she seems to start to warm up when I open a bottle for her too.

At halftime she gets chatty. "So tell me about the girl."

I take a long slow swig. "What do you want to know?"

"I'm of the female species, Paulie. I want to know everything. How'd you meet her?"

"Ma knows her from church. She teaches Sunday school."

Elle practically spits up her beer. "You're dating a Sunday school teacher? Does she know your background?"

I give her a stern look. "That's irrelevant."

She rolls her eyes. "She may not agree with you on that point, bucko. You were a total man-whore."

"You know, you're a little hard to figure out."

She takes a sip of beer. "How so?"

"Well here you are this badass tomboy, Elle. And last week's Tinder Elle was all sexy and provocative. And then I've also met apple pie, Elle . . . sweet as sugar."

"Hmmm," she says.

"So which one is the real Elle?"

The corners of her mouth slowly turn up. "All are! There are lots of sides of me and I like it that way."

"Indeed."

"Is that a problem for you? Which Elle do you like best?"

I immediately know I can't be honest with her and tell her that I really like them all, so I cop out. "I'll never tell," I reply with a forced grin.

Her eyes narrow with a suspicious look and she turns back to the TV.

"So what's the Sunday school teacher's name?"

"Lourdes."

"Hmm, interesting name."

I nod. "Hey Elle, seriously I need to talk about this girl. Can you be straight with me?"

Her expression turns more somber and she nods. "Okay, sure. What?"

"So Ma thought she was perfect for me, and I take her out. And it's okay, nothing great, but she's nice enough."

"So you weren't attracted to her?" Elle asks with an arched brow.

"No," I admit. "Not really."

She nods, looking a little smug. "Go on."

"I mean we don't even kiss after two dates, and I'm not even sure I care and then . . ."

She waves her hand at me to continue.

"She asks me to come for dinner at her place."

"Ooo, so what was that like?"

I realize that I'm relieved to finally have someone to talk to about this, so I lean back into the couch, and tell Elle everything.

The creepy crucifix paintings, the absinthe that made me not-right in the head, and I conclude with the presentation of the holy water for virtual virgins.

Elle holds her hand up in front of her like she's stopping a speeding train. "Wait a minute. Wait! What the hell is a virtual virgin?"

I shrug. "I was actually hoping you could tell me. She had this holy water she wanted me to sprinkle on her—"

"Of course she had holy water. Did she have one of those BDSM crosses in her bedroom to hang from?"

"This is serious, Elle."

She bites the tip of her tongue. I sense she's trying to hold back a laugh or loud guffaw.

"So she wanted you sprinkle holy water on her, get her all wet and then deflower her . . . take her virtual virginity?"

"She did."

"How'd that work out for you?"

"I already told you, I didn't touch her."

"Not even a kiss with tongue?"

I shake my head. "Nope. No tongue. No kiss."

"Geez, I don't feel so bad now. You turned down another chance for easy sex. Should I worry about you?"

"No, don't worry about me."

"But what if after all this you go gay? Don't get me wrong, I love my gay boys. But you and all your hotness, and the anaconda need to stay on our side of the fence."

"I keep telling you, you don't need to worry about me and other men."

She rolls her eyes. "Yeah, I've been told that before."

"So what about Stephan?"

"He's not gay. Don't let the meticulous side of him fool you. The way he fucks, he's straight-up man."

My fingers tighten around my beer bottle. "So where are things going with you two?"

"He asked me to go to Maui with him. He has a condo there."

I feel a little sick. "Are you going?"

"Hell yes. Why wouldn't I? I've always wanted to do it on the beach."

"So is this getting serious? You know . . . between you two."

"I'm serious about the sex. Is that what you mean?" "That good?" I can barely hide the jealousy in my tone.

"Multiple orgasms. We were up all night the last time he stayed over."

"Awesome."

"Don't be that way, Paul.

"What do you mean?"

"You sound forlorn. It could have been you, you know."

"Yeah?"

"But you like those Sunday school teachers. Well at least the idea of them, even if that one didn't work out. And you know what . . . now that we're buds, I'm with your mom. I want a nice girl for you who deserves a guy like you."

"What kind of guy is that?"

"A good man. One who loves his parents, is handy and can fix your sprinklers and stuff. And of course, one who will watch football with you."

As I drive home that night I have to wonder why hearing from Elle that I'm a good man just makes me want to be bad again.

My elbow is firmly planted on my drafting table as I stare out the window. I've been inspired with this new landscape design for a library garden in Orange County, but this stuff with Elle is distracting me. I really need to get my shit together and focus.

My head jerks back to my desk when my phone vibrates. Talk about timing . . . it's a text from Elle. My good intentions of focusing just flew out the window.

Aloha handsome!

I sit up tall as I gaze at the screen. I'm jazzed to hear from her even though I hate knowing that she's with the Viking.

What? You're already in Maui?

Yes I am. I don't mess around. I'm a woman of action.

I feel the jealously scorch my insides as I imagine her in his arms. I'm surprised how much it burns.

Good for you. Is it everything you hoped?

It's paradise. What's not to like?

Have you had sex on the beach yet?

No. Apparently Mr. Clean has an issue with sand. He doesn't like it against his skin.

HE DOESN'T LIKE SAND? You're in Maui for God's sake.

Sigh. I know.

Does he leave the hotel room?

For meals and when we take strolls on the beach he wears those goofy water shoes.

HE WEARS WATER SHOES FOR WALKS ON THE BEACH?

Would you stop with the shouty caps?

Water shoes aren't manly, Elle.

I know, but he doesn't wear them in bed.

Hey, what's he doing now?

He's on a business call. I think I'll go prance in front of him in my bikini. Last time I did that he got off the phone right away and we never made it downstairs. ;-)

There's that burn again. I don't want to let her go. I don't want to think about him fucking her in paradise.

Do you miss me? I'm about to delete that mushy crap but my traitor finger hits send.

Yes . . . lots! Bikini worked! Gotta go xo

Thursday's family dinner is tense. Ma has never looked so fed up with me. She purses her lips as she gives me the once over. Even the bun in her hair seems wound extra tight.

"What do you mean Lourdes is not your type? She's pretty and she's a girl. That's your type."

Trisha snorts.

Ma's face grows more flushed. "Maybe she's too good for you."

I push my dinner plate away. Thanks to her hounding me, I've lost my appetite. "If that's what you want to think, be my guest."

"Was she not attentive enough? I know how you like women to dote over you. She seemed very eager when you two met."

I look up with as stoic face as I can muster. "Oh she was attentive all right. But there's good attentive, and not so good attentive. She was more the latter."

Ma pokes her finger out at me. "Must you speak in riddles, boy? Explain what that means!"

Trisha smirks. "Ha! I bet she didn't fawn all over him, like most girls do. It was a big blow to his massive ego."

"Do you realize that you sound like an irritating twelve year old, Trisha?"

She ignores me which serves to confirm my observation.

"So, Ma, it looks like your two-for-two is zero-for-zero in the matchmaking department," Trisha says.

Dad throws a concerned glance Patrick's way and I notice Patrick's expression fall. Just seconds later he excuses himself from the table mumbling something about needing to get back to work.

When he's left the room Ma hisses at Trisha. "Do you ever think before you open your mouth, Trisha?"

"What? You raised us to always tell the truth."

"Yes, but there are times it's better to keep your mouth shut. If you haven't learned this by now I wonder if you ever will. You hurt the poor boy's feelings."

Trisha shrugs and continues eating.

I push my chair back. "I'm going to go check on Paddy."

Dad nods.

When I get to his room his door is closed. I can't believe that my older brother still lives at home. No wonder it's hard for him to date. What kind of woman can be okay with that? I knock.

"It's open."

I step inside, and glance around. The *Star Wars* and anti-motivational posters of his younger years are gone, now replaced by world maps and posters from different countries. It takes some re-adjustment on my part even though the rest of the room looks pretty much the same. He turns and notices what I'm looking at.

I point to the pictures. "These are interesting. I don't remember seeing them in here before."

"No I put them up this year."

"What's with the maps and pictures from exotic places?"

"I really want to travel. I've got a plan to go somewhere different every year."

"Oh yeah?" I ask surprised. Patrick never seemed the traveling type. "So where will you go first?"

"I just booked a trip in the fall to Morocco."

This is a revelation. I never thought my brother had an adventurous spirit. "Wow. That's so cool. Who are you going with?"

His gaze drops down to his computer screen and he skims his fingers back and forth over the keyboard. "No one. I'm going by myself."

My stomach sinks. Why did I have to ask him that? "Well you know, what's great about that is then no one can tell you what to do."

He smiles, seeming to appreciate the encouragement. "Yeah, that's what I told Ma and Dad."

"Some people are a pain in the ass to travel with. I went with that girl Bethany to Vegas about five years ago, and when we got there all she wanted to do was shop. We had a big fight right in the middle of the Caesar's Forum mall."

His eyes grow wide. "Oh, that must have been awkward."

"I'll say. She stormed off, then locked me out of our hotel room, and I headed home early."

"Oh man! Yeah, so if when I'm in Morocco, if I want to spend all day at Ben Youseef Madrasa no one can harp on me about it and then lock me out of the room."

"Uh huh," I agree, not asking for an explanation of this place he's mentioned. Evidently he's done a lot of research. I sit down on the edge of his bed. "Hey, Patrick? Can I ask you what happened with Elle?"

There's a long pause while he stares into space. I'm almost ready to change the subject when he replies.

"I thought she was enjoying our date. She seemed to like the exhibit, but at the end of the afternoon, when I asked her out again, she said no."

I can see the disappointment in his eyes and it makes me feel bad for him. "I'm sorry, dude. Did she say why?"

"She said I was a great guy but her heart already belonged to someone else. She was hoping we could be friends."

My stomach sinks. Is it more serious than she's been saying with the Viking? I thought he was only for sex. Maybe she hasn't been straight with me.

Patrick looks oddly relieved by my reaction. "So you're surprised?"

"Yeah, I am. She's been seeing this guy, an architect for a few weeks, but I didn't think she was that into him. I guess I was wrong."

"So you talk to her a lot?"

"Well, we're pretty good friends. Why?"

"Just wondering. She seems great. Why haven't you asked her out?"

"When we first met I thought she was everything I needed to avoid."

"She is really different than the girls you used to hang out with. What do you think about her now?"

"I think that we make great friends. And that's probably a good thing since apparently the kind of guy she goes for isn't anything like me."

Patrick doesn't respond but he looks deep in thought.

"Hey, Ma has the pound cake you like for dessert. Let's go have some, okay?"

He nods and gets up. I pat him on the back, and ruffle his hair, all brotherly-like, before we walk down the hall.

His sandy brown hair is thick and the mess I've made of it gives him an edge. "You should always wear it that way," I say. "Chicks like it like that . . . mark my word."

"Okay," Patrick says with a shy smile. He stops me right before we enter the dining room. "Hey, I'm sorry that Lourdes didn't work out either."

I nod. "Thanks, man."

"Was she really that weird?"

I roll my eyes and shake my head. "You have no idea. Tell you what? Let's go out for a drink next week and I'll share the story."

"I'd like that."

CHAPTER EIGHT

SPIN CYCLE

I don't know what's wrong with me. I can't stop thinking about her. Something about the idea of Elle in Maui is the sharp snap of a match being lit. I feel the wave of heat every time I think of her with him and it burns.

What if she really is in love with the Viking? I haven't heard from her in three days. I start second guessing my decision not to sleep with her when I could have.

I can't stop myself from imagining all the ways I would take her on the beach in Maui, rolling over the dunes and fucking her slow until every inch of our bodies was covered with sand. I'd drive her over the edge with the pounding waves drowning out our moans.

For hours after we would shake the sand out of our hair, and feel the burn of sex on our skin. I can almost smell the salt and faint whiff of coconut simmering off her warm body.

Just when I think I'm going to start shopping for airline tickets to the islands to steal her away from him, she texts me.

I can't even Paulie . . .

What does that mean exactly?

I wish she'd called instead of texted. I really miss hearing her voice and all her little sighs.

I'm really relaxed and so tan, the most glorious bronze tone.

And all this swimming has done wonders for my thighs and my ass is so tight . . . I may never return to the mainland.

I guess the trip has loosened her up again to toy with me.

Don't be such a tease.

But I like teasing you.

Is that how it is? That's cold.

No it isn't . . . it's hot. And furthermore I went and bought a teeny tiny white bikini today and I'm pretty sure I have never, nor will ever, look this good again. So you don't just like me, if you could see me you'd want me. Badly. I'm certain your resistance over screwing me would crumble.

It's hard to say if I would've crumbled since you aren't around to show me.

Take my word for it.

Pictures or it never happened.

How can I shoot a full-length picture of myself? If I ask Stephan he will get suspicious.

Have you ever heard of those magic pieces of glass called mirrors? They work astounding well for full-length selfies.

Of course! What was I thinking! Give me 5 . . .

I pace back and forth across my living room until my phone finally pings. My fingers tremble as I press on the tiny jpeg of her and wait for it to go full size.

Oh. My. God.

I fall back into the armchair and brace my arms so I can study this picture indefinitely.

She texts when several minutes pass with no response from me.

Well?

You're right.

About what specifically?

It's a good thing you aren't here.

Because . . .

That tiny bikini would be in tiny shreds on the floor.

Sigh. That's so hot Paulie.

Well, you're seriously hot. Surely you know this.

Mmm maybe. But I really like hearing you say it.

Something about the flirting in her texts is making me wild. It's bad enough that just looking at her bikini shot has me all worked up, but her teasing has resulted an epic hard-on. It's frustrating because I have to keep stopping fisting it to reply to her texts. Thank God for voice command on this phone, 'cause I want to just close my eyes and imagine her straddling me with her tits in my face as she grinds over me.

Hey Paulie . . . will you swim with me in the ocean sometime?

I'll swim with you anywhere if you wear that bikini.

I wish Stephan was fun like you.

I'm glad he isn't. It makes me extra awesome.

I'll say. Do you know what he's doing right now?

On another business call?

No, he's following the room maid around supervising her work. He's done it every day. It makes me want to scream.

I bet. But I don't want to talk about him, I want to talk about you.

I also want to tell her how much I miss her but that wouldn't be cool considering everything.

Hey, Paul, I know we're just friends and all but will you be looking at my hot bikini picture later when you get off?

I swallow hard. She knows me so well.

What makes you think I'm not looking at it and getting off now?

Are you?

Yes.

Pictures or it didn't happen.

Use your imagination.

Believe me, I am.

Time for me to finish what you started, naughty tease.

Me too. Xoxo

I remember that she mentioned an important set of meetings in the following week so I'm assuming she's back home, unless the Viking pulled a fast one. I keep hoping she'll call or send me more dirty texts, but nothing. So on Tuesday I drive by her house early evening and don't see any sign of her, but when I do the same Wednesday I see her on her porch with a watering can, moving from one flower pot to another.

She must have just come from work because she's wearing one of those tight business-like navy skirts and a white fitted jacket thing that shows off her golden tan. I let out a long sigh and either I'm having a caffeine reaction, or my heart is racing just at the sight of her. I roll down the window and lean my head out.

"Hey lady! Haven't you heard we've got a drought going on?"

She holds her hand up above her brow to shield the sun until she spots me.

Grinning, I wave.

She puts her hand on her hip and shakes her head. "Mr. Sprinkler is chastising me about using water?"

I park and step out of my car. "So what if I am?"

"You want to come regulate me, Mr. Official Guy?"

"Maybe I will." I amble up to her front porch and flash a pretend harsh look. "How much water have you used with this activity?"

"Ha! Not enough!" she exclaims as she steps closer and tips her can in my direction. "You know what? You're distracting me, and when I'm distracted my aim with the watering can isn't so good," she says with a flirty side-glance.

I pretend not to notice that's she's watering my feet and before she's figured out my plan, I try to wrestle the can out of her hand. The resulting struggle creates a splash that soaks the front of her jacket.

I expect her to shriek and jump back, but instead she slowly unbuttons her jacket and opens the front, revealing the sheer white blouse she's wearing underneath. We both stare at each other and then down at her chest as the water that splashed down her neckline does its magic.

Hot damn. If this were a wet T-shirt contest, she'd win, hands down.

I can't help but stare with a lascivious grin.

"You like that, don't you?" she asks with an arched brow.

"You bet I do."

She nods her head toward the front door. "Wanna beer?"

"Sure."

As I follow her I'm mesmerized by how good her curvy hips look in that skirt, and the click of her high heel pumps on the wood floor. "Is that how you dress for work?"

"Yes, I've just come from a meeting."

I imagine all the business men leering at her and it pisses me off. "It's kind of sexy, don't you think?"

"You think this is sexy?" she asks, turning to me.

"I do—and especially now," I say, looking down where the thin fabric is clinging to the top of her breasts like a second skin.

"Well, that doesn't count. When the jacket is on it's essentially a business suit."

I shrug. "Maybe it's just you. You have this ability to make everything look sexy."

"So how was Maui?" I ask after settling down at her kitchen table.

"Beautiful. It was good to get away."

I nod and glance down, resisting picking at the label on my beer bottle.

"So, was it everything you'd hoped with the Viking?"

She shrugs. "It was fine. A mix of good and not-so-good—you know what I mean?"

I nod silently even if though I really want to know what she means by that. I remember my conversation with Patrick that made me think she'd fallen in love. If that's true she certainly hides it well.

"Did you get your sex on the beach?"

She makes a cute little face. "I had to get him liquored up and really worked into a frenzy to even get down to the beach. I was determined . . . sex on the beach has always been on my bucket list."

I have to wonder what else is on her bucket list. Is there anything on it that I could give her?

"So you said it was mixed. What was the good part?"

She twists a strand of her long hair in her fingers. "It's hard to explain. But something about being on the shore made me feel kind of raw and wild. It was like I was on the edge of the earth with the moonlit waves crashing at our feet. It made me feel like an animal in the wilderness. I devoured him."

My damn cock starts to get hard imagining raw and wild Elle, which is just an abomination since the Viking is involved. *Traitor cock!*

"Did he like being devoured?"

"Apparently, until in my passion, I kicked up the blankets and coated him with sand. You'd think I'd set his hair on fire the way he leapt up and squealed like a little girl."

I throw my head back and laugh whole-heartedly.

She smiles at my reaction.

"So was that the end of it?"

"Hardly. No, I taunted him then and we argued which resulted in him fucking me hard, which was really hot. It was so hot and aggressive that I got rubbed raw from the sand."

I feel annoyed at the idea of it and hold up my hand. "Too much information."

"Believe me, there's nothing sexy about sand abrasion."

"Way too much information," I groan.

"Well, have you done it on the beach?"

"Does in the ocean count?"

"You did it in the ocean?"

"Yeah, you sound surprised."

She sighs. "No. Just jealous."

"Should *I* be jealous? You're the one who just had a love connection in Maui."

She looks up at me with wide eyes. "Are you?"

I shrug. "Maybe, just a little."

Grinning, she punches me on the shoulder. "Oh you!" She settles down on the stool next to me and takes a sip of her beer. "So I want to ask you a favor."

"Okay . . ."

"It's a big favor—really big."

"Do you have another burned out light bulb in some heavy ass light fixture?"

She shakes her head. "No, it's a much bigger favor than that. I'd really appreciate it if you could take me to my bestie's wedding this September. I mean, I know weddings are torture for dudes—"

I jump in before she goes on. "Sure, I'll take you."

"And it's formal . . ." She makes a grim face like she's really trying to talk me out of it.

"Awesome. I look hot in a tux. Besides, I love weddings!"

Her mouth falls open. "You love weddings?"

"What's not to love? It's a big party and everyone's happy."

"You're killing me with this, Paulie. Are you toying with me? I thought all men hated weddings."

"Not this man." I glance over at her and watch her wiggle with delight in her seat. She appears so happy and relieved.

"Hey, so why me? Why not the Viking?"

She twists her beer bottle in her hand as she looks down. "You're more fun."

I'm tempted to drill her for more information but I decide to let it go. "And I'm extra fun at weddings."

"Good, I'll be needing fun."

I notice the tightness around her eyes. "Yeah?"

"My ex will be there with his new girlfriend. He's the Best Man at the wedding."

"Oh, damn. That's awkward."

"You have no idea," she says with a frown.

"Well, I'm your man. I'm going to dote on you like you're the best thing that's ever happened to me. That ex is going to be full of regret for what he lost by being an inattentive asshole."

"You're willing to do all that for me?"

"Yeah, I'm a good guy. Remember?"

She lets out a long sigh. "The best."

Several weeks later I find my mind wandering during my Sex Addicts meeting when it occurs to me that Elle hasn't mentioned the Viking in well over a week. Maybe that initial thrill of getting laid whenever you have an itch has faded. Maybe his crazy ass obsession with cleanliness has finally gotten to her.

Should I feel guilty that I'm happy and want him out of the picture?

Hell no.

Elle deserves better. She's an amazing woman and not just

because she's gorgeous and loves sex. It's because she's smart, strong, straight-talking, and more fun to be around than any woman I've ever known.

She needs a man who appreciates all of that glory. She needs someone like me who understands her.

"Paul!" Jim calls out.

I snap to attention. "Yeah?"

"I just asked you a question."

"Sorry, got stuff on my mind." I look around and am stunned to realize that in my stupor the meeting ended and everyone but Jim is gone.

"That broad?" he asks like that's a bad thing.

"Her name is Elle," I answer with my jaw so tight that I have to ungrit my teeth. "And she's not a broad. She's an amazing woman."

"Is that so? You were completely checked out at this meeting. I thought you had a handle on this, man. You've worked so hard to get control over your obsessive behavior. I hate to see you backslide now."

"I wouldn't call this backsliding."

"What would you call it? You know what she's about and that she isn't what you need. Have you gone over the edge already?"

"You want to know if I've screwed her," I say, my fury building. I know my rage isn't really toward Jim, but myself. What happened to me in my life that I have to sit in this church basement with a bunch of losers wondering when they can get home to their bottles of lube and porn DVDs? I'm better than this, damn it. Surely there can be worse things than being insatiable about having a desirable woman in my bed.

He nods. "Yeah, I do. You signed up for this, man. You know very well what this program is about. Have you been able to control yourself or not?"

I fold my arms over my chest and pull my shoulders back. "No."

Jim shakes his head and his expression looks tired. "I knew

it. Can't you see that she's become your obsession? You're whipped. Pull yourself together, man, before you're off the program."

"I'm not off shit," I say way too loud considering I'm in a church. I feel like my head is on fire and that the rest of me is seconds away from combusting. "This is the thing, Jim. I haven't touched her. But I want to, damn it. I want to more than anything I've wanted in my life."

His expression is muddled. "So what are you saying?"

I lean over, my fists tightening as I struggle for a breath. *Holy fuck.* When it all hits me it feels like my knees will give out.

"I'm saying that it's not just the sex anymore, damn it. I'm falling for her. I can't stop thinking about when I'll see her next. So do me a favor, don't fucking say anything about this being wrong, because to me, everything about her is right."

"You're falling for her?" he asks like I haven't made myself clear. "Maybe you've confused blue balls with infatuation."

I want to punch him . . . badly. How dare he belittle what I now know is one of the biggest realizations of my life? This is a game changer. I want Elle. Yeah, I want to have all the sex with her, but for the first time in my life I want her in my arms in the morning too. I want to watch her wake up, and smile when she sees I'm there.

"Does she know how you're feeling?"

I shake my head and the insecurity starts creeping in. What if this isn't welcome news to her? She seems very comfortable with us being friends. Besides I've already rejected her too many times. "What should I do?"

"If you really think this isn't just about screwing her and that you want something more, then you should man up and talk to her. If she doesn't feel the same, it's best you know now before much more time passes and you get crazy in the head."

That night I make up my mind to take Elle to dinner to talk to her about how I'm feeling. I'm going to play it kind of cool so she doesn't feel cornered. Even if she is afraid to be rejected again, I can give her time to ease into the idea.

Or if she feels the way I do, things could happen fast. I grin to myself realizing that this is the best I've felt in a long time.

I consider taking her to a nice restaurant but then decide to be low-key. When I call to ask if she'll come with me to my favorite barbeque place in Korea Town, she seems open to it.

"Is that where you pick out all your stuff in a bowl and they cook it in front of you?" she says.

"Yup, and this one's really good."

"Sounds like fun. I've always wanted to try that."

I'm encouraged by how upbeat she sounds, and clearly she wasn't already booked with the Viking or a Tinder hook-up so that's another positive. "I'll drive. I'll pick you up at seven."

That evening when I get to her house there's no answer even though her car is in the driveway. I try to call her from my cell phone but it just rings and goes to voicemail. This isn't like Elle. Worried, I let myself in the side gate and walk to the backyard to see if she's sitting out back and didn't hear the doorbell. The yard is empty and my anxiety goes into over gear when I notice the French doors facing her yard are open. I approach the door cautiously and peek inside.

The house is eerily still until I hear a tiny snore. I step inside so I can walk around to face the couch. Curled up into the pillows and covered by a fluffy blanket is my dinner date. She's so damn cute I can't help but smile.

She also looks so peaceful that I don't want to wake her, so instead I settle into the adjoining love seat and peruse the new stack of books on the table. I smirk as I read the back summaries. At least she's consistent in her taste. I'm particularly puzzled by the one where the guy has one hand on his bare chest and his other hand down his pants that are half undone—although in fairness I can't tell what he's trying to grab. Maybe it was his keys and he missed his pocket.

I glance over at Elle who is still deep in slumber so I crack open the cover. Maybe once I start reading I'll understand why this dude, Steele, likes to have his hand deep in his pants.

This book starts out slower than the last one. The first chapter doesn't have any sex at all, but that all seems likely to change when Steele is released from prison after serving time for vehicular manslaughter. Well, at least I now understand why his hand was in his pants. Self love is the best choice by far if you're in prison.

So his childhood bestie, Ricky, who happens to be a real hottie now, picks him up in her battered pick-up and agrees to let him stay at her place until he gets back on his feet. Naturally she's a bartender by night and dancer by day.

By chapter two she helps Steele get a job doing maintenance at the dance studio although apparently he spends more time watching Ricky dance from the sidelines than actually cleaning.

By chapter three there's still no sex just a lot of uncomfortable staring at each other's body parts and Steele thinking dirty thoughts.

I'm really losing interest. Finally I notice that Elle left a bookmark further back in the book, and when I go to check it out it's noticeable that the spine is loose at this section. Apparently my little vixen has read this part more than once.

And I can see why. Three pages in and my cock is wide awake. So much for Steele and Ricky being besties. I guess the ten previous chapters leading up to this one had enough tension to fuel a number of epic sex scenes in a row. Even I'm worn out by the last scene that involves dirty dancing, and shower sex so wild it sounds dangerous. I'm guessing by the fold in the page that Elle really liked this scene, too.

I glance over at her just when her eyes flutter open. From the way her eyes bug out when she sees me and her mouth falls open, I guess I've startled her.

"Oh my God! How long have you been here?" she asks, as she lifts herself upright. Her hair is doing a wild dance all over her head and she has the pillow's texture imprinted on her cheek.

I smile at her. "A little while. I didn't want to wake you, you looked so peaceful."

"That was nice of you."

She stretches her arms up over her head and my eyes trail down to the little patch of skin revealed where her shirt lifted. Her skin looks velvety soft. I wonder how it'd feel to touch it, even press my lips against it . . .

"I've been sleeping on and off all day." She lets out a huge yawn.

I reach over and rest my hand on her cool forehead. "You don't have a fever."

"No, I feel fine. Just tired I guess." She spies the book in my hand. "Hey, were you reading my smut again?"

I hold up the book. "Yeah, the ex-con one. I think I found your favorite chapter. I didn't know you were into ex-cons."

"I'm not usually. This one just had special qualities." She gives me a wink. "I'm starving. Let's go eat!"

We're loaded in the car when she turns to me. "Hey, how into the barbeque thing are you?"

"I'm not married to the idea, why? Would you rather go somewhere else?"

"I'm craving a Double-Double something fierce."

"In-N-Out?" I ask, scrunching my face. I immediately think of how unromantic those white Formica booths are and realize that this night isn't going the way I'd hoped. But I look over and her face is lit up. How can I turn her down?

"Could we?" she asks with those big doe eyes. Her hair is still crazy and I reach over to smooth it down.

"Okay, sure," I say.

She claps her hands like a kid and I grin as I pull onto the street.

I've never seen Elle eat like this. She's suddenly a truck driver in a petite package. She polishes off the Double-Double, a chocolate shake, her fries, and half of mine. I finally pull the fries away. "Slow down. You're going to make yourself sick."

She snags another fry and waves it toward me. "Yeah, and can you believe I was throwing up this morning! Fast recovery, right?"

"What do you mean you were throwing up? Did you eat something bad?"

"I guess so. I've been off all week. Maybe I'm fighting a little virus or something. I just want to sleep and eat all the time."

As I watch her drain her milkshake my mind starts to wander with disturbing thoughts. I've been around women enough to pick up on the myriad of weird body stuff they suffer through due to their crazy, ever-changing hormones. What she's just described sounds like a particular combination of symptoms. *Oh Jesus*. Could she be pregnant? As soon as I think of it I feel like I've been kicked in the stomach. Is fate this big of a bitch . . . is this the worst timing in my life? The night I was finally ready to ask her for more, could be the night where her life turns another direction without me in it. My fingers tighten along the edges of the tabletop.

"What's wrong? You look freaked out." Her smile fades the longer I don't answer her question.

What do I say? I pull my straw halfway out of my soda and then slide it back in several times while my head spins. At this point telling the truth is the only road worth taking.

"Could you be pregnant?"

She drops her fry. "Pregnant? No, of course not."

"Are you sure? Birth control isn't infallible you know."

She folds her arms over her chest. "I'm sure. I'd know if I were pregnant."

She glares at me like I've told her she was stupid or something. I wish I felt better hearing how confident her answer was.

"Okay. Sorry I said anything. Shall we?" I ask as I gather up our ravaged remains to throw away.

She nods, a faraway look in her eyes.

We're half way out the door of In-N-Out when she turns to me. "Hey can we swing by Krispy Kreme on the way home?"

Good Lord, this woman.

Far be it from me to get in the way of her eating frenzy. "Sure thing."

We do the drive-thru but then I decide to pull over so I can watch her devour another round of food. It's entertaining. She keeps smacking her sugar-coated lips and she moans with each bite.

She's halfway done with her maple bar when her mood suddenly shifts. Her eyebrows knit together like she's trying to figure out a complicated problem. She turns to me. "Wait a minute. What's the date again?"

"It's the fifth, why?"

After frantically dropping the doughnut back in the bag, she rummages through her purse until she pulls out her cell phone. She swipes the screen, her fingers a blur. She looks up at me with an expression of horror and then back down to the screen.

"What?" I ask. She's freaking me out.

"I'm a week late," she whispers.

"Are you sure?"

She nods, tears already forming in her eyes. "Yeah, I've been in such a fog this week that it hadn't occurred to me. Oh my God, Paul. What if you were right? What if I'm pregnant?" Her expression is twisted with fear like she's suddenly trapped inside a horror film.

My heart is pounding. This isn't how I thought this evening would go at all. She looks like she's slipping down a slippery slope and needs something to hold onto.

I rest my hand on her shoulder and squeeze it before I start up the car. "Let's make sure first."

"Where are we going?" Her hands are pressed against her face.

"The drugstore."

The whole drive she is rocking in her seat chanting, "Oh my God, oh my God," over and over.

It reminds me of when I did this for my sister her first year of college when she was dating that asshole football player. Luckily her test came out negative. Maybe Elle's will, too.

When we get to Rite-Aid she's rocking so hard I'm afraid she'll hit her head on the dashboard.

"Oh my God, oh my God . . ."

I realize that she's in no shape to go inside. "Elle, I'll be right back. Okay?"

She doesn't respond, just keeps rocking.

I dart out the door and into the store like a man on a mission. I rush down several aisles before I find the potentially preggers section. With the sanitary napkins just to my right, it only takes a few seconds to be reminded that this is no place for a man. I scan the options: Early Detection, First Response, Clear Blue . . . blah, blah, blah. I grab three different choices and head to the front of the store hoping Elle hasn't passed out in the car yet.

Why there's a line at Rite-Aid at nine at night, I have no friggin' idea. Yet it's my lucky day when my Tinder trainer and pal, Gabe, gets in line behind me with a twelve pack.

"Hey, dude. How's it going?" he asks, and looks down at what I'm holding before I have a chance to tip it away from his view.

Fuck.

I glance over to the check out stations and curse the old man in the jogging suit that's demanding a price check.

"Hey, Gabe. I'm good, and you?"

He leans forward. "Well, well, look at that. You gearing up for daddyhood man?"

Damn it all!

"No, man, this is for a friend. I swear."

"Sure, sure," he says and gives me a grin.

The jogging suit guy finally finishes up. "Hey Gabe, please don't say anything to Dad. I swear this isn't my kid."

He nods and pats me on my back right before I step forward.

"No worries, dude. This is just between us."

Back in the car, Elle has added trembling to the rocking and chanting. I place the bag on her lap to buckle my seatbelt and she shoves it off onto the floor. Yeah, this isn't at all how I thought tonight would go.

"I'm not peeing on a stick, Paul."

"You're going to have to, Elle. You need to know for sure."

"I'm going to wait a few days. Maybe my cycle is off because of traveling."

I nod. "Maybe. And you said you were really careful about birth control, right?"

"So careful. And Stephan was meticulous about it."

"Okay, so this test is just for peace of mind. If your birth control was meticulous, then you should have nothing to worry about."

"Right, right. We went through two boxes of condoms."

"I really didn't need to hear that," I grumble.

"We even used one on the beach."

"Awesome." I can't hide the sarcasm in my voice.

She takes a sharp breath. "The beach!" she wails.

I swerve to the right before gaining control of the car again. "What? What?"

"The sand, the pounding! The condom was messed up when it was over."

I want to ask more specifics but I'm sure I can't stomach it. I don't need to reply though because we've just pulled up to her house. I rush around, open her door, and extend my hand. "Come on. Let's go."

She paces the living room while I tear open the first package and read the instructions. "Let's get this done," I say, pointing towards the guest bath. When she opens the door I hand her the stick. "Pee on this part for five seconds."

I look her in the eyes and all I see is terror. I can't blame her. In a few minutes her whole life could change. When the door closes I fold my arms and lean back on the wall across from the door. A nervous minute passes and all I hear is silence.

I step up to the door. "You okay?"

"I can't pee," she cries out.

"You've got to. Mind over matter, Elle. Think of waterfalls or something."

"What?"

"Just pee, damn it!"

"Asshole," I hear her mumble.

A minute later the door opens and she hands me the wand. After slipping the cap back on it, I lay it flat on the counter. "Okay let's walk away for five minutes."

She nods and heads to the kitchen. With the stiffness of a zombie she takes a bottle of beer out of the fridge, opens it, and hands it to me. It's not hard to miss that she hasn't taken one for herself.

"So, busy day tomorrow?" she asks.

I blink at her. She wants to talk about our schedules? Okay, I'll play that game.

Besides, her vacant expression tells me that she doesn't give a shit about what my day is like tomorrow but she needs to be distracted.

"Yeah, pretty busy. You?"

"Yes, I have a presentation to a new client I really want to work with."

"Well, good luck with that."

She chews on her thumbnail and nods toward the bathroom. "How much more time?"

"A minute and a half." Her color is shifting to a grayish hue.

"Oh no . . . I think I'm going to be sick."

She rushes toward the bathroom with me right at her heels. When she curls over the toilet, I sweep her hair off her face and hold it back as she hurls.

So much for that In-N-Out dinner and maple bar. At least she's quick about it.

"You okay?" I ask as she wipes her face and flushes the toilet.

She goes to the sink and rinses out her mouth. "How much more time now?"

I glance at my watch, reach out and carefully pick up the wand, and hold it toward the light. It reveals two distinct stripes. That second little stripe indicating positive, feels like a needle jabbed in my heart. I turn away from her so she can't see my expression. I have no fucking gameface at this point.

"What?" she whispers.

I hold up the stick. "Positive." I feel like I can't breath and it's not even my kid. She wasn't looking for this. I can't even imagine how she's feeling.

"Positive?" she asks in a distraught voice. I hear her choke back tears.

I nod and try to swallow down the lump in my throat. Luckily, I look over at her before she sways and then starts to crumble. I catch her just in time and pull her tightly into my arms. It breaks my heart when she presses her face into my chest and lets out a sorrowful cry. I sweep my arm under her knees and lift her up.

She's full on sobbing by the time I carry her to the living room and sink down onto the couch, still holding her tightly against me. I slowly run my hand across her head and down her back over and over, imagining what this experience would be like if it were my kid. Would she feel differently than as distraught as she seems to be right now? Would she want our baby as much as I would? I ache because I wish it were mine and that's messed up to even be thinking about when she's so defeated by the news.

My shirt is soaked and my arm numb by the time the tears quiet. She tilts her face up to look at me.

"What am I going to do, Paul?"

"I would think you'd want to take a little time to figure out what your heart wants you to do."

She lets out a long sigh and nods.

I can't help but be tender with her. My heart is broken—not just for what we could have been, but for the tough decisions she has ahead of her. I brush her hair off her damp forehead.

"I must say, Elle, I think you'd make an incredible mom."

I watch two streams of tears slowly make their way down her cheeks. "I'm not so sure I would," she says quietly. "How could I properly take care of a baby with my irregular work schedule and travel? There are some events where I have no idea when I'll get home."

"But what about Stephan? He would be helping."

At the mention of his name she squeezes her eyes shut and grimaces. "Stephan," she sighs.

"What? This baby is his responsibility, too."

"Yes, but can you imagine? He'd seal the baby in a germ-free bubble. Besides, he's the least fatherly man I know."

"I'll take your word on that. You'd have a super clean baby for sure." I try to give her a warm smile. "He'd probably wear surgical gloves to change a diaper."

"Oh I can promise you that he'd never change a dirty diaper."

"He might surprise you. Fatherhood changes people. I have a friend from college that could be such an ass, but when his son was born he changed completely . . . at least around his kid. He's a total mush head now."

She lets out an awkward laugh.

"What?"

"I just remembered my junior high health teacher telling us to never sleep with someone unless you think they'd make a good parent. She was only trying to scare us out of sex, but now I see the wisdom in her words. I should've listened."

"Don't be so hard on yourself. I know better than anyone that the need for sex can make us do things we wouldn't necessarily do."

She nods and leans into my chest again.

"You just need to tell him so you can figure the rest out. Hopefully, together," I say.

"Okay," she whispers.

Her eyes glaze over and I wonder what she's thinking deep in her heart. Elle is a worldly woman. I don't need to tell her that there are several choices she can make regarding the baby. It's not my baby, nor my body, so I intend to support her with whatever she chooses.

She makes an effort to sit up and I help her until she's upright with her legs hanging off the couch. "I think I need to go to bed," she says.

"Yes, get some sleep. You can call Stephan tomorrow."

When we get to her front door I turn to face her, placing both of my hands on her shoulders. "Will you let me know how the·

talk with him goes?"

She bites her lip but nods. "Yes."

I run my hands down her arms. "I want you to know that I'm here for you, whatever decision you make. Just promise me you won't sell yourself short. I meant what I said. You'll be an incredible mom."

She brushes new tears away and steps up close so I can wrap my arms around her. "Paul, what would I do without you? Your kindness means so much to me. You're such a good friend."

And I'll never be more than that now . . .

My chest hurts as that raw truth hits me.

"Good men make good friends," I say with a hug. "I'll call you tomorrow."

I hold it together as I take several steps down her walkway and turn to wave good- bye. But I clench my fists all the way to the car and my jaw is locked as I pull my door shut. In the silence of my car I finally let out my frustration.

"Damn it all," I yell as I slam my forehead against the steering wheel. "Why? Why?"

I want to punch my fist through the windshield and then track down the Viking and beat the crap out of him for having a timeshare in Maui when he hates sand. It's all his fault that I no longer have a chance with Elle.

I feel a stinging in my eyes and I flip down my visor mirror. *What the hell? Are those tears glazing my eyes?* I never cry. I point at my reflection. "Don't you dare cry, asshole. Don't you dare!" I slam the visor back up.

As I fire up my engine my mind goes dark places. How tragically ironic that the night we learn that Elle has a new life growing inside of her is the same night my hope, for the life I finally realized I want, has died.

CHAPTER NINE

THE HERO

The next two days at work are living hell. I'm worried about Elle, and not sure what I can do to help her. She texts me to let me know she's meeting with the Viking after work on Tuesday. She promises to text me whether he took the news better than she'd hoped, or worse.

Stephan isn't the only thing I'm concerned about in regards to Elle. I'm worried she isn't taking good care of herself and my internet research has shown that her health habits in this first trimester are key. At lunch I go to the pharmacy in the building across from our office and get a recommendation from the pharmacist for pre-natal vitamins. As I pay for the purchase it occurs to me that she may have trouble keeping them down. I hope she does better with them than she did with her Double-Double.

By early evening Tuesday I find myself lingering behind at work and doodling at my drafting table while I try to imagine how I would take the news if it were my baby, and not the Viking's. I know I'd be a better dad than him. As soon as the kid was old enough I'd start taking him to the park so we could play in the sand box barefoot together. Hell, I'd buy a sandbox for our house, and I sure as hell wouldn't be caught dead in those pussy water shoes.

Our kid would know sand, and messy hand paintings and food all over their little face. We'd pitch tents in the living room, and there'd be Lego pieces under every piece of furniture or tucked into every cushion crevice. I'd smile at every sticky fingerprint because I'd know that they were like footprints in the road proving I was on the right path with my life.

I pick up my phone and check it again. Nothing. By 7:30 I can't take it any longer and I text her.

You okay?

She responds almost immediately.

No.

Is he still there?

No.

I'm on my way.

I curse him the entire drive over. *Motherfucker.* How could he leave her alone after the news she just shared? My hate for him hits new levels. I plot revenge the entire ride over so that I hardly notice the drive. When I arrive the front door is cracked open and I find Elle in the living room sitting in the corner of the couch.

She looks terrified, like a little girl accidently left behind at the bus depot.

I hate seeing her like this and I'm so amped up I can't sit down. "What happened?"

She curls forward and rubs her fingers over her scalp nervously. "Well, to start with he said it wasn't his."

Motherfucker did not!

"Classy. Did he forget that you were in paradise together when it happened?" "According to him that doesn't mean for sure it's his."

I grit my teeth so hard my jaw hurts. "So what's he saying, that you got it on with the cabana boy in Maui?"

"I have no idea what he's thinking. He insists it wasn't him, and he also disputes that there was a problem with his condom."

"That's big of him. I think all of those cleaning products have gone to his head.

But what can you expect from a man who is afraid of sand?"

"You know, I didn't expect for a second that he'd be happy about the news, but I didn't think he'd stoop so low as to say it couldn't possibly be his."

"He's a dirty scumbag. Don't let all those bottles of sanitizer fool you."

"I told him that I'm more than willing to do a paternity test if he needs reassurance, but I'm sure it's his."

"So what plan did you guys make?"

"Well he left without any kind of plan. As a matter of fact, he said not to contact him and that his lawyer would make sure that he was not responsible for any child support."

"Are you serious? What kind of man would do this?" I ask as I feel the fury work its way up my neck.

She looks up at me with the saddest eyes I've ever seen. "Not a good man."

Pressing her hands over her face, she starts to cry. I sit down on the couch and slide my arm over her shoulder so she can lean into me. "I'm so sorry, Elle."

She silently nods as the tears stream down her face. We sit like that for a few minutes and then she clears her throat. "What am I going to do?"

"Just take things one step at a time, that's what my dad always says. Hey, how about a walk? It'll be good for you." I want to say it'll be good for the baby, too, but I stop myself.

We're silent and walk almost to the corner before she turns to me. "This was a good idea. I needed to get out of the house."

"Me too. When we get back let's burn some candles to get the Viking stink out of your home."

The corners of her mouth turn up the tiniest bit. "Good idea."

Two kids wiz by us on their bikes and I watch them until they turn the corner. I've always liked this neighborhood but now I'm seeing it in a new perspective. It's a family kind of place. "This seems like a great area to raise a kid in."

"It is. That's part of what drew me to living here. I know I don't come off as the most maternal person because of my up-bringing, but do you know when I was little I was fixated on being a mom? I had a baby dolly that I treated like a real baby. I had a little stroller for it and everything. I loved taking care of it."

It makes my chest hurt to know she had a dream and life sucked the beauty out of it. "I bet you were a cute kid."

She smiles. "I'll have to show you pictures some time."

"I'd like that. So you make it sound like your attitude about being a mom changed over the years."

Her expression falls. "I blame a lot of that on my mom. She was always telling me how much work I was, how she couldn't get a good job or make decent money to support us because she had no help raising me."

"Where was your dad?"

"Apparently off drinking somewhere. There was a point where her schedule changed at the restaurant she worked at, so she had no choice after school but to drop me off at one of those youth center places with strange people lurking around. I'd have a paper bag with a sandwich and juice box for my dinner. I was only in the second grade.

"Luckily the director of the center took a liking to me and she took me under her wing. She gave me little jobs and taught me how to be strong and self-reliant. It was probably around that time, where I was spending time around kids that were neglected, that made me realize maybe I wasn't meant to be a mother. If my mom couldn't handle it, why would I think I could?"

"And what do you think now?"

She lets out a long sigh. "That's what I'm trying to figure out."

"You know Elle, sometimes the best way to learn is from poor examples that teach you what *not* to do."

"I suppose you're right. Unfortunately, I have a long list there."

"And you aren't your mother."

"Thank you. I hope not. I don't want to end up bitter and

angry at the world like she is."

"That director lady was right . . . you're strong and self-reliant."

She loops her arm through mine. "So enough about me. What about you, do you want to have *a* kid one day?"

I shake my head.

Her expression falls. "You don't?"

"No, I don't want a kid, I want a whole lot of kids. You know those reality shows with the super-sized families? When I was younger I wanted a super-sized family. We would be our own village. How cool would that be?"

"You're insane," she says with a laugh. "That's a baby factory, not a family."

"But I'd have my own posse."

"You say all this like it's a good thing."

"I used to be a camp counselor—four years at Camp Yallani. I loved the little tykes. The more little ones swarming around me, the better."

"Sounds like chaos."

I grin. "Managed chaos."

"So you better get moving on this big idea. You're getting a little old to have a super-sized family."

I let out a long exaggerated sigh. "I know. I've had to downsize my dreams."

She purses her lips. "Plus you have to find a woman with breeding tendencies who has lots of ideas for first names that start with the same letter. That's the rule with big families, right? Something like: Timmy, Terry, Teresa, Tess, Thomas, Taylor, Toodles . . ."

My eyes grow wide. "Toodles?"

She nods. "Catchy, right? You need at least one wacky, far-out name."

"Sorry . . . Toodles is a no. And you've nailed the biggest issue. It's not easy to find women who will let their vejays be clown cars."

She sputters a laugh and her cheeks turn hot pink. "Yeah,

great point. Good luck with that."

It's great to see her happy even if it's just for a minute.

I glance up and realize that we're almost back to her house. "I'm going to walk you in and then I'll take off. You ate dinner, right?"

She gazes off in the distance. "No. I didn't have a chance."

I give her a stern look. "You know I'm not going to put up with that."

"Aren't you the bossy one?"

Once we're in her kitchen I fish through the fridge and pull out some stuff. "I'm going to scramble some eggs so you get protein."

She slaps her hand over her mouth and shakes her head. "No eggs! Just the idea of them makes me gag right now."

I put the egg carton back in and continue with my foraging. "How about some fruit and yogurt?"

"I think I can handle that, thanks."

I quickly cut up the fruit and mix in the yogurt, then slide the bowl over to her. "Eat up."

She digs in. "Mmm. This is good!" She waves her spoon in the air.

"Awesome." I settle on one of the stools and lean my elbows on the counter while I watch her eat. It's a glorious thing to behold, especially when she licks the spoon clean and runs her tongue across her sweet lips.

I suddenly remember something. Grabbing my jacket, I find the bottle of pre-natal vitamins in the pocket. As I return to the kitchen I remove the protective seal and get the bottle open before shaking out a vitamin. After setting it on the counter, in front of her, I pour her a glass of water.

"What's this?" She holds the capsule between her fingers and lifts it to the light.

"A pre-natal vitamin. The pharmacist said this is the best brand."

Her jaw goes slack and her eyes fill up with tears so fast that it makes my eyes bug out. A second later her lower lip starts to wobble and she looks unsteady.

I lean forward. "You okay? You suddenly don't look so good. You can wait to take the vitamin if you're worried it will upset your stomach . . ."

She does this weird wave of her hands and then lets out a sob before slinking off her stool and fleeing the room.

I'm stunned. What did I do wrong? Maybe I was too pushy. The website I was reading warned me that her hormones are in flux and she could be prone to wide swings of emotion.

I gingerly walk to the doorway and pause so I can listen carefully for her. I hear crying with the occasional wail. *Damn.* I must've really fucked up.

Gathering up my courage, I step into her room.

"Elle?"

The only reply is a sob and she turns away on the huge bed. In her vulnerable state this bed feels like it could swallow her up.

"I'm sorry I upset you . . . really sorry. I'm just trying to help, and . . ."

She sits up and turns around, staring at me like I've lost my mind. With her puffy eyes and crazy hair she looks positively unhinged.

"Sorry!" she yells. "You're sorry?"

I jam my hands in the back pockets of my jeans and shrug. "Yeah, I'm sorry I upset you. I didn't mean to."

She sits up taller on the bed and bends her knees so she can fold them against her chest and then she takes several deep breaths. "I'm not acting like a crazy woman because you upset me, Paul. I'm crying because I just can't believe you."

I extend my arms out in frustration. She's going to make me work for this. "But I haven't lied about anything."

Her head falls until her chin is touching her chest. After a few seconds she lifts her head back up and observes me with sad eyes, then holds her hands out toward me. "Come here."

I step closer and take her hands in mine. She pulls me down until I'm sitting on the edge of the bed and I hike up my knee on the mattress so I can turn toward her.

"Look at me," she commands.

I do, and I see a fierceness in her eyes. I can sense that everything about Elle has changed. In her expression I see a mama lion, a woman who's invincible.

"What?" I whisper.

She scoots toward me and her grip tightens over my hands.

"I need you to understand something."

"Okay."

"No one. No one, Paul . . . has ever treated me like you have."

The tears are streaming down her face now and I have to turn away. It's so much emotion . . . a blazing fireball. It's more than I can take.

She yanks hard on my arm to get my attention again. "No one has ever been so kind, so supportive . . . Paul you bought me and my baby pre-natal vitamins. I am speechless."

Well, technically she isn't speechless since she's still talking but things seem to be going my way now, so I keep my mouth shut.

She wipes both hands across her face to catch the torrent of tears. This isn't her most attractive moment, but even in a state of despair, I still think she's beautiful.

She quiets so I decide to speak. "It was easy for me to do and the vitamins are really important to start early in the first trimester. I'll send you the link for the study I was reading—"

Fisting the front of my shirt, she yanks me toward her. "Are you paying attention to what I'm saying?"

"I'm trying—I swear."

"It's your kindness Paul. You're amazing, and I will adore you forever for what you've done for me. You've given me more than hope tonight. You've made me *believe* I can do this and be all right."

Okay, this is good. This seems to be going better now. I decide to run with it.

"*You're* the amazing one, Elle. I know you will be more than okay."

She crumbles back onto the bed and starts sobbing again.

Holy hormones! I'm starting to see that this is not a job for the weak-willed man. I need to be strong.

I flop down on my back next to her and despite her protests, I tuck her into the crook of my arm. She cries and cries while I make cooing sounds to try to calm her. I'm sure all this upset isn't good for the baby.

"You really think I can do this?" she asks.

"Absolutely. I hope you don't mind me asking . . . but can I be Uncle Paul? I may spoil the little tyke a bit."

She sobs again. *Geez*

"You would be Uncle Paul?" she asks in between tears.

"Yeah, I'd love that. And I can take care of the baby when you need help. Hell, if we get my parents on board they'll want to babysit. My mom is absolutely wild about babies and small kids."

"I really like your parents," she says in a soft, sleepy voice.

I skim my fingers lightly over her back, back and forth, as I feel her settle into me. "Yeah, they may make me nutty at times but they're really good people."

A minute later I realize her breathing is deeper and she's fallen asleep. We lie together like that for a long time. I like her in my arms and I like being with her on her bed. It might be wrong to feel this way under these circumstances, but I can't help it.

I replay in my head all the emotions she shared with me tonight, from despair to hope and back again. I didn't think she had it in her to be so emotional, but despite that she seems to be holding on. I try to picture her as a young girl being left at that kid's center without her mom or friends and it gets me in the gut. Maybe her mom just couldn't see a better way, but I have to think there could've been one.

Despite all that Elle rose above her circumstances and made something of herself. Now I'm more impressed with her than ever.

It's just past midnight when my eyes open with a start and I realize I've dozed off. Elle's curled even closer to me now, and I have to gently scoot away as not to wake her. I wander into the kitchen and find a pad on the desk so I can leave her a note.

Morning sleepyhead.
It's just past midnight as I write this and
I'm going to head home. You're deep in slumberland.
Let me know in the morning how you're doing.
I'm just a phone call away.
*   ~ Paul.*

Back in the bedroom, I carefully remove her shoes, open the folded blanket at the foot of the bed, and drape it over her. I prop up my note on the bedside table so she'll see it as soon as she wakes.

It's lunch time when my phone prompts and I look at the screen to see it's her.

"Hey Elle, how are you feeling?"

"Nauseous but otherwise okay."

"I put that fruit and yogurt in the fridge last night. Can you try to eat that?"

"I'll try. How are you doing?"

"Fine, doing the work thing . . . figuring out tree installations. Are you working today?"

"I slept straight through my first call of the day so I decided to cancel my meetings and take the day off. I've made an appointment with my OB/Gyn."

"Good, I'm glad you're going. Do you need a ride?"

"No I think I can swing it. But thanks for the offer."

"Any time."

"I was thinking I'd like to cook you dinner. Are you free Friday night?"

"Sure, what's the occasion?"

"To thank you."

I rub my chin as I try to figure out what this is about. "For what?"

She lets out a happy sigh. "For everything."

"That's kind of vague."

"Okay, how about for being a good man."

"It's a little wide-sweeping, but I'll take it."

"I promise on Friday to be more specific."

I grin into my phone. "Excellent. So call me later, okay?"

"I will."

I feel good all day. Really good, like my life is in order and I'm grounded to something bigger now. But how can the chaos of Elle's accidental pregnancy and my compulsion to be her port in a storm, make me feel so settled? It's freaking weird.

I decide not to be an idiot who questions everything and just go with it. Elle texts me in the afternoon to let me know the appointment went well and the good feelings expand with the news.

I take a longer run after work and skip my beer that night. It's like I'm a new man, the kind of man I can actually feel positive about.

By the time I arrive for dinner Friday this new scenario between us is feeling normal. Elle's been impregnated by a Viking, and I've traded my dream future as her passionate boyfriend for being a doting uncle to her baby. I'm not sure why it seems to make sense but it does, like we've stepped into an alternate universe and find that it's not bad at all. When she opens the front door I hand her a book on pregnancy for working women and a little stuffed lamb instead of a bottle of wine.

Judging from her reaction to the gifts, I'm totally rocking this uncle thing.

She clutches the gifts to her chest and kisses me on the cheek. "I hope you're hungry."

"Famished."

She sits me down in the kitchen and pours me some wine while she finishes up the beef stroganoff.

"So what did the doctor say?"

"Well first of all she said I'm in really good health which bodes well for the pregnancy. She said I can keep up with my exercise routine as long as I don't push it."

"You mean the balls and straps?" I narrow my eyes. "Are you sure that's okay? I'm not sure I like that."

Laughing, she shakes her head. "No, I'm staying away from the balls and straps, but I also do the cross country ski machine, so I'm going to keep that up."

I let out a relieved breath. "Okay. Good to know."

"And she was very impressed with your choice of pre-natal vitamins and diligence in getting me on them right away."

"Well I'm determined to be a do-the-right-thing kind of guy."

"Indeed."

"So when do you see her again?"

"In four weeks. It's the appointment after that we hear the heartbeat."

I look up at her expectantly. I wonder if she'd feel weird about me coming along. "That's really cool," I say as I glance down and take a bite of the salad she's just put in front of me.

"Would you like to come?"

My head pops up and I can't stop myself from grinning ear to ear. "Yeah! That'd be great." After taking another bite of my salad I ask, "So what else did she say?"

"We talked about the challenges of being a single working mom. So she talked about building a support circle. It takes a village, and all that . . ."

"Right," I say, nodding.

"I'm still scared out of my mind, but she reminded me that women all over the world do it every day. There are some good daycare places around here and with my flexible schedule I'll have more quality time than a lot of working parents."

"There you go," I say encouragingly.

She takes a long sip of her water. "And we talked about sex."

My mouth falls open and I set my fork down. I thought we were done with that subject for quite a while. "What about sex?"

"Why I want it all the time now."

I feel the blood drain out of my face. "But you wanted it all the time before. You mean you want it even more now?"

"I do. She says it's the hormones, but how am I going to manage all of this raging physical need?"

Oh dear God.

"Please tell me you aren't going to start up Tinder again."

"Oh no!" She looks alarmed. "That would be crazy."

"Good. You were scaring me."

She pulls her shoulders back and straightens up. "And look. My boobs are bigger. I guess they're going to be huge by the time I deliver."

"They were already pretty big."

"And they're really sensitive, but in a good way."

In order to know this, she must be touching them a lot.

I can imagine her touching herself way too vividly in my head. I'm sure I'll be imagining her skimming her fingertips over her breasts and softly pinching her nipples while I'm in the shower tonight.

"Um, wow, that must be cool."

"Except that I want to touch them all the time."

"Even now?"

"Especially now . . . well, you know, since we're talking about it."

I lean back in the chair to adjust myself. My jeans are too damn tight right now. "Well, don't let me stop you. Be my guest."

She cups her hands over her breasts and squeezes a few times with her eyes closed. A huge smile spreads across her face as she lets out a satisfied sigh. "Oh, that feels so good."

This woman . . . Am I in in a dream—like one of my dreams when I was twelve and obsessed with breasts?

I feel kind of drugged watching her, like the walls in the room are wavy and her large, amazing breasts are all I can see.

My hard-on is getting painful. "You know you're making me crazy, right?"

She drops her hands down and bites her lip. "Sorry about that."

"You should be. You know about my issues," I say with a mock stern voice.

"I got carried away. It's just all so fascinating how different my body feels."

"So how are you going to manage this? It's not like you can be touching yourself in public."

"I went sexual relief shopping after the appointment."

She carries over from the desk a bag from a bookstore and starts lifting out the contents. Each new book looks smuttier than the last.

I nod. "Impressive." Frankly I'm just so relieved she won't be looking for real sex in the world at large that I'm in full support of her lack of regard for fine literature. "Well, you've got hours of fun ahead of you with that selection."

"Wait, I'm not done. I also went to the Pleasure Chest."

"The dildo place?"

"Oh they've got everything."

"But I thought you already had a vibrator."

"I do, but I'm afraid my deluxe rabbit has to be put out to pasture for a while. It's just too intense and I'm ultra-sensitive right now."

"Back in the day one of my hook-ups showed me her rabbit. That thing is crazy! Is what you usually use?"

She winks. "I like it intense, but now it's just too much."

I lean back in my chair. "Wow."

For a moment I allow myself to imagine what it would have been like if we'd met during my wild days and before she was married. Without a doubt the sex would've been mind-blowing.

I watch her open up the package for the simple vibrator, unscrew the back and slide the batteries inside. She turns it on and strokes it, then gives it a nod of approval. "Much less intense."

"Are you going to demonstrate it for me?"

"You wish," she says with a teasing tone while glancing down at my plate. "Hey eat up. Your Stroganoff is getting cold."

Chapter Ten

Against the Wall

The following Thursday as I drive to my parents it hits me that I should've planned out better how I'm going to break the news to them about Elle. I really have no idea how they're going to handle it. I work on the breakdown of how I imagine their thoughts will run:

Strike one: she's a divorcee

Plus one: she baked an apple pie and brought it to our house for dinner

Plus two: she went out with Patrick

Strike two: she rejected Patrick

Strike three: she got knocked up out of wedlock

Plus three: she's having a baby and Ma says babies are gifts from God

As for the issue that I'm going to be Uncle Paul? I have no idea how they'll rank that surprise.

My head is spinning. So instead of creating a strategy of how to tell them, I down a beer soon after arrival and have another before dessert is served. It's loosened me up enough to bolster me with a false bravado.

During a rare quiet pause in the conversation I share my big news rather nonchalantly.

"Hey, guess what?"

Dad takes the bait. "What, son?"

"I'm going to be an uncle."

My parents push their chairs back in unison with such force that the table pitches forward. They almost knock Trisha over trying to hug her and I instantly realize that being spontaneous was a sucky idea. I have given them the completely wrong idea and Trisha is giving me the *"you will pay for this asshole"* look in a profoundly convincing way.

"Paddy, Paddy . . . We're going to be a grandparents!" Ma yells, even though we are all within feet of her.

I leap to my feet. "Wait! Wait a minute! It's not Trisha!"

In unison their gazes move to Patrick and back to me.

"What are you talking about, Paul?" my father asks. He's not amused with my shenanigans, and obviously he wants some answers.

"It's Elle."

Patrick gasps and Trisha snorts.

"Elle?" Ma says. "What does that have to do with you being an uncle?"

"The guy she was seeing wants no part of it so I told her I'd help."

"Help how?" my sister asks.

"Yes, what exactly do you mean by help?" My dad asks with a scowl on his face.

"I bet he's in charge of diapers because he's so full of shit," Trisha says.

"Shut it, Trisha," I growl.

She points at me. "Don't even . . ."

"Paul? Help how?" my mother says in a stern tone that I recognize. If I don't start making sense soon I'm going to be in the doghouse for sure.

"You know . . . just being supportive. We're good friends so I calmed her down after the guy was an ass about it."

My father shakes his head. "Ass indeed. What kind of man can he be?"

My fingers instinctively curl into fists. "Don't get me started.

I want to beat the shit out of him."

"Goodness. You *are* supportive," Ma says as she studies me.

"I am. I did some research online and bought her pre-natal vitamins."

Patrick jumps in. "Those are very important."

"How do you know that?" Trisha asks with an arched brow.

He shrugs. "Doesn't everyone?"

I glance over at Mom and her expression has softened. She looks at my dad, and then back at me. "You bought vitamins for her baby?"

I nod. "It wasn't a big deal. I'm happy to help her. She's a good woman, Ma."

Patrick nods.

"She is," Ma agrees. "Poor lass to be in such a situation. It's a lot for one woman to manage—too much really."

"And a baby needs a father," Dad says.

His words sting because no matter how supportive I am, being an uncle is nothing compared to being a dad.

Ma turns to Patrick and Trisha. "You two, we need a word alone with Paul."

"Why can't we hear?" Trisha asks.

"Do you really need to ask that? You and your agitating comments . . ."

"It's part of my charm," Trisha remarks with a grin.

Patrick stands up. "Come on, Trisha, let's go do the dishes."

Ma waits until she hears the water running in the kitchen before she turns to me. "Paul, we want to know, is there something going on between you and Elle that you aren't telling us?"

I can't help but squirm in my seat. "No. Why do you ask?"

"I just can't imagine why you would take this on if you aren't involved. Saying you are going to be an uncle is a serious business. You can't just flitter in and out of the wee one's life."

"I'm not the flittering type, Ma."

Dad rests his hands on the table. "We know that, son, but you haven't known Elle long. Do you really know what you are getting into? She's embarking on the biggest job and responsibility of her life. And although I'm very sympathetic, how will you handle it if she asks too much from you?"

"That's not her style. If anything she tries to do too much on her own, when she should ask for help."

Ma twists her hands together.

"Do you think badly of her for this unplanned pregnancy?"

"No," she scoffs. "That's life—mistakes happen, but a baby is a gift regardless.

And Elle is a lovely woman who's been married . . . she's not a sixteen year old girl who was careless."

"And we've always liked her," Dad chimes in.

Ma nods. "She just needs to make the best of it, and it sounds like she's trying."

"She is," I agree.

Ma gives me a stern look. "Okay, but how are you going to meet a girl and have your own family if you're so busy being uncle to Elle's baby?"

"And what if the father changes his mind and decides to be with Elle after all?"

"Believe me, he's a whack-job . . . I really don't think that's going to happen."

"But you can't know that for sure," Dad says.

I stand up and push my chair back. "Look, I appreciate your concern for me, really I do . . . but the bottom line is that I truly care about her and she really needs my support. I figure the rest will be worked out in time."

"Please be careful, son," Dad says.

I nod and then Ma steps up and hugs me tightly. I can't read the hug: is it tinged with worry, protective urges, pride or disappointment? Perhaps it's a mix of them all.

The following week we're back at In-N-Out because Elle has a craving. She must be very brave to eat another Double-Double so soon after the last one's untimely ending. With each bite she moans, closes her eyes, and smiles so it seems like things are going well. Honestly, watching her eat that burger is the closest thing to watching porn but everyone's clothes are still on.

When she finishes it she elaborately licks each finger, and I keep having to look away.

"What?" she asks before pressing a napkin over her lips to blot the ketchup that remains.

"Oh nothing."

"Then why do you look uncomfortable?"

"Do you always moan that much when you eat?"

Her cheeks immediately blush pink. "Was I that loud?"

"Uh huh. That would have made a great sex scene soundtrack."

"Oh no! I'm horrified."

"Don't be. It was hot. I'm sure every man within hearing distance of our table has a hard-on right now."

Her eyes grow wide. "Do you?"

"What do you think?"

She sits back in her seat. "Well, at least I've still got it. I thought men didn't find pregnant woman sexy."

"Oh, that's so 1950. I've seen some very sexy pregnant women."

"Like who?"

"Well, you for one."

"Really? Be honest now, you just lust after my big boobs. Besides, I don't even look pregnant yet. Let's see how you feel when my belly gets round."

"Will you let me touch it?"

"My voluptuous chest?"

"No. Your round belly."

"Sure. Anytime." She pats her tummy gently and smiles.

"Paul?"

I glance over to see my sister's friend, Holly, holding a tray and standing at the edge of our table.

Awkward. I wonder how much of that conversation she overheard.

"Hey, Holly. Long time no see."

She glances at Elle. "Is this your girlfriend?"

While I'm thinking of an equally rude and invasive retort, Elle jumps in. "No, we're just good friends. I'm Elle by the way." She gives Holly a little wave.

"Hi there. I was just wondering because Paul never returned my call about coming with me to the reunion next month."

"But you weren't even in my class. Why would I go to that reunion?"

"Because you promised me when you wouldn't go to the prom with me that you'd make it up to me one day."

I bite the inside of my cheek so I don't laugh out loud. "Surely you didn't think I meant that?"

"So you were lying?"

"Absolutely. I really didn't want to go to the prom."

I leave out the 'with you' part.

I see Elle's eyes twinkle as she takes a sip of her shake. She's enjoying this way too much.

"I think you should go to the reunion with Holly," Elle says.

Traitor!

How could she do this to me after I volunteer to be her baby's uncle?

Holly lets out a little "Woo-hoo!" and with the way that the other patrons are staring at us, I'm feeling like our booth has become the center of the In-N-Out universe. *Can we leave now?* Don't get me wrong, Holly is actually quite attractive, but the girl never shuts up and I'm pretty sure I've never heard her discuss a single thing that was of interest to me.

"Hollyeee," we hear some chick screech from across the bright white expanse of booths and mini-tables.

Holly waves at her Neanderthal friend who yells across restaurants. "I've got to scooch. I'll call you, Paul. And great to meet you, Elle!"

And a second later she's gone.

I squint my eyes and shake my head. "Scooch?"

Elle shrugs. "Does that mean to go somewhere?"

"It sounds like that thing dogs do when they drag their butts along the ground. I actually could see her doing that."

She nods. "It's such an ugly word."

"And can you tell me what I did to you to make you do something so hateful to me?"

Her expression falls instantly from amused to mournful. "Hateful?"

"Enlisting me in reunion hell."

"Oh, listen to you! You make it sound like torture."

"I promise you, it would be if I went. And I'm not going."

"I know you aren't going." She has a sly grin that makes me smile.

"So you were lying to her."

"Of course, what else would get her to shut up and leave us alone? You're with me, and she has a lot of nerve coming over here and fawning all over you."

She's jealous. The idea of this makes me unbelievable happy.

"Oh man, I love you!" I say, and then grit my teeth. Did I really just use the big L word like some lovestruck pussy boy? "I mean, I love that you did that," I correct quickly.

She takes a sip of her shake and nods. "She *is* pretty in a *'trying way too hard'* kind of way, but she's not for you."

"Who *is* for me?"

You, you, you . . . my brain whispers on autopilot.

She gets a faraway look in her eyes. "We'll see."

We're at Elle's house curled up on the couch in our third attempt for her to stay awake long enough to watch *Baby Boom* with Dianne Keaton. My sister shocked me by loaning me the DVD two Thursdays ago after family dinner night. She shoved it at me while I was leaving.

"Here, watch this with Elle."

I held up the DVD case and studied it. "What's it about?" Although with the name *Baby Boom*, I was pretty sure it wasn't a

Star Wars kind of flick.

"She's a career woman who suddenly has to take care of a baby. And you remind me a lot of the Sam Shepard character."

"Is he an asshole, or something?" I ask since she always seems to have the lowest opinion of me.

"Nah. The opposite really. He's calm and steady and just naturally looks out for her . . . like you're trying to do for Elle. I really like his character."

I stop and turn around, realizing this is a moment I need to pay attention to. They come so few and far between. "So are you saying I'm a good guy, Trisha?"

"Maybe," she mutters, glancing down and twisting her watch around her wrist.

"And are you saying that you like me?"

She looks like she's holding a hot plate in her hands and has nowhere to set it down. "Well, I wouldn't go that far."

I nod and open the front door.

She clears her throat. "Well, maybe just a little bit."

I let out a low laugh and give her an awkward hug. "Well, whatever you're saying . . . thank you."

"You're welcome."

I'm a few steps into the walkway when Trisha calls out to me. "Hey Paul?"

"Yeah."

"I'm really am proud of you for how you're helping Elle."

I gaze at her intently and the corners of my mouth edge up as I nod. "Thanks, Trisha."

So Elle and I are watching the movie and are at the part where Sam Shepard meets Dianne in his veterinary practice in rural Connecticut. Elle suddenly turns to me.

"Tell me about your work."

"Okay. What would you like to know?"

"Do you enjoy it?"

"Most of the time. I love the creative part where I'm envisioning the design, and the thrill of creating something people will see and appreciate. I'm still one of the mid-level men on the design team so far, but I plan to work my way up."

"I'm sure you will."

I appreciate her blind faith in my ability.

"You know, like any work, there's stuff I can't stand about it: difficult clients, boring status meetings, budget cuts mid-way through projects."

"That sounds like my job."

"So then, what do you like about your work?"

"I think it's the challenge of pulling off events when there are so many ways things can go wrong. I like the strategy of fig-uring out a game-plan, and I have really good vendors I've de-veloped relationships with. I love the adrenalin when the event starts and we're all amped up . . . showtime!"

"It does sound a bit like live theater," I say.

"It is in some ways. My busy season is going to start soon. Which reminds me . . . I think I'm going to have to shop for new business clothes already. All those Double-Doubles caught up with me. My pencil skirts are too tight."

"Well you've been eating for two. Are there pregnant clothes for career women?"

She grins. "You mean maternity clothes? I'm not sure, but wearing those ugly slacks with the expanding waistline is a hard limit for me. I'm going to try to buy regular clothes, just bigger for now."

"Promise me that you aren't one of those women that goes out wearing a skin-tight knit dress in her last months where you can see the baby kicking—the thing is so revealing. I really don't need to see that from total strangers."

"No one does. I promise I won't do that."

"Thank you."

She lets out a long yawn. "You sleepy?"

"Yeah, always these days. I'm lucky that it's been my slow time at work since I'm so tired all the time."

"So what's your busy season like?" I feel a surge of worry that it's going to sound like too much in her condition.

"Long hours, lots of stress. I have no idea how I'm going to get through it without my coffee."

"So you really stopped drinking coffee? I'm impressed" She looked at me like I was nuts when I first told her she should wean herself off of it. Luckily her doctor re-confirmed what I said.

"Oh man. It was rough. Good thing you didn't see me those first few mornings. I miss the coffee a lot more than the booze. Nine months is a long time."

"It is, but you're being strong for the baby. See, you're already a good mom."

She leans her head on my shoulder and smiles. "I guess you're right. I want to be a good mom, Paul . . . more than anything."

"And so you will be."

CHAPTER ELEVEN

THE HOT SEAT

"Are you really sure about this Paul? Really? Oh my God, I'm freaking out."

Parking in front of my parent's house, I turn toward her. "Why are you freaking out?"

"Your parents are very traditional people. They must think very poorly of me for being in this situation."

"Well, I'm not going to lie and say they think it's great that you are having a baby without a husband, but they respect the fact that you are doing the best you can. We talked about it. They've always liked you, and they still do."

"How do they feel about you . . . well, you know, helping me so much . . . and being 'the uncle'?"

I grip the steering wheel as I try to think of what to say so that she isn't uncomfortable. She could easily take what I say the wrong way and I don't want to upset her. "They want to make sure I'm helping you for the right reasons."

"Are you? I mean, I think you are, but only you can say for sure."

I nod. "I am."

"But they're still worried, aren't they?"

"Maybe a little."

"That I'm taking advantage of you?"

I point to the house. "Hey, what do you say we shelve this

deep-feely stuff for now and go chow down? I swear they're going to be nice to you. They really like you."

She folds her arms over her ample chest and side-eyes me. "Okay, I'll agree because I'm famished. So you get a break now, but we're discussing this later."

When we get out of the car she retrieves the dessert she baked from the backseat.

"So is that your apple pie?" I ask, my mouth already watering.

"No, this time I made strawberry cheesecake."

My eyebrows arch and let out a low whistle. "See there, we haven't even finished the first quarter and you're already ahead in the game."

"Oh my goodness gracious!" Ma exclaims as she clasps her hands over her heart. Her cheeks are pink and she looks positively blissful. "You shouldn't have, Elle! You should be resting, not baking."

Ma really should've been an opera singer. She's so theatrical with her booming voice and dramatic gestures.

"But baking is relaxing to me, Mrs. McNeill. Besides, Paul told me strawberries are your favorite."

"They are indeed. Come in, come in, and call me Millie, lass."

There's a little bustle at first with all of the overly exaggerated greetings. Finally Dad gets Elle settled on the couch with a glass of water, and so far there's no weird vibe. Even Patrick doesn't seem totally awkward about seeing her again.

During dinner, Dad keeps passing the lamb chops to Elle and I've lost count how many she's eaten. It's starting to get a little obscene.

Meanwhile Patrick and Dad are talking about the stock market while I watch Elle eat. Suddenly Trisha pipes up.

"Hey, Paul, did you hear who Ma ran into at the bank?"

I look over at my mother, who's busy buttering her bread.

She gives Trisha a stern look and shakes her head, then glances at Elle. Ma's reaction makes me curious as to what's going on.

"Nope. Who was it?"

"Melanie Milstead," Trisha replies with an edge of defiance in her voice.

Ma's eyes grow wide with fury. My sister has a knack for stirring things up.

The intensity of the feelings that buzz through me is surprising, a mix of intrigue, frustration, and longing. *Melanie Milstead* . . . the girl that got away. Even after all these years hearing her name still gets to me.

Ma lifts up the big bowl to her right. "More mashed potatoes anyone?" she asks with an exasperated expression. Dad picks up the cue and grabs the bowl and offers more to Elle.

Patrick sets down his fork. "Hey, I remember that girl. You had a big crush on Melanie Milstead in high school. You talked about her all the time."

"Um, yeah. That was a lifetime ago," I respond.

He nods. "Wow. How's she doing?"

Ma sighs with resignation. "She seems fine. She's just moved back to L.A. after working in New York for a few years. I think she said in design."

"Yes, she's a graphic designer," I say.

Elle looks over at me with a curious expression.

"So Ma says she asked all about you," Trisha teases.

"Really?"

Ma shrugs. "I told her you were working for Sater and Gates and she was impressed."

"That's nice," I say, my palms sweating. I can't believe just the idea of that girl still makes me nervous.

"She gave Ma her information so you could contact her," Trisha states.

"Contact her? Like a date? Are you going to do that?" Patrick asks like it's a column of numbers that aren't adding up.

"No! I'm not going to ask her on a date!" I answer emphatically.

"Why not?" inquires Elle, seeming genuinely intrigued.

My mouth twists as I try to think how to change the subject. "Well . . ."

"Ask her out," Elle says.

I lean back. I sort of thought that Elle wouldn't want me dating other women, while I'm helping her with her baby-centric life.

"Really?" I ask.

"Sure."

I study her face and see no sign that she'd care if I go out with Melanie. It bugs me. I want her to care.

Elle gives me a smile. It looks a little forced, but I'm not sure. "It might be fun to see her."

"Lots of fun," Trisha comments.

"Maybe I will," I reply, testing the dark and murky waters. I don't share that I could never get Melanie to go out with me before, so I'm not sure why she would now.

"Good." Elle says as she finally pushes her dinner away. Her plate has enough bones to qualify as an archeology site.

"Maybe she'll be a good design contact," Ma suggests.

"You said she really has her life together. Didn't you, Ma?" Trisha says.

Ma scowls at her.

From the way Elle's eyes darken I can tell she's taken offense. She smooths her napkin over her lap. "You should definitely be dating a woman who has her life together," she says in a clipped tone.

"And you two aren't a couple, right?" Trisha asks, gesturing toward Elle and me. My sister is ever the helpful one. Maybe this was her idea to test us to see if we could be a potential couple, and Elle and I have failed.

"Oh no! Not together in any way. We're just friends," Elle assures her.

I don't like the tone of Elle's voice . . . like being with me would be about as much fun as a root canal.

"I'll call her tomorrow," I say with a tone indicating that I'm done with them figuring out my life while I sit and chew on a lamb chop.

After dinner Dad and I do the dishes. I suspect he's as relieved as I am to get away from all the female hormones for a while. We left Patrick in there, but I'm sure it's a chance for him to learn fascinating new things about that perplexing species.

When we rejoin the clan Ma has pulled out the photo albums and is showing Elle our baby pictures.

"Oh, Paul. You were the cutest baby! I mean look at these chubby cheeks!" Elle exclaims.

I shake my head. "Yeah, I've seen those. I think I'll pass."

"Look at those thick thighs," Ma coos. "He was insatiable, I could never feed him enough."

"Do you even hear what you're saying?" I ask, not hiding the frustration in my tone. "I'm going to hurl that album out the window if you go on any more about my insatiable feeding for fuck's sake."

"Paul!" Dad snaps.

"I love seeing these pictures of you," Elle says. "You look like you were such a happy baby, and your mom told me all about your delivery."

"You were already trying to get out before we got to the hospital, Paulie. You were always on the go."

"Why is no one listening to me?" I say into the void.

"Is your baby's daddy a big, strong man like our Paul?" Ma asks.

Elle studies me like she's sizing me up.

"Well, he's taller, but not built like Paul. He's long and lean."

Ma nods. "I prefer a big man, but as long as he isn't fat. Because a fat man will only get fatter."

"Word to the wise," I mutter, rolling my eyes.

"Well, you were right," Elle says as she buckles her seatbelt.

"See, I told you they would be welcoming. I think Ma was in

heaven talking about babies all night."

"They really couldn't have been nicer. I really like your family, Paul."

"Well you can have them."

"Don't be that way. I mean I know the breastfeeding thing must have been awkward for you, but I think it's kind of cute."

"Cute? What in the world is cute about breastfeeding?"

"I'm going to breastfeed the baby."

Alarmed, I look over at her. "Why would you do that when bottles make so much sense?"

"Make sense? Don't you know how much healthier it is for the baby? Look how good you turned out."

"Just promise me you won't keep doing it to where it becomes a freak show. When the kid can come up and tell you he wants it, and then lifts your shirt and yanks at your bra, it's time to stop."

It's her turn to look alarmed. "Ewww."

I shake my head. "Exactly."

The next mile or so we're both silent. I'm deep in thought and assume she is too. I finally glance over at Elle for a second to make sure she's all right. As it happens she's squeezing her boobs and I almost lose control of the car.

"What are you doing?" I ask, my throat suddenly as dry as the Sahara.

"Checking."

"Care to elaborate?" I ask with a smirk.

"I'm checking to see if my boobs got bigger."

"Since when?"

"Since this morning."

"They grow that fast?"

She shrugs. "It seems like it." She thrusts her chest out. "Here, you want to see for yourself?"

Her words make me die a little inside. I want to feel her up so badly, but I can't. She doesn't understand my issues with self-control. One minute I'd be sizing up her breasts as I fondle them, the next I'd have her pinned down across the front seat with her panties pulled off.

"No thank you," I say, my steely gaze focused on the cars in front of me.

"It's because of this Melanie person being back in town that you won't touch my breasts, am I right? I could tell that she wasn't just any 'ol girl when Trisha brought her up. Was she one of your sex girls?"

"Sex girls?" I ask, perplexed.

"Like number three of your foursome?"

"Ah no, she was not, nor would ever be one of my sex girls." Elle's eyes narrow. "So she was more?"

"More or less, depending on how you look at it."

"What does that mean?"

I clear the gruffness out of my throat. "I was crazy for her, but she always refused to go out with me."

"You're joking, right?"

My stoic expression falls. "No joke, I swear."

"How in the world could she refuse you? Is she gay?"

I have to smile at her apparent high regard for my desirability.

"Nope, not gay. Just very picky."

"But you're the entire package. And with the anaconda, you're the entire package plus!"

"Is there ever a time where you aren't thinking about sex, Elle?"

Her cheeks blush pink. "No, not really."

"Well, she turned me down more times than I can count. I found out later that she preferred older men. She was particularly drawn to the prestigious designers."

"Ah, so she's ambitious."

"Very. How did you know?"

"It's the only way any of it makes sense. She turns you down for some older guy who can help her move ahead. Only now that you're getting somewhere with your career can she be bothered." She huffs and looks out the window.

"Kind of judgmental, aren't you?"

"Maybe. But if she can't appreciate *all* of your amazing

qualities then she doesn't deserve you."

"Is that so?" I ask, trying not to make my tone sound too playful.

"I could find you a much better woman than Ms. Melanie."

"So what? You'll be my pimp?"

The irony that the one woman I've made up my mind I want, is the same woman determined to get me someone else, is not lost on me. If our situation wasn't so crazy, I'd really be gutted.

She grins. "I'll be your pimp, and you're my baby uncle. We're so damn modern."

"So what kind of girl will you pick for me?"

She looks up to the side and purses her lips. "Let me see. First of all, I'm thinking a big, curvy girl."

That wasn't what I was expecting. "Why?"

"So she can handle you. You know . . . all of you."

She is obsessed with the anaconda. I guess it works because it's obsessed with her.

"Well, I dig big, curvy girls so I'm okay with that. Will she have big tits?" I ask this crude question to throw her off, but she doesn't even blink.

"Most likely, those two things tend to go hand in hand."

"What does she like to do in her free time?" I ask.

"Exotic dancing," she answers, without missing a beat.

I nod. "Good."

"Yes, she'll have the moves."

"Is this someone I can bring home to meet the family?"

Her lips pucker into a little pout as she taps her chin with her finger.

"Maybe on second thought she's not an exotic dancer."

I nod, fighting back a grin.

"And she can't be a ballerina, they're too stiff."

"Yeah, I like my women bendy."

"I know! Your parents are Irish . . . she could be an Irish dancer!"

I let out a guffaw. "Ha! Have you ever watched Irish dancing?"

"Sort of."

"It's all jumping up and down."

"So . . ."

"Didn't you say she had big tits?"

She bends over laughing. "Oh my God! Jumping up and down is not good for the girls!"

"Not that I'd mind watching that, just saying . . . but it could be really uncomfortable for her."

"Good point. Okay, I'll keep thinking."

I'm almost to her house when Elle turns toward me. "So what does this Melanie look like?"

"Mmm. Back in the day she was long and lean, gorgeous smooth skin, a mysterious smile, and the biggest blue eyes. But it was the way she carried herself that set her apart—she seemed aristocratic."

"A mysterious smile?" she says with her lips pursed. "What does that mean?"

"Like she knew something you didn't."

"What's my smile like?"

"I don't know. I've never thought about it."

She folds her arms over her chest. "Oh I see. She's mysterious and I'm forgettable."

"That's not what I said."

"You may as well have said that."

"Is this a hormone thing? Because you're acting unusually nutty."

"Unusually nutty? So I'm always nutty, but right now even more so."

My brows knit together and I shrug. "Yeah, I guess."

"So do I amuse you with my nuttiness?"

"Usually you do, but not so much right now. But don't worry about it. I was reading about pregnancy and I'm sure this is your hormones going haywire again."

She doesn't respond, and when I glance over I see a dark red flush running across her face. That can't be good.

She points out her window. "Pull over!"

I swerve to the side and skid to a stop. If she's going to up-chuck dinner I sure as hell don't want it in my car. As soon as I hit the unlock button, she swings the door open wide.

But instead of leaning into the curb she pops out of the car, turns and slams the door shut.

Luckily the window is partially rolled down so she can hear me yell out, "Hey! What are you doing?"

"This nutjob is getting away from you, Mr. Critical."

My mouth falls open. "What did I do?"

"Oh, you didn't do a thing. It's all me. And I'm sure it will be an incredible relief to get away from nutty me and take out the exquisite Miss Melanie with the perfect skin and 'together life'."

She does quote marks in the air to emphasize her point before continuing.

"I'm sure *Melanie* won't be hormonal and demand massive In-N-Out meals because she accidently got knocked up. *No!* She'll probably suggest the hippest new restaurants where they serve little aristocratic portions. And I can bet that Ms. Perfect won't be feeling up her own boobs at inappropriate times, since unlike me, she has hot guys lined up that want to feel them for her."

Oh man, she's gone off the ledge. I better try to reason with her. It isn't good for her to be this upset.

"What are you talking about? Those Tinder guys wanted to feel you up. I bet if you called them they'd be happy to do it again."

She juts her hands on her hips and gives me a look so harsh that it makes me wither inside.

"Awesome response, Paul, to make me feel even better in my state of hysteria. That was epic. Thanks for the suggestion that I do Tinder hook-ups while pregnant. That's so appreciated."

Sheesh. "I didn't mean you should do hook-ups!"

Holy mother of all hormones! Someone hand me a shovel, so I can dig myself deeper into this hole.

She's riffling through her handbag and then pulls out her phone and starts tapping at the screen.

"What are you doing?" I yell. I'm losing my damn patience with this woman.

"Tinder."

I can feel my fury burn all the way up to the tips of my ears. "Put your phone away, Elle," I growl.

"No."

She starts walking in the opposite direction so that I have to shut down the engine and jump out of the car.

"Where are you going?"

"Home."

"Get in the car!"

She takes several steps toward me with that diva walk she did when we first met, but rather than opening the door to get back in she points at me.

"I've changed my mind about you, Paul."

I let out a long sigh. "Yeah?"

"You aren't good."

I freeze in place as she stares me down. Is she fucking serious with this? This feels like more than just hormones gone haywire. Her expression tells me that she's beyond pissed off and ready to draw blood.

"You're a bad man."

"Really? So now I'm bad?"

She shrugs half-heartedly like she's undecided but she's also not taking it back. Doesn't she know that she's gone way too far? I'm pretty sure I deserve more than this hormone-driven shit show.

She may not really mean it but she's hit my sore spot. She could've taken a dull knife and carved a hole in my chest and it would've hurt less. Is it my turn to get dramatic back because I feel like I can't breathe? I've tried so hard to be what she's needed me to be, so what the hell? She's the last person I expected to knock me down, and bring into question what I've feared about myself all along.

I turn and look away, staring down the deserted street. Everything looks colorless and I shiver even though I'm not cold.

What can I possibly say to her? I glance back to see if she has any remorse for what she's said, but she's already halfway down the street. My heart sinks down low. It's hard keeping it suspended in my chest when she's taken part of it with her.

Her words echo over and over.

If I'm a bad man, then I do what a bad man would.

I let her go.

Chapter Twelve

THE WRAPAROUND

On Tuesday Ma calls and I steel myself as I pick up the phone. Ma's got stellar skills for knowing when something's up.

"Hey, Ma."

"How's my boy? Are you having a busy day?"

"Yeah, super busy." *So can we get off the phone now?*

"And how's our Elle?"

Our Elle? Oh, it's more serious than I thought. They're attached to Elle and her baby now, so how do I tell them that Elle went nuts and decided I'm not good enough to be an uncle anymore?

I can't handle the onslaught, so I lie.

"She's good. She really enjoyed dinner the other night."

"Yes, she was so sweet about it when she called the next day to thank me."

I desperately want to ask how she sounded but it would give me away.

"She told me how kind you've been to her, and what a wonderful man you are. It made me proud, Paul."

"She said that? Really?"

"Indeed she did. You sound surprised."

"I guess I am. Sometimes I make her mad."

"No! *You?*" she says in a highly exaggerated tone.

"Okay now," I warn.

"You know what? She also said that she doesn't know how you put up with her."

"Sometimes it's not so easy."

"I know, but I still told her not to be so hard on herself. When you're pregnant everything becomes emotional and dramatic. Things will calm down."

"Will they?"

"Yes, they will."

"So I'm wondering, how did Dad deal with this with you?"

"He just let me be, have my fits and then he would bring me flowers. Why don't you take Elle some flowers tonight? Nothing like flowers to smooth out the rough edges."

"I'm not her husband, or even her boyfriend."

"I know that, but you're her close friend, aren't you?"

My mom is clairvoyant and I sense she knows Elle and I had a blow-out. It would be creepy if it weren't so cool. Either she's psychic or Elle told her so.

"Got it. Thanks, Ma."

"You're a good man, Paulie."

"I'm glad you think so."

"I do."

The florist seems to understand completely. I sense I'm not the first man asking for an apology bouquet.

"Let's make this happy!" she says enthusiastically as she meanders, collecting stems from tub after tub of colorful flowers.

I nod absentmindedly when she shows me the assortment she's gathered. I don't even ask the price. If this warms up Elle to me, it's priceless.

"So what did you do?" she asks as she winds ribbon around the wrapped flowers.

"I'm not sure," I reply honestly.

"Well it can't be that bad if you don't know why. I bet this will fix it."

"You really think so?"

"I do."

When I arrive at Elle's place her car is in the driveway but she doesn't answer the door. Wondering if she's napping again, I go through the side gate to check to see if the back French doors are open. To my surprise I find her kneeling on her lawn messing around with the sprinkler head. I'm immediately bothered. *What? I'm not good enough to fix her sprinklers anymore?*

I move a little closer and then stop to watch her. Her tongue is poking out the side of her mouth as she twists the head and pushes on it, then pulls it back out to study it.

"What are you doing?" I call out.

She looks up with wide eyes and her mouth agape. Her attention then shifts down to the flowers and she sits up straight. "Fixing stuff. What are *you* doing here?"

"Oh you know, I happened to be in the neighborhood . . ." I give her a crooked smile.

"Are those for me?" she asks in an unsteady voice.

I'm tempted to tease her and say that *'no, these are for another woman,'* but then I remind myself that that kind of humor got me in this trouble in the first place. So instead I hold the bouquet out in front of me. "Yes, they're for you."

Instead of smiling her lower lip quivers and she blinks rapidly. "I don't deserve any flowers, I should be giving you flowers."

I watch a tear skate down her cheek and I shake my head.

"I don't want flowers, Elle. I just want us to get along. Besides, I've missed you."

"I've missed you, too."

She gives me a soft smile and I feel a surge of relief and genuine happiness to see her again. It's just been a few days but I've missed her a lot. I step right up to where she's working and hand her the flowers.

"They're so beautiful. Thank you," she says as she accepts them. I kneel down to examine what she's working on. Lying next to the sprinkler set-up is a mangled head. It looks like someone went after it with a machete.

"The gardener again?" I ask.

She nods. "I don't know how he even does it. Like we talked about last time, he must have some seriously repressed anger issues."

"I'll say." I pick it up and examine it before glancing over at her. "So speaking of anger, are you still mad at me?"

"You? No! I'm mad at myself."

"Well, if you're not mad at me, why didn't you call me?"

Her gaze drops down. "It's complicated."

She keeps twisting the new sprinkler head in her hands so I take it from her, and screw it in place. "Done."

I stand back up and brush off my jeans, before offering my hand to her. "You got any beer inside?"

"Sure," she says and I follow her into the house.

We're sitting at her kitchen table. I'm nursing my beer and she's taking tiny sips of her chamomile tea. I finally ask the big question but this time I have to get an answer. "So why didn't you call me?"

She casts her eyes down and folds her hands in her lap. "I was embarrassed and I've been building up the courage to call. All that stuff I said to you was so stupid."

I nod. "I agree." When I smile she play punches me in the shoulder.

"I was kind of crazy, wasn't I?" Her eyes roll back and forth to emphasize her point.

"Not just kind of," I answer, giving her my best, startled, wide-eyed look.

"How crazy?"

"Mmm, somewhere between wacked out and bat-shit."

"Nice."

"So did you get it out of your system? Are we okay now?"

"I think so. You know, it was really big of you to come by here and bring me flowers."

"I've been worried about you. I wanted to make sure you were okay. Besides there's a good game on this weekend and I was hoping to watch it with you. I love how you yell at the television."

"So I can yell at the TV instead of you?"

"That's the plan."

Releasing a long sigh of relief, she rests her chin in her hand. She looks deep in thought and her expression gets somber again.

"I'm a mess," she says softly. "I'm still stunned by all of this. My marriage ending was nothing compared to the shock of this unexpected pregnancy."

She's never talked much about her marriage and it makes me curious. "How long were you married?"

"Eleven years."

My eyes grow wide. "Wow."

"I know . . . and by the end I was so unhappy that I was relieved it was over."

I scratch the back of my neck. "That's a long time to be married if you were unhappy."

"Oh, it wasn't always that way. When I met Daniel I was young and naïve, while he was self-assured and commanding. His protective demeanor made me feel safe. I never had that growing up, and I craved it desperately, so in the early days I was really happy as we started to build our life together."

"What happened to change things?"

She stares out the window for a moment and then her focus shifts back to me. "The best way to describe it is that I gradually grew into myself. I became more confident and independent, and he didn't like it. Eventually he started to try to control me by undermining my confidence, and once he realized he couldn't lord over me anymore, he belittled and shunned me."

I can feel my blood pressure rise as my temples pulse. "What an ass."

She nods. "So I left our marriage feeling angry and with a fierce determination that I could take care of myself. Unfortunately, I also left with my faith in relationships destroyed. Looking back, I think Tinder appealed to me because I felt in control and could ask for and get what I wanted from men with no complications." She lets out a bitter laugh.

"What?" I ask.

She waves her hand over her belly. "Could anything be more complicated than this? Obviously I'm still naïve, and now I'm floundering."

"I know this has been a rough time, Elle. Don't be too hard on yourself."

"It's just that I'm so overwhelmed. The universe dealt me an unexpected hand that's changed my entire life. Every single day from now on is different than what I'd planned."

I nod. "That would freak anyone out, believe me."

"Freak out or not, I've got a little life to look after, and the only thing that I know for sure is that this baby deserves more than me—more than knowing their life is the result of contraception failure and a dad who couldn't give a shit about them."

Reaching over the counter, I take her hand and squeeze it. She doesn't let go of me but instead holds on and winds our fingers together.

"You aren't giving yourself any credit. You make it sound like you're unfit to be a mother."

"Aren't I? I think I'm horribly unfit."

"Hell no. To start with, you aren't a crack whore . . . so major points for that." I give her a big thumbs-up with my free hand.

"You always say the sweetest things."

"I know, I have such a way with words. But seriously . . . you're an amazing woman. So smart and spirited . . . you've got such a big heart. This baby is so damn lucky."

"How can you say the baby's lucky?"

"Because you care so much. You're making changes in your life so this kid will have the best chance. I admire your courage and determination."

"Oh, I'm not that brave."

"Yes, you are."

"Paul, you don't know what I'm like inside. I lie in bed and I worry about everything. How will I know what's the best thing to do?"

"Best thing? Like what?" I ask.

"Like I was reading that it would be beneficial for the baby to sleep with me—that it soothes them."

"Sleep in the same bed? Aren't babies supposed to sleep in cribs? I mean that sounds dangerous. I, for one, flop around like a beached walrus. What if you roll over on them in your sleep?"

"Exactly! And I've never changed a diaper, let alone bought one. Hopefully there's a YouTube video about how to do that stuff. As for baby food . . . it's a mystery to me. I checked it out at the grocery store and it looks like space food. Then I can't even, with the car seats . . . I'm realizing that figuring them out requires a degree in engineering. And I overheard two women talking last week about how getting into pre-school is harder than college for God's sake. Then there's the books!

"What about books?" I ask.

"Well, what do I read to the baby that won't terrorize them? I had bad dreams for years over Hansel and Gretel. Cannibalism isn't cool, you know?"

She's starting to make *me* nervous. Her eyes grow wide as she remembers something else.

"Did you know that some kids get seizures from playing certain video games? My God! How will I know what to do?"

"Isn't it like anything in life? You learn one thing at a time. What about talking to other moms. Do you know any?"

"Well, none of my friends have kids yet. We're all career women."

"Then we'll go find you some mom friends."

She gives me a lopsided grin. "We will? And where do we find these mom friends?"

I shrug. "I don't know. In the park or something. I always see a lot of them in the park huddled together . . . or how about online! Isn't there like a Tinder for moms or something?"

She almost spits up her tea and I have to pat her back to calm her down.

"Mom hook-ups?" she sputters.

"Yeah!" *Damn, I have good ideas.*

"You're a gem, Paul."

I suspect she thinks my ideas on this subject are ridiculous, but she appreciates the effort.

"I know. How about Sunday before the game we go to one of those baby stores? I bet the people that work there know a lot."

She blinks rapidly, but thankfully I don't see any tears. "You'd do that?"

"Sure as long as you don't jump out of the car and yell at me."

"Deal."

That night as I lie in bed, I remember the charge I felt just seeing her again, and I'm pretty sure she was feeling the same. She looked stressed out and depressed when I saw her from a distance in the yard, and once we'd talked things out and got past that stupid argument, her real smile returned.

It feels like there's some of Elle now in every part of me . . . she's on the edge of every thought . . . her laugh, the teasing look in her eyes, and the way she curls into me whenever we're on the couch together. Tonight she laid her head on my chest as we watched some show. It could have been anything on TV, but all I cared about was that I was there with her and how weirdly perfect that felt.

Now that she's pregnant I know I shouldn't be thinking of sex with her, but I do . . . all the time. She's always turned me on but now it's different. There's something primitive about it, like I'm a freaking tiger desperate to mate her. Is this some crazy male hormone thing? I should Google that shit.

Everything that I'm attracted to in a woman is accentuated now, her curves and full breasts make me wild. Then her vulnerability, which belies her fierce inner strength, makes me protective of her. I don't want to just claim her as mine, but I want the baby to be mine, too. I feel attached to that kid already. Is that wrong?

I want it all and I have to face that I may never be satisfied until I get it. I also have to face that I could also end up with nothing. It's in fate's hands now.

The visit to the baby-stuff store on Sunday ends up being a kick-ass idea on my part. Our salesperson, Naomi, is so amped up to have a baby newbie that she goes above and beyond. By the time we leave the store Elle has a priority list of purchases and although I find the whole thing anxiety producing, Naomi seems to make Elle calm.

She has a big smile on her face when we finally get in the car to go home and see the game.

"That was the best idea ever, Paul," she says as she squeezes my arm.

"Yeah, I'm a genius."

"Can you believe how nice that Naomi was? All that time she spent with us and we didn't even buy anything."

"Yeah, she reminded me of my mom. Some women are just ga-ga over babies—not just theirs . . . anyone's."

"So did it bother you that she kept referring to you as the dad?"

My chest swells but I don't want her to know how not only did it not bother me, but I liked it—a lot.

"I noticed you didn't correct her." I glance over and see her sly smile.

"Well, it's not her business. We don't have to explain anything."

"Did it bother you?" I ask.

"No, I liked it. Believe me, I wish you were the dad." My heart practically explodes in my chest. *I could be.*

If I only had the courage to say those words. Still stunned from her honest confession I finally respond, "Really?"

"Of course. You're awesome. You'll be a great dad one day."

"Thanks. I plan to be a great uncle, too."

Her expression falls a little when I say 'uncle'. It gives me hope that one day I really can be the dad.

It's no surprise that Elle passes out curled up next to me in the fourth quarter of the game. The Trojans are kicking Arizona's ass, and after a while I'm just embarrassed for the Wildcats. I'm starting to doze off myself when Elle suddenly wakes with a start and sits up. Her eyes are wide.

I rub her back. "Hey, you okay?"

She nods but she still looks startled. "Yeah, just really weird dreams." She points to the television. "Did SC win?"

I nod. "They slaughtered them. I'm glad you missed it. Honestly it was painful to watch."

She lets out a sigh of relief. "Okay, good." She settles back against me.

"So what kind of dreams did you have?"

"Disturbing. I'd rather not relive them. Okay?"

"Sure."

She's pulling on the ends of her hair and I know her well enough that something I'm not going to like will soon follow out of her mouth.

"So I want to ask you something," she says in a serious tone.

"Okay."

"Will you do me a favor and go out with that girl Melanie?"

My head drops down so I can go eye to eye with her. What the fuck is this about?

"Because?"

"Because I want you to find your happiness. And right now you're putting a lot of your time into helping me. Don't get me wrong—I'm so grateful for all that you've done. I don't know what state I'd be in right now without you. But I can't be selfish. I want all the good things for you."

"What makes you think that Melanie will be all that good for me?"

"I don't know that she will be, but you were crazy about her. Right?"

"That was a long time ago."

"But I could tell when her name came up at dinner that she's still in your thoughts. Just the mention of her visibly got to you."

I shrug. "We all hold onto all kinds of stuff. Who knows? Maybe it would've been great or maybe we would've been all wrong for each other. She could be an epic bitch in a relationship."

"Maybe. Maybe not. I'm just asking you to find out for once and for all."

"Is this a crazy hormonally inspired idea?"

She smiles. "No. I feel very calm right now."

As we stare at each other I wonder if she's right. Maybe I should just do it so I can let go of the teen-angst curiosity that has stayed with me all these years.

"Please," she says.

"Okay," I huff.

"I have rules though."

"You do, huh?" I ask with an arched brow. "That's rich, Ms. Bossy Pants. What are your rules?"

"If you sleep with her right away I don't want to hear about it."

My eyes narrow as I watch her fold her arms over her chest.

"Well, I would've thought you'd want to hear all about it. So why not?"

"I'd be jealous, of course. Think about how hard I tried to get you to sleep with me before I gave up."

"Gotta say, I feel like I'm being set up here for some major girl drama."

"No, I'll be good, I promise. Just no hot sex talk. I'll let you know when I'm ready to hear it."

I shake my head. "You're crazy Elle."

She smiles and winks. "But you like me enough to put up with me."

"Yeah, I suppose I do."

Chapter Thirteen

Woman On Top

I decide to call Melanie Monday afternoon. That seems like a neutral time. It's not a sexy time, and it can't come off as anxious since my mom gave me her number over a week ago. I get her voicemail.

Hey, Melanie, it's Paul McNeill.

Mom gave me your number after you guys ran into each other. She said you've moved back to L.A. Let me know if you'd like to meet for coffee or drinks. It'd be cool to catch up.

I leave her my number and realize that my heart is thundering after I end the call. *Damn.* I'm really not in the mood to get ignored by her again. But she made the gesture, so she sure as hell better return my call. The text arrives ten minutes later.

Hi Paul

How about drinks tomorrow night at Osteria Mozza. 7pm.

As I reply that I'll see her there, I realize all the implications that her choice suggests: her choice of restaurant is on trend, in sophisticated and hip Hancock Park, highly ranked food, and expensive as all hell for a plate of spaghetti. That's Melanie. She's probably never eaten at In-N-Out.

I arrive early to the restaurant so I can pick our seating and have my bearings before she arrives. I'm swirling the Jamisons whiskey in my glass when a feeling comes over me. I just know under my skin that she's here. Sure enough I turn and it's as if there is a beam of light just above her as she gracefully works her way through the crowded bar. I'd forgotten how tall she is, and between the long platinum-blonde hair, and her sleek ivory dress, she stands out in a crowd—not just stands out, she fucking glows. All she needs is a long flute of champagne to finish the picture of how the better half lives.

She gives me a quiet smile as she approaches, and slides into the chair next to me before I have a chance to pull it out for her. She looks amazing. Not that I expected anything less but every gesture seems perfect. Like the way she sweeps her sheet of satin hair over her shoulder so it cascades down her back.

I smile at her. "Good to see you, Melanie."

"And you," she says with a nod as the bartender approaches. "Martini, extra dry, extra olives on the side."

The essence of the Melanie I remember is still there, but now just more polished and confident if that's even possible . . . more of everything, really.

"New York was good to you, I take it. You look great."

"Thanks, New York was amazing. It was hard to leave since I found I'm really more of a New York kind of girl. Believe me, it had to be a huge opportunity to get me back here."

"I'm sure. So where are you now? Mom couldn't remember."

"Christopher, Roth, and Reiss. They were especially interested in me because they've just landed two huge corporate identity projects. It's all very exciting. We have meetings in China week after next."

"Did you do a lot of traveling in your last job?"

She nods before taking a long sip of her martini. "Quite a bit, especially to Australia. Our partner agency was there."

"Cool. I've always wanted to go there."

We order small plates from the bar and feast on mussels, octopus, and several exotic cheese presentations as she tells me about her favorite projects. I realize when we order our second round of drinks that she hasn't asked me a single thing about myself. I also haven't smiled other than those fake smiles you give when you want people to think you're interested in what they're saying even though you're not.

"Do you travel much for work?" she asks, and I have to regroup to realize that she's actually addressed me.

"Not really unless you call trekking down to Orange County traveling. We mainly do projects in this region, although the partners are doing a big project in Dallas."

"So how did you end up in landscape architecture as opposed to building architecture? Wouldn't that be more lucrative?"

"I suppose, but I've loved trees and working the earth since I was a boy from hanging out with my dad on jobs. Besides, there's lots of cutting edge design happening in landscaping. A good design enhances the building."

"Your dad's a gardener, isn't he?" she asks, her gaze wandering off to some people at the bar.

Her tone is condescending like there's something wrong with what he does.

"He's an irrigation specialist," I reply.

"Irrigation. Right," she says nodding with an intent look on her face. "So do you think you'll stay in L.A.?"

"I imagine so. My family is here, and I like L.A. It suits me."

"Hmm, interesting." She waves the bartender over for a third round. I really feel that two was plenty but before I can say anything the bartender has turned away and starts preparing our order.

She's a few sips into her fresh martini when I finally see her loosening up. Up until now this tall drink of water has had quite a tolerance for gin. I'm hoping the conversation gets more interesting now that she's getting a little more relaxed.

"So did you have to leave a boyfriend in New York?" I ask taking the final bite of burrata from the plate of cheeses.

She's fishing the rogue olive out of the bottom of her glass. "He's one of the reasons I came out here. I was tired of waiting for him."

"Waiting?"

"He's married, and kept telling me he was leaving his

pathetic wife."

I feel a wave of disgust. "Oh, that kind of waiting."

"And I'm sure she suspected us . . . I mean, all those late nights we *'worked'* together on projects. I think she just didn't want to let him go."

"You worked together?" I have to focus to keep my expression neutral, as much as my stomach is turning. The illusion I had that Melanie is perfect has just faded like a photograph left in a sunny window. Every edge to her is now faded and undefined.

"He was one of the partners. I got spoiled with those long trips to Australia and having him all to myself."

"Wow. That's quite a story."

"And I know he wanted me. I'm sure of it. But he just was afraid of the divorce and how it would affect his kids."

Oh Jesus. She's unbelievable.

"Right. So he has kids?"

"Four kids! Can you believe it! One's just a year old. She got knocked up with that one when I was on a business trip without him. It was just another one of her desperate attempts to hold onto him."

Wow. So now a man having sex with his wife is cheating on her? The wife did not impregnate herself. He would've had to want to have sex with his wife. I guess she can't accept that.

"So that must have pissed you off."

"You have no idea. I broke up with him for almost a month that time."

"Why did you get back with him?"

"He needs me. I'm who he should be with—he's an incredible, dynamic man and she's just a housewife."

"Actually, she's a mom, and that's a big job . . . with four kids that's a really big one, I bet."

"Whose side are you on?" she asks with a stern expression. I suddenly notice that up close her skin isn't so smooth after all.

"Side?"

"Oh, let me guess you want kids, too."

"I do. So I take it you don't."

She purses her lips as she shakes her head. "No, I don't."

As I watch her sip the last of her drink I marvel that I was once so crazy for this woman. She just seemed so intriguing compared to the other girls in high school. She projected the feeling that she had important things ahead of her and the talent and confidence to get her there. And I have to admit that she was the only girl I ever wanted who didn't succumb to my charms, so that made her all the more desirable in my eyes. Now that I've got her full attention she's a two dimensional woman with apparently no soul, and not the slightest bit interesting to me.

She looks up at me with one eyebrow arched like she knows a secret. "So I've heard quite a bit about you, Paul."

Wait . . . did she just bat her eyelashes at me? *Oh hell no.*

"Yeah, what did you hear?"

"That you're quite the beast in bed."

I almost spit out the ice cube that's been rolling around on my tongue.

She leans toward me and speaks in a soft voice. "It is true that you partake in orgies?"

I watch the flush of what I sure as hell hope isn't arousal crawl up her long neck as she bites her lip, waiting for my answer. "Why do you want to know?"

She chews on the tip of her olive pick. "Because I'd like to try that."

"Really?"

"Yeah, I've been with women before. My college roommate turned me onto the wonders of that scene, but I've only ever done one-on-one."

I'm speechless. Melanie is bi. That'd be really hot if I liked her a lot more than I do right now.

"My boyfriend that I just mentioned really likes to watch me with another woman."

"Really? How modern of him." I gesture to the bartender for the check.

"What's the most women you've done in one orgie?" she asks, leaning even closer.

"I think the stories about me have been exaggerated." I hand the bartender my credit card without taking time to open the folder to check the bill.

"Well, I've heard straight from the source about your many talents." I feel the tips of her fingers graze my knee as I slide the credit card back in my wallet.

So is this why she wanted to see me? I'm not even sure in my craziest times that I would have fucked her after hearing all that I did tonight. I may have screwed women I didn't have anything in common with during my sex fiend days, but I never screwed someone I didn't like.

I manage to get her outside claiming a really early morning at work. We're standing next to the building at the valet station—waiting for my car and her Uber—when she suddenly turns and leans into me, pressing me against the building.

"Why don't you come for a drink at my place?"

If I push my disappointment with her aside, I can't deny that it feels really good to have a beautiful woman this close to me after two dry years, but there's no way I'm going to her place.

I choose a vague reply. "Tonight's not the night."

She leans her face into my neck and skins her teeth along my stubble while she slips her hand into the back pocket of my jeans. She moans as she squeezes my ass and pulls me against her. "We could have such a good time," she whispers.

My head starts swimming, it's been so damn long since any-one has rubbed against me like I was the flint to their flame. I shouldn't be surprised when she kisses me. Honestly, I'm trying so hard to focus on her home wrecker ways, and not her naked with another woman, that I don't see her next move coming as her tongue slides in my mouth and tries to take control of mine. She's moving over me like hot lava and with the resulting roar in my head I barely hear the valet clearing his throat and jingling the car keys.

Holy hell.

My eyes pop open and I peel her off me so I can hand the guy a ten and get my keys.

"You sure?" she asks as the Uber driver tries to get her attention.

I do what I did so many times back in the day and it makes me feel dirty but I do it anyway—the McNeill brush-off. It's all in the presentation. I take her chin in my hand and run my thumb back and forth along her jaw, while looking in her eyes like I'm peering into her soul. "I'll call you," I say just loud enough for her to think she heard me right but can't be sure.

I may be a liar too, but at least it's to avoid hurting someone.

She winks with the thrill of what she imagine is up ahead, and turns on her heel before sliding into her ride.

I take a deep breath to get my bearings as the Uber guy drives off.

Thank God. *Free at last.*

I'm numb the next day. How do you process so much shit at once? The girl that had lingered on the edge of all my fantasies as a young man, has now taken a swan dive right into never *ever* land. I should be relieved to be free of all of those years of frustration but I'm more pent up than ever.

The feelings remind me of Chelsea, a girl I was really into my first year of college. I sat next to her in the History of Landscape Architecture class and we started talking. I'd never met anyone who had such similar taste to mine and shared my passion for landscape design.

She was beautiful too, in that quiet way that didn't shout for attention. We had coffee after class once in a while, and we even studied together, but every time I'd ask her out for anything not involving schoolwork, she'd brush me off. I was falling for her, and her disregard of my obvious interest in her was making me crazy.

Right after our quarter-finals there was a department party, and I was hoping she'd show up so I could finally connect with her the way I'd hoped. Well, she showed up all right. Not only was she wearing a short skirt and make-up, she hard- core flirted with at least half-a-dozen upperclassmen, but avoided me completely. I was initially confused, then gutted, and finally angry.

I left the party that night with a thick shell cemented over my heart, and a redhead from our program on my arm. By morning, I felt high realizing that wild sex with strangers could be my crack. My days of chasing the *right* girl were over. The new me embraced the pleasures of being with all the wrong girls who put-out, and never made me feel like I wasn't important enough. Instead these girls made me feel like a porn star and my ego inflated like a hot air balloon.

Unfortunately, for me casual sex, like crack, was incredibly addictive. My constant craving for release, led me into an insatiable obsession that I may always struggle with. I'm not sure what would've happened if my Dad hadn't forced me to get my shit together.

As the afternoon passes it weighs on me that Elle called me late last night and didn't leave a message. She knew where I was going and probably now wants a full report. Do I tell her about the kiss with Melanie, as disingenuous as it was? I'm not sure if she'd be happier if I had found a love connection, or disappointed. That mysterious part of her is usually a turn-on but right now it's just unsettling. It's too soon for me to upset her again. I'm determined to tread carefully so I decide to wait to call her until I'm ready.

But when I get home from my after-work run she's sitting on the stair leading to my front door chewing her thumbnail. I'm sweaty, winded, and gross.

Great . . . just great.

She grins and gives me a little wave. "Hi Paul!"

"What are you doing here?" I ask, not hiding my alarm. I've never given her my address. It's not like where I live in Beachwood Canyon is around the corner from Studio City.

Her eyes grow wide. I guess that isn't the greeting she was

expecting. "I was waiting for you."

I peel the sweaty shirt away from my chest. "I can see that. Are you okay? Everything okay with the baby?"

"Yeah, it was a rough day at work but we're okay."

I finally remember my manners. "Do you want to come in?"

"Are you sure? You act like you don't want company." I can tell she's trying not to not assume anything.

"How'd you get my address anyway?"

"Your mom. By the way she wants me to remind you that there's no family dinner this week. They're going to visit your aunt."

I nod. "Yeah, I remember." I jog up the steps until I reach her and I hold out my hand. "Let's go inside. I just have to jump in the shower."

She nods. "While you shower, do you have anything I can eat? I was so busy I didn't have time today."

"Elle," I say in a stern voice.

She holds up her hand. "I know, I know."

"You have to take care of the two of you."

"That's why I'm asking if you have any food."

I let us in the house and head to the kitchen. "How about a turkey and cheese sandwich?"

"Perfect. Thanks." She leans against the kitchen counter as I wash my hands and then watches me throw the sandwich together. I pull out some grapes and carrot sticks from the fridge and make a pattern with them around the plate before handing the sandwich to her.

She grins. "That's so pretty."

I shrug. It's no big deal and she needs to eat fruits and vegetables. "It's the designer in me."

While she eats I gather the clothes I'm going to change into so she doesn't have to watch me walk through the apartment naked. I know she probably wouldn't mind that, but we're still on unsteady ground so it's better to play it safe. She's humming a little song in between bites when I head to the bathroom and it makes me smile.

But I'm not even out of the shower for a minute and preparing to shave when she knocks on the bathroom door. I quickly pull a towel around my waist and yank the door open.

Her mouth falls agape as her gaze scans from my shoulders, across my chest, and then lingers right where the towel is wrapped tight. What did she expect?

Her cheeks turn pink as she looks back up to me.

"Your body," she whispers.

"Yes?"

"It's amazing. And you're so tall and handsome too. You could model you know."

"Uh, definitely not my thing, but thanks. I'm glad you think so."

There's a tightness of anticipation in my chest. It wouldn't surprise me if Elle reached forward and tugged at the towel. I start to get hard just thinking about it.

She blinks, I blink. *Damn,* I want to kiss her so bad.

She sighs and looks at my shoulder and then just beyond.

What's she thinking? "You want to take a shower?" I ask, hoping she knows I'm teasing.

"With you?" She actually looks hopeful.

I tip my head sideways and give her a half-smile before I shake my head.

"I just showered, where were you then? I would've liked having my back soaped up."

Her eyes light up. "Just your back?"

She glances down as if she knows the damn towel is starting to tent, but then she reaches out to hold onto the door jam.

"You okay?" I ask, trying to get her to look up at my face.

She nods and clears her throat. "Sorry to interrupt, but I'm kind of dizzy. Do you mind if I lie on your couch?"

"You don't need to ask that, of course you can."

"But it doesn't look like a couch you lie on."

I roll my eyes knowing she's right. That's what I get for buying a designer sofa. All looks but no comfort.

"Do you know why you're dizzy?"

"I over-did it today."

I gesture to the doorway just past where we're standing. "Please lie on the bed. I'm pretty sure I made it this morning."

She nods and turns toward the bedroom.

After I finish pulling on clean jeans and a T-shirt, I check in the kitchen and grab her unfinished sandwich and a glass of milk. I find her stretched out on my bed with her eyes closed. I set the stuff down on the side table and rest my hand on her calf.

"Hey, you okay?"

She silently nods without opening her eyes.

"I brought your sandwich in. Why don't you eat some more?"

"Are you mad I dropped by?"

"No, I'm not mad. Just surprised. But now that you know where I am you can drop by whenever you want."

The corners of her mouth turn up and her eyes pop open. "Really?"

I scoot her legs over and sit on the edge of the bed. "Sure."

She sits up and picks up the glass of milk, and taking several long sips she starts back in on the sandwich. While she eats she regards my bedroom, and seems to be taking everything in with great interest. It makes me see my stuff with a fresh eye.

She points to the black and white prints framed on my walls. "What's with all the photos of bridges?"

I tip my head as I scan the images. "I think they're fascinating. Bridges get you places. If they weren't there you'd have a hard time going to those places."

She looks at me with a surprised expression, like I have a milk mustache I forgot to wipe off or something.

"What?"

"That's really great. I didn't know you were so deep." She winks at me.

"Oh, I'm deep, so deep—an endless well really. I'm surprised you didn't pick up on that until now."

I'm glad to see her looking better.

"Well, now I know. And I like your place. It's cool. Not

exactly like I imagined."

"And how did you imagine it?"

"Not so thought out. Everything works together design wise . . . it's pretty sophisticated for a dude."

"You still think I'm your sprinkler man, don't you? I'm a designer, remember?"

"Well that explains the sage-colored walls and couch you can't lie down on."

I fold my arms over my chest. "Are you really going to shame me for my couch?"

She bites her lip. She looks like she's holding back a grin. "Nah. You know I love designer stuff."

"I'll say. Look at your place."

"Watch out. I'm feeling hormonal."

I drop my arms down to my sides. "Thanks for the warning."

She pats the spot on the bed next to her. "Come sit over here."

When I sit on the opposite side of the bed she slides a little closer to me.

"So which is your favorite bridge picture?"

I don't even pause to think about it. "The one of the Golden Gate Bridge. I love how it's rising out of the fog. It's like you don't know where you're going to end up or how you got there."

"But because it's a steady bridge you trust that it's going to be okay on the other side," she says quietly.

I nod.

She slides farther down on the bed and I follow suit.

"So how was your date last night?"

"Is that why you came over?"

"Well you didn't return my call, so I figured something big must have happened."

"What if it did? Would you be happy?"

Her eyebrows knit together like she's thinking really hard, but finally she says softly, "Yes, I would be happy."

"Well yeah, something really big happened." I'm about to tell her what a let- down the evening was when she jumps in with a true Elle inquiry.

"Oh my God. Was the sex phenomenal?"

"I promised you we wouldn't talk about that."

"But I need to hear."

"Why?"

"If I can't have mind-blowing sex at least I can live vicariously through you."

"And what if it wasn't mind-blowing?"

"Make something up, damn it! And make me believe it."

"But I promised not to do this!"

She grabs my T-shirt in the center of my chest, makes a fist of it and pulls hard until we are face-to-face.

"To hell with the promise! I need it, Paul. I was up all night imagining it."

Her cheeks are hot pink and I remember the hormone warning. At this point I'd tell her anything to keep her calm considering the shape she was in when she showed up here.

"Okay, I'll tell you if it's really what you want."

She nods and lets out a sigh. Her fingers loosen on my T-shirt.

Where do I start with this fiction story? At least the first detail can be honest.

"So Melanie and I met at Osteria Mozza."

She shakes her head firmly. "I don't want to hear about the restaurant unless you had sex in the bathroom."

This woman.

"So no build-up? Got it."

"Yeah, get to the good stuff."

"We'd both been drinking and the flirting was really intense, so when we got out to the valet stand she pushed me up against the building and ground all that sexiness up against me."

"In front of everyone?" she says with her mouth agape.

"Oh yeah. I bet I could have fucked her right there and she would have gone for it. She dug her hand into my back pocket and grabbed my ass like she meant business."

"Was the anaconda awake?"

"Hell yes," I lie.

"Oh God, I bet she liked that."

"Judging from the way she grabbed onto it and moaned I would say so."

"Hot damn. So there was grinding and what else? Kissing?"

"Naturally."

"Is she a good kisser?"

"Incredible kisser." I'm full on lying now. *What the fuck?*

She sighs. "Oh man, I love great kissing."

"Yeah, it was so hot."

"Was there lots of tongue action? Was it so good you got dizzy?"

If she only knew how *not* dizzy I got. "My head was spinning it was so hot."

"Oh God," Elle says as she unbuttons the top button of her shirt.

"What are you doing?" I ask, trying not to get alarmed.

"Don't worry. I'm just trying to get some air on the girls. I'm burning up."

"Do you want some ice cubes to suck on? I've heard pregnant ladies like that."

Grinning, she shakes her head. "So did you go to her house or yours, or wait! You didn't do it in the car, did you?"

"Oh course not!" I respond, pretending to be offended. "I'm classier than that on a first date."

"What about by the fourth or fifth date?"

"Anything's possible by then."

She chuckles. "Okay, but back to last night . . ."

"So we went to her place." My mind scrambles to make up where she lives but Elle takes care of that reminding me that extraneous details are frowned upon.

"Did you go straight to the bedroom?"

I nod. "Most of her clothes were off by the time we got there, and damn she is fine. What a sexy body."

Am I imagining things, or did Elle just snarl and bare her teeth?

"Of course, Ms. Perfect is fine. Don't worry about the chubby pregnant hormonal girl over here. Let's hear about her perfectly flat stomach and long, lean legs."

"Geez, Elle, next time we do this can you give me the rulebook first? How am I supposed to know what you want to hear versus what will piss you off? Besides, what the hell do you mean chubby? You're not chubby."

She runs her hands over her hips and rolls her eyes. "Whatever. So did she worship the anaconda?"

"Are you asking if she dropped to her knees to blow me?"

She bites her knuckle and nods. I'm really wondering if this is a good idea.

She looks so excited but this could implode any second.

I let out a low whistle. "Yes, she did and she sucks cock even better than she kisses."

"Did you run your fingers through her hair, and watch?"

"Naturally. What? You thought I'd close my eyes while that was going on?"

"My ex used to close his eyes."

"And . . ." I prompt while waving my hand.

"He's an idiot!" She grins.

"Believe me, Elle, if your mouth was on me I'd never take my eyes off you."

I'm picturing it in my head and the heat moves down my chest straight to my groin.

She curls closer to me . . . too close. "Damn, you know how to make a girl feel great."

"Well, I mean it." And if she only knew how much I did mean it . . . how she was the only woman I fantasize about doing that with now. Elle's pretty lips on me . . . *oh man.*

"Did she swallow?"

Geez.

Knowing I have to prolong my story, I shake my head. "No, I needed to fuck her, so I lifted her onto the bed."

Elle is pressing her thighs together rhythmically. "Did you crawl over her like a wild beast?" She undoes another button on her shirt and pulls the collar further open.

"Is that what you would want me to do, Elle?" I ask, my gaze falling from her hooded eyes, to her flushed neck, to the sheen of perspiration at her cleavage now exposed.

She reaches over and digs her fingers into my forearms. "Oh, yes. That's what I would want."

"Well I did that. And she started to beg for it, so I pulled her legs apart and rubbed myself against her to make sure she was ready for all of me. Cause you know . . ."

"Oh God, she must have been so wet. I am," she groans.

My eyes bug out. "You're wet?"

"Hell yes. I've never been this turned on."

Now that I think of it, neither have I. But I don't want to tell her that. This is confusing enough as it is. I'm trying to find the brain in my foggy head—since all the blood is below my belt—when I suddenly feel her hand skim all the way up my fly. There's no question anymore for her as to whether I'm aroused or not. I've never been this hard. As a matter of fact, I'm surprised my cock hasn't done a Hulk move and busted out of my jeans.

"Wow, Paul," she moans.

I'm barely holding on at this point.

She closes her eyes and takes several deep breaths like she's trying to calm herself down. I'm not sure I'll ever be calm again.

"Should I stop?" I ask in a ragged voice.

"Please don't stop," she gasps.

"Where was I?"

"So did you fuck her hard? How did she like it?" Her hand wraps around her flushed neck.

I imagine Elle spread out on the bed under me, and the look of want in her eyes. I know for a fact that I've never wanted anyone more. *What if?*

My impatient friend squeezes my arm. "Well?"

"Did I fuck her hard? No, not at first. Slow. I fucked her slow. I wanted to let it build so she'd feel everything. I wanted to watch her and see what she liked."

"Of course you did," she says with an envious sigh.

"And I kissed her, and gave her breasts the attention they deserved. She liked that a lot. It made her wild."

She runs her hands up her torso and over her breasts, which only pulls her shirt open further. "Oh . . . I bet she did. Did she let you know how good it was?"

"She begged for more and thrashed and moaned a lot . . . so yeah."

"Were her legs wrapped tightly around you?"

"Naturally. Her movements were in perfect rhythm with mine. It was unbelievable."

"Please tell me you kissed her breasts, too?" She undoes another button.

We're in the danger zone now. I'm already imagining I'm doing all of these things to Elle and not Melanie. I'm not sure how much restraint I have left in my reserve. I want her desperately.

I lean in closer to Elle's face and look her in the eye. "I didn't just kiss her breasts. I sucked them."

As I look at her I find myself licking my lips, they're so dry from my deep breathing.

The intensity must be too much because she shuts her eyes and turns away from me. I see a tear make its way down her flushed cheek. I slowly run my fingertip along its wet path to take it away as my mind tries to process where I screwed this up. Just because she said she wanted to hear about the sex, doesn't mean it was the right thing for her.

"Elle?"

She's taking short, choppy breaths and a sudden fury explodes in my chest. Why did I go along with this? Any man in his right mind would know this was the worst idea ever.

Rising up on my elbow, I gently take her chin in my hand and tilt her face back toward me. "Elle. Elle," I say softly, "what's wrong?"

She shuts her eyes and shakes her head, which sends new tears cascading down her face.

"Please tell me what's wrong? I'm sorry. I thought you knew

I was making up that stuff. I swear, Elle, it didn't go like that at all."

"Really?" she asks with wide eyes.

"Really. I promise."

She shakes her head. "Don't be sorry. I'm just sad because I want all that and who knows when I'll ever have it again."

The tears fall faster now.

"You mean sex?" I ask.

"Not just sex. It's being intimate, and being touched. I'm just wired that way, Paul. I need to be touched. It grounds me. It's only been a matter of weeks and I feel like part of me is dying inside."

"I can touch you," I say, in a lame attempt to soothe her. I run my hand up her arm and squeeze her shoulder.

She sighs and it's the saddest sigh I've ever heard. "I adore you for that, but I want my body touched."

"How about if you got massages. I know a place that's supposed to be great."

She looks at me like she can't decide whether to laugh or cry. She runs her fingertips up and down my forearm. It sends an electrical charge right through me.

"Will they massage my boobs?"

"What?" I ask, trying to keep my eyebrows from darting into my hairline. The hormones have clearly rendered her with temporary insanity. What woman gets a boob massage?

"That's what I want more than anything. I want my boobs touched."

I clear my throat. "Um, I'm pretty sure this place doesn't do that. And places I know that will I wouldn't ever take you to."

"You could do it, you know. You could touch them." She bites her lip and looks up at me.

That doesn't help—at all.

"That would be really difficult and complicated for me," I stutter. She's pregnant and hormonal for God's sake. My physical desire for her is so far past my craving to get off with a hot woman. I'm desperate to make love to her, but every choice I make now, no matter how tortured, has to be what's best for her and the baby.

She takes my hand in hers and slides it over her chest. "It's really not that complicated. Pretend I'm a mannequin."

"Right, a really chatty mannequin," I say as she moves my hand over her chest in broad circles while I desperately try not to glance down.

As her movements continue her expression softens, almost melting. She looks positively blissful and it keeps me from doing the right thing and pulling my hand away. I realize that there's heat emanating from my hand, like one of those creepy faith healers I've heard about. The question is, am I healing her or is she healing me?

A moment later I feel flesh against flesh and I look down to see that she's opened her shirt completely and my hand is resting just above her cleavage while she unhooks the front of her bra.

Oh good God.

"Elle," I groan.

"Please, Paul. Just a minute or two. Please?"

When our eyes meet she looks hopeful yet full of fear that I'll turn her down. I know she needs this but how dangerous is it for me to be the one to give it to her? The thing that makes up my mind is wondering if not me, who? That's unfathomable to even think about.

As I slide my fingertips down between her luscious breasts and circle her torso I take in her perfection. She is completely vulnerable and exposed, and her trust in me takes my breath away.

"You're so beautiful," I whisper.

Her breath catches as my right hand moves up to cup her breast, so full and perfect. When my left hand cups the other breast her back arches up to meet my grasp. I am gentle and slow as I touch her, and her tears are still flowing but I know it's different now. She's smiling like I've never seen her smile before.

I love her breasts. They're my new favorite part of her as I palm and squeeze them and she sighs with contentment below me. Her skin is exquisitely soft and her nipples a ruby rose. I avoid touching them, even though I ache to. It's just more than I can handle.

The next time I look up at her I can no longer remember tired, defeated Elle that sat on my top step waiting for me. This angel is luminous, her eyes softly shine and it's taking everything I have not to run my lips along all her curves, marking her with my trail of kisses.

I press my lips against her ear.

"I'm going to need to stop," I say with some urgency. I'm starting to lose my composure. I fear I'll be pulling her panties off any moment if this doesn't end.

She nods with understanding. She takes the edges of the bra in each hand and as I start to pull my hands away so she can close the clasp she gazes up at me.

"Can you just touch my nipples once?"

I can't say no. With each hand still cupping a breast I run the pads of my thumbs over their peaks, and she shudders with such a moan that I feel like I'm going to lose it without even being touched.

I regretfully pull my hands away and she slowly fastens her bra shut and then fastens her shirt back up.

"Oh wow," she says with a smile.

"Is that a good wow?"

"An all caps, bold font with several exclamation points, kind of wow."

"I'm glad to be of service."

"You have no idea how much I needed that. Can we do that on a regular basis?"

"I'm not sure that's a good idea."

"Really? I think it's the best idea ever."

"It's not that I don't want to make you happy but this is a lot for me to handle."

She gestures to her open shirt. "I warned you they were bigger now."

"It's not that. Well, you know . . . I'm a man, Elle."

She nods with a very serious expression. "And you have needs?"

"Yes, I do."

"I could help with that," she replies with an arched brow.

"That's not what I'm asking for. I just want you to understand that touching you is . . . exciting. And when I get excited, all bets are off. You don't know what I can be like."

"I wish I could see you like that."

I shake my head at her.

"You know what? I'm going to give you something that I'm pretty sure isn't what you want but I think you need."

"Oh yeah? What do you think I need?

"Affection."

The idea of expressing affection isn't high on my radar. I imagine her patting my head and giving me a teddy bear. "Is that so?

"It is. And I want to give it to you. Here, close your eyes and relax."

This woman.

"Can you tell me what the difference between affection and sex is?" I ask. I'm really not sure.

"Seriously?"

"Yes. I wouldn't ask if I didn't want to know."

"But, you don't know?"

"I guess I don't."

"Affection is from the heart."

"So what are you going to give me?"

"Close your eyes."

Teddy bears be damned . . . my mind goes all kinds of wild places, happy places, Elle touching me in ways she hasn't before.

She taps me on the chest and I realize that not only are my eyes not closed, they are wide in anticipation.

"Eyes closed, please."

"I like when you ask nicely."

She takes her fingers and gently brushes them down my

eyelids until my eyes are shut. I feel her fingertips skim down my cheek and along my jaw.

"See, that's nicely," I say.

"Mmm, hmm."

I'm acutely aware of every sensation: the way her body is leaning into mine, her subtle fragrance, and the tickle of the ends of her hair brushing along my forearm.

"What are you going to do?" I ask impatiently.

"Shhhhh."

I feel pressure on my torso as she leans in closer to me and my heart starts thundering. I also feel pressure in my chest like I can't catch my breath I'm so wound up to see what she's thinking.

When I feel her soft lips brush against mine, it takes everything I have not to open my eyes. She pulls away as quickly as she arrived leaving me aching for more. I hold still as a statue. This can't be it. There has to be more. I'm not even sure I'm breathing as I wait to see what happens next.

My reserve either inspires or challenges her, and she hikes herself up higher and her leg folds across my thigh. I grasp my hand in the bend of her leg to secure her against me.

Everything is different when her lips press against mine and seem to melt. She's kissing me gently and slow, but the emotion I sense behind it feels like it's important to her and I kiss her back with the same intensity. My arm slides around her to pull her close and her breasts press against my chest. Every second of this is unbelievably great, and I never want it to end.

Kissing Elle is unlike any kiss I've ever had. I've never felt so much . . . not just in the obvious places, but inside my chest. It's fucking unreal. I run my fingers through her hair and kiss her back from the heart. I can sense what it's doing to her and I like it.

Just when I think more has to happen she pulls away and snuggles into me.

Damn.

"How was that?" she whispers.

Words can't define how I feel so I respond simply. "I liked it."

"Me too."

We lie silently for a few minutes while I trace my fingers over her back and try to figure out what to make of what just happened.

"Can we do that affection thing on a regular basis?" I ask.

She smiles and for a brilliant moment the room lights up.

"Maybe."

I think of the look on her face when I told her I couldn't handle touching her regularly. "Payback?"

"Maybe." But then she reaches up and kisses me on the cheek.

What the hell are we doing? This is the weirdest relationship I've ever been in. What's even worse is that I don't just like it, I'm starting to *need* it. I need *her* and I've never been in this situation and it scares the fuck out of me. She's pregnant with another man's baby. I'm on the sidelines, hoping I'll get called into the game to be quarterback before the fourth quarter. *What if I don't?*

"Hey, Paul," she whispers with a sleepy voice.

I can tell she's going to fall asleep in my arms again and I want her to. "Yeah?"

"You know all that stuff you were saying about your favorite photograph of the bridges?"

"Yeah. What about it?"

"How you said it's like you don't know where you're going to end up or how you got there, but that it's a steady bridge and you trust that it's going to be okay on the other side?"

I nod. "I remember. Why?"

She sighs and rests her open palm on my chest.

"You're my bridge."

CHAPTER FOURTEEN

TIGHT SQUEEZE

I press the phone tighter against my ear. Elle sounds tired and her voice is unusually quiet as she cancels joining me for dinner with the family tonight. There was no family dinner last week so it's been a while since she's seen them.

"Are you sure you can't come? Ma's making beef stew because you said you liked it so much last time you were over."

She lets out a frustrated sigh. "I wish I could come, really I do, but I have hours of work left tonight."

"But it's already five. This isn't good for you." I can't help pressuring her—I really don't like that she's working so much. She's been looking exhausted way too often lately.

"I know, but if I don't get this done tonight, tomorrow's event could be a disaster."

"Elle . . ."

"I know—the baby. I'm trying to do all the right things but if I don't stay on top of my jobs I won't be able to take care of us. At least the day-after-tomorrow I can take the day off and I plan to sleep all day."

"And eat full meals."

"Yeah, that too."

There's a long, silent pause.

"You still there?" I ask.

"Yeah, I'm here."

"What is it?"

"Stephan called me."

For a second I can't find my voice but then I clench my fists and the rage starts burning through me. "What'd he want?"

"I didn't talk to him. He left a message saying he wants to meet, and he didn't sound very friendly."

"Meet? What the fuck? He's been silent for all these weeks and now the fucker wants to meet?"

"I know," she says in a wavering voice. "What am I going to do?"

Let me beat the living crap out of him. I sure as hell hope she didn't already agree to see him.

"What do you want to do?" I ask.

"I don't want to talk to him, but what if he doesn't take no for an answer?"

"He can't force you. I won't let him anywhere near you."

"Maybe if I just don't reply he'll fuck off."

"Yeah, that might work," I say, even though in my gut I don't believe that. What if the asshole is having second thoughts about the baby?

"I could tell him that the baby isn't his after all so he doesn't need to worry about it anymore."

The tone of her voice is unconvincing. Knowing how honest Elle is, I doubt she could follow through with this strategy.

"Could you really do that?"

There's a long pause. "No. What should I do?"

"Look, you need to just deal with your work tonight. Try to push it out of your mind. You don't have to reply immediately. Who knows? Maybe he won't call again."

"Okay." Her voice is soft and she sounds vulnerable. It makes me want to protect her.

"I'm going to check on you later. I want you home by nine. Okay?"

"Yes, sir."

Later at dinner Ma notices I'm distracted. "What's the matter, Paulie? You've hardly eaten."

I push my stew around with my spoon. "Elle's baby's dad called her today and wants to meet."

I glance up in time to see Ma and Dad share a concerned look.

"This is the scoundrel who denied it was his baby?" Dad asked with a scowl.

I nod.

"Does she know what he wants yet?" Ma asks.

I shake my head.

The mood at the table shifts like a black veil just settled over us. It even feels like the overhead lights have dimmed.

"Does Elle have a lawyer?" Patrick asks.

"Well I know she must have a divorce lawyer. If they can't help her I'm sure they would have a referral," I say.

"What if you adopted the baby?" Trish asks.

To my surprise no one argues with her.

"Adopt the baby? But we aren't even married."

She shrugs. "A quick trip to Vegas could solve that."

What has happened to my straight-laced, traditional family? I feel like I accidently sat down at another family's dinner table.

Dad holds up his hand. "We're jumping the gun here. First of all, you can't just adopt another man's baby. Elle needs to see what the man wants and decide how she feels about it."

Ma nods in agreement despite looking miserable about it. I know they were both afraid this would happen.

"Are you sure it's his? Is it possible it's yours?" my sister asks. I bet that knowing my history she assumes we slept together early on.

I shake my head and her expression softens.

I'm really moved that my family likes Elle enough to be pulling for her. They get on my nerves a lot, but right now I'm grateful they see the good in Elle that inspires them to want the best for her.

After dinner I join Dad in the backyard patio while he drinks his after-dinner hot toddy. We've had warm weather this week and even in the dim light of dusk the yard is full of color with the fuchsia and apricot bougainvillea, roses and wall of violet trumpet vines.

We don't talk for a while, just sit, comforted by the melody of familiar sounds. I hear Ma washing dishes in the kitchen, old-lady Margaret's loud TV playing *Jeopardy* next door and the faint whiz of traffic from the nearby freeway.

Dad finally looks over at me. "How are you holding up, son?"

I lean forward and twist my hands together. "I was doing okay, but now I'm not so sure."

He nods. "What are you most worried about?"

"This is hard to admit, because it's stupid of me . . . but I've been getting attached not just to Elle but to her baby, too—really attached. And now if the dad is involved, I may be forced out of the picture and I can't stand the idea of that."

"That's not stupid, Paul. It makes perfect sense to me."

"It does?"

"When you love a woman like you love Elle, you care more about them and their needs than your own. You want to share all the parts of your lives."

He knows I love her. I must wear it on my sleeve.

"It's that obvious?" I ask quietly.

"It is to me. I've never seen you like this." He turns his gaze to the evening sky. "It's what I'd always hoped for you . . . finding a good woman like Elle. I just wish it wasn't such a complicated situation."

"Me, too." I take a deep breath relieved to be honest about how I feel.

We sit in silence another minute before I turn to him.

"So you really like Elle, even despite all this stuff you know . . . being divorced, then this pregnancy?"

"I do like her. I always have. I think she just needs the right man to love her."

He looks up at me intently and doesn't say another word, but I feel like I can read his thoughts. It reminds me of the look he'd give me when I was young before an important race. That look gives me the confidence to not just give up.

Elle must have listened to my concern on our earlier phone call because she calls me at nine to assure me that she's home. She sounds so damn tired but I do my best to cheer her up.

I check in with her late the next morning. We have a broken-up conversation because of interruptions from the convention director over issues with the room set-up. Despite that she's able to get enough conversation in to let me know that Stephan called her again that morning and she didn't answer. I want to rage but I keep my mouth shut because I don't want to upset her more. She already sounds really stressed out.

That afternoon she texts to say he tried again. *What the fuck? And what the hell can I do about it?* I call her to tell her just to get through the day and we'll figure out how to deal with him later. Once I'm assured she's calmer, I throw myself back into my library garden project that has a deadline looming, hoping it can get my mind off things.

When I finally leave the office, I text Elle and tell her I'm picking up dinner. She sounds grateful and requests chicken noodle soup and cheese blintzes from Art's Deli on Ventura Boulevard. Comfort food sounds like just the thing for both of us.

She pulls open her front door before I even ring the doorbell. "You're here!" She gives me a hug before pulling the bag out of my arms. "I'm starving."

"Did you eat today?" I ask as I follow her in. I'm glad to see her spirit is good.

She makes a face, scrunching up her nose. "Does a smoothie for breakfast and protein bar for lunch count?"

"Elle," I say in a stern voice.

"Oh, and I had a yogurt and some almonds when I got home."

"You're so L.A." I point to the kitchen table. "Sit down, I've got this."

She grins and winks. "Okay, Mister Bossy Pants."

"Well, someone needs to take care of you."

She leans on her elbow, cupping her chin with her hand as she watches me with a tender expression. I divide up the soup, and dig spoons out of the silverware drawer.

"You sure have a lot of stuff in here," I remark after noticing how packed all the cupboards and drawers are.

"I like cooking and entertaining," she says as she checks the soup to see how hot it is.

"Do you cook that much?"

"Not as much as I'd like to. I used to dream of having a kitchen full of friends and family."

I let my gaze wander through the kitchen and into the adjoining dining room as I consider what's behind what she just said. It's like she's set the stage for what she hoped her life to one day be. The way she described the beginning of her marriage, I'm sure divorce was never part of her master plan.

She has a great three-bedroom house with a barbeque, garden, and fire pit perfect for s'mores. It's near good schools with tricycle-friendly sidewalks, yet when I leave tonight she will be completely and utterly alone.

It occurs to me that what she desired her future to be isn't much different than what I've intended to find. The difference is that I was still searching when I met her, and she thought she'd found it with her ex, only to lose the dream and stop hoping that it even can exist for her.

I'm not actually hungry but I force myself to dig into the soup so she follows suit. I roll my eyes internally realizing that I've turned into my Irish mother wanting to make sure she's fed.

She starts eating and I'm relieved to see she seems happy with her dinner. I love watching her move her tongue over the spoon after each bite, her eyes rolling back while she sighs. It makes me wish I were a spoon.

"What?" Her eyes are wide like I caught her doing something naughty.

I shrug. "Nothing. It's just fun watching you eat."

She eats all her soup and a blintz before her eyes start to droop.

"Poor baby, you're so tired," I say.

She nods as she lets out a long sigh. "Hey, we were going to talk about what to do with the Viking."

I can't help fighting back a smile. It's the first time I've heard her refer to him that way and I love it. "Fuck the Viking, you need to rest," I say with more force than I'd intended.

She bites her lip as she studies me. "You're so sexy when you're mad."

I shake my head and look down. "I'm mad all right. You rest tonight and we can work it out tomorrow."

When she stands she wobbles before pushing away from the table. I take her by the shoulders. "Steady, now."

She nods. "If you don't mind, I think I better get ready for bed. I'm going to crash any minute."

Does this mean I get to put her to bed? I hope so. I can only imagine what Elle sleeps in. I imagine it isn't much, coverage wise.

She emerges from the bathroom with her face scrubbed pink and a minimal sleep garment. It looks like she's pulled on a short slip for a twelve year old. It falls dangerously high on her toned thighs and the thin strap keeps slipping off one of her shoulders. I have to look away as I focus on doing the alphabet backwards.

"Am I tucking you in?" I ask, trying not to focus on the way her bare breasts look draped in silk.

"Tucking?" The corners of her mouth turn up.

I nod and narrow my eyes at her. "You heard me correctly."

"Too bad. I thought you said something else." She rubs her hands over her face. "I guess it's just as well, I'm exhausted."

I follow her into the bedroom watching the silk skim her ass as she walks.

Even in her exhaustion and despair this woman is really something. I've been reduced to such a sap because everything about her is beautiful to me.

Lifting up the cover, she slides down between the sheets. When she's settled I smooth the blankets down and sit on the edge of the bed.

She gazes up at me with her sleepy eyes and rests her hand on my knee. "You're amazing . . . such a catch. I still can't figure out why some awesome girl hasn't snagged you yet."

I smile at her. "Maybe I'm difficult to snag."

"Hmm. No doubt."

"I can tell you that hooking up is a hell of a lot different than dating. Dating is much more complicated."

She sighs. "I think it's all complicated, even when you try to keep it simple."

"In L.A., hook-ups are a dime a dozen, but someone real who I know would stand by me through thick and thin is hard to find." I say.

"As you know, when my marriage collapsed I was intrigued with the idea of hook-ups." She slides her hand under her head and pulls her hair out until it fans over the pillow.

"Why, Elle? Why just hook-ups? Was it really only about control?"

"I don't know. I guess my heart and ego were so bruised by Daniel that I couldn't imagine making myself that vulnerable again. I just needed to feel that I could turn someone on as much as they could turn me on. Is that awful?"

I shake my head. "No, not at all. I just think you deserve more."

She rubs her hand over her belly. "Well even if I was willing to risk my heart again, no one is going to want me now."

"You know that's not true."

"Regardless, it doesn't matter. Now that that part of my life is over I realize that hooking up wasn't the thrill I thought it'd be either."

"You sound like you're done with it."

Her eyes grow wide. "Well, of course I am. How does a working woman with an infant do hook-ups?"

"Babysitters?" I ask, testing her.

She shakes her head. "Are you serious? I couldn't do that even if I wanted to. I'm done with all that. I deleted Tinder off my phone."

I have to steady myself, the flood of relief surging through me almost knocks me off my feet.

"Do you think you'll ever go back to hooking up?" she asks.

I shake my head. "No way. I didn't like myself much during those years. It's just much easier getting myself off and not feeling like an asshole all the time."

She coughs and her cheeks flush pink.

"You okay?"

She bites her lip. "Oh man, don't do that! Don't casually mention you getting yourself off without giving me a warning or something." She pushes the covers down to her waist and moans. "Now I'm all worked up and hot."

"What? You know I take care of myself. We've talked about it."

"We've sexted about it . . . not talked about it when you're here in the flesh sitting on the edge of my bed."

Sighing, she turns onto her side so she's facing me. "You need to distract me. Tell me a bedtime story."

"What kind of bedtime story?"

"A sexy one of course. How about one of your sex-capades from your past."

"How will that be distracting?"

"You're real and in the flesh. A story is a fantasy. It's like escaping into my erotica novels."

"Okay. Can I add flourish to this story—have some fun with

it?"

She nods, a grin spreading across her face.

"Okay. Once there was this guy . . ."

"Named Paul," she adds.

I fight back a smile. "Who loved sex . . ."

"And he wanted it ALL the time," she says enthusiastically.

"So after hooking up with all the hot babes that didn't hold his interest, he searched far and wide for an amazing and unforgettable maiden who loved sex as much as he did."

"And once he found her they'd never get out of bed," Elle adds for me.

"Never?" I ask, worried. I'm not sure if this story is going south with a couple of agoraphobics with dirty sheets.

"Well, I exaggerated a bit . . . of course they get out to shower and go to nice restaurants and stuff."

I nod. "Okay, I can deal with that."

"You know she'll have to go to the gym, too. She needs to be in great shape for all that sex."

"They both will, so gym memberships are a must. And she can't be too thin. Paul likes something to grab onto," I say. It sounds weird referring to myself in the third person.

"Or too fat," she adds.

"She has to be just right."

"So where does Prince Paul go to find his maiden?" she asks.

"Oh, he's not a prince."

She makes a face. "Maybe secretly he is."

I laugh. "How about he looks for her at the gym?"

"That's good! There are tons of gyms in L.A. . . . so he searches from one to another."

"He searches from Calabasas to Pasadena, Long Beach to Burbank."

She shakes her head and purses her lips. "That's too much! He'll be stuck in traffic, living on the 405! I say it's from the Westside to Silver Lake, Culver City to North Hollywood."

I roll my eyes. "Whatever. So are they going to be working out next to each other in the gym? That's usually not a sexy place to me."

She taps her chin. "I know! They meet in Zumba class! That's sexy."

"Zumba? That Latin dance thing where you shake your ass a lot?"

She nods with a grin.

"Oh, hell no! I'm not doing that."

"Please. This is my bedtime story. Don't you want me to like it?"

I scowl. "What does *Paul* have to wear?"

Her eyes light up. "You know those lycra running pants? He can wear those."

I arch my brow and fold my arms over my chest. "Oh really?"

She pushes my knee. "Don't you see, you're the prince, so naturally you have to show off your perfect package."

I huff. "Naturally. But if you dress me any more gay than that we're going to have to change the story line."

She laughs with abandon and I realize that I'll wear lycra pants anytime if it lightens her spirit like this.

"So is there a big Zumba Ball or something where he sees her from across the gym?" I ask.

"Oh, that's good! Maybe it's the ultimate Zumba Celebration or something and the moment he sees her dance he's captivated."

"By her sexy body?"

"Yes, and the way she moves. She can swivel her hips like none other."

I rub my chin. "Okay, I like where this is going. So he goes and dances with her or can he just watch?"

Her eyes narrow in concentration. "Well, it doesn't really work like that in Zumba—couples don't dance together, but we'll make an exception."

I shrug. "Why not? We've already bastardized the hell out of this story."

"And then just when they really get going, her cell phone alarm goes off and she has to run out of the gym . . ."

"And in her hurry, her gym shoe falls off," I add.

"And the poor prince doesn't know that the evil gym owner hates the girl for being a sexier Zumba dancer than her, and so before she runs out of the gym the witch owner has her drink a poison energy drink—apple flavored of course."

"Look at you, smashing up fairy tales."

She grins. "I know, awesome, right!"

I had no idea Elle had such storytelling swag and it inspires me. "So before she can even make it to her orange Prius, she passes out into the arms of the balding Viking who puts her in his minivan—"

"He didn't drive a minivan!" Elle squeals.

"Shhh. And he drives her to the land of no sand where he locks her in his dungeon."

"What story is this now?" she asks.

"It's your story but I'm telling it my way now, okay?"

"Okay, then what happens next?"

"The prince rushes to the parking lot, and the seven dwarf valet guys tell him about the Viking and how they couldn't stop him, but Chewie got a picture of the minivan's license plate."

"There's no dwarf named Chewie!"

"There isn't? Whatever. So the prince has a magic cell phone with tracking devices and he jumps in his turbo Ferrari and tears the fuck out of there."

She nods excitedly. "That's so hot. He still has her shoe, right?"

"Yeah, yeah. But this prince dude is taking no prisoners. So when the Prince gets to the Viking's McMansion in Woodland Hills, he goes all Mortal Combat on the fucker and beats him with his vacuum cleaner then douses him with 409 and Windex."

"Oh, the prince is so badass," she says with a satisfied smile. "So he saves his girl."

"Hell yes! He breaks her out of the dungeon and gives her a hot kiss so she wakes up from the poison energy drink, and then he carries her out in his arms to her freedom."

She sighs. "Did he make her try on the gym shoe first to make sure it was her?"

I tip my head and give her a wary look. "Do you really think he's going to take time to do that when he can't wait to fuck her?"

"Oh yeah, and now we're getting to the good part."

"So back at his palace . . ." I begin, my mind gearing up for the sex scene.

"Which is a split level mid-century, maybe Neutra?"

"Or Lautner," I say, appreciating that Elle knows her modern architects.

"I love their houses with walls of glass," she says.

"Is the prince with glass walls an exhibitionist?"

She cups her chin in her hand. "Hmmm, I don't know if exhibitionism is sexy or not."

"Prince Paul is super sexy, so let's say he has glass walls but the house is surrounded by a dense enchanted garden with birds of paradise, orchids, mango trees, and weeping violets so no one can see in."

"Oh yes," she moans.

She seems so delighted with the story and it makes me wonder how she'd like the sex to go now that they're in their mid-century perfection. "So what do you think would be hot to happen next?"

"Well, she was Zumba dancing and then kidnapped, so she must be all sweaty. I think the situation calls for a shower in his historically accurate master bath."

Showering together is sexy, and I'm charmed by her practicality and nod to good design. "Okay, so he sweeps her through his front door and carries her to his bathroom."

"While whispering in her ear that he's going to take care of her."

I blink several times at her suggestion. It's interesting that my self-reliant career woman's fantasy has a man taking control and taking care of his woman. How decidedly un-modern of her.

Elle is looking exhausted but waves her hand at me impatiently. "Keep going!"

"He sets her down and begins removing her clothes, kissing

her bare skin as each piece of clothing is pulled off."

Elle's fighting back a yawn but she still squirms. "Mmm. Yes . . . I can feel it."

"His kisses trail along her neck, down between her breasts, and across the top of her belly as he drops to his knees."

"Hot damn, the prince is on his knees! Is this where he peels off her bottoms?"

I clear my throat since my voice is getting rough. "Yes, it is. And when he's done and she's completely bare, she's even more beautiful than he imagined."

Elle's hands grip the edge of her blanket.

"He drags his fingertips over her hips. His hands cup her ass as he imagines what it would be like to taste her."

Elle runs her hands up along her neck. "Yes, tasting . . . lots of tasting! I want that," she whispers.

I immediately get distracted imagining tasting Elle. *Hot damn.*

"Hey, wait a minute!" Elle says, her eyes grow wide with a suspicious look. "Are you sure you aren't secretly a romance writer? This is starting to sound like one of my books."

I arch my brow at her. "Did you forget that I've read a couple of your books? Believe me, I wouldn't have come up with this stuff on my own. I'm just tailoring it to our story and with no freaking words like *moist folds.*"

"Oh my God, Paul! You're so awesome. Well, whatever inspired this . . . don't stop now. This story is h-o-t, hot!"

"Okay, let's see where was I before I was rudely interrupted?"

"You had her naked and all worked up. Is he naked, too?"

I pretend smack her thigh. "Be patient!"

I focus again, picturing the couple in front of the shower. It's not a coincidence that the naked girl looks exactly like Elle. I clear my throat to continue.

"He leads her to the shower and he's burning up with want for her."

"She wants him, too!" Elle cries out.

I nod, trying not to laugh at her outbursts. "He turns on the shower and leads her under the spray of the water, before stepping back to take off his clothes."

"Oh yeah . . ." Elle purrs.

"Her gaze follows his hands as he pushes off his pants."

Elle fist-pumps the air. "The anaconda is finally free and it's huge!"

My head drops to hide my amusement. I haven't seen her enjoy anything this much in weeks. I better read some more of that crazy shit since I sense this isn't the last sexy bedtime story I'll be telling Elle.

"She stands waiting for him as the water cascades over her lush breasts."

"Lush?" she asks with a snicker.

I frown. "You don't like lush? So what kind of breasts are we talking about: plush, perky, pillowy?"

"Ewww! What do pillowy boobs look like?" she squeals.

I fold my arms over my chest and roll my eyes.

"Okay . . . let's stick with lush. Go on, go on!" she says as she cups her breasts with her hands and squeezes.

I let out a huff. "He pulls her forcefully into his arms, desperate to have his lips pressed against hers."

"Oh my God! Can you imagine the epic kiss? The tongue action!"

"Well, yeah. I'm about to tell you about the tangling of tongues."

"I can already feel it . . . from my head to the tips of my toes, and most distinctly between my legs."

"Well why don't you tell me about the epic kiss," I tease.

"I'm not a writer like you evidently are, but if I were her I can imagine what it would be like to be held in your strong arms while the water poured over us. And your kiss would be a claim, marking me as yours. Your kiss would be a proclamation that I was not just your present, but your past, and future too."

My eyebrows shoot into my hairline. "Wow, poetic, Elle. You've sure read a lot of that stuff. Hell, we could write it together."

She grins. "See! You've inspired me."

"So keep going."

As she gets a faraway look I can suddenly see how exhausted she is. Reaching out, she grabs my hand and squeezes it before letting out a long sigh.

"You look really tired. Maybe this is too much?"

"Actually, you're right. I think this is all I can handle tonight. Besides I want to go to sleep with the image of that epic kiss."

"Are you sure? I was getting ready to really amp it up."

"I know, and this isn't the end of our story. We'll continue it next time when I'm fully awake and ready for all of your sexiness."

"I know. The sexiness can be overwhelming." I wink at her.

Her expression suddenly gets serious.

"What's going on inside that pretty head of yours?"

"Thank you for tonight."

I shrug. "It was no big deal. Besides, I've had fun."

"But you're always doing stuff for me, and what do you get out of it? You're the least selfish person I know."

"You're making me sound like a saint. Believe me, I'm not. I just like hanging out with you. We have fun."

"We do," she agrees but still seems unconvinced.

"So enough about how amazing I am. I'm going to head out before you light a candle for me or something."

She studies me for several long seconds and then finally nods.

"Okay, but mark my word, Paul. Someday I'm going to do something extraordinary for you. I have no idea what it is yet, but it's going to be grand."

"Is that so? Why?"

"Because you deserve all the good things. You're the best man I've ever known."

"I think you're overstating things but thank you anyway. You're pretty easy to be good to."

Her eyes go soft and glaze over.

I stand up because I don't want her to cry. I can tell her

hormones are on high alert and she needs her sleep. "So you ready to crash?"

She nestles down lower under the covers, yawns, and nods.

I lean over and kiss her on the forehead. "Sleep, princess. I'll check in with you tomorrow from Orange County."

She winks. "Goodnight, Prince Paul."

The entire friggin' drive to Orange County I'm wondering what to do about Elle. She's on my mind all the time now and I sure as hell don't treat her like 'just a friend.' She has to wonder what I'm up to, and why I can't seem to leave her alone. But more than anything I wonder if I should tell her that I'm crazy about her. Well, not just crazy for her, I'm crazy in love with her.

Then I know that sharing my feelings could just freak her out considering all she's facing with the baby and the Viking harassing her. She needs my support and friendship right now more than anything. Plus she's said several times that she has no intention of falling in love with anyone, so am I ready for a one-way conversation on that topic? If I freak her out with my declaration she may just push me away. I can't risk that. In my book an unfulfilled heart is better than a broken one.

By the time I get to the Newport Beach library I'm relieved to have something else to focus on. There's a series of meetings planned for the day because thanks to bureaucracy, anything that involves the city planning is a hundred times more complicated than independent projects.

I check in with Elle after lunch, right before the meeting with the board, and her spirits are good.

"See, aren't you glad you stayed home and rested?" I say.

"Actually I had to go to the convention center to deal with some outstanding issues but I'm about to head home, I swear."

Oh, this woman.

I'm careful not to chastise her. "Well, if you're working at least you sound happy about it."

"I'm happy because I just met someone who could change my life."

My inner freak-out makes my whole body seize up. She met someone? At the fucking convention center? I clench my fist and focus on trying to keep my voice regulated. "Yeah, who was that?"

"Her name is Donna and she runs one of the top nanny agencies in L.A."

I let out my breath in a wave of relief.

"Nanny agency? That's an auspicious meeting."

"I'll say. We started chatting at the snack stand, and you aren't going to believe it, Paul, but she had a similar story to mine. She had her kid out of wedlock and was at a loss how to manage everything. She ended up leaving her corporate job to start the agency so she would have more flexibility with her child."

"All this was revealed at a snack stand?" I ask, not hiding the marvel in my voice.

"We're women, Paul, that's what we do."

"Well, that's awesome."

"So she has a soft spot for women like me. We really hit it off and she said she will send me her best people when I'm ready to hire someone."

"Wow, that's terrific."

"How's your day going?" she asks.

"It's about what I expected. Everyone is trying to water down the design by committee. What is it about palm trees? Everyone wants palm trees. Can we get past the cliché and move on?"

"You don't like palm trees?" she asks.

"It's not that, they're fine. It's just that there are other trees that deserve a chance in Southern California, don't you think?"

"If you say so. You're my landscape designer guy."

"Ha! You didn't call me your sprinkler man. I've gotten a promotion in your mind."

"Don't fool yourself. You were already at the top of the heap."

CHAPTER FIFTEEN

THE HIGH DIVE

I'm in my car just a few blocks from finally getting on the freeway to head home when my phone vibrates. It's Elle. I pull over to dig my headset out of the glove compartment and by the time it's on, her call's gone to voicemail. I'm about to call her back when my phone rings again. It's not Elle's style to call repeatedly, something must be wrong.

"Elle?" I ask.

There's a muffled sound and then what sounds like a sob.

"Elle? What happened?"

I barely recognize her voice it's so weak. "I got served papers."

I'm tempted to pull over again as I tightly grip the steering well. "Served by who?"

"They're from Stephan's lawyer."

"When did this happen? You were on top of the world just a few hours ago."

"I know," she wails. "The guy rang the bell just minutes after I got home. He must have been outside waiting for me. What do I do Paul?"

I'm trying to merge on the freeway and I'm going too fast. I have an overwhelming urge to get to her, but with the rush hour traffic this could take a couple of hours. I keep glancing at my car's clock. "What did the paperwork say?"

I hear the rustle of papers and sniffles. "It's a summons and a complaint."

"Lowlife fucker," I growl.

She starts crying again and I feel like the raw flesh of my heart is being torn apart. "What Elle?"

"He's demanding a paternity test. I just looked it up and the kind he's demanding is very invasive, and there's a chance of miscarriage from the procedure."

"Well, fuck that. I won't allow it!"

Elle is gracious enough not to point out that as the pseudo-uncle, I have no claim on what happens with the baby.

"And if paternity is established he wants partial custody."

"Oh for God's sake." I keep gunning the car's engine I'm so full of fury. What will a clean-freak asshole do with a baby? It's unbearable for me to think of him alone with the kid for ten minutes, let alone for days at a time.

"What am I going to do, Paul?"

"We're going to fight it, that's what!"

"I can't ask you to take that on with me," she says with the most strength I've heard in her voice since she called.

"You didn't ask me. It's what I want so let's not even waste our energy talking about it. I'm all in."

She cries harder and I can hear everything in her tears: she loves this baby and she's afraid of the baby's father. I have to protect her, and I'll do anything to make sure the two of them are safe. It's all that matters to me.

"Where are you? Are you almost home? What if he comes by here?" she whispers.

"Damn. I wish I were almost home. I'm still at least an hour or two away. Is there someone you can call?"

"No. You and your family are the only ones who know about it."

"I'm calling Trisha."

"What?" she asks, her voice laced with disbelief.

"Believe me, there is no one on Earth you want on your side in a crisis more than my sister. I don't know if it's the firefighter training or what, but she will stop at nothing to make sure you're safe."

"I don't know," Elle whispers.

"And her best friend is a top lawyer. Trust me. Okay?"

"I guess so."

"He what the fuck, what?" Trisha barks into the phone.

"Exactly. He tells her he wants nothing to do with it and now he's trying to take control."

"Well, we aren't putting up with that."

I smile. I knew she'd be like this. My sister may not be good for much, but she counts for two people in the tough times. She didn't even hesitate when I asked her to go check up on Elle until I make it back to L.A.

"And call Jeanine, will you?" I ask. Her best friend, Jeanine the lawyer, is tough as nails like Trisha. She helped me once when a girl I'd hooked up with started harassing me.

"As soon as we end this call," she says, her tone all business.

I let out a breath of relief. "Good. I'll call you to check up in an hour. Meanwhile call me if anything else comes up."

"Will do."

"Thanks, Trisha. I owe you."

"Just get back safe," she says.

The last thing I remember clearly before the bottom fell out was a call from Trisha when I was inching along the fucking 5 freeway due to an accident in Downey. My stomach was already churning but Trisha's tone took everything down a notch darker.

"Did you know Elle's been cramping since yesterday?"

"No. What does that mean?"

"Hard to say yet, but I'm pretty sure it's not good. I've been trying to keep her calm but I just made her call her doctor. She's on with her now."

"Is something wrong with the baby?"

"I hope not."

I don't like her ambiguous answer. Why the fuck did today have to be the day I was in Orange County? I feel so hopeless. "What can I do?"

"Just keep your focus and get here as soon as possible. Meanwhile I've faxed the legal documents to Jeanine for her to review them. If I need to take Elle in to be checked I'll let you know so you can meet us there."

A surge of emotion wells up in me. Elle can't lose the baby. She just can't. "I'm going to kill that fucker for upsetting her," I rage.

"Paul," my sister snaps at me.

"I mean who the fuck does he think he is?"

"Paul!" she practically yells.

"What?"

"You need to calm your ass down, and for God's sake don't bring any of this anger home. She needs us calm and focused. You hear me?"

She's right. I've never appreciated Trisha more. "Yeah. I'll be calm for Elle. I promise."

I'm still on the 5 approaching Griffith Park, and close to the 134 when I get a text from Trisha to meet them at a women's clinic on Van Nuys Boulevard. She instructs me to call her once I park and she'll meet me outside. I'm desperate for some shred of hope to hold on to and her text sure as hell didn't give it to me.

When I finally park and get out of the car, my hands are trembling as I text Trisha. I'd been praying the entire last endless leg of my journey, but when I see the drawn look on Trisha's face I realize that God must not have heard me.

She walks straight up to me and grabs my forearm. Her sad eyes look even darker with the mascara smears.

"It's happening fast," she says.

I swallow hard, forcing down the surge of despair. "She's losing the baby."

Trisha nods as her grip on my arm tightens.

I fold over, my palms push against my knees to keep me

from toppling over. A sharp shudder runs through me.

"No." I don't even recognize my voice. It sounds like it's been dragged against asphalt.

Her hand rests on my upper back. "I'm so sorry, Paul."

I take a sharp breath at Trisha's tenderness. The baby may not be my biological kid, but I realize that it isn't just my parents who understand what Elle and her baby had come to mean to me.

I stand back up and look at Trisha. "Elle?"

"It's hit her hard, Paul. That's why I wanted to get to you before you see her. She needs you to be strong."

"And there's nothing they can do?"

Trisha shakes her head. "It's common in early pregnancies, up to twenty percent miscarry. There are various reasons why it happens."

My hands curl up into fists. "It's because of that fucking Stephan."

"The dad?"

I nod, feeling like my grimace is permanently etched across my face. I've never had a burning desire to see someone's demise, but I have it now. If I didn't know that Elle was inside this building and needed me, I'd probably go after him tonight.

Trisha sighs. "Well I'm sure all the stress he caused didn't help anything, but these early miscarriages are usually caused by a chromosomal abnormality."

I start to pace back and forth trying to get my bearings. I can't even believe this is happening. Of all of the times I've thought of Elle and the baby, this scenario never crossed my mind.

"I don't want to hear about any of that, Trisha. I just need to see her. Can you show me where she is?"

She turns and walks toward the door, and when she realizes I haven't followed she stops and turns. There's a measured look between us, as if she knows that once I see Elle my heart will be battered, but I need to pull myself together. I nod and walk toward her, as the fragments of the future I was reaching for fall behind me.

When I step into her private room the first thing I notice is the quiet stillness. There are no monitors beeping, no hopeful chatter of visiting family, just the silence of loss. Elle is turned on her side away from me and I try to imagine what I can possibly say to her.

I clear my throat as I approach her. When I reach her side of the bed, her arms are crossed over her chest and her eyes pressed shut. She looks like a battleworn soldier who lost the war.

I lean over and press my lips against her forehead. "I'm here, Elle," I whisper.

Her eyes blink open and she looks completely broken as our gazes meet. She presses her hand over her mouth. "I lost the baby, Paul," she cries as tears slide down her face.

"Shhh, I know." I take her hand in mine and hold it firmly. "I'm so sorry, Elle. I wish I'd been here."

She shakes her head. "Don't say that. You've been here all along for us, more than anyone, and you're here for me now."

I nod. "I am. And I'm not going anywhere. I want to help you get through this."

She closes her eyes again. "I have no idea how to do that. I feel like I've lost a part of me . . . it's like every dream I had for my baby and our future together will haunt me the rest of my life."

I think about the dreams I had, too . . . maybe they were fantasies, but they felt real to me. My favorite was imagining the three of us at the beach, Elle holding the kid's right hand, and me the left, while we swing the little one over the ocean swirling around our feet.

Without letting go of her hand, I reach behind me and drag the chair as close to her bed as possible. We let the silence and pain wrap tightly around us. All I can do is hold onto her hand while she cries, knowing these tears are the beginning of a river we will wade through. There's no other way.

After a few intense minutes the tears slow down and she closes her eyes. I rest my head on the mattress next to her thigh.

The weight of defeat is swallowing me and I frantically blink back my own tears. I need to be tough for her, but it's hard, damn it, when I feel broken too. Elle seems to sense my spirit falling and without opening her eyes, she gently places her open hand on my head.

It's in this intimate moment that the door opens and Trisha sticks her head inside.

"Sorry. Elle? They're ready. Do you still—"

Elle doesn't wait for the rest of the question. "Yes," she says.

Trisha gestures for me to join her. "Come on Paul, we'll wait down the hall."

I try to hide my confusion and concern from Elle, figuring whatever she's made her mind up about I need to trust.

I lean into her. "I'll be out there. Tell them to let me know when I can come back to you."

She nods. "I will."

I slide down into the waiting room couch and press my hand over my eyes. These fucking florescent lights are making me edgy. The last thing I need right now is everything in this bleak place brightly lit and defined when my mind is so dark.

Trisha lets out a long sigh as she sits down next to me.

"So what's happening in there?" I ask.

"It's called a D and C. It's finishing what nature started. At least she won't have to deal with possibly a few weeks of bleeding after this."

I press my lips together. The mystery of women and what they have to deal with has never felt more overwhelming to me. I know Elle is resilient, but everyone has their breaking point. I need to be ready in case this is hers.

CHAPTER SIXTEEN

TABLE FOR TWO

Grief is a shadow that clings to you especially in the quiet darkness. You can run but that fucker is attached to your heels looming behind you, ready to swallow you up.

Grief is also the language Elle and I speak now, it's the language of no words just the hollow echo of her empty belly as we sit side-by-side on her couch, watching mindless comedies to fill the evening hours.

Once she's back at work, I check on her every afternoon as she moves from one meeting to another. She seems busier than ever and she finally shares with me that she's been pushing hard to pick up more clients so her schedule is always packed.

I get it, but it doesn't keep me from worrying about her. The night I took her home from the clinic is now just a fuzzy collection of the fragmented actions—Elle leaning against me as she signed off on paperwork, carefully loading her in my car like she was a porcelain doll, and tucking her into her bed at home while making sure she took her pain meds. My care was all I had to offer so I did the best I could, even sleeping on her couch so I could check on her throughout the night.

She was asleep, when in a wave of rage and despair, I pulled a number of items out of her purse. With my phone I took a picture of the hospital paperwork with the miscarriage diagnosis, procedures and charges. Then I opened up her phone to recent calls, scrolling down until I found that motherfucking Viking's name. I copied his phone number onto the text I'd written, attached the photo, and hit send.

Maybe it wasn't the smartest thing to send a text threatening him if he ever contacts Elle again, but at least he has hard proof that the baby he was suddenly trying to claim, lost its chance at life that night. As much as I wanted to track him down and beat the shit out of him, far more than that was the determination to make sure Elle didn't have to deal with him again in her sorrow.

That text and other emotional parts of that night I've filed away in my brain but they sneak up on me at unexpected times, temporarily stopping me in my tracks. I'm sure it happens with Elle, but she does her best to hide it from me. Knowing her, she thinks I've put up with too much already. Maybe she hasn't realized yet that when it comes to her there's no *too much* for me.

I know we need to push ourselves if we're going to get past this. After a few weeks I start testing her.

Hey, you want to go to that new restaurant on LaBrea?

Did you hear about the latest DeNiro film? It's playing at the ArcLight and it's supposed to be great.

Did you know they're doing tours of Frank Lloyd Wright's Hollyhock House again? Wouldn't that be cool?

All of my suggestions are met with an unenthusiastic shrug. "Maybe later," she says.

I decide to give it more time, but one evening she points out a picture in a magazine spread. "What do you think of this?"

I look over her shoulder. "The Getty Center garden? It blew my mind first time I went. I love the bold choices. It's amazing that they allowed Robert Irwin to realize his vision."

She smiles. *Damn I've missed that smile.* "Will you take me to see it?" she asks.

I push back a grin. I don't want to risk her changing her mind by thinking I'm expecting too much. "Sure. How about Saturday morning?"

"I'd like that."

She's wearing a sundress and sandals when I pick her up at ten thirty. It feels like her mood is the lightest it's been since before losing the baby. Perhaps she's pushing herself to try to find her new normal. Her hair is pulled back in a ponytail and she has sunglasses pushed on top of her head.

"Hey, pretty girl," I say when she steps up to me for a hug.

"Hey, handsome."

She plays with the radio as I drive, and I let her. She finally settles on an Ed Sheeran song and leans back in her seat with a smile. "It feels good to get out."

"Well, wait until you see the garden."

After we get off the tram from the parking lot, I take her hand and pull her along, heading directly to the Central Garden, pointing out the ravine and stone waterfalls along the way. I have trouble containing my excitement. For some reason it never occurred to me to bring Elle here, and the fact that it was her idea makes it that much sweeter.

"Wow," she exclaims when we finally reach the focal point of the gardens.

I start pointing to various plants and design elements and explain that everything was designed to reflect color and light.

"Those are interesting," she says, pointing to the teepee structures that have fuchsia petals feathering out of their tops.

"I know. That design fascinates me. They're custom designed bougainvillea arbors."

"They look like abstract art."

After circling the garden twice, I take her where they've carved a quote of Irwin's in the plaza floor. *"Always changing, never twice the same."*

She studies the words for a minute before looking up at me. "Boy that could be my motto this year, too. My life was one thing, then it changed direction completely, and then it flipped me over again."

I squeeze her hand. "It's been a lot."

"Too much," she says quietly. "What's the saying? *The Lord giveth and the Lord taketh away.* I don't think God or the universe thought I deserved a baby."

I look over at her, alarmed. The entire time I walked through this journey with her, I never thought she'd take the miscarriage as punishment.

She's staring at the vast view in the distance. It's a sunny, warm day and everything felt kind of perfect until this moment.

I step in front of her so she looks at me. "You deserve a baby, Elle." She shakes her head and casts her gaze down. I slip my fingers under her chin and lift it until we are eye to eye. "Yes, yes you do."

"But we don't always get what we want, do we, Paul?"

There's a long weighted pause where I try to respond, but I can't find the words and she doesn't back down. I finally decide it's time to change things up. I pull her back toward the museum buildings.

"Where are you taking me?" she asks with a wary expression.

"I made reservations in the nice restaurant."

Her somber mood lightens a bit. "That sounds good."

We order wine right away and have almost finished our glasses before our lunch order arrives. I order another round because I can tell the wine is doing its trick and helping us both relax. It feels good to let loose with Elle. I keep teasing her and she giggles so much that I have to remind her to eat.

I love seeing her eyes sparkle and her cheeks turn pink as she recounts that day she first found me in her yard.

"What did you think when you saw me down on my knees on your grass?"

She arches her brow at me and runs the tip of her index finger along the rim of her wine glass. "You know what I thought. If I didn't make it clear that day, surely now that you know me, you know exactly what I was thinking."

I take a sip of my cabernet. "What a handsome devil I am?"

"Ha!"

I feel wounded. "What? You didn't think I was handsome?"

She sets down her glass indignantly. "Are you fishing for compliments or something?"

I shrug. *What is wrong with me?* The wine is making me act stupid, but I can't help it . . . I need to hear that she wanted me.

"Oh for goodness' sakes . . . it was *because* I thought you were unbelievably gorgeous that I had two thoughts in my head."

I instantly feel better. "Okay, what were the two thoughts?"

"The first was trying to estimate how long it would take to get you in my bed. The second was wondering if I'd replenished the condom stash in my nightstand drawer."

"So confident," I tease, as my mind tries to process the idea of us fucking for hours.

"I was until you totally burst my bubble. I think I sat in stunned silence for about twenty minutes after you turned me down and left."

"Wow, so I was an exception to the rule."

"And you still are."

She takes a sip of her wine and winks at me.

"Well don't think I left easily that day. I almost caved and blew my two year record."

"Really? I know the very instance! It was when I told you to take out your cock so I could lick it! I think I was on my third or fourth beer by then." She grins widely and I take a second to glance around our table to see if anyone is listening to us. She's getting a little loud.

"What?" she asks.

"You may want to quiet down a bit, I think everyone including the guy in the corner over there heard you."

"Oh stop!" she says with a laugh.

"But you're right . . . that was one of the times I almost caved."

She folds her arms over her chest. "And for the record, I wouldn't have just licked. Oh noooo . . . I would have sucked."

And there she goes . . . my girl with the filthy mouth is back. I could howl with relief I'm so happy to see her again.

She gives me a flirty smile that is unabashedly seductive.

"You like that, don't you? I can see it all over your face."

"Forget my face." I glance down between my legs.

"The anaconda," she whispers as her eyes close with pleasure.

"Yeah, he really loves your filthy mouth."

"Maybe one day you'll let my filthy mouth love him. I still can't believe we haven't had wild sex, Paul."

I swirl the wine in my glass. "I thought you liked us as friends."

"I'd like it better if we were friends with benefits."

"Hmm."

The waiter brings over the check. I glance up to note that there are a lot of people waiting to be seated. They must want to turn our table. Maybe it's just as well. If we continue on like this I could lose control and we may end up screwing in the parking lot.

As we wait for the tram to take us to my car, Elle throws me a curveball. "So Tuesday I'm flying up to Stockton to see my mom."

I can't hide my surprise. The only time she spoke of her mom was when recounting her less than idyllic childhood.

She shakes her head. "Believe me, I don't want to go but she's having heart surgery and needs someone to take care of her."

"And you're the only one who can?"

She nods. "The only one who's reliable. I resent having to take care of her again, but if I don't go and something happens, I'll never forgive myself."

"How long will you be gone?"

"Hopefully just a week. It depends on how it goes. She's a mess."

We're quiet on the ride back to her house. When I walk her to the door she doesn't invite me in since she has to get a proposal done for work.

Our hug feels different. It's a little bit sweet like the old days and a little bit sad knowing I'm not going to see her for at least a week.

"I want daily reports," I say as I push her sunglasses up on her head so I can see her blue eyes.

"Yes, sir. And don't forget that the wedding is in three weeks. Have you gotten your tux yet?"

"No, I promise, I'll do it this week. Take care of yourself, okay? Safe travels."

She smooths down the front of my T-shirt. "I promise . . . and I'll be home before you know it."

That following Thursday, I finally return to the family dinner after missing a month of them while I looked after Elle. My parents didn't give me any shit about it because they knew that Elle took comfort in my company and she needed quiet, peaceful time to heal, not the emotional chaos that our family dinners can be.

I've just let myself in the front door when Ma drags me to the kitchen.

"What's up?" I ask.

She puts her index finger up to her mouth. "Shhh."

"Okay, what?" I whisper.

"Patrick is bringing a girl to dinner."

I fold my arms over my chest. "Did you set this up?"

Ma waves her arms dramatically. "I certainly did not. This girl is a *hippy*."

She spits out the word like it's dirty.

Now that's unexpected. "He's interested in a hippy?"

"He's not just interested, they're dating. They may have already had s-e-x."

She whispers the letters and I have to suppress a laugh.

I hold out my hands. "Well, that's what people who like each other do."

"Not you and Elle," she points out.

I close my eyes and count to three. There's no point in arguing with my mother before the evening even begins. I respond the only way I know how.

"Yeah, but we're weird."

"Well, you might want to figure that out. I like Elle. I think she's good for you."

Is she teasing me, or is this my mother's way of suggesting that I get together with Elle?

I let Ma get back to cooking and head to the living room where Trisha is arguing loudly with Dad about politics. The evening is showing great promise for being a hot mess.

I'm finally able to distract Trisha away from politics with an update about Elle, including the latest news that she's in Stockton with her mother to help her after her surgery.

Dad looks uncomfortable hearing about the bypass surgery and he excuses himself to check on Ma.

"Is he okay?" I ask Trisha.

"His doctor just put him on cholesterol medicine. Between that and the knee surgery, he seems to have finally realized that he's an old man and it's all downhill from here."

"Geez, Trisha. You didn't tell him that, did you? You make it sound like his days are numbered."

"Face facts, Paul. It's just a matter of time for all of us."

"Well aren't you Suzy Sunshine."

She shrugs. "I'm a realist. Life is hard and then you die."

If she keeps going on like this, I'm going to need a stiff drink. It occurs to me that the night she spent helping Elle probably only supported her bleak outlook.

I'm about to change the subject when the front door opens and Patrick steps in with a shit-eating grin on his face. He's followed by a woman in a long gauze skirt and Birkenstocks. He takes her hand and leads her into the living room.

I have to focus on not letting my mouth gape open. Apparently what we have here is the perfect example of the saying that opposites attract.

"Umm, Paul, Trisha, I'd like you to meet Skye," Patrick says.

I glance at the girl and then back at Patrick. Who is this

Patrick? How could he look so different in just a month? His hair is longer and messy like he just had wild sex and finally got out of bed. *Holy hell! What if he did?* Clearly the S-E-X agrees with him—he looks great. I decide not to chide him about the African print shirt he's wearing . . . at least for now. Instead I focus on Skye.

"Hi, I'm Paul." I reach out to shake her hand and notice she has that henna stuff painted from the top of her hand all the way up to her elbow.

"Hi, Paul."

She doesn't seem to have any make-up on and her wavy hair falls almost to her waist. What do you bet that she doesn't shave her armpits? That's just not okay in my book, but unless she starts wearing tank tops when she's around us, it's not my problem.

Trisha clears her throat. "I'm the sister, Trisha."

As they shake hands, Skye nods. "Yes, I've heard all about you."

Heard about Trisha? Been warned about Trisha is probably more like it.

Trisha gives Patrick a dubious look.

Skye addresses Trisha again. "Hey, your husband's a floral designer, right? That's so awesome. I work in a flower shop in Silver Lake."

Trisha seems pleased that someone finally refers to Mikey with some regard. "Yes, his shop is in Burbank. He does a lot of work for the studios."

"Cool," Skye replies before leaning into Patrick. He wraps his arm around her waist.

"Let's go meet Ma and Dad," he says to her. She nods and gives us a little wave.

"So this is the first time you guys are meeting her? I ask Trisha, wondering how Ma knew she was a hippy.

"Yeah, a couple of weeks ago he showed us her Website that tells about her yearlong trip hitchhiking around Europe."

"Well that explains why Ma is spooked by the idea of her. So how in the world did those two meet?"

"He was asking questions on some travel blog that she answered. They start having longer conversations and realized they live in the same area. Next thing we know he's a vegan and won't wear leather shoes or belts."

"Vegan? Ma must love that. And how does he keep his pants up?"

"He's wearing some kind of rope belt. I mean, what the hell is happening to him?"

The high point of dinner is when Dad gets his portion of the casserole Ma baked for our meal. He has a repertoire of about twelve dishes that he prefers for dinner and he immediately discerns that this isn't one of them. He pokes the goopy pile with his fork. "What the hell is this?"

Ma narrows her eyes and purses her lips. "It's vegetable casserole."

Dad keeps pushing the lumps around. "Where's the beef?"

"There isn't any."

"We aren't poor, woman! This isn't the potato famine. I need my meat."

Patrick squares his shoulders. "Dad, Ma knows that you like your meat. But she made this especially for me and Skye. We're vegans."

"What's a vegan?" Dad asks.

"We don't eat any form of animal products," Skye explains.

His brows knit together. "No meat? You eat milk and cheese though, right?"

Patrick shakes his head. "Nope. Milk and cheese are animal products, Dad. "

Dad turns to Trisha, and whispers. Since I'm next to them I can hear their conversation. "Is this a cult? Do we need to be worried?"

"No. It's not a cult, although it may as well be."

"There are several vegans at my work," I say trying to lighten the mood.

Trisha nods and turns to Patrick. "Between vegans and

gluten-free people, you guys are trying to take over our food chain. It may just be an L.A. thing but half of the selections in my favorite bakery are now vegan or gluten free. What the hell?"

Patrick jumps in. "It's healthy. And Dad, you're trying to cut down on your cholesterol. Eating vegan is a great way to go."

"I don't think so," he replies as he pushes his plate away.

Trisha rolls her eyes, Ma growls, and I try a bit of the grub. I may not like it but I'm relieved that I don't gag.

Skye looks nonplussed.

I turn toward her. "Sorry, we're not trying to be rude, but we're kind of traditional with our food."

She smiles. "That's okay. I'm used to it. My parents don't like it either, and Patrick warned me that you guys aren't vegan." She turns to Ma. "But I think it's very sweet that you went to all this trouble for us."

Ma smiles. Points for Skye . . . obviously she's clever. I'm sure you can't survive hitchhiking around Europe without street smarts and people skills.

"I reserved my tux," I tell Elle the next day on our phone call. "You got black right?" she asks.

"No, it's white with an Elvis cape and rhinestones. What do you think? Of course it's black."

She laughs. "Thanks for doing that. I bet you cut a fine figure in a tux."

"Yeah, I look all right. The saleslady that helped me was very enthusiastic. She took her time measuring my inseam."

"I bet she did. I would've too if I were her."

I imagine Elle on her knees measuring between my legs and I get flustered. My grip on my phone tightens as I try to focus on something else.

"So what are you wearing? I never asked if you were a bridesmaid."

"No, I'm not because of the awkward situation with my ex

being best man. She's having her sister stand up for her."

"That's good. So that means you get to wear whatever you want. Wear something sexy."

"Is that a command or a request?"

"A little of both," I admit.

"Hey, I've got bad news. I may not be coming home Sunday. Mom's having a reaction to the medication and I'm taking her to the doctor this afternoon. Depending on what he says, I may have to extend my trip. Thank God she has Internet, at least I've been able to keep up with all of my work while taking care of her."

"No!" I say with more force than intended.

"What? Is something wrong?" she asks.

"It's just that I miss you."

"Really? I miss you too."

"And I've been working on our fairytale."

"Ooo. Are they still in the shower?"

"No, they've moved into the bedroom."

She sighs. "I can't wait to hear it."

"Well, hurry home."

"I promise I'll do my best."

"Oh before I forget, Patrick and his new girlfriend have invited us to a concert."

Her voice goes up an octave. "His girlfriend? When did this happen?"

"I'm not sure but he's all in, and it appears that she is, too."

"What's her name?"

"Skye."

"Really? Like clouds in the sky, Skye?"

"Yup, and as Ma pointed out to me privately before they showed up, she's a hippy. I didn't really need the explanation. It was evident the second I saw her."

"Ha! Well that explains the name. I'm looking forward to meeting her. Where are we all going?"

"Some kind of tribal drum performance. She's turned him into a vegan and everything. The sex must be phenomenal to be willing to stop eating meat for this girl."

"You know, I've got to say, I always suspected your brother had it in him to be wild. He just needed to find the right person to bring it out of him. Sounds like she's it."

The next day the tone of our conversation is completely different.

"You okay?" I ask when she answers my call with a subdued voice.

"It's a hard day," she says.

"Your mom?"

"She's wearing me out, but it's not that. I was putting in upcoming event dates on my calendar this morning and saw something upsetting. I still haven't stopped crying."

My mind races to wonder what could upset her so much. I didn't miss her birthday, did I? "What was on your calendar?"

"I saw the doctor's appointment where we would have heard the baby's heartbeat. I forgot to take it off my calendar after, well, you know . . ."

The pain in her voice takes my breath away—it's a kick in the gut.

"Oh, Elle."

"I wasn't fully awake when I looked and for a moment I was confused, like I was still pregnant. Why didn't I erase that appointment? I'm hurting so bad right now."

I can picture the tears running down her face as she cries and it twists me up. It pisses me off that she's so far away when she needs me.

"Maybe you weren't meant to erase it. Maybe it's part of the grieving process. Life can kind of suck that way. Like Ma cries every Mother's Day that she lost her mom."

"Oh no, I didn't even think about Mother's Day. How will I get through that?"

"I don't know. All I can promise is that I'll be there with you."

Almost a week passes before I'm finally winding through the Westside neighborhoods trying to get to LAX at rush hour so that I can pick up Elle on her return home. I've got it for this girl bad because I sure as hell wouldn't go to LAX this time of day for anyone but her.

It was hot today and the heat still shimmers off the asphalt. I've got my windows all open, so depending how you embrace the sounds of L.A., at every stoplight I'm either serenaded or assaulted with mariachi or rap music from nearby cars. My favorite is when the base is so loud that my car literally throbs with each beat. I bob my head mindlessly.

I'm on the final stretch of La Tijera Boulevard when my phone chimes.

"Where are you?" she asks with a wicked teasing tone. I'm surprised how much just knowing she's close gets to me.

"Exactly where I should be. Where are you?" I reply.

"I'm about to hitchhike up Century Boulevard. We got in thirty minutes early."

"How did that happen? Isn't the flight like thirty minutes?"

"Yeah, something like that. By the time I got my Bloody Mary and pretzels there was a flight attendant, right behind the one who served me, asking for my empty glass."

"That's messed up."

"I know, right? I've got to warn you, I drank it really fast and now I'm loopy. So don't hold anything I say in this conversation against me."

"Okay."

There's a long pause.

"Did you miss me?" I ask.

She groans. "Sooo much."

"What do you miss the most?"

"Well, in a perfect world I'd say your anaconda. But you don't let me play with it, so I'll say your story telling."

"And I've got more stories to tell, but right now I'm heading up Century and I don't see you hitchhiking."

"Okay, I was joking. I'm standing in front of the United

terminal and fending off an army of suspicious indie drivers with tinted windows. You better get here quick before one of them sweeps me off my feet."

"I'm pulling into the airport from hell right now. I may never forgive you for this rush hour crap and not flying into Burbank."

"Well I come bearing gifts so don't write me off yet."

She's not hard to spot, being a gorgeous woman in a sea of forgettable people. She's also the sexiest woman I've seen since she left town. As a result my inner sexy radar, which is still finely tuned from my hook-up days, spots her a terminal away. She's barricaded herself behind a sea of baggage. What is it with women and their poor packing skills?

When I pull up to the curb she drops her folded arms and pulls her sunglasses lower to peek over the top. She gives me a big grin.

"Well, it's about time."

I grin back. "Don't you start . . ."

I get out of the car, and before I can even get to her she propels herself off the curb and into my arms. I grab onto her tight, completely overwhelmed to be holding her again.

"Welcome home," I say with my lips pressed against her neck and just loud enough to be heard over the airport din.

She settles into my embrace. "Glad to be back."

We load up the bags and we haven't even gotten out of the airport when she rolls up her window, gestures for me to do the same, and then turns on the air.

I arch my brow at her. *Bossy woman.* "You want to drive, too?"

She slides down in her seat and kicks her shoes off. "Nope."

"Was your mom sad to see you leave?"

"Hardly. There's no apartment big enough to house our two personalities. I'm sure she'll miss me taking care of everything for her, but she definitely won't miss my sass."

"I don't know. I missed your sass. By the way, my family misses you too. Ma asked if you'd come for dinner Thursday."

She smiles and looks out the window. "Sure. I have a new dessert recipe I want to try."

"And Sunday I thought maybe we could go to Descanso Gardens."

She makes a face. "From Friday on, my life is not my own. Stella's wedding stuff goes full force then."

"But I thought the wedding was a week from Saturday?"

"It is, but women don't just show up at a wedding, and although I'm technically not part of the wedding party, I'm still her best friend. There are many rituals we must act out leading up to it."

"Like what?"

"There's the spa day, then make-up and hair trial runs, the special wedding shower for the out-of-town relatives that missed the official shower . . . shall I go on?"

I shake my head. "Did you do all that crap when you got married?"

She rolls her eyes. "Yeah. I didn't want to but Bridezilla Stella made me. And since I've been a total bestie-fail with her wedding, I really need to step up this week."

"Damn. I'm so glad I'm a dude."

"I'm glad for that too." She nods and winks.

CHAPTER SEVENTEEN

THE CHALLENGE

"What's in the big bowl?" I ask Thursday evening when I pick up Elle before driving us to my parent's place. She's holding it in her lap like it's something precious.

"You'll see. It's a surprise."

"You're such a tease," I say.

"And this is news to you?"

When we step into the kitchen Ma approaches us with a big grin.

"Ah, we've missed you, lass. I'm so glad you came tonight."

"Me too," Elle replies as they hug.

"Did you hear that our Patrick met a girl and he's a hippy now?"

"I did indeed."

"They're up in his room meditating," Ma tells us with a roll of her eyes.

"Meditating?" I snicker. "Sure they are. You keep telling yourself that, Ma."

"Believe me, I'd rather he was shagging her. Whenever they *meditate* they burn that God-awful incense stuff that stinks up the entire upstairs. As a matter of fact, Paulie, can you go up and get them? Dinner is almost ready."

Before heading upstairs I hold up the bowl full of Elle's mystery dessert. I'm tempted to rip a hole in the foil cover to see what it is. "Where does this go?"

"Let's put it in the refrigerator until it's ready to be served," she says.

Ma's eyes grow wide. "What did you make this time, lass?"

"Irish cream and berry trifle—and I put extra strawberries in it just for you, Millie."

Ma's hands fly up to her cheeks as she lets out a joyful cry. "You did not!"

"I did so," Elle says with a grin.

Ma wraps her arm around Elle's waist and squeezes her before looking up at me. "Paulie, I love this girl!"

A warm feeling shoots through me as my heart silently agrees, *I do too, Ma. I do too.*

Based on the *'What, no meat!'* drama with Dad from our last dinner, Skye brought stuffed potatoes for her and Patrick, along with extras in case we aren't too freaked out by the tofu gravy. All of us but Elle politely pass on the travesty that looks like a potato that ate its vegetable neighbors and then threw up on itself. I may want Skye to feel welcome, but even I have my culinary limits.

Ma serves beef stew, knowing that it's a favorite of Elle's. Ma isn't too subtle as to which of the two girls she prefers.

"So Paulie says that between your job being busy and taking care of your mom that you've been working hard, Elle," Dad says before taking a roll from the basket and passing it on.

I watch her pretty smile fade to a serious look. "Yes, it's helped to be busy."

"Of course," Ma replies.

"I think it's important not to be busy," hippy girl chimes in. "We have a tendency to fill every working hour with business to prevent really feeling all the deep thoughts that fill our soul."

Patrick nods like the zombie hippy he's become.

Trisha turns to Patrick. "What in the hell is she talking about?"

Skye leans forward. "Feeling, Trisha. Feeling everything and living every day like it may be your last."

Trisha turns to Patrick. "Are you guys high?"

Patrick turns pale as an unbalanced spreadsheet. "Don't be rude, Trisha! Of course we aren't high."

"Not now at least," Skye says with an expression so neutral I can't fully tell how much she's fucking with us. She turns to Elle. "Don't fill your days with work, Elle. It sucks the life from your soul. Ask yourself why you are so unhappy that you have to fill your emptiness in such a way."

The entire room goes silent.

Elle's devastated look should say everything to hippy girl, if she'd just pay fucking attention.

Patrick leans over and whispers something in Skye's ear. I watch her cheeks redden as she looks down and folds her hands in her lap. She closes her eyes for a few seconds, and when she opens them she looks over at Elle.

"I'm so sorry," she says softly.

"It's okay. You didn't know," Elle replies.

Dad makes a feeble attempt to pass the rolls again. I can't help it . . . I'm mad enough that I wish Skye would take one and then choke on it. I'm not as forgiving as Elle is.

Elle stands up. "Dessert, anyone?"

We all chime in and I rise to help Elle gather stuff.

She slides the trifle bowl out of the fridge as I watch. I then step up to her, take the bowl out of her hands, and set it on the counter before pulling her into my arms. I kiss the top of her head and hug her tightly, swaying slightly side to side.

"I'm sorry," I whisper.

She nods. "I know. Me too."

"You okay? I'm starting to regret making you come tonight."

"Don't say that. I wanted to be here."

"That stupid stuff Skye was saying made me want to stuff her in the stuffed potatoes."

"It wasn't stupid, there's some truth in what she's saying."

"But she hurt you. I could see it on your face."

"True . . . but she didn't know about the baby."

"Still . . ."

"I will say, it's a little naïve of her to think you can go through life and not be busy and work hard if you are going to support yourself. Life is expensive."

"Damn right." I grab a beer out of the fridge and after taking a swig, Elle pulls the bottle out of my hand and takes one before handing it back to me.

She shrugs. "Maybe she'll end up living in a commune or something, and not need cell phones and internet service. But that will never be me. I want more out of life, not less."

I realize as she says it that I want more for Elle, too. She deserves it.

"I admire how hard you work," I say.

She smiles. "Thanks. I feel the same about you."

"I can't help but worry about Patrick. I hope Skye doesn't make him too freaky. It's like an alien landed in our neighborhood and now she's trying to abduct one of our own."

"I think he's finding himself. Maybe she's good for him. She can loosen him up and get him to try things he never would have."

I think about tofu and chanting and shake my head. "The sex better be great."

"Well, judging from how happy he looks with her, let's assume it is."

Realizing we better rejoin the family before they send out a search party, I gesture to the dessert. "Shall we?"

She smiles and peels the foil off the top. I peek over her shoulder.

"Whoa! Is that pudding or something?"

"It's a little bit of everything good . . . so yummy."

I gather up the bowls, and follow her back out to the dining room.

Dad seems excited. "Is that trifle, lass?"

Elle nods with a grin.

Dad and Ma share a look. I can only imagine what they're

thinking. With every moment like this I know Elle is settling deeper into their hearts.

She stands above the bowl as she serves it up. She even remembered to bring separate servings of just the fruit for the vegan freaks. I watch her with pride.

Damn, she's amazing.

When I take my first bite, my eyes roll back in my head as I groan.

"You like it?" Elle asks with a demure smile.

"Hell yes! It's fit for a prince!"

"King," Patrick says. "You mean fit for a king. That's the saying."

The corner of Elle's mouth curves up and she winks at me.

I notice Skye studying us and I sense more awkwardness up ahead.

"How long have you two dated?" Skye inquires.

I'm still watching Elle as I answer, "We aren't dating. We're just friends."

Elle smiles at me, and it's a mysterious smile. I can't tell what's behind it. I'm then reminded of the time she yelled at me because of what I said about Melanie's mysterious smile.

"Wow," Skye says.

Patrick's brows knit together. "Wow, what?"

Skye nods toward us. "With the energy sparking between them, I would've never guessed they were just friends."

Damn right.

Hippy girl finally got something right.

Elle does the dishes, and I dry, while Ma deals with the leftovers.

"I hear you two are going to a wedding a week from Saturday," Ma says to Elle.

"Yes, my best friend Stella."

"So when are you going to marry my Paulie?"

Both Elle and I snap our necks in Ma's direction. Elle laughs. I'm not sure whether to be offended by that or to join her.

"Is he going to ask me?" Elle says. The way her eyes are

dancing, she looks amused.

"He better," Ma huffs.

"I'm sorry to disappoint you, Millie, but your son has no interest in marrying me."

"I have to disagree. Paulie seems quite taken with you."

What the hell? Thanks, Ma.

"Besides, I'm done with marriage. I think I'm meant to be single. And Paul knows that. He's still searching for his nice girl who isn't a handful like me."

I throw down the dishtowel and pound my fist on the counter.

"Does my presence here count for anything? Why are you two talking like I'm not here?"

Ma continues to ignore me as she replies to Elle, "Well, I'm not giving up hope. Maybe you'll change your mind in time."

Elle glances over at me and winks.

What the hell does that that wink mean?

When did she become so mysterious?

"So that was fun," Elle says when we get in the car to leave.

"Yeah, loads," I reply with a huff.

"Aww come on."

"Why is it that I become the butt of everyone's humor when you're over?"

"Maybe because you're so fun to tease."

"Awesome."

"Your mom sure got you riled up trying to get you to marry me."

"And you were no help with that."

"Why does she want you to marry me so much?"

I roll my eyes with a dramatic flourish. "I have no idea really. It's especially baffling because you're so unattractive and unappealing. The grandkids would look like trolls."

She seems to be fighting back a smile. "Go on."

"And you don't get along with anyone thanks to your incredibly sour personality."

"Yes, I can believe that. I can barely stand to be around myself."

"See what I mean? Oh, and your desserts suck."

"Yeah, that explains why you had three helpings."

I shrug. "Well, I didn't want to hurt your feelings. You know how emo you get. Let's not even talk about that."

She lets out a long dramatic sigh. "Well, it's just as well that I'm undesirable to you because I would never marry the likes of you anyway."

I roll down the car window. It's getting hot as hell in here.

"And why would you never marry me?"

She gazes out the window. "I'm not telling."

What the hell? "That's not playing fair. I told you—why won't you tell?"

"I don't think you could take it."

I pull the car into her driveway and park. We sit in silence for a minute. I tap my fingers on my knee but she's still not talking.

"Okay, thanks for dinner." She pops out of the car and walks to her porch before I can figure out what she's up to.

I move quickly to catch her before she can get her key in the door. Reaching over, I press my palm against the lock so she can't push her key into it.

"Why?" I say in a low voice as I lean into her, my chest against her back.

"Why, what?" She doesn't turn, just jingles the keys in her hand.

"Why would you never marry me?"

When she turns around and looks at me, I study her expression to try to figure out what she's thinking. It doesn't feel like joking anymore.

"You really want to know?"

"I asked, didn't I?"

There's a long pause as she studies me.

"The thing is, even if I were the type of girl that wanted to get married again, I wouldn't marry you because I don't think you're interested in sex anymore. I know you were once, hell you were obsessed with it, but then something happened to you. I'm not sure what, but what you're doing just isn't natural."

"Really?" I ask, folding my arms over my chest as I step back from her.

She nods. "And I need sex . . . a lot. I need it all the time. I threw myself at you countless times, and despite your low opinion of me, most men think I'm really hot."

I don't like where this is going and I squint at her. "Is that so?"

She folds her arms over her chest mimicking me. "Yes, sir, it is. Yet despite that, you didn't just turn *me* down, but you turned down that goth girl who was begging you for it, as was that Melanie goddess. Any normal man would have screwed all of us just for the easy sex. But you walked away so easily . . . without a second thought."

"You think you have me so figured out."

"Well, what other reasonable conclusion can be made?"

I drop my arms and storm across her porch, but instead of marching down to my car, I turn and walk back toward her.

"You have no idea."

"Well then, explain it to me."

My fingers tighten into fists as I turn to pace the porch again. How can I explain anything when my feelings of love and lust for her get so tangled up that I can't see which way is up anymore?

How do I tell her that at dinner tonight there was a point that I was completely lost with want for her?

We had just finished eating and my sister was going on about something when Elle sat up straight and swept up her hair behind her head.

Something about the way her arms were lifted drew my focus to the curve of her neck and the way her breasts looked so perfect—they were calling out to me to be fondled. I immediately pictured her in this pose again, but under me in bed and naked . . . her hair making waves over the pillow.

As I watched, she let her hair fall back down over her shoulders and reached for her glass—I don't even think she knew I was looking at her and that just turned me on more. I started to fantasize crazy thoughts of slipping from my chair to under the table, and passing by the sea of legs until I got to hers. I would press my lips to her bare knee and slowly pull her legs apart so I could trail kisses up her inner thighs.

Shaking my head of the memory, I try to focus back on what I'm going to say to Elle to explain myself. I keep pacing.

On my third stride across the porch she sighs and sits down on the bench. I can't read the worried look in her eyes. Does she regret that she turned my teasing of her into something so personal for me . . . something I'm not sure I understand enough to explain?

Most of the time she thinks I'm a good man but she has no idea how *not good* I was back when I spent every free hour hunting for sex. I was such an asshole and I'm scared that fucker is still buried inside of me just waiting for the trigger to inflate my dirty lust again, expanding like a hot air balloon, pushing out all the good that has filled me.

Elle doesn't understand that she's the motivation that makes me want to be good; she's transformed me. Yet I still don't trust if we get intimate that the darkness won't prevail.

I run my fingers through my hair and make fists of it, tugging hard. I'm protective of her so it weighs on me that I was an asshole when I played the field. The quest for that surge of euphoria as I got off, ruled me.

Tonight when that idiot Skye started babbling that inner soul crap about burying empty feelings and I looked over to see Elle's expression, I was angry. As Elle blinked back tears I could feel in my bones how she was suffering the loss of her baby all over again, just when things had started to get better.

In that moment I wanted to go sweep her out of her chair, and pull her tight in my arms. With her pressed against my chest, I'd carry her away to a quiet place where we could find our peace again.

I glance over at her patiently waiting on the bench for me and I want to yell in frustration for all the words I can't say. Does she really mean it when she says she's done with relationships? I've never even come close to having crazy intense feelings like this about anyone . . . what else could it be but love?

Does a love like this break you, or put you back together again?

I finally stop pacing and approach her. She looks up at me with wide eyes.

"Elle, I'm sorry."

The corners of her lips turn down. "Why?"

"I can't talk about this right now. I need some time to figure stuff out."

She tips her head as she looks at me. "Can I help you? I'd do anything to help you."

I shove my hands in my pockets. "Thank you. I think I just need some time to get my head on straight."

"Alone time?" Her brows knit together.

"Yeah, that would be best."

She casts her eyes down at the ground and I notice her hands tighten on edge of the bench. "Does this mean you won't come to Stella's wedding with me?"

I slip my fingers under her chin and lift up so she's looking at me.

"I'm taking you to the wedding. I promise."

Her eyes have a gray tint, like the blue color has faded along with her spirit. "Thank you."

I sit down on the bench next to her. "Look, you've got a crazy week ahead with all the wedding stuff. Just focus on that and a week from Saturday I'll pick you up and I promise we'll have a great time."

Standing up, I reach for her hand. "Come on, let's get you inside."

She joins me and takes a step toward the door but then turns and puts her arms around me. I hug her back, and from that gesture she sinks into me and runs her hand down my neck until it rests on my chest.

"I'm so sorry if what I said hurt you. You're the last person in the world that I would want to hurt," she whispers.

"It hurt. But you've got to be honest with me."

She presses her eyes shut tight at my words. "I'm selfish. It's just sometimes I lie in bed and imagine us together. I remember how turned on I was when we kissed that one night and how perfect it was when you held my breasts in your hands. And then I fantasize about how it would feel with you inside of me . . ."

My heart is thumping. *Why is she doing this to me?*

"Elle," I gasp.

"I don't even read my erotic books anymore, I just think about you."

I run my hand down her back and it takes everything I have not to slide my hand down to her ass and tug her against me.

She leans farther into me and the heat between us is overwhelming. I've never wanted anything more than to pull her into the house and make love to her all night. The undercurrent of my passion for her is off the charts. Surely she can sense it burning through me.

I can feel everything so acutely—her breasts against my chest, her leg sliding between mine and pressing in all the ways I want her to.

She skims her lips against my neck. "I can feel you, Paul. I can tell that you want me . . . or at least your body does."

I swallow thickly as she rubs against where I'm already so hard for her. "Is just sex enough for you?" I ask in a low voice.

She looks up at me with a hopeful expression. She's misread the tone behind my question. "Enough? Sure it's enough. That's all I want."

I shouldn't be broadsided but I am, and I can't make sense of any of this. The one thing I know is that sex with Elle without the rest would never be enough for me. I gaze at her, hoping to get a glimpse of anything more.

She pulls away. "Damn. I'm so selfish. You said you needed some space and I throw myself on you. I'm sorry."

It hurts like hell to agree but I nod. "Just a little time. Okay?"

She takes my hand and squeezes it. "Okay."

After the door closes behind her I walk slowly back to my car. I'm so damn pent up. In the old days I would have gone directly to a club I used to frequent on Sunset Boulevard where my choice of hook-ups was a given.

Instead I head home for the longest shower of my life.

CHAPTER EIGHTEEN

PLEASE AND THANK YOU

It's a long weekend and I try everything to get a grip. I even go to church Sunday afternoon and sit in a pew for almost an hour hoping to get answers that I can't figure out on my own.

By Monday I've got to face the fact that I still have nothing. We've flipped the traditional man/woman paradigm. Elle wants the sex with friendship, I want the love and complete relationship. How the hell did I end up being the needy one?

Tuesday, Elle texts me a picture of a horrific puffy, purple dress with ruffles and rhinestones. I can't help but laugh at the accompanying message.

> *This is what I won't be wearing Saturday. Thank God I'm not a bridesmaid.*

> *Why do they want a bridesmaid to look like a sparkly bunch of grapes?* I respond.

> *I have my theories.*

> *Well, good thing you aren't wearing that. It'd be a deal-breaker for me.*

> *Oh, you're not getting out of this wedding mister. Remember you promised.*

And I always keep my promises.

She replies with a smiley face.

Wednesday morning—after a night of almost no sleep due to thinking about Elle—I consider going back to my Abstinence Until Love meeting, but then I realize I don't even belong in that group anymore. I must be cured of my obsession with sex. Like Elle said, I've turned down three women recently that most men would be thrilled to screw. No, that apparently isn't my problem anymore.

Instead what I need is EA—Elle Anonymous, since she's become my obsession. She's my constant craving, the cool water for my unquenchable thirst. I don't know why I thought a self-imposed break from her was a good idea. It's making me fucking crazy.

I literally have to grip the steering wheel extra-hard when I pull out of my garage so that I don't turn my car in the direction of her house. In my weakest times, which are upwards of a dozen times a day, I pick up my phone and bring up her number just to see the picture of her I loaded there. This is followed by a battle of wills not to press the call button.

Yeah, I've become one of *those* guys.

Of course her little teasing texts only make things worse. Wednesday's late-night text features a picture of what appears to be a wicker trash can shaped like a frog. She hasn't attached an explanation.

What the hell is this? I text.

We've been drinking and voting on the tackiest wedding gifts Stella and Brandon have gotten so far. She has some distant relatives that apparently have a sense of humor.

So is this the winner?

It gets my vote, she replies.

Damn, I need to find my receipt. I got them the same thing. Do you think they could use two?

She doesn't reply immediately, but when she does her response is golden.

Bwahaha! I just read your text to the girls and Stella spit up her Cosmo.

I grin as I text back.

Girls that I can make laugh and spit up Cosmos are my kind of girls. This wedding is going to be a blast.

Another minute passes and a picture shows up on my phone of a group of women laughing and holding up martini glasses like they're toasting me. The blonde in the middle holding the wicker frog must be the bride, Stella. I scan the faces until I see Elle and she's blowing me a kiss.

Damn, I love that girl.

But then Thursday night she provokes me by sending a picture with the group of them in front of one of those male stripper shows on Santa Monica Boulevard. It's followed by a shot of her grinning and holding up a bunch of crisp five dollar bills.

Waiting to go in! she texts.

I grind my teeth for a minute before I can calm down enough to respond. If she's going to provoke me, I'm giving it back.

Okay. See you inside.

Oh yeah?

Didn't I tell you? I'm part of the show.

Then I'll make sure and save some fives for you.

Okay, but don't expect special treatment or anything. I'll be working all sides of the stage.

Is that so? I bet you're popular.

Well I don't want to brag or anything.

You know what? I don't want all these horny women crawling all over you.

Really? I promise to keep my G-string on.

Oh hell no. Put your loose jeans on and get your butt home.

I love that she sounds jealous.

All right, but you don't know what you're missing.

That's the thing, I do.

It's radio silence Friday and I try not to let my stupid imagination go wild. Saturday morning she texts asking me to pick her up at 5:30 for the wedding, and I'm amped to know I'll be seeing her within hours.

I can't believe it's been over a week. I surrender to the fact that I didn't figure anything out in our time apart, and I'm giving up trying. I'm as lost as I was the first time I set my eyes on her.

I take my run in the early afternoon and come home to shower and figure out the tux. It's a long time since I've worn one but I have to admit, my last glance in the mirror before I set out to get Elle is pretty satisfying. I look damn good if I do say so myself.

I grab the flowers I bought this morning. I'm not sure if they're the right thing to be giving her considering our ambiguous status, but can you really go wrong with red roses? They're the essence of romance and women love that shit.

I'm nervous as all hell when I ring her doorbell, and damn if she doesn't answer. It really would've been nice for once not to troll through her side yard. Glancing at my watch, I realize I'm twenty minutes early. I guess I was more distracted than I realized. I decide to go in the back and hope the French doors are open so I can wait inside.

When I step in her house I can hear Elle singing—wailing really, at the top of her lungs. I vaguely recognize an old Annie Lenox song and she's into it. I laugh to myself when she misses a high note but owns it anyway.

When there's a pause in the song I call out her name but she doesn't answer and starts in on the song again. My gut tells me that I really should let her know I'm here, and enjoying her note-worthy performance. Hopefully she won't be too horrified to know she's had an audience.

I approach the bedroom suite since that's where the singing is coming from and when I reach the entrance to the bathroom hallway I can't take another step. Hell, I can barely breathe, and my grip tightens on the bouquet of roses.

She's turned away from me, and swaying her hips as she sings. A second later she rests her foot on the edge of the bathtub and slowly smooths lotion over her leg in long strokes.

I swallow thickly as I watch. If it weren't for the tiny pale lace bra and panties she's wearing, she'd be nude, and my carnal reaction is similar to when she sent that white bikini selfie from Hawaii. I'm so instantly aroused that I'm almost disoriented. Reaching out, I rest my hand against the hall doorjamb to steady myself.

I watch her run her lotion-filled hands up her neck in slow motion, down her arms and over her hips. I wish it were my hands sliding over the soft skin of those curves. She stops sing-ing and now hums as she turns to the mirror, and pulls a clip out of her hair so that it cascades around her shoulders.

I'm overcome with the most powerful jolt as I realize that seeing her like this in the flesh is more than I can handle. It's pushing me off my cliff. All of these weeks I've been dangling from the edge with my fingers slipping and losing their grip, my legs wildly waving try to find a toehold in the jagged rock of our friendship—but I can't fight it anymore. I'm not even sure when I finally let go, what direction I'm going to fall.

I tilt back against the doorjamb, trying to catch my breath, and silently watch her. When she looks up and sees my reflection in the mirror, her lips part. My heart is thundering so hard that I can barely hear her gasp.

She half turns and looks back at me over her shoulder. She doesn't act embarrassed or try to hide. She studies me with a curious expression but I sense from the hunger in her eyes that she's as turned on to see me as I am to watch her. It's incredibly sexy that she's so comfortable in her own skin.

The corners of her mouth edge up just slightly. "How long have you been standing there?"

"Not long enough."

Her eyes grow wide as her gaze moves down my body. "Wow."

"What?" I ask.

Her cheeks are tinged pink and her eyes narrow. "Look at you. You're so handsome."

I straighten up. "You like the tux?"

"I like you in it. You wear it well."

I nod toward her state of undress as I pull on my lapels. "I'm feeling really overdressed. Maybe I should take the tux off."

"Is that so?" she says in a low voice with an arched brow.

I notice her nipples are hard as I think of all the ways I'd like to touch her, starting there. As she watches me I don't know if she can tell how aroused I am, but from the way the flush has moved down her neck, and how rapidly her chest is rising and falling, I'm guessing she's getting worked up, too.

I nod. "Look at you. I could be as bare as you in a matter of seconds."

Please say yes. I'm aching for this.

"So now you're teasing me? We're supposed to leave in fifteen minutes or we'll be late for the photos."

My mouth is dry as she places her hands on her hips. The swell of her ass holds my attention as she pivots. I want to take a bite of that perfection.

"We don't *really* have to go, do we?" I reach up, wanting to loosen my tie.

For a long pause she looks like she's going to come to me,

but then she shakes her head and steps back instead. "Yes, this is one instance where bailing is not an option. Stella would never speak to me again, so please stop provoking me. You're making me crazy with want for the very thing I can't have right now." She picks up a silk robe that's draped on the edge of the counter and pulls it on, tying it shut with a defiant stare.

Damn.

She walks toward me. "Are those roses for me?"

I hold them up for her and she takes them with a smile. "They're beautiful, thank you."

"Are you sure about this?" I can almost hear the pleading in my voice.

She pushes my shoulder. "Quit toying with me, big boy. Go make yourself busy while I pull myself together."

I nod and back out of the room, but damn it's hard to finally take my eyes off her.

A few minutes later she joins me in the den. Her long, dark grey dress accentuates all her best assets, including her curvy hips and full breasts. I let out a low whistle.

Smiling, she turns for me. "You like?"

I give her an enthusiastic thumbs-up. "Now that I see you in that dress, I'm extra glad you aren't a bridesmaid."

"Believe me, me too."

"Honestly though, I preferred what you were wearing a few minutes ago. But this is a close second."

"What's gotten into you? A week away from me and suddenly you're amped up with all this flirty, sexy talk." She waves her hand. "Not that I'm complaining or anything."

"Yeah, I missed you."

Her expression softens. "I missed you, too. But we've got the night ahead to have fun."

I stand up and straighten out my jacket. "Let's do it!"

When we pull up to the Ebell Club off Wilshire Boulevard, the valet takes the car. Elle links her arm through mine as we walk through the Mediterranean courtyard looking for the wedding group. The coordinator approaches us and explains to Elle where the bridal party is with Stella. She also lets me know that some of the men are at the bar.

"You don't mind if I leave you for a while? They want to get pictures of us helping Stella get ready."

"Yeah, you told me about that. No problem. I'll hang with the guys."

As I search for the bar I wonder if I'll find her ex, Daniel, there. Of course he doesn't need to know who I am in relation to Elle . . . not yet, at least. I plan to show him later in a very vivid way.

But apparently Daniel and some other friend are helping the groom get ready, so I get a beer and chill with Jack and Erik. These dudes aren't as happy to be here as I am, and they're taking away my mojo with all of their complaints about wearing tuxes and that they're missing some movie screening. I'm relieved when Elle finally comes to find me, and the energy from the party starts amping up as more and more guests arrive.

"Isn't this place cool?" Elle asks as she takes my hand and pulls me into one of the empty ballrooms with the carved ceilings, huge arched windows, and antique chandeliers.

"Yeah, very cool. I looked it up the other day. It was built in the twenties as a social and philanthropic club. The architectural style is impressive."

"And I'm finally free to enjoy it with you," she says.

"So what were you girls doing all that time?"

"Oh you know girls, we like to make a big production of these things. We fawned over her make-up and hair, and helped her get dressed. We may have had some champagne."

I smile at her. "You seem a little buzzed."

"It was Cristal."

"Fancy."

She steps closer to me and pulls at my lapels. "So are you going to dance with me later?"

"I'll dance with you now." Grasping her hand, I lift it up and guide her so that she slowly twirls full circle.

"Ooo," she gasps as I pull her back into my arms.

"Where did you learn that?"

"Ma. She told us that all young men should know how to dance. She taught Patrick, too."

She presses her hand to her cheek. "That's so sweet."

"She intended to raise fine gentlemen."

"Well *I* think she succeeded."

While being serenaded by the faint melody from the ballroom next door, I take Elle for several spins around the room. We move smoothly together like we were meant to be in each other's arms and dance. I don't say anything as I look at her, but something about being here with her to watch two people get married makes me want to tell her everything. I want her to understand how she's turned my life right-side up, and how I've never been happier than when I'm with her.

Maybe tonight she'll agree to more with me and we could finally start writing our own dramatic romance novel. Our prologue would be part comedy, part tragedy, crossed-wires, friends to lovers, and everything in-between. I'm sure the main part of the book will be full of steamy erotica and obsessive devotion. Finally, I'll make sure we finish our novel our way, with a happily ever after.

When the music fades we wander back into the smaller room that is set up for the ceremony with large overflowing flower arrangements and ornate candelabras. This shindig is fancy as all hell. People are starting to take their seats so we do the same. When the minister, groom, and best man file in I get a firm elbow in the side.

Elle didn't need to alert me. She should've figured out by now that meeting her ex was near the top of my list for reasons to come to this wedding. I'm disappointed as I study him and realize there isn't a whole hell of a lot to make fun of with the man I've been calling an idiot. He's good looking and has that confident air. *What an asshole for being more impressive than I'd been counting on.*

I mean come on, universe, give me something to work with here: ears that stick out, acne scars, a soft jawline, or at the very least he could be bowlegged. But no. I've got nothing but Mr. Tall, Dark, and *look at me, I'm handsome.*

I glance over at Elle as she watches him with narrow eyes while pretending not to. When his gaze starts to scan the seated guests she turns toward me and takes my hand.

"That's him, right?" I whisper.

She nods. It bothers me that she looks nervous. Where's the pissed off Elle who never said anything nice about the guy?

I give her a smile and squeeze her hand. "You okay?"

She shrugs. "This is really awkward for me. I may be drinking a lot later."

"Thanks for the warning."

"Can you imagine if you hadn't come with me? I'd be a wreck."

My eyes grow wide. "I don't even want to think about that."

The ceremony is okay if you don't mind a bride that looks more like a Vegas showgirl. Her dress has so much sparkly shit on it that she's blinding as she wades through the rose petals littering the aisle. I'm half expecting her to slip and land on her ass, but her dad is holding onto her tight. I'm sure he's thinking the same thing.

Meanwhile I'm willing to bet money that the bride's tits are going to make an appearance. The sparkly dress probably weighs so much with all that fancy crap on it that it can't help but droop down bit by bit with each step until the girls are almost clear to break free.

Good thing Ma isn't here as she went off at my cousin's weddings about her sagging dress. I overheard her drilling into my sister that there's a reason for straps on bras. Have wedding dress designers lost sight of that?

Meanwhile the groom looks scared out of his mind. Well I would too between my bride's tits about to flash our entire posse, and being bedazzled by her damn dress. This is no way to start a marriage.

Like church services, I pretty much tune out the vows. Instead I watch Elle as she listens. The way she reacts to everything is fascinating, her expression shifting one moment to the next from sad to happy, and inspired to confused. I guess girls really pay attention to this stuff.

After the kiss, which goes on so long there are cat-calls and whistles, the happy couple leaves the room and we file out behind them for cocktails and hor d'oeuvres on the patio. I've just stuffed an oversized meatball in my mouth when Dashing Daniel, the ex, and his poor replacement for Elle, step up to us. I decide to refer to him from now on as DD. His woman looks like she'd rather be at the bar getting a lemon to suck on.

"Elle," DD says with a fake smile.

Elle lifts her hand and gives him a little feeble wave. "Hi, Daniel."

I can't help but be irritated. *Come on, Elle! For fucks sake, you can do better than that.*

"I'd like you to meet Veronica." The woman with the tight smile nods her head and gives Elle the once over. All I can think of is that she reminds me of the Veronica in the Archie Comics that my sister used to read.

"Nice to meet you," Elle says with a false sincerity. I suspect that she'd secretly like to push the sour-faced bitch who just hooked her arm through DD's into the fountain right behind them.

Dashing Daniel holds out his hand to shake mine. "And you are?"

"Paul McNeill, Elle's boyfriend." I shake his hand firmly— really firmly.

I don't even need to turn to Elle, I can feel the delight come off her in waves. She loops her arm through mine. "Paul's a landscape architect," she states proudly.

Yup. *Sprinkler man has left the building for good.*

DD pulls a card out of his tuxedo pocket and hands it to me.

"Excellent. I do property development and I have a project coming up that may interest you."

Veronica nods her head and her helmet hair nods with it. "Sycamore Falls?" she asks. DD nods briskly.

What an ass. Who brings business cards to a wedding? I take the card, smile and nod too. "Thanks. I'll be in touch."

Just when I'm at a loss what to say next, another douchebag guy interrupts us to tell DD that there's someone he wants him to meet. They excuse themselves and move across the courtyard.

Elle let's out a deep breath and pulls her arm out of mine. "Thank you," she says.

"For what?"

"All of it. Saying you're my boyfriend. Being gorgeous and classy. Not saying what I know you wanted to."

"Yeah, and what's that?"

"I'm guessing that the word *idiot* would be involved."

I grin at her. "You know me so well."

I notice she's chewing on her thumbnail.

"So do you think she's pretty?" she asks in a soft voice.

"Veronica?"

She nods. For some reason Elle looks a little insecure.

"She's all right I guess, if you like the pinched face look."

Elle lets out such a loud guffaw that some wine splashes out of her glass. Luckily I dodge the wave of cabernet.

Pleased to see her enjoy my response, I share my other reference for her ex's girlfriend. "You know, when I was young and got bored I used to read my sister's Archie Comics, about that group of kids in high school. I thought Veronica was an uptight bitch. I'd pretty much say the same about this Veronica."

"Archie Comics! I read those," Elle exclaims.

"Betty was the one I liked. She was a cutie and kind of sexy. Fourteen-year- old me imagined pulling on her pigtails while I screwed her."

"Naughty boy," Elle says finishing off the wine she didn't spill. "I bet Betty gave good head too."

When I laugh it's my turn to spill my wine, but alas my glass is empty. "Damn, Elle, you and your filthy mouth! And meanwhile Veronica was hanging with that rich gay dude . . . was it Reggie? Well honestly, he reminds me of a teenage version of your ex."

"Me too! And not just in looks! Truthfully I'd screw Archie, or even Jughead before I'd do Reggie, knowing what I know now."

I tip my head at her. "You'd do Jughead? The dude that wore a crown?"

She giggles. "On second thought, maybe not."

A waiter comes by, and after taking our glasses he gives us fresh ones. I raise my glass to her. "Here's to more laughs and spills tonight."

She lifts hers. "Here, here."

"I've got to say, I thought it was tacky when your ex gave me his business card. Is he always like that?"

"Always working? I bet you thought I was exaggerating. Well, I promise you, I wasn't."

"Wow. That sucks."

She nods. "It does. I did't care how much money he was making. I mean I work hard, but I want to have fun, too. Otherwise what's the point?"

"Exactly."

"You know that's how I ended up with the house. He got it cheap because it needed a ton of repairs. He lied to the old lady who sold it to him and said he'd move his "family" in when all along he planned to tear it down and build a McMansion. When the neighbors found out about it they fought him hard with the city council."

"Good for them," I say. "Those kind of developers are despicable."

"Yeah . . . and he doesn't know that I gave them ammunition to fight him. I love that house and I hated what he did to that sweet old lady. Eventually he gave up fighting them and let me have the house in the divorce instead of a bigger chunk of his money."

"So you won and the neighborhood won, too."

She nods. "And the best part is the neighbors all love me for it."

"You're a clever woman, Ms. Elle Jacoby."

She stands up straighter and her smile lights up the courtyard. "Thank you."

Elle looks off to the far side of the gathering, apparently making sure her ex isn't close by. "So Stella's fiancé, I mean husband, told her that Daniel and Veronica met at work."

"Really? DD and Pinchy?"

She blinks at me rapidly. "Excuse me?"

"Those are my new nicknames for them."

I love watching her laugh as I explain the references. This time it takes her almost a minute to recover.

She presses her hand over her stomach after she's caught her breath. "Pinchy evidently is a mortgage broker."

I nod. "She looks like one."

She steps close to me and kisses me on the cheek while squeezing my shoulder. "I can't believe you! I was dreading tonight and I'm having the best time."

"I told you I loved weddings. The material to work with is endless."

So whomever is paying for this shindig is loaded. Dinner is big portions of steak and lobster. I pity the pale-faced vegetarian girl sitting across from me with her tragic steaming plate of vegetables. This is probably the best wedding food I've ever had. The wine is also flowing freely so we're feeling no pain.

Elle was nervous about giving her speech but she does a super job, telling cute, single-girl stories from her and Stella's party years that segue to her being overjoyed that Stella has found her prince. She looks relieved when she sits back down at our table.

I lean in close to her. "You did great!"

She glances over at me with big eyes. "You really think so? You aren't just saying that?" she whispers.

"I swear. And may I also say that you are by far the prettiest girl here."

She turns to look at me and studies me silently with her lips pressed together and her eyebrows scrunched. *Why is she suddenly so serious?*

"What?" I ask.

"I don't know. You're different tonight. What's up?"

That damn girl-radar. She's onto me. I stumble to recover. I don't want to give up my game just yet.

"Nothing's up. I'm just having fun. This is a great wedding!" I give her a goofy grin, and after watching me for another long second she takes a sip of wine and settles back in her chair.

Pinchy comes over to our table to say something to the woman sitting directly across from us. The woman nods and Pinchy heads back to the wedding party's table.

"I wonder if she's really smart," Elle says with a pensive look on her face.

"Why do you care?" I ask.

She shrugs. "Oh, I don't really, but Daniel always made me feel like I didn't work hard and that I wasn't smart enough."

"You?" I ask, not hiding my disbelief at the dickwad's gall.

She drinks more wine and I'm worried we're about to head down emo road. When she isn't looking I move her glass over behind mine.

"He also thought something was wrong with me because I liked sex so much."

"Well, I think something was wrong with him because he didn't," I reply.

"He implied once it was low class."

"Chalk up number forty-seven on the idiot tally."

"The final straw was that he kept putting off having kids even though he understood how much I wanted them. He knew about my insecurities from my childhood, and told me he didn't think I could handle a baby."

My fingers curl into fists and I feel my pulse pounding in my forehead.

She looks over at me with an alarmed expression. "What,

Paul?"

"You need to stop, okay? Because right now I'm amped up enough to beat the shit out of him and then he won't be Dashing Daniel anymore unless he has deep pockets for plastic surgery."

She gasps and shakes her head.

Resting my hands on her shoulders, I rub my thumbs over her soft skin. "Please change the subject, okay?"

She blinks rapidly and then her eyes dart around nervously before she leans into me. "I've got it. Did you hear what outrageous thing the Bruins did to the Tommy Trojan sculpture yesterday?"

I grin and gesture for her to bring it on.

That's my girl.

Lots of wine at weddings can lead to some clueless dancing and this wedding is no exception. While out on the dance floor I've finally discovered the second thing DD doesn't do well, after being a crap husband . . . is dancing. He looks like he has a Paul Bunyan-sized stick up his ass. I take great pleasure in watching him embarrass himself.

It's a different story on our side of the dance floor. I know I'm a good dancer, and Elle's an even better one, so her sexy moves inspire me to be my best. I catch people watching us move together. *Yeah, take notes people. This is how it's done.*

When the music finally slows, I'm so charged up that my nerve endings are sparking. There's an awkward moment when Elle asks if I'd rather sit the slow stuff out but I answer her by pulling her into my arms.

I shake my head at her slowly as we start to sway. "You're not getting away from me."

"Who said I wanted to?"

The corners of my mouth turn up. I'm liking this. There's a feeling in the air, a current of possibilities as Billie Holiday serenades us under the golden light. I'm just buzzed enough to feel reckless but not wrecked, and I've got the most beautiful woman in my arms. I'm liking this a lot.

She trails her fingers up the buttons of my dress shirt and tugs on my collar which pulls the shirt open where I've undone a few buttons. "Hey, where's your bowtie?"

I nod back toward our table. "In my jacket pocket. Why? Are you missing it?"

"Nope. Not one bit . . . I like your sleeves rolled up. You and your sexy, strong arms."

"You know I wasn't teasing earlier, right? You're the most beautiful woman here."

She grins. "Well, except for the bride of course."

"Bride, what bride?"

She pushes me on the shoulder and gives me a side look. "If I didn't know you better, I'd swear you were working on getting laid tonight."

"Hmmm," I say as I slowly spin her around. "What if that wasn't all I wanted?"

"You know you don't have to work it so hard with me, right? Just say the word . . ."

"What fun is it if you haven't worked for it . . . earned it?"

"Earned? Let's not even go there . . . I owe you so much. Everything really."

Leaning into me, she rests her head on my chest and I hold her tighter as we take small steps.

I don't know if this weird feeling comes over me because I'm in an unfamiliar place and surrounded by people I don't know, or that we're dressed like movie stars at a premier—but I feel like I've stepped into a different reality. I close my eyes and rest my chin on top of Elle's head, trying to get my bearings. She holds onto me tighter as if she senses I need reinforcement.

I have a dreamlike image behind my closed eyes and I see myself running at a steady pace through an endless, dimly lit tunnel. I can feel my chest rise and fall, the pounding of my feet on the unpaved ground and my laser focus as I look ahead trying to see the end of the tunnel and finally find my destination.

My eyes pop open and I take a sharp breath. It all hits me hard. For two fucking years I've been running . . . running away from who I was but never certain where I was going. But right now I can feel the surge of relief from figuring out the answers to what I've been searching for. I've finally arrived where I'm supposed to be. It's like that goddamned tunnel ended at the doorway to this ballroom and there was Elle, lit from behind like a vision, waiting for me.

I pull back from Elle, intending to ask her to come with me out to the patio so we can talk, but her attention has shifted to her ex and his girl as they dance not far from where we stand. She looks distressed.

"Elle, look at me," I instruct as I skim my fingers across her lower back.

She glances at me briefly and then her focus moves back to DD and Pinchy.

I cup her chin in my hand. "Come on. He isn't worth your attention, Elle. Stop looking at him." I run my thumb across her chin and she sighs.

"Look at me."

Her eyes grow wide as she studies me. "Yes?"

"Repeat after me . . . He is nothing, Paul is everything."

She gives me a coy smile like she thinks I'm playing with her. "He is nothing. Paul is everything."

I tip my head back and look down at her with narrow eyes. "Say it like you mean it."

"He is nothing, and Paul is everything!" She smiles. "And for the record, I knew that already."

I nod. "Good."

"I was just remembering something I'd rather forget, but that's all gone now."

I watch her gaze move over my face, down to my chest, and then back up to my eyes.

"What?"

"The way you're staring at me. I remember that look."

"You do?"

"Yes. You look like you want to kiss me."

I take a deep breath as I study her lips, imagining how they'll taste. I bet they'll be sweet as all hell. She breaks my concentration by biting her lower lip.

"Well?" she asks, her eyes searching mine.

I nod and take a deep breath. "I do."

She blinks and tries to pull back but I hold onto her tighter.

Her eyes become stormy. "Please don't tease me with this again, Paul. I don't think I can take it."

"Do I look like I'm teasing?"

She studies me and the longer I don't back down the more she relaxes into my arms.

"You have to know that I've always wanted to kiss you . . . and I'm not talking about just the affectionate kind of kiss," I whisper as I run my hand up the back of her neck until her head is cradled in my hand.

Her lips part as her gaze searches mine. "Really?"

I answer by pressing my lips against hers and the feeling is perfect. Once the kiss starts I immediately know that all bets are off. I just let go of the edge of the cliff and I'm flying.

Judging from Elle's reaction, she's flying with me. This is way different than that first kiss we shared on my bed. With this kiss we're sharing each other's secrets, and while people continue dancing around us, we're in our own world.

Damn, how I love her in my arms. Her soft lips are full and lush, and move perfectly with mine. I feel her fingers slide up the base of my neck and bring me closer—every part of her is projecting heat as she presses against me: her breasts, the rest of her body, but most of all her lips. The intensity of her passion is wild, like any minute she'll forget where we are and her hands will be all over me.

Maybe I'm okay with that. Who am I kidding, I'm more than okay with it—it's exactly what I want.

When we finally pull apart to breathe she gives me the most blissful smile, like she's coming down from an orgasmic kiss.

"Epic," she says.

"Epic," I agree.

I look up and notice the ex glaring at me. Giving him the

most shit-eating, satisfied grin I've got, I run my grabby hands down over her curvy hips, then rest them just above her ass.

How that asshole could have given this woman up will baffle me the rest of my life. He's the Grand Poobah of idiots. Seriously, when you look up *idiot* in the dictionary, his picture should be there.

Leaning closer to her, I press my lips to her ear and whisper, "Poor Pinchy, I think DD is jealous that you're mine."

She laughs so loud it's kind of a shriek and then looks over at the ex and Pinchy, and back at me. "You're right," she says as she bites my earlobe and grabs my ass.

I love this girl.

"So am I yours? Really, Paul, or is this for show?"

I give her what I'm pretty sure is a smoldering look. "Let me get you home and show you. It's time to blow this popsicle stand."

She glances back at our table with an ecstatic grin. "Let me grab my purse."

Something occurs to me and I turn to her. "Stella won't write you off if we leave a little early?" Frankly I don't give a shit about bailing early, but I don't want Elle to lose her best friend.

She shakes her head and winks. "Nah, we talked in the bath-room after dinner. She said that with someone as hot as you, she couldn't believe I'd lasted that long. We understand each other. Just give me a minute to tell her that we're leaving."

I nod and she dashes off. As I watch her disappear into the crowd by the main door I feel someone brush against me.

I turn to see her ex. Judging from his point of focus he was watching Elle hurry through the room too. He has a smirk on his face.

"Still a bitch in heat," he mumbles.

Every muscle in my body tenses, and I spin around. My glare hardens as I stare him down.

"What was that?" I growl.

He sways and I can smell the sour stench of bourbon as I lean into him.

"You heard me. Take it to a motel, and if you're smart, when you're done you'll leave her there."

Raw adrenaline courses through me as my fingers curl into fists and my eyes focus on his lower jaw where I intend to pummel him first. Through a haze of rage I see Pinchy rush up beside him and grab his hand. My arm tenses as I hold back my punch.

I grit my teeth. "You know you're going to pay for that," I say to him with a snarl.

"What's going on?" she whines.

"I'm going to beat the crap out of your pussy boyfriend," I spit as I grab him and my fingers curl around his throat.

He's cursing and flailing which just pisses me off more. My fingers dig under his collar and twist until his bowtie is strangling him and I yank him forward. "Outside," I growl.

I've dragged him several feet forward with Pinchy squealing behind me when I see Elle rushing toward me.

"What happened?" she asks as her fingers graze my forearm.

Twisting his collar tighter, I shake my head. "This ass has quite a mouth on him, I'm going to take him outside and teach him some manners."

I see a fire flare up in Elle's eyes as she bites her lip. What do you bet she thinks this is hot? The ex's shock is wearing off and he's growling and putting up a fight. I need to keep moving so I don't lose my grip. Jerking him forward, I take another step.

Jumping in front of me, she presses her hands against my chest. "Did he slut shame me again?"

"Damn right. I may have to kill him."

"Let go of me, asshole," he sputters in a squeaky voice. His face is turning purple.

Elle's face is flushed as she turns toward him, and before I even realize what's happening she swings her leg back and full on kicks him in the shin.

Damn, those fancy shoes she's wearing are pointed.

He yelps like a puppy.

When she leans into him, I tighten my grip. "You think you're all that, but you can't hold a candle to this man. He takes care of me in *every* way." She arches her brow at him to make her point and turns and winks at me.

"Let him go, baby. He's *so* not worth it."

"You sure?" I ask, twisting my fist tighter as I brace for the regret I'll feel letting him go.

She steps back and reaches her hand to me. "So sure. Come on, sexy, let's get home."

My heat of fury morphs into another kind of heat as I see the desire simmering through her.

I loosen my grip on his collar and shove him with enough force to send him stumbling backwards. We don't even look to see if he falls as I grab her hand and move forward, picking up speed until we blast out of the ballroom, dodging guests as we go.

When we're outside on the landing I stop her for a moment and turn toward her. "You okay?"

She guffaws and then curls over laughing. "Okay? That was awesome!"

"Really?" I wish I could laugh but I'm still so amped up.

"Well I may have messed up my big toe, kicking him. But hot damn, Paul! I've never had a man defend me like that. It was so hot . . . straight out of one of my books, fucking hot."

I pull her into my arms because I'm really needing to feel all of this woman pressed against me. "Glad to be of service," I whisper in her ear.

She looks up at me, her gaze full of lust. "I have never want-ed anything as much as I want you right now."

"Me too," I gasp.

We rush down the stairs to the valet stand. I wave my car ticket in the air like it's on fire. A compassionate valet, who with once glance at Elle seems to understand my plight, runs off at full speed to get my car. That dude is getting a good tip.

Elle is so anxious she's bouncing on her heels. "Stella and Brandon snuck off and did it in the bridal changing room right before the cake cutting. She and I are two peas in a pod."

"Well that explains one thing . . ." I say as the valet pulls up, I hand him the twenty, and we jump in the car. "That's the most relaxed and happy I've ever seen a dude look to have cake smashed in his face."

CHAPTER NINETEEN

EDGE OF HEAVEN

I'm a little frustrated when Elle insists on us going to her place since it's ten minutes farther than mine, but she makes it worth my while by groping me in ways I've never been groped. I'm going to add Magic Fingers to my list of affectionate nicknames for Elle, right after Filthy Mouth.

I take on the winding road over the hill of Laurel Canyon like a race car driver. Luckily, it's late enough that the traffic is sparse, either that or God is finally looking out for me. It's a good thing we're both buckled in tight because I'm pretty sure I take a few of those curves with two wheels instead of four. Elle shows off her upper body strength by holding on even tighter, with a death grip on the passenger handle, and the other on my thigh. For that part of the canyon ride she doesn't full-on grab my cock, perhaps for fear that I'll lose control of the car, but once we're on the flatlands of Studio City the game goes into overdrive.

I tear into her driveway and almost forget to turn the engine off as I'm peeling her hands off me long enough for us to get inside. She leaps out of the car and I'm right behind her, unzipping her dress as we wobble across her front porch.

We haven't even closed the front door when the dress becomes a grey puddle in the middle of her living room. Leaping into my arms, she wraps her legs around me, and I swallow back a yelp when her sharp high heels dig into my ass. The pain is instantly forgotten however when I press her against the wall. It's all just too fucking good. I take a moment to revel at the feeling of my hands groping her ass as she does some kind of Zumba thrusting move against me.

"Well, here we are," I tease as I gasp for a breath.

"And just in the nick of time," she says with a groan.

I bite my way up her neck until I'm kissing her again. I'm so fucking hard for her. The rough two years of being pent up, with every desire shoved down until I was almost dead inside, is finally over. Now my desperate need for her is a flash fire raging through me.

I start to yank my fly down so I can fuck her against the wall when my sex- fogged head clears enough to remember that this is Elle, not just any hook-up, and it has to be different with her.

"What?" she asks when she notices that I've stopped opening my fly.

"I want to take you to bed," I say in a rough voice. "Now."

She wraps her arms around me and tightens her legs so she's clinging onto me. As I storm out of the room I reach behind me and knock her stabby high heels off. I plan to have her completely naked as soon as humanly possible.

I'm breathless by the time I've carried her to her bedroom and right before I drop her on the bed she pipes up.

"Um, remember that time you told me that you wanted to fuck me so hard that I wouldn't be able to walk the next day?"

"Yeah," I say as I lower her onto the sheets.

"Can you do that?" Her eyes go half-mast and she sighs. "I'd really like that."

"Believe me, baby, that's the plan."

"Oh yes," she moans.

I wrap my hands around her ankles and pull her legs down so she's closer to me. Meanwhile she peels off her bra and stretches her arms over her head. Every move she makes is seductive, and I'm pretty sure she knows her breasts look spectacular when she does that, but I appreciate the gesture nonetheless. I cup all that softness in my hands and claim them.

"Mine."

She stretches over and grabs at my hard-on, still trapped in my tuxedo slacks.

"Mine," she says.

That works for me.

I practically rip my shirt off as she watches.

She lifts up so she's leaning on her elbows like she needs a better view of my slacks coming off. She bites her lip and I notice the sharp rise and fall of her chest.

I take my time unzipping my fly and she starts waving her hand at me.

"Come on now . . . hurry up! Do you know how long I've waited for this? I finally get to see if that bad boy is everything I've dreamed of."

"Should I feel objectified? I'm sensing that you only want me for my cock."

"Well, no that's not entirely true," she says with a wink.

With my fly undone, I lower my slacks slowly as I watch her eyes grow wide.

She lets out a low whistle. "Praise the Lord and baby Jesus!"

I choke back a laugh. The Lord and baby Jesus being mentioned in reference to my cock is a first for me, but I don't mind when she looks so excited. It's like she's about to get on a brand new ride at Disneyland. I'm going to buckle her in and show her that this ride was worth the wait.

Looping my fingers under where her panties are clinging to her hips, I pull down. My breath catches when I finally see her bare. When I rub my hands up her legs, she opens them, welcoming me.

I gaze at her smile and the way her cheeks are glowing pink. She's glorious. "Oh damn, Elle, you're so beautiful."

She lets out a long sigh. "You're beautiful, too. If you're half as amazing in bed as you're good looking, I'm never going to let you go."

I join her on the bed and pull her into my arms. I love kissing this woman, and now skin-to-skin, with my hard cock pressed against her belly, and her hands gliding over my body, it's perfection.

I do all I can to put off being inside of her, because I know it's going to be unbelievably intense and I doubt I'll be able to hold off for long—the first time anyway. The anticipation alone has me on a knife's edge. So I kiss her long and hard while sliding my fingers between her legs. She trembles with every touch and stroke. She's the most responsive woman I've ever been with and we're only getting started. I take her nipple between my lips. I tease and suck slow at first but then hard, and she bucks, crying out with pleasure, her hands in my hair pulling me closer.

"Oh please," she cries when she can't take it anymore. She pushes my shoulders so I lift up before she points to the nightstand. "The condoms are in there." Seconds later I'm kneeling between her legs, slowly rolling it on while she watches.

She pouts. "It's a shame to have to sheathe all that magnificence."

"One day," I say, holding back the emotion in my voice, "we won't."

I lean over her and she takes my cock in her hand and rubs it against where she's wet for me. It feels amazing to finally have her under me, moaning and begging for me to take her.

For a fuzzy moment I remember that we need to talk so I can finally tell her everything, but we're both explosively pent up and the sex train has left the station. . . there's no stopping this now.

I lift up and kiss her as she strokes me. My lips trail along her jaw until I'm biting her earlobe and working my way back to her sweet lips. My hands glide over her curves so I can memorize every part of her. We already have our own rhythm as if our bodies are doing a slow, erotic dance.

The next time she rubs me against her I push my hips down, my ability to take my time with her falling away from me. I need to be inside of her, finally knowing what it is for her to be completely mine.

Her eyes are full of wonder as she spreads her legs open

wider. "This is really going to happen, isn't it? You want this. I swear I'd given up hope."

"Never give up on me." I position myself and begin to push. "I've always wanted you . . . I've imagined this a thousand times."

"Only a thousand?" she says with a sly smile as she swivels her hips.

I'm too distracted to smile at her teasing. All of my focus is on working my cock inside of her. It's so tight, which is only uncomfortable for about three seconds and when her body adjusts, I push further into her and cross the borderline from cautious to elated. Seriously, the feeling once I'm completely inside of her and we begin to move together is life-changing. What is my life that this gorgeous woman who makes me laugh, is also my best friend and my sexual equal? She's the modern day Eve to my Adam—it's just us naked, with all the time in the world, and a bed big enough to live on. Does anything else really matter?

"Oh Christ, Elle," I say in between short, choppy breaths.

She looks transported and already covered with a sheen, while she chants indiscernible outbursts. I love her filthy mouth even more when we're in bed and she's going on about how fucking great I'm making her feel. In true Elle form, she doesn't just grab *me*, with her other hand she keeps touching her luscious breasts and squeezing them. If her intent is to make me wild, she's succeeding.

I slowly pull out, and with my next thrust I push her hand away and take over touching her breasts. Her hands move to my ass and she grabs on and grinds up against me. A second later she reaches up and bites me on the shoulder.

I bristle from the sting. "Hey, what's that for?"

She gives me a wide-eyed look. "How could you deny me this glory all this time? I may never forgive you."

I stop thrusting and release my grip on her hips so I can tease her back. I look at her with an arched brow. "Is that so? You aren't going to forgive me? So, this is it?"

Her eyes narrow and her lips press together. "No! I didn't

say that!"

"Okay, then hold on, baby, here we go."

I'm swept up into my desperate lust and I consume her, my movements more powerful with each thrust as she begs for more. Is she human? I've never known a woman who could take it this intense and love it. I'm so turned on I feel like I'm about to implode.

When she starts to come I realize it first from the look in her eyes, wild with lust and a brighter blue. She's reached that perfect place and I've taken her there. As I join her, the adrenaline courses through me, lighting my fuse. Knowing that I love Elle amps every sensation up tenfold and with our final thrusts I explode.

It doesn't take either of us long to recover. I feel like I'm wrapped in a force field 'cause Elle's got me plugged in. I wasn't even sure I'd still have it—two years of abstinence seems like a sure way to lose your game. But with Elle I'm as much of the beast as I used to be, only better because it's all for her. Hell, I love this woman and I'd do anything to see that sexy, blissful gleam in her eyes. I rub my hand up and down her arm and kiss her shoulder.

"You okay?"

She sighs dramatically and shakes her head. "No, I'm not *just* okay . . . I'm magnificent . . . I've never had sex that intense." She throws her hands up toward the ceiling and then lets them fall again. "It was epic! I'm just waiting to get the feeling back in my legs so we can fire up round two."

That's my girl.

She grins at me while stroking my chest with her fingertips. "You okay with that?"

I shrug. "I suppose we could do it again. There's no good football games on, anyway."

She hits me with her pillow before I have time to tackle her. I finally wrestle the pillow out of her hands and tuck it under my head as I lie back.

"So tell me, sexy girl, do you always come like that?"

"Like how?"

"It was pretty wild. All the screaming and writhing . . . the way you were fisting the sheets I thought you were going to rip them apart."

"Doesn't everyone get wild?"

I can't tell if she's joking or not. "Ah no. Not *that* wild. That was definitely a first for me."

She gives me a side-glance. "Did it scare you?"

I laugh. "In a good kind of way. It turned me on."

"Really?"

"Oh yeah, something fierce."

She smiles as she circles my nipple with her fingertips. "I think everyone should just go full throttle and experience bliss like that. The world would be a better place."

I chuckle imagining it. "That would be something all right."

This woman . . . she's one of a kind and she's mine.

I like round two even better, if that's possible. One minute she's raking her fingernails up the inside of my thighs and teasing me. A minute later she's straddling me and making quite a show of working my cock inch by inch until it's inside of her.

I lean back with my arms folded under my head and watch her slowly roll her hips, lifting up and rocking down, farther and farther until I'm all the way in.

Damn. She looks as good moving over me as she feels.

Her breath catches and I worry that she's still tender from the way we went at it earlier. I run my hands over her hips and squeeze her gently.

"You okay?"

Biting her lip, she nods. "This is crazy good. You're bigger than my rabbit."

"Why do you keep comparing my cock to animals?"

She grins. "I love animals, especially when they're wild."

While she finds her rhythm I get distracted watching her. She's so damn beautiful. My gaze runs down from her wavy hair, past her lush lips now parted, to her full breasts and tight pink nipples, down across her curvy hips and ending between her legs where we're joined. As she looks at me with lust-filled eyes, she rocks her hips so I can see just where she lifts up and then sinks back down over my cock.

I run my hand over her breasts and slide one hand down to stroke her clit. She shudders and leans into me, close enough that I can kiss her breasts.

"Oh yes," she groans. She looks down to watch me shift to her other breast and tease her nipple with my tongue. As her nipple hardens I pull it in between my lips and gaze up at her with hooded eyes as I suck.

The tension slowly builds until there's blinding intensity. The storminess in her eyes makes me thrust up powerfully as her hips sway, and when she tightens over me I can tell that she's coming undone. My hands cup her ass and pull her down over me again and again.

"Paul," she gasps.

"That's right, gorgeous girl. Give it to me," I whisper in a rough voice.

Her nails dig into my shoulders as she arches back and starts to cry out. Her hips still undulating, our gazes are locked . . . all that matters is watching the magnificence of her pleasure as it peaks, her body flushing pink as she moans.

I've never felt so powerful or satisfied by giving a woman what she needs. She collapses down on top of me and I hold her tight.

"Oh my God, oh my God," she chants.

Smiling, I bury my face against her neck, trying to ignore that my cock is still throbbing inside of her. She needs a minute.

Or apparently not.

"Your turn," she whispers.

"You can take it?" I ask, smoothing her damp hair off her face.

"What do you think?" She arches her brow and gives me a willful look.

I roll us to our sides, pull out of her, and check the condom. *All good.*

"I think I want to look at that perfect ass of yours. I'm taking you from behind."

"Mmm," she moans.

She submits as I roll her to her stomach, grasp and angle her hips up with one hand, and ease her legs apart with the other.

Once I'm on my knees I take a moment to rub my hands over her ass while my cock presses against her.

She spreads her legs farther apart and rocks her hips up higher to welcome me. I don't need to be invited twice.

"You ready, baby? This is going to be hard and deep."

"So ready," she whispers.

I start slow, one hand balancing me on the mattress as I lean over her, the other guiding my cock inside.

"You're so wet," I groan once I've filled her.

"Thanks to you," she says with a sharp breath.

I begin to move, slow at first until we adjust to each other, then harder as I pull her tight against me. I slip a hand under her to tease her nipple and then trail my fingers down to stroke her.

Her filthy mouth takes off again, and it just gets me more worked up.

It isn't long before my hands grip her shoulders as I take her full force. We're both slick with sweat and I rake my teeth against her neck and growl as I get close to my edge.

"Too much?" I gasp as her body snaps forward with each thrust.

"Never."

She moves under me like she dances, every undulation leading me, calling me to her. I rise higher and take her hips in my hands, blind with lust as every nerve ending sizzles, with my final thrust I roar.

I barely remember how I ended up flat on my back with Elle in my arms. All I know is that I've never been more spent or satisfied.

"How'd I get here?" I groan, only half joking.

"You sort of passed out. I had to roll you over." Leaning over, she grabs a water bottle off the nightstand and offers it to me. I lift up and take a few swigs.

"Where'd you get that?"

"From the kitchen. I made a run after I used the bathroom."

My mouth falls open. "Holy hell, I did pass out."

She grins. "Well it's no wonder. I'm going to call you Beast Boy from now on."

"Filthy Mouth and Beast Boy . . . we make a fine pair," I murmur.

"A very fine pair," she whispers before turning off the light and settling back down into my arms.

I vaguely remember kissing her on the forehead and pulling her closer before sleep takes me again.

Chapter Twenty

FACE TO FACE

"You smell like sex."

I'm pulled out of the depths of sleep and I blink several times.

"What?" I ask as I rub my eyes.

She trails kisses across my chest and give me a lazy smile. "You smell like sex."

I chuckle. "Well, it's no wonder." I lean into her. "You do too."

Grinning, she eases her folded leg over my thigh. "I know. Isn't it glorious? The best smell ever!"

"Well, it's distinct." I blink again, noticing how dim the light is in the room. "What time is it anyway?"

"Five-thirty."

"In the morning?"

"Yes, you've been sleeping like a bear. It's no wonder you have no sense of the time."

"Haven't you been sleeping?"

"Not a wink. I'm too excited!"

"What about?"

"Sex!"

This woman.

I bite back my smile. "What about sex?"

"Isn't it obvious? Now that I've got the best lover of my life,

I'm imagining all the sex ahead of us. I was making a list in my mind of all the things I want to try. As a matter of fact, there's a sex show coming up at the Convention Center and I thought we could go and see all the latest stuff."

Stuff?

"Oh really?"

She nods with a sincere look. "Yeah, that's where Stella got the crotchless sex swing. They had the part where it hooks up installed over their mattress in their bedroom."

What the hell?

"Stella has a crotchless swing over their bed? I wonder if it's got that sparkly shit on it?"

She laughs. "Ha! Probably."

I point up to her light fixture. "Wouldn't hanging a swing over your bed conflict with your heavy-ass Venetian light fixture?"

She taps her fingers on her chin. "Good point. Well, we could hang it in the guestroom."

I'm tempted to ask her how it works but I don't want to give her a false sense of encouragement. I may be a beast in bed but I don't do crotchless swings.

She runs her hand down my thigh. "Speaking of crotchless, do you have any chaps?"

I'm starting to get concerned. Why is everything starting to sound like a bad theatrical production?

"Leather chaps?" I ask to check her level of sincerity.

She nods.

"No, my leather chaps got messed up when I tried washing them. All the fringe started coming off."

She purses her lips. "Hey, are you making fun of me?"

"Maybe just a little bit."

She play pouts, pulling the sheet up to cover herself, and folds her arms over her chest.

"I don't like it when you make fun of me . . . especially when I'm so excited about something."

I lift up on my elbow and gaze down at her. "Aww, don't be

mad at me, Elle. The chaps thing just took me by surprise."

All of this reminds me of when she wanted me to dress up as a construction worker. "Hey, have you read any cowboy erotica?"

She nods. "Montana Bound is one of my favorite BDSM series."

I purse my lips together. "I see. And the cowboy . . ."

"Rusty," she fills in.

"Rusty wore chaps?"

"He wore them a lot, although it was only in the bedroom where he wore them without jeans underneath."

"Right, right. That's where the crotchless part comes in." I purse my lips together and try to imagine how such a scene would play out. "I have cowboy boots," I offer.

She smiles. "Well, that's a start."

I run my hand over her shoulder and down her arm. "I'm not really a dress- up kind of guy. Other than appreciating a woman in beautiful lingerie, I really prefer naked sex without a lot of gadgets."

"You don't think that's boring?"

I push back from her, my eyes wide with surprise. *"Boring? Were you bored earlier?"*

"You know I wasn't. I've never been more excited."

"Me neither. Just remembering it is getting me excited again."

She takes her hand and slides it down until I feel her fingers wrap around me. My cock pulses in response and she moans.

I press my lips against her cheek. "You turn me on so much." I ease her sheet down to her waist, kissing her across her shoulder and up her neck as my hand cups her breast.

She runs her fingers up and down my cock. "You have no idea what hearing that does to me."

"And we don't need a swing, baby." "Yeah?"

"All I need is you."

As we lie together we touch each other slowly in the quiet light of dawn. I gently brush her hair to the side so I can caress her cheek. When our lips meet and we kiss it feels different, like we're even more connected. Not that I'm surprised, but it means a lot that I'm sensing it so strongly from her.

It's time. I've got to tell her.

Taking a deep breath, I pull back so we're lying side-by-side facing each other. I look into her eyes and take her hand.

"What?" she asks, squeezing my hand gently.

I take a second, hoping to calm my nerves. "I just thought you should know . . . I mean, I've wanted to tell you . . . but I guess I was worried you'd freak out . . . so please don't freak out . . ."

She claps her hand over her mouth and there's panic in her eyes. "Oh God, what is it? Are you moving away?"

"What? No!"

"Do you have some rare incurable disease?"

"Hey, hey, hey . . ." I say gripping her arm. "It's nothing bad. Why did you assume it was?"

"I don't know. Maybe because you're stuttering and you look like you're either going to throw up or cry."

I laugh, and then laugh harder until I roll over and hold my stomach. I'm so fucking smooth. For the first time I'm going to tell a girl that I love her and she thinks I'm going to throw up instead.

"Why are you laughing at me?" she asks with a frown. "Now I'm getting annoyed."

"No, don't get annoyed. I'm laughing at myself, not you, and I'm an idiot." I roll back on my side to face her.

"So what's going on?"

"It's just that—"

"Stop," she says placing her hands on either side of my face. "It's me. Elle. Just tell me."

"I love you," I blurt out.

She looks at me kind-of stunned. Maybe she isn't clear on this yet.

I shake my head in frustration. "What I'm trying to say is

that I'm *in love* with you—*that* kind of love. You know, the deep kind of love that people write songs about." I place my hand on my chest.

She gets quiet and glances down. "Oh, I see. You're *in love* with me."

My stomach twists up as I wait for her to look back up. "Is that a bad thing?"

She narrows her eyes as she studies me. "Is this a new thing? I mean, did you just figure it out and now think it will mess everything up or something?"

I swallow hard. I have to be honest. "No, I've known for a pretty long time."

"Why did you wait so long to tell me?"

"Well, I was going to tell you, but when we found out you were pregnant it wasn't the right time. I guess after that we had to find our footing again with so much changing. I was waiting for the right moment."

"I see."

"I'm starting to realize that maybe this wasn't the right moment."

She gives me a little smile and inches closer to me. "Maybe it was exactly the right moment."

She silently stares at me for a long time, or at least it feels that way. Then I notice there are tears starting to stream down her face.

I reach over to brush one away. "What is it, Elle?"

"I'm *in love* with you, too," she whispers.

"Are you crying because that's a bad thing?"

She sniffles. "No, it's because I never thought that someone would love me again, especially the way *you* do."

"Oh, baby," I whisper as I pull her into my arms. "You're amazing. How could I not fall in love with you?"

She answers with a kiss that shows me she loves me even if she hadn't said the words.

I answer back by easing on top of her so I can feel her underneath me when I return the kiss, and I make sure it's one she'll remember.

"So this is a good thing," I say when our lips part.

"Definitely."

"And is *this* a good thing?" I kiss her again and adjust my body between her legs as she slowly eases them apart. My cock seems to slide into her of its own free will, like it knows where it should be. Maybe I gave it a little help, and she did too, but still it was cool it felt so natural.

"Such a good thing," she whispers. She has a vulnerable look in her eyes and I see that the tears haven't stopped. I kiss them away and then move to her lips where the kisses continue as I slowly make love to my Elle.

I think this kind of lovemaking is new for both of us—there's nothing hard about it yet the passion is even more intense without being wild. It's as if our bodies are confirming the thoughts we shared. I'm acutely aware of the way she's touching me, like I'm a treasure she's unwrapped.

All of it is such a turn-on, and I'm stunned to realize that I'm close to coming and we never put on a condom. I lift up on my arms and she looks down to where I'm sliding in and out of her, and she gasps. She circles the base of my cock with her fingers and then strokes herself.

"Oh, Paul, I'm so close," she says with wide eyes.

I swallow thickly. "Me too, baby, but we don't have a condom on."

She shakes her head. "Don't worry. My doctor put me on the pill."

"So we're okay?"

She nods and continues to stroke herself. The flush is running down from her cheeks, along her neck and over her chest.

She nods and bites her lip as the intensity builds, drawing each other to our edge. I'm so deep inside of her.

"Oh my God, Paul," she cries.

I can feel everything; it's powerful, not just her starting to come but how this is more. This is love.

I don't speed up, so as I come inside of her every sensation is amplified. It's crazy intense, and for a second I wonder if my heart has stopped, but then I realize that it's wildly beating.

When our gazes meet, I sense that she realizes everything between us has shifted. I understand now why this love thing is such a big deal. It's an opening of your heart, and you have to be brave because it's magnificent but terrifying, too.

The only thing I know for sure is that from this moment on nothing will ever be the same.

CHAPTER TWENTY-ONE

THE BALANCING ACT

We fall asleep and when we wake up I realize that we're not just stuck to the sheets, but to each other. As I try to peel myself off of her, I laugh and she opens her eyes.

"Where you going?"

I flop back down. "I had this idea that I'd go find some food in your kitchen, but I can't be bothered."

"You hungry?"

I nod and rub my hands over my face and through my hair. "Yeah. I should probably take a shower too but I don't have any clean clothes with me. I'm going to have to leave some in your closet so I'm prepared after our next marathon. I'll be one of those guys who brings over a few things at a time and suddenly I'm living here."

She tips her head as she looks at me. She suddenly feels far away.

What's that about?

"Hey, you'll come to dinner at the folks this Thursday, right?"

She glances over at the clock. "I think I can come. Let me check my schedule."

She has to check her schedule?

She smooths the sheets over her legs. "Do your parents know?"

"Know what?"

She waves her hand back and forth between us. "You know . . ."

"That I'm in love with you?"

She nods.

"Yes, they do. I've got to warn you, now that we're *together* Ma is really going to amp up the marriage thing."

There's that faraway look again.

"Oh."

"Is something wrong?"

"I guess I'm just feeling overwhelmed. Like everything is moving so fast. You know I haven't wanted to be in a relationship."

I feel like she just kicked me in the gut, and I reel back. "Are you saying that hasn't changed?"

"Not exactly. I love you, truly I do, and the sex . . . well, it's phenomenal. But that doesn't mean I want to suddenly set up house and be a full-on couple."

The blood in my veins goes cold. "What do you want?"

"I don't know . . ."

"I think you do."

Looking up at me, her expression is hopeful as she bites her thumbnail. "I was thinking we can be like we've always been, but with sex."

"So friends with benefits?" I grit my teeth.

She smiles like I'm going along with it. "Yeah, like that."

"I see," I say as I step out of bed. My stomach is churning and I'm sure as hell not hungry anymore. My instinct to flee that developed during my player days kicks in. It used to be when the girl got clingy after sex I'd get moving. The weird thing now is that the roles are kind of reversed, which actually makes me feel even more uncomfortable.

Searching for my clothes, I find them crumpled up on the floor. I pull on my boxers and shake out the slacks before pulling them on.

"What are you doing?" she asks, with a bewildered look.

"I think I'm going to get going. I really need a shower and clean clothes."

"You could shower here. We could take one together. I've always wanted to try shower sex."

Wow. It's all about the sex. For a brief moment I regret sleeping with her, but then I remember how awesome it was and I get over it.

"I'll take a rain check," I say as I button up my shirt.

She gets out of bed, grabs her robe from the closet, and pulls it on.

As she ties her robe shut she looks up at me. "You know, I'm still a little foggy from all the sex and no sleep but can you tell me what's going on—why you're upset and rushing out of here? Can we talk this out?"

"I'm just tired," I lie.

She arches her brow at me. "You can do better than that."

"What about you? You seem so distant all of a sudden. At daybreak we were in each other's arms confessing our love for each other, and now a few hours later we're besties with benefits."

She sits of the edge of the bed and stares out the window. "Maybe all that 'couple talk' you were going on about when we woke up made me uncomfortable."

"Yeah, I picked up on that. Like it's the last thing you'd ever want."

She holds her arms out and her eyes are wide. "But you've known since you met me that being part of a regular couple again was the last thing I wanted."

I can't argue with her. She's only speaking the truth.

I nod, and sit down on the opposite side of the bed.

"And you've always known what I wanted," I say.

"True . . . I just hoped . . ."

"As did I," I admit. "Somehow I thought that if you loved me enough you would decide you wanted more after all."

"So we were both wrong," she says with an incredibly sad tone to her voice.

I lean forward and drop my head in my hands. My elbows are digging into my knees as if I'm trying to hold up the weight of the world instead of just my fat head.

A creepy feeling edges up my spine. "Is this about you wanting to still do hook-ups? Because this is making me feel like I'm just another one of your Tinder guys."

Her mouth drops open and her eyebrows shoot up. "No! How can you even ask that? Besides after last night you've ruined me for anyone else."

Her answer only makes me feel the smallest bit calmer. "Oh, this really sucks," I groan.

"Can't we just take things as they come?" She almost sounds like she's pleading but that doesn't make me feel any better.

I consider the idea as my forehead presses into the palm of my hand. It's not the worst idea. If we just act like friends who are in love and have a lot of sex, won't we eventually evolve into being a couple? Before you know it we could have a couple of kids and a Spanish bungalow in Larchmont Village or Toluca Lake.

Sitting up, I glance over at her. She looks as upset as I feel. I want to go to her, but I know I'd regret it later.

Instead I stand, and pick up my jacket and shoes before clearing my throat.

"Look, we're both exhausted and overwhelmed. I think we both need some time to think about things."

"Time?" Elle asks, looking scared. "I don't like the sound of that."

I let out a sigh. "I know. I don't like it either. Here's the thing, after two long years of abstinence and those crazy meetings, two years of occasional dates with women who didn't excite me at all, I've finally found what I want and I'm not settling for less. I want *you*, Elle."

"I want you too," she replies. Her voice sounds like she's holding back tears.

I shake my head. "You know what I'm about. I want it all . . . including the emotional intimacy and connection. I want to know that you're my future. This is a hell of a lot more than sex to me and I can't believe that's all this is to you."

Her voice gets quiet. "And if I can't be who you want me to be, that's it for us?"

I consider what she's asked carefully before I finally nod and look over at her with sad eyes. "It just wouldn't make sense, if what we want is so fundamentally different."

"No," she whispers. I notice there are tears in her eyes but as much as I want to, this time I can't be the one to dry them.

I shake my head. "Damn love."

"What do you mean?"

"Everything would be easier if I hadn't fallen in love with you. Now I'm getting why all the tragic songs are about how love hurts."

"Don't say that, Paul. Love should be beautiful."

I'm so tense my jaw locks. I'm getting frustrated and mad, which makes me feel stubborn. "It's not so beautiful right now, is it?"

She casts her gaze downward. "I don't know what to say."

"Look, let's just think about things . . . take some time, okay?"

Her whole face is drawn and her expression forlorn. "And then what?"

"We can agree right here that if one of us has a change of heart about the bigger picture we'll let the other know."

I sound more positive than I feel. I'm getting dizzy the longer I sit here and let the magic we had last night be swept aside by today's new reality.

She lets out a ragged sigh. "It's not going to happen, Paul. You're not going to suddenly decide that I'm worth letting go of your big dreams of a *together* wife who wants a big family."

"It doesn't have to be a big family. And I'm not looking for, what did you say once . . . a complacent wifey. I want *you* but you have to be more than a bestie with benefits. I need a lot more than that."

She wipes off her tears with her robe sleeve but I can see from her wary look that she isn't buying it. "I understand that you need more," she whispers.

"I do," I say.

"I wish I had it to give. I feel hopeless about that kind of love. And even if I could be that intimate it doesn't change the facts. This seems to be my history and my destiny. I've never gotten what I wanted or needed in a relationship, and it may be because I don't deserve it. Maybe this is just how it's going to be for me."

Why can't she believe in me and that things could be different with us?

I think what hurts the most is knowing that she actually believes what she just said. Sometimes you have to fight for what you deserve, but what can I do if she doesn't think she deserves to be loved for who she is? How can I get her to see in herself what I do?

I walk over to her and pull her into my arms. Holding her tight, I kiss the top of her head as I silently hope that she'll come to believe that she can be loved completely—not in fragments that if pieced together would complete the puzzle that is Elle. She *is* more, and I'm willing to wait some time for her to realize that we're worth fighting for. I don't want to settle for a lesser version of who she can be.

I know in life you have to take a stand for what your true beliefs are, but when I walk out of this house my heart will be blown apart by not holding onto her.

"I've got to go," I whisper.

She nods and steps back, staring at the ground. She doesn't even look up at me when I move away, and turn to leave. I glance back one last time before I pass through the bedroom door. I see tears and I see her arms wrapped tightly across her chest like she's holding herself together, but I don't see my Elle that I held last night. And I know as I walk out that door and get in my car that I never may again.

I'm about two days into this "let's think about things" break/

break-up when I start to wonder if it was all some kind of bullshit drama that people in love do just to keep each other on their toes.

I can't sleep and I can barely eat, but hot damn, I sure as hell am holding onto my pride like a big man, waiting for my little woman to come to her senses. It's all starting to feel surreal and ridiculous. I start questioning everything . . . like maybe I'm okay not having a bunch of kids and instead settling for a semi-girlfriend who loves sex as much as I do.

But then I see one of those commercials where the goofy dad is trying to change the baby's diaper while the mother is trying to wrangle the other kids into the bath, and the dog is barking . . . that family chaos thing that commercials make look better than it ever is in real life.

In the final shot the family is all cuddled together on their couch appearing content, and he and his wife give each other this look. It feels intimate and full of the kind of love I imagine I'd feel with my wife, the mother of my children.

I know my logic of an insurance company commercial affecting my life choices may be misguided but I can't help it. That final image of the dad surrounded by his children and adoring wife reminds me I'm never going to stop wanting that kind of life.

Wednesday I call my parent's place to tell them I won't be over Thursday night. Ma picks up.

"Why aren't coming for dinner, Paulie? I was going to try Elle's lasagna recipe you went on about. I was hoping you'd bring her."

"Well Elle's kind of the reason."

"What do you mean? What's wrong?"

This is harder than I thought. I swallow back my frustration. "It's just that I'm not seeing Elle for a while."

"Why in the world not? You two are such close friends. You

know how much we love her."

I feel awkward. There's no easy way to break this to Ma.

"Yeah, about that close friends thing . . . Remember that we were going to her friend's wedding?"

"Yes."

"Well it was one of those nights, and one thing led to another . . ."

"Oh my. Frankly I'm not surprised. So how does a couple go from that to not seeing each other anymore?"

"I don't know, Ma. I'm still kind of baffled myself over it."

"You were attentive, yes? You better say yes, or I'll smack you."

"Of course I was. It wasn't being intimate—it all went to hell when I told her I was in love with her."

"What do you mean? That doesn't make any sense. That should've made everything even better."

"I know. I'm still trying to figure it out. She says it's not that she doesn't care about me, she does . . . but she doesn't think she's meant to be in a relationship."

Ma is eerily quiet.

"You still there?"

"I'm here. So that's what she said?"

"Yes."

Ma lets out a long sigh. "Poor lass."

"You feel bad for *her?*"

"I feel bad for her because she must not value who she is. She was already in a relationship with you . . . a grand one. Anyone could see it. She's a fool to let that go."

"I don't know what to do. I'm so messedup, Ma."

"I know, and I'm sorry, my boy—very sorry. She isn't thinking clearly. There must be a way for you two to work this out. Let me pray on it. You should, too."

Ma thinks prayers cure everything, but at this point what do I have to lose?

"I'll try, Ma. I promise, I'll try."

It's just past nine o'clock Thursday night when my phone prompts. I'm surprised to see it's my brother. He must have gotten an earful from the folks about the tragic turn my life has taken.

"Hey, Paul. Ma told us about what happened at dinner to-night. I thought maybe it'd be good for you to get out. Are you free tomorrow night?"

"Would Skye be coming?" I'm not trying to be rude but I can't take that woman right now.

"No, just us guys."

I let out a sigh. I'm really not in the mood to go anywhere but it's a big deal for my brother to put himself out there and of-fer, so I agree. Besides I'm going nuts after work, during the long empty hours at night.

"Okay. Musso and Frank?" he asks.

I roll my eyes. This notorious restaurant is seeping in Hollywood history and is relatively unchanged over the years. It's almost a hundred years old, which by L.A. standards pretty much is equivalent to the Ice Age. It's his favorite place and he insists we go there every year for his birthday instead of getting presents. I don't know if it's the old Hollywood vibe that he likes or what, but the whole place has stopped in time. Far be it from me to crimp his style.

"Seven's okay?"

"Yeah. See you there."

Patrick is already in his booth when I arrive. He always asks to be in this section so his favorite waiter, Al—who's an old, cranky bastard—can wait on us. Apparently they have a special connection that I'll never figure out. Al always argues with me about what I'm ordering.

"Medium-well," I answer when he asks how I want my steak.

"Rare. It's better," he says as he scribbles in his pad.

Screw you, old man.

We're halfway through our old-school martinis when it hits me that Patrick ordered a burger.

"Hey, what happened to being vegan?"

He shrugs. "I can't give up my meat."

"But what about Skye?"

He starts to turn red as he fidgets with his silverware. "Um, I don't eat it around her."

"You dog!" I say with a laugh. "She doesn't know, does she?"

He shakes his head.

"I tried, I swear I tried," he insists.

"Hey, I'm not going to give you any shit about it. A man needs his beef, right?"

He nods looking relieved.

"So then what about the rest . . . the meditating and weird clothes?"

"That stuff is all right. I don't mind the meditating. Actually I kind of like it, but I almost blew it last night when I fell asleep while she was chanting. I don't think she was amused."

"But she's peaceful and all-accepting, right? So I'm sure she was cool with it."

"Oh, she's feistier than she looks. I was making fun of the weird art on her vision cards the other day and she got pissed."

"So what is this then? Is she someone you're serious about?"

"I don't know if I'd say serious yet, but she's pretty great. She's really sweet to me. Besides, it's part of my plan to expand my horizons."

"Like the travel you were telling me about?"

I think about how much Patrick has changed lately and realize it's good to focus on someone else's relationship for a change.

"Exactly."

"Well that's cool I guess. How about the sex? Is that expanding your horizons too?"

His face turns a brighter shade of red. "Have you ever heard of Tantric sex?" he asks.

"No."

"Look it up." He leans forward with an intense expression and lowers his voice. "It will change your life."

My eyes grow wide. Whoa, Paddy's got it going on. Good for him. No wonder he's putting up with the incense and rope belts. I lift my martini glass in a toast.

"Here's for expanding your horizons."

Grinning, he lifts his glass to join me. "Here, here."

Grumpy Al brings out our food and we dig in. I'm almost done with my steak when Patrick brings up my situation.

"So can you tell me about what happened with you and Elle? Ma said something about her telling you she didn't want to be in a relationship."

"Yeah, she told me that the first ten minutes after we met, but I kind of forgot that small detail the closer we got."

"What are you going to do?"

"I don't know, but I better figure something out because I'm missing her so much that it's making me crazy."

Patrick finishes off the final bite of his burger, pushes his plate back, then taps his fingers on the table. He squints like he's deep in thought before looking back up at me.

"I'm going to tell you something, and I'm going to get in trouble for telling you, but I think it's worth the risk."

"Is it about Elle?"

He nods. "She called me today to ask about you. I didn't tell her we were meeting and I agreed not to tell you this, but this is the second woman in a week I've lied to so whatever . . . I'm going to hell."

My stomach starts flip-flopping and my hands are getting clammy. "Is she okay?" I ask.

"No. To be honest she sounds worse than you. She hasn't been able to work all week."

I let out the breath I've been holding. "Damn." I realize I feel even lower knowing that she's bad off, rather than being an asshole and relieved that she's struggling too. If that isn't love, then I don't know what the hell is.

"So what did you say to her?" I ask.

"That she should give you guys a chance."

"How did she react?"

"She was quiet. And then I reminded her that despite the fact that she told me she was falling in love with you months back, you guys never had the chance to be a romantic couple. Because of circumstances you were always just friends."

"Wait a minute . . . did you just say that she told you she was falling in love with me months ago?"

He nods and gives me a sheepish look. "At the end of that date we had."

"Why didn't you say anything? I thought you were talking about the Viking when you talked about her being interested in someone else."

"I promised her. I swore I wouldn't say anything."

I press my hand over my forehead and moan. "I can't believe it . . . I had no idea. I mean, I knew she wanted to sleep with me, but never anything more than that. Oh man, what a mess."

"Messes can be cleaned up, you know."

"So how did you end the conversation?"

"Well she told me she was scared to fail again. I told her that sometimes the only way to deal with an issue is to face your fears head-on. Why not do the work so you can be the best version of yourself?"

"Whoa, Patrick, where did you pick up all this stuff?"

"It's from a book I read last year about conquering your fears. It inspired me. That's the reason I'm doing stuff like planning trips, and dating someone like Skye. I'm done with being worried of what people think of me, that I'm not good enough for the things I want."

My mouth drops open. I knew my brother wasn't a stud, but I had no idea he used to have that much self-doubt. I'm impressed with this new Patrick. "Never sell yourself short, man. You're the real deal."

He sits up straight, pulls his shoulders back and gives me a satisfied smile.

"So I told Elle about the book, and she gave me her email so I could gift it to her for her eReader. She promised to read it."

"I hope she does."

"I really want you two to figure this out. You're great together."

"We are." The one thing I know for sure is that it always felt so right to be with her.

I study Patrick as we get up to leave. I'm proud of him, and I really appreciate the advice he gave Elle. Now if she only takes it . . .

That night I lie in bed exhausted but amped up. The idea that Elle had loved me from early on, yet kept it a secret is blowing my mind. With each toss and turn in my bed I relive our various adventures through a different perspective.

I still can't believe that she insisted I take out Melanie, then showed up on my front porch to hear if my high school dreams had finally come true. I try to imagine the heavy feeling in her heart thinking I could be in bed with this woman who had every potential of blowing Elle and my intense connection apart.

Well, that shit didn't happen. Melanie couldn't hold a candle to Elle.

No one can.

I keep replaying my conversation with Patrick in my mind, and I can only conclude other that I can't force the outcome of this situation. Elle needs to figure out if she can handle me.

I think she can. And I know for sure that I want to handle her.

At eight forty-two Sunday night I get a text and I almost drop my cell phone when I see who it's from. I press on her name so hard that I'm surprised I don't shatter the screen. There's no message, only a picture, and when I open it it's a photo of the Brooklyn Bridge. The memory of Elle lying in my arms while we talked about my bridge photographs, and her gesture of sending this, gives me hope.

I wonder if she knows me well enough now to guess that I love the Brooklyn Bridge. I met up with a college friend in Brooklyn a few years ago. We had pizza at Grimaldi's and then we walked across the bridge toward the Big Apple—the massive expansiveness of it made me feel like a giddy Munchkin headed to the Emerald City. It was one of those experiences you never forget. I don't think the world had ever felt as big as it did that day.

I spread the image open larger on my screen and study it, trying to figure out if there is significance to why she sent this particular bridge. Does she know it's grand but under repairs? I'm clueless and it puts me at a loss with what to say. Finally, I realize she's probably nervous waiting to see if I'll respond so I reply.

Nice bridge

She texts back immediately. This bridge looks strong and solid and it made me think of you.

I laugh out loud. That's not a good sign. Maybe she doesn't know about the flaws.

It's impressive but it's under repair for cracks and holes. Being strong and solid doesn't mean it doesn't need work. I'm a good example of that.

But I thought you and the Brooklyn Bridge were perfect.

Nope, not even close. How about we pick a shorter bridge so we can get from one end to the other faster?

Shorter?

I do a Google search and bring up an image of a famous bridge in Venice, Italy. I send it to her.

The Rialto Bridge in Venice . . . it's stone and has survived for centuries. Plus its shops are enclosed so we can take cover, even in a storm.

That's a really good one, she replies.

I picture her sitting in her house, biting her lip as she taps her screen and it's a sharp reminder of how much I miss her.

I take a big breath as my fingers glide over the screen's keyboard.

I liked being your bridge, you know. I miss you, Elle.

I miss you too.

A minute later a picture pops up that she labels, The Bridge of Sighs. I look it up and see it's actually the Hertford Bridge that links two buildings at Oxford University but is nicknamed after another famous bridge in Italy.

Good thing you picked the Oxford one. The Bridge of Sighs in Venice had a prison on one end, and interrogation room on the other.

Oh no! I picked this one because it's really short, enclosed—so we're protected—and it has great style.

That's my Elle—she's more focused on the style than ending up in prison.

It's very inviting.

Exactly . . . I wanted a short, inviting bridge for a reason.

Yes?

I was hoping we could talk in person tomorrow.

Okay. We could do that.

Could you come over after work?

I'll be there at seven.

I'll be ready.

I'm not sure what *ready* means, but I sure as hell am going to find out.

CHAPTER TWENTY-TWO

THE BRIDGE

When I pull up in front of her house early the next evening, I pause for a moment and run my fingers through my hair a few times. Even though it hasn't been long since I was here, it's like her house is a mirage and I'm not sure I should believe it's actually there and she's inside waiting to talk to me.

I slap the dashboard with my hand. "Get a grip, dude," I say out loud to myself right as some lady walks by with her dog. She looks back at me, alarmed. I sigh, roll up my window, and get out of the car to head in before I freak anyone else out.

Of course Elle doesn't answer the door. *Well at least she's consistent.* I shake my head and walk to the back.

I'm not even out of the side yard when I hear the hiss of sprinklers and cursing. *What the hell?* I round the corner.

Not only are the sprinklers going, but the sprinkler that we first became friends over is a geyser and Elle is on her knees trying to force the sprinkler head into it. Why the hell are they even running at this hour?

To top it off she's wearing a dress that I've never seen and her hair is swept off her face. Why doesn't she just shut the system off? She's getting soaked for God's sake.

Her face is red and she's sporting the biggest frown. I can't help but feel sorry for her as she curses like a sailor and pulls the head back up and throws it in the bushes. It's right after it disappears into the foliage that she looks up and sees me standing there.

"On no! You're here!"

Wasn't she expecting me at seven?

I tip my head and glance over at the bush that swallowed the sprinkler head.

"What are you doing anyway? Is this why you wanted me to come over?"

I'm teasing but damn, this is weird. This isn't the greeting I was expecting at all.

She shakes her head with a grimace, then feebly stands up and tries to pull her wet skirt away from where it's clinging to her legs.

Stepping closer, I observe that she's wearing nice shoes and she has make-up on. Or she was, but now her face is really wet and her eye makeup stuff appears to be sliding off.

As I gaze at her with wide eyes, she seems to realize what she must look like. She runs a finger under her eye and cries out softly when she sees it's covered with black goop. She reaches into her pocket, pulls out a wet tissue, and wipes off the worst of it.

"I had plans," she wails.

"I'm sorry they didn't work out."

Her focus moves from one end of the yard to the other, then back at the geyser and she lets out a sorrowful sigh.

"Can I help?" I ask.

She nods and so I retrace my steps to the side yard, open the panel, and shut the system down. There's the slow fizzle of the sprinklers shutting off and then silence.

After rejoining her, I nod toward the bush. "I'll fix it later. I'm not really dressed for doing hard labor." I grin at her and she seems to relax a tiny bit.

"You look really nice," she says as she studies me.

"Thanks."

The corners of her mouth turn up a little. "You're wearing tighter jeans."

I shrug. "I wanted to put my best foot forward, so to speak."

She nods, fighting back a smile. "Thank you for that."

I look over to the chaise lounges and gesture in their direction. "You want to sit down and talk?"

"Should I change first? I must look awful."

"It's up to you, but I think you look great all wet."

I love that I finally see her full smile. She walks toward the sitting area and points for me to sit across from her, but I settle down next to her instead.

As we sit silently she twists her hands together. Damn, she's going at it so intently that it looks like she's going to pull her fingers off. She's making me anxious. Reaching over, I wrap my fingers over hers.

"Don't be nervous. Just tell me what's on your mind."

She leans back and takes a deep breath before curling forward again. "Stella yelled at me. And she got really loud."

Okay. That's out of left field but I'll go with it.

"I thought she was on her honeymoon?"

"They were in the car on the way to the airport."

"I bet her new husband liked that."

She laughs softly. "He's used to stuff like that with Stella."

"Well he's a better man than me then. So what did she yell at you about?"

"That I should get over myself."

I don't respond. *I mean, what the hell can I say about that? That I agree with Stella?*

"She also yelled that if I let you get away she'll never speak to me again."

I raise my brows as I turn toward her. "Never?"

"She tends to exaggerate. But I'm sure I'd never hear the end of it."

"Well I guess I'm glad to have her on my side."

"And then there's your brother . . ."

I decide I'm going to cover for Patrick and play this like I don't know they talked. "What about him?"

"He gave me a book."

"Really? What kind of book?"

"Umm, inspirational, I guess? It's actually pretty good. It's helping me get over myself."

I stretch my legs out. "So are you over yourself yet?"

"Not completely, but I want to be."

Okay. That's something.

"Well, that's half the battle. And what does *getting over your-self* entail?"

"Deciding that I'm not going to let the disappointments and failures in my past define my future."

I nod slowly. Sounds like that book Patrick got her was worth every penny. But still something bothers me. I don't trust anything that feels like a magic fix.

"And just reading a book is going to make you figure out what you want?"

She shakes her head with an earnest look. "No. Anyone with half a wit knows this stuff already. The book just reminds us how to walk toward it—otherwise the possibility seems overwhelming and so far away. So I can take one step at a time. Right? I don't have to figure it all out at the same time."

"Sure." I nudge her shoulder. "Rome wasn't built in a day."

She smiles, and I notice that her eyes have their twinkle back.

I wave to the wet lawn. "And what was this all about?"

"It was my attempt at a grand gesture."

"It was grand all right."

She sighs. "I had the timer set so we'd be out here having our talk and then the sprinklers would go off. But the clock on the thing must not have been set right, so as I finished my hair I hear them start up in the backyard."

"Damn clock."

She nods. "And then when I rush out here, since I can't seem to do anything without some kind of drama, the gusher is going. So I go to the control box and I'm normally good at timers and such, but I couldn't get the damn thing to shut off, probably because I was so agitated. Then I tried getting that stupid head back into the hole so this wouldn't be just a colossal failure and you saw how well that worked out."

I let out a low whistle, secretly enjoying that at least *that* was a problem I could easily fix for her.

I clear my throat. "So walk me through the grand gesture part of all of this. What part did sprinklers running have in that?"

She bites her lip. "Well now it sounds kind of kooky, but at the time I thought it was a cool idea. It's a lot of symbolism. We met over sprinklers."

I grin. "Yes, we did. And what a meeting that was."

She rolls her eyes. "I know. I was so classy. Me and my filthy mouth."

"Are you kidding? You completely captivated me."

"Likewise." She gives me a grateful smile. "So see, it takes us full circle, we started out here not knowing that we could possibly have a future together . . ."

"And now we're here to decide if we do?" I ask.

She takes a big breath. "Yes. But it's not just that. Water is symbolic of cleansing."

I pull on the edge of her wet hemline. "And it looks like you were baptized."

She nudges me back with her shoulder. "Hmm, maybe I was."

She scoots away from me so she can turn and face me more head on. Her eyebrows knit together and she suddenly looks serious.

"Sunday morning when you walked out of my house, I crumbled. I wanted to run after you but it was like my legs wouldn't work. In my heart I knew I'd do anything to be with you, but my head kept stopping me with doubts like hurdles that seemed too high to jump over."

"Hurdles?"

"Like what if I can never be everything that you want?"

"What if you already are?" I reply.

Her eyebrows relax and she sighs, but then she starts blinking.

"But what if over time, I'm not enough for you . . . and you get tired of me?"

I have to press my lips together to keep from laughing. *This handful of a woman thinks she may not be enough for me? Oh good Lord . . . does she have no sense of how extraordinary she is?*

I suddenly feel a fury burn in my chest. I want to beat the hell out of her dad, her ex, the Viking, and any man who ever made her feel that she wasn't worthy . . . wasn't enough.

I reach out and take her hand. "We aren't teenagers, Elle. We've both been out and about in the world and have known a lot of people. You're the most exciting, fun, sweet, sexy, awesome woman I've ever met."

She tugs at my hand. "You forgot smart."

"Yeah, you're smart, and I'll add sassy, too."

"And you like that I'm sassy?"

"Are you kidding? I love it."

She sits up taller. "You know what? I've started realizing that I deserve you. Some people may look at me right now and think, she needs this man but doesn't deserve him. But I do deserve you."

I press my lips together so I don't grin. "And why's that?"

"Because I'm a good woman and I love you with all my heart, and want to be my best for you."

"Yes, you deserve me and I'd be damn lucky to have you."

She glances down at our hands where my thumb is rubbing across her palm.

"So do you think you'd be willing to take a chance with me, knowing I've still got all this stuff to work out?"

"Yes. I'm all in. What about you? Are you willing to take a chance on me? I mean, I hate to break this to you, but I'm not perfect."

She shakes her head. "Damn. I thought you were."

"Nope. Not even close."

"Well, we'll just have to agree to disagree," she says winking at me.

"Yup. We'll take one step at a time and figure it out as we go along. So you're going to be my girl?" I ask as I edge closer to her.

"Yes, I'm all in."

My relief is intense as she presses her lips against mine. This is the kiss that steals my heart. She's got me now, no matter what lies up ahead. It's the kiss that closes the door on our past, and flings the new one open for our future.

And believe me, I can't pass through it quick enough.

Within seconds she's on my lap and we're lip-locked, her hands in my hair, across my shoulders, on my chest . . . filling me up with love until I'm overflowing. It's so emotional that we don't even grope each other and start pulling off clothes.

This feeling is more intense than that early morning a week ago when we shared all the feelings that we'd hidden from each other. This time we've been tested. We sunk to the bottom and separated, but now we've surfaced together and we're moving toward the horizon up ahead.

"I love you, Elle," I whisper when we part to catch our breaths.

She's glowing, her joy palpable. I'm going to bronze that damn book Patrick gave her and put it on our future mantel.

"I love you, too."

"So am I still your bridge?" I ask, only partially teasing.

She places her hands on either side of my face and gazes at me with a look so full of emotion it overwhelms me.

"You were never just my bridge, Paul."

It's weird, but just like my parent's way, I sense what Elle's going to say next before the words leave her lips.

"Yes, you're my bridge but also my heart, my future . . . and my destination."

Those words are everything. I pull her back into my arms.

She eases closer and lets out a contented sigh. "I've finally arrived."

I smile from the inside out as I take her hand in mine.

"Welcome home."

Also by Ruth Clampett

Animate Me

Mr. 365

Work of Art~Book 1 The Inspiration

Work of Art~Book 2 The Unveiling

Work of Art~Book 3 The Masterpiece

Many thanks to those of you that
take a moment to leave a review
~ it's much appreciated.

Acknowledgements

I love our community of indie authors, bloggers and readers and am so grateful for the wonderful friends I've made that support and encourage me with my work. I've met the most amazing people who have embraced not just me, but my daughter Alex, and our lives have been richer for it.

Thank you Lisa Fortunato, Glorya Hidalgo, Azu Sandoval, and beta Amy Marxen Jennings for reading and giving notes on the rough draft of Wet and making me believe I had something special with Paul and Elle. The continual encouragement from my dear Lost Girls has meant so much, as has cheerleading from Alex, DJ, Kellie, Suzie and Elli.

I so appreciate my content editor Angela Borda who gives me tough love when I need it, and rewards me with side notes that make me laugh out loud. You make this challenging process of content editing something I look forward to.

It was such a delight to work with Heather Maven on Wet. You bring such a smart understanding of characters and their voices to the beta process. Your feedback was a gift.

Heartfelt thanks to Neda, of Ardent Prose PR, who shows great care and enthusiasm for my work and pushes me out of my promotional comfort zone—which is exactly what I need.

Jada! You hit it out of the park with this bookcover! This is our sixth book to work on together and I think we make a great team. Thank you for approaching every project with passion and great ideas.

Thank you Flavia Viotti and Meire Dias of Bookcase Agency

for your continued support. You ladies rock.

Many thanks to Melissa of There For You Editing for cleaning up the error of my ways…and to Christine of Perfectly Publishable for doing a terrific job formatting.

I've been so lucky meeting amazing readers like you that I've connected with either through social media or at author events. If we haven't yet met, I'd love to hear from you.

With a full heart I thank you for inspiring me to share my stories.

About the Author

Ruth Clampett, daughter of legendary animation director, Bob Clampett, has spent a lifetime surrounded by art and animation. A graduate of Art Center College of Design, her careers have included graphic design, photography, VP of Design for WB Stores and teaching photography at UCLA. She now runs her own studio as the fine art publisher for Warner Bros. where she's had the opportunity to know and work with many of the greatest artists in the world of animation and comics.

Wet is Ruth's sixth book, following Animate Me, Mr. 365 and the Work of Art Trilogy. She lives in Los Angeles and is heavily supervised by her teenage daughter, lovingly referred to as Snarky, who loves traveling with her mom with a sketchbook in hand.

Connect with Ruth

www.RuthClampettWrites.com

Twitter
www.twitter.com/RuthyWrites

For book stuff:

Facebook ~ Ruth Clampett Writes
www.facebook.com/RuthClampettWrites

For a more general stuff:

Facebook
www.facebook.com/RuthClampettWrites

Instagram
www.instagram.com/Ruth_Clampett